MARAUDER

GANGSTERS OF NEW YORK, BOOK 2

BELLA DI CORTE

Bella Di Corte

Editing by: Alisa Carter

Cover Designed by: Najla Qamber Designs

For the Connollys and Ryans of the world...

"Hearts are not had as a gift but hearts are earned. By those who are not entirely beautiful."

— W.B. YEATS

INTRODUCTION

Marauder is the second of three books set in the savage world of the **Gangsters of New York series.** Each book can be read as a standalone, but they are all based in the same world.

Reading Order:
Machiavellian
Marauder
Mercenary

There are other families mentioned from other criminal world books, but those books do not have to be read to enjoy **Marauder**, either.

For reference, a list of each family, along with important names and how they are related, can be found at the beginning of **Marauder**.

THE
FAUSTI
FAMILY

Faustis who are either mentioned or make an appearance in Marauder:

Luca Fausti (incarcerated) is the eldest son of Marzio Fausti and he has four sons: **Brando, Rocco, Dario,** and **Romeo.**

Rocco Fausti is married to **Rosaria Caffi.**

Tito Sala, MD is connected to the Faustis by marriage. He is married to **Lola Fausti.**

Scarlett Fausti is married to **Brando Fausti.**

There's a drawn-out feud between the Faustis and the Stones in the **Fausti Family saga.**

MACHIAVELLIAN

Mac "Capo" Macchiavello & Mariposa "Mari" Flores

.

KELLY

Ronan Kelly:

He was the head of the Kelly Family

He has two sons: **Cashel 'Cash' Fallon Kelly** (mother, **Saoirse**/*ser-sha*) and **Killian 'Kill' Patrick Kelly** (mother, **Saoirse**).

He was married to **Molly O'Connor Kelly**. Molly's brother has a son, **Rafferty (Raff) O'Conner**, who works for **Cash Kelly**.

Other important families and names:

<u>Ryan Family:</u>

Keely Shea Ryan and her four brothers: **Harrison, Lachlan, Declan**, and **Owen**.

<u>The O'Connell Family:</u>

Maureen O'Connell and her two grandchildren: **Connolly** (**CeeCee**) and **Ryan**.

Father Patrick Flanagan is a family friend of the **Kelly Family**.

<u>The Grady Family:</u>

Cormick Grady was the head of the **Grady Family**.

Brian Grady is the younger brother of **Cormick Grady**.

Lee Grady is the son of **Cormick Grady** and the nephew of **Brian Grady**.

The McFirth Family:

Susan McFirth used to work for **Ronan Kelly**. She has a grandson, **Colin McFirth**.

Colin McFirth is the grandson of **Susan McFirth**, and he works for **Cash Kelly**.

If you are familiar with the **Fausti** *Famiglia*, then you will be familiar with the history between the **Faustis** and the **Stones**.

Scott Stone lives in New York, but he has ties to the **Stone Family** in Louisiana. They are in the **Fausti Saga**.

MARAUDER

noun

1. a person who marauds; a raider.

FOREWORD
CASH

"Some men are born more animal than man. It's just who they are, what's running through their veins," the old man used to say.

He'd tell me that bad men don't know they're bad, and they usually don't believe it when they're told. In the eye of the beholder, the end always justifies the means. In our world, *it is what it is.*

So let me ask you a question: Does the end always justify the means?

Stealing to stave off hunger?

Lying to protect the one you love the most?

Cheating to win so your worst enemy doesn't?

Killing to save your life? Or hunting for the one life that means more than your own?

You see, all of these scenarios have one thing in common.

Stealing.

Lying.

Cheating.

Killing.

They're all considered wrong. One is even a mortal sin.

Yet, depending on the scenario, you are excused from this wrongdoing, the sin, in the eye of certain beholders.

Reality—how different it looks through different eyes.

Even Robin Hood was a fucking villain, depending on who you ask.

Ask me. I'll tell you.

The world sees me as a marauder.

You cross me, and I'll return the favor by pillaging your village for whatever the fuck I want. I'll find the one thing you hold dearest and rip it away from you like a babe from his mother's breast. Then I'll starve it. Let the one piece of you die a slow death, and watch as you watch, and there's not a damn thing you can do about it.

Is Robin Hood the villain or the hero? It depends on who you ask.

Ask me. I'll tell you.

The Hood just knew how to spin the story.

Now you tell me: How do you see me? *Remember this question.*

I'll give you time to see how I spin the story before you answer.

I give you permission to begin now.

Ready.

Set.

Fucking go.

1

CASH

The cell rattled as the door opened, and I stepped out
of the cage.

"Make this the last time we see each other, Cash
Kelly," the guard said. "You've graduated with honors."

I grinned, and a few minutes later, I took in my first lungful
of fresh air in three thousand, six hundred, and fifty days.

This animal was finally relieved of rattling cells and steel
bars. Or as the guard had said, I'd finished school, which meant
that I'd served my time and was now a free man in the eyes of
the law.

It took me ten years to graduate. A detective by the name of
Jeremiah Stone busted me on some bullshit charge of racke-
teering, when he knew damn well I should've been booked and
charged for two counts of murder. I'd killed the two men—or as
I called them, wasted space—that were in the car when my
father, Ronan Kelly, was slaughtered in broad daylight.

Charging me with the less honorable crime was Jeremiah
Stone's way of saying *fuck you* to the son of the man he despised
—my old man, Ronan Kelly, or as he was known on the streets,
Maraigh (MA-RAH, murder or slay in Irish). Stone had chased

him relentlessly and could never catch him. Not until my old man fell to the cement, never to get up again. So Jeremiah Stone disgraced me by refusing to admit to the world that I killed the men who murdered my father in cold blood.

Reminiscing about everything that led up to my imprisonment only brought me to the letter in my hand. I'd gotten it a week before my release, and it was the only thing I'd saved from my time behind bars. I read it every morning, every night, memorizing the words by heart like some sad poetic rhapsody.

Killian, or as I used to call him, Kill. He'd written the letter, breaking the bond not only between brothers, but twins. He apologized in the letter for not coming to see me in ten years, for leaving without saying goodbye, and for the long goodbye that was going to follow.

My twin brother, my blood, half of me, never wanted to see this sinner again because of what had happened the day my old man was killed. The bullet that was meant for me had paralyzed him. He'd never walk again. Instead of seeking revenge, though, Killian had decided to join the priesthood in our native Ireland. He wanted to save souls instead of stealing hearts.

I didn't have an issue with his life choice. A man should live his life as he wanted. My problem was with his hypocrisy. If there was one type of person I couldn't stand, it was a fucking hypocrite.

Killian had decided to use his new-found awakening to go from one prison to another—saving lost souls in Ireland—but his own flesh and blood wasn't good enough to see in the light of day. He'd taken it to heart when our old man said that we were day and night; my brother sang while I stole the air from lungs.

Still, he was out there saving sinners, and the dark half of his life—me—wasn't even worth talking to. Maybe he felt I was beyond saving.

He was right.

Killian knew I wasn't through with the world I belonged in, and it wasn't through with me. I'd claimed my revenge on the men who killed my father, but I still hadn't had the pleasure of getting my revenge on the men who set the wheels in motion. The downfall of my entire life.

Two men.

Jeremiah Stone and his son, Scott Stone.

It wasn't the older Stone that I had my sights on any longer. He had retired once his son had been promoted to detective. No. It was his son, Detective Scott Stone, who my eyes were on —eyes that belonged to a marauding green-eyed tiger. My spirit animal, the old man used to say. Our stripes were a natural part of who we were. Mine were earned in battle; his were given at birth.

"If you want to hurt your enemy," my old man had said to me once, nodding to the tiger basking in the sun at the Bronx Zoo, "you go after what he keeps locked in his heart. Death is not the worse fate he can face." He chucked his chin toward the animal once more. "That fate—his heart being locked up, not able to run free with its instincts—is the worst fate for that animal. And our circle of men, down to our marrow, we're nothing but a bunch of animals."

It was time that the marauder of Hell's Kitchen, *me,* reclaimed the streets that belonged to us, and at the same time, find out what Scott Stone had been up to. Find out what he kept locked up in that heart of his.

Once I did, I'd steal it from him.

2

KEELY

Only those who have tasted the saltiness of true grief can understand how sweet the other side is. But if bitterness lingers too long, the other side always tastes too sweet. Enough to turn the stomach.

I could usually find balance between the two, but December... I sighed, and my breath billowed out of my mouth in a cloud. In December, I felt nothing but open wounds, and I tasted nothing but salt. Salt that never seemed to clean the wounds. No amount of tears could ever heal what I'd lost. Instead, they aggravated the old wounds, making them deeper and angrier.

Leaning down, trying not to be too morbid, despite my surroundings, I placed a bouquet of lilacs and baby's breath on the cold ground before the grave.

Purple was her favorite color. Green was mine.

It made sense back then, and it made sense in that moment. She was the twin who would always be victorious in life. I'd forever be the envious one. *Of her.* Even at five, jealousy had been a bitter pill to swallow.

"I wonder if that's true for all twins," I wondered aloud.

"One is *this*, will be *this*, will do *this*, and the other one is *that*, will be *that*, will do *that*."

"In my experience, that's true."

I whirled around so fast that a gust of wind moved between me and the man suddenly standing close to me. Something that sounded like *"shit-a-motha-fooker-wooooo!"* left my mouth in a garbled rush. My heart felt like it was in my throat, and my hand shot up, covering the area so it wouldn't jump clear out of my mouth. "You—" I was about to lay into the stranger, curse him even in a cemetery, but the words died in my throat.

My eyes flew up—*yeah, up*—and crashed into the eyes of a green-eyed man who no doubt had trouble running through his veins. It was at odds with how well he was dressed, like a businessman. He wore a custom-made suit and a hat that looked like it came straight from another time. Even through the thick mist of a dreary day, his green eyes seemed to sparkle with mischief and something else, something predatory and dangerous.

"I should punch you in the face for scaring me like that!" I whisper-hissed. Yeah, I might not be as big as this guy, but being a tall girl with curves gave me the courage to not back down. And being raised with four brothers didn't make me timid, either. I was rough, and if I had my bow and arrow, I could take down any predator that was after me.

Unfortunately, my bow and arrow were stowed in my junky-ass car parked across the cemetery. And this predator could take me down, even if he had to fight a little to put me out for the count.

His eyes narrowed, but he didn't say anything for a minute or two. Somewhere between then, I realized a bottle of whiskey dangled from his fingers, along with two shot glasses. "Roisin Ryan was your sister."

That mouth of his was a mixture of Irish and New Yorker. He had a soft lilt, and when he said "Roisin," it came out as

"Ro-Sheen." Which was the correct way to pronounce her name. Being in an Irish cemetery, I wasn't surprised at his accent. Still, I wasn't expecting him. At all.

"Why are you ignoring what I said?" I wasn't ready to answer his question, so I deflected.

"About punching me in the face?"

"What else?"

He sighed. "Are you going to do it, darlin'?"

After a shiver tore over me at the way he said, *darlin'*, I looked around. "No, only because this is not the time nor the place. I would, if we were anywhere else—"

"But we're not," he said.

I studied him for a minute; he seemed to be studying me, too. I wondered what his smile was going to be like. I just knew, *knew*, that his grin, or his smile, was going to be charming, at odds with those dangerous eyes. Men like him never made sense.

"It's just rude to scare someone like that," I said after another minute had passed. "This is a place where people come to find peace. And it's hard-earned. You should announce yourself, or at the very least, make noise. Clear your throat. Something."

He cleared his throat.

Smart ass. "But no. You asked me if Roisin Ryan *was* my sister. She *is* my sister."

"She was little," he said.

At least he had a brain and could keep up with the conversation. I was trying to think nice thoughts, I really was, because I could be too hard on people. Especially men. My Mam always told me I was too hard on them. She said that I had probably told my soul mate to go to hell at some point in my life. Seeing as he was too scared to disobey me, he probably did.

I nodded. "She was five. Car accident."

"Your twin."

This time I narrowed my eyes against his.

Droplets of water collected on his long black lashes, making his eyes seem fiercer. In the smoky cold, they seemed emerald, but when the sun hit them, I was willing to bet they'd be closer to chartreuse. The oddest color I'd ever seen, but honestly, the most beautiful. And even though he'd only spoken a few words, something about him oozed charm. The same charm I was willing to bet matched his grin.

It was hard to tell if he was trying to charm me or not, and what was even harder, was trying to explain the way he looked at me. He was studying me, but in a way that only seemed to bring up more questions. It was the oddest fucking thing I'd ever experienced. It took every ounce of my self-restraint not to pinch him, to make sure that one of the old ghosts around the cemetery hadn't decided to talk to me.

Or maybe one of the statues. He carried the strength of one —a perfect, carved stone in a graveyard.

I would've called him a martyr, but he was far from it. He didn't seem like the type of man to sacrifice himself for anything, even something he wanted. *Because he probably always got what he wanted.*

"I had a twin, too," he said.

That brought me back to the present. To him. "Is he or she here?" I looked around, feeling foolish after I did, because it wasn't like he was going to introduce me.

"He," he said. "But nah. My old man is. He's buried—" He turned a little, pointing in another direction. "Kelly's the last name."

"Ah," I said, motioning to the bottle of whiskey and the glasses in his hand. "Come to have a drink?"

"You can say that. It's been a while since the Old Man and I had a chat."

"It's cathartic sometimes."

"Must be the same reason you come to see Roisin."

For the first time in sixteen years, I felt a sense of warmth settle over me, and I shivered when it clashed with the cold. I'd never felt anything but chilled to the bone when I came here, but in that second, my blood heated, even if only for a second. I motioned to his hand again. "I might need a drink first before we get into that."

He lifted the whiskey bottle, set the two glasses on Roisin's tombstone, and poured a glass. He offered it to me, but I shook my head. "It doesn't seem right," I said. "She was only five."

He gave a curt nod before he threw back the whiskey. His throat worked with the fire assuredly moving down his tongue. "I've always been the devil," he said.

It took me a moment to make sense of his comment. "Your twin was the angel—"

"Yeah," he said. "It's all good, though. The old man had the best of both worlds. He had two different sides to consider before he made final decisions."

"I'm sorry," I said. "That you lost your brother and your dad."

"Life," he said. "It's the most unpredictable thing, but most still try to control it."

"It's a wild animal," I said, and meant it. "Sometimes it's better to let it run wild."

"You let life run you?" It didn't really seem like a question.

"No," I said automatically. "I'm a fighter."

"Knew it," he said, and then the corner of his mouth turned up into a semblance of a smile. It was a grin that was as cocky as it was charming—a fucking winner that stole my breath.

"Unless it comes to death," I said, refusing to stop the conversation because he had somehow gotten underneath my skin, like the cold, for a brief second. "How can you beat death when it holds all the cards?"

"Hundreds beat diseases every day."

"Those are fights worth taking on. But I think we all need a certain amount of grace, too. Grace to let go of things we no longer have control over. Let it run wild. Because when we do —" I shrugged "—sometimes we run to a better place."

"Remember that," he muttered. Then he seemed to study me a bit harder. "Tell me about Roisin."

I turned to look at her space, seeing a picture of me on her grave, though it wasn't me. We only shared the same reflection. "Like I said, car accident. I had thrown a fit about her getting the lead in some Broadway show. I threw such a fit that I held my breath and passed out. It was the first time I'd ever done something like that. So my grandparents offered to take Roisin so she wouldn't be late. My parents took me to the emergency room because they thought something was really, really wrong with me. I was diagnosed with a temper tantrum. None of us made it to her show that night. They were hit on the way."

"Half of you died with her, and nothing's been the same ever since."

"It's almost unexplainable to someone who doesn't share that kind of bond. You understand." I looked up at him, and even though I expected it, it still shocked me—his eyes had softened some. Then, in an instant, they hardened. They were so hard that it almost felt like he was stoning me with his thoughts.

I opened and closed my hands, feeling uneasy all of a sudden. Cold. Warm. Cold. Warm. I had thought it was the weather, and maybe having someone to share this moment with, but I came to the conclusion that it was him. He was sending me weird vibes.

"I gotta run now, Mr. Kelly. Have a nice chat with your old man."

"Ms. Ryan," he said, tipping his hat, watching me as I left.

I hustled to get out of there, feeling out of breath by the time I reached my old car. Something about the way he said my name led me to believe that in his mind he was actually think-ing, *Take care, Ms. Ryan. I'll see you soon.*

How the fuck was he going to see me soon when he didn't even know me? I hit the gas harder than I ever had before, my old car wheezing with complaint, trying to outrun his memory, but even after I got home, I still felt like he was watching me. He was as beautiful as he was threatening.

He'll get an arrow in his ass before he comes close to me or mine.

Then another thought slammed into me, harder than anything ever had before, and I had to sit down and catch my breath.

Why would Roisin send someone like *him* to *me*?

3

KEELY

In moments of complete weakness, sometimes I had talks with Roisin in my head. After the accident, when she was ripped from my side, I cried nonstop. I couldn't stop crying. I was five, and my best friend in the entire world had left me all alone with a house full of boys.

Harrison, Lachlan, Declan, and Owen.

Only twelve months after Owen was born, the twins, also known as RoKe, made our arrival into the world. If anything, Roisin and I had always irritated the boys, but it was always *us* doing whatever it was against *them*.

My sister's death came, and even at five years old, I knew that half of me had died with her. And I desperately wanted it back. I wanted to feel whole again. So I started having conversations with her.

I refused to let anyone else hear me, so I carried the chats on in my head.

It was about that time my Mam said that I stopped talking. I didn't remember not talking. Maybe because the conversations in my head with Roisin were enough. But I did remember asking her to send me another sister, another her, so the hurt in my heart would go away.

The spring after Roisin left me, I knew she had heard me. I had been outside with Harrison when I saw a little girl with a blue butterfly clip in her hair standing in our next-door neighbor's yard. I had no idea they had kids, but Harrison told me they had adopted her. The little girl had been there since December, but she rarely came out of the house.

Jocelyn, who was our next-door neighbor, stood next to her and introduced us. She called the girl Mariposa, and she told us that in Spanish *mariposa* meant *butterfly*.

Mariposa shook her head and said, "My name is Mari."

I'd refused to answer, but she kept looking at me anyway.

"When's your birthday?" she tried again. Her words came out different from mine, and back then, I couldn't place it. When I got older, I realized she had had an Italian accent, but she was trying not to. Jocelyn kept correcting her words when she said them in Italian, though she said Mariposa was fluent in Spanish. We never heard her speak a word in Spanish.

"September," Harrison had answered for me. "When's yours?"

"October," Mari answered.

"Oh, that's right! You're only about two weeks apart!" Jocelyn had said, trying to push us closer together.

"You hear that, Kee?" Harrison nudged me. "You and Mari are only two weeks apart."

Harrison told me that my eyes had lifted after, and I took Mari's hand and dragged her inside of our house.

From that point forward, Mariposa Flores became my sister. And it was around that time that I started becoming what Mari called a "fixer." Someone who had to fix all of the problems in the world, "the world" being my family. Mari included.

I never told Mari this, but the reason I started talking to her that day was because I knew Roisin had sent her to me. To be my sister of the heart. I was older than Roisin by two minutes. And when Jocelyn had announced that Mari and I were only two weeks apart, in my heart I knew Mari had come to live on Staten Island because I needed her.

Turned out, she needed me, too.

Her parents had died in a car accident when she was five, and she had gone to live with Jocelyn and her father, who everyone in the neighborhood called Old Man Gianelli. Old Man Gianelli died somewhere in that time, and then Jocelyn died when Mari was ten. After that, there was no one to care for her, so the state put her into foster care.

Again, half of me seemed to disappear. So I started holding my breath again. I refused to stop unless Mam found her.

I had held my breath and lost my sister. Maybe if I held my breath again, Mari would come back.

She did.

My Mam found her.

For the most part, though, my Mam tried to keep us apart. She was concerned that I was using Mari to replace Roisin, and she didn't like it. She said it broke her heart that I'd found a replacement for my twin. Even as the years went on, Mam still kept Mari at arm's length. She said Mari was trouble, and that she was going to bring it to our door. The tea leaves told her.

Trouble or not, and even if Mam could never understand, Mari would always be the sister of my heart.

None of us ever told Mari about Roisin, though. I didn't want to. I worried that Mari would think I was trying to replace my sister, and then she would doubt what we shared was true.

Mari had issues with kindness, but somehow, she accepted it from me. For the most part. I knew there was a story there, about why she rejected it so fiercely, but the beautiful thing about Mari and me—we were good at keeping our secrets, but they never broke us apart.

For the longest time after Mari came into my life, the

conversations with my sister came to an end, but every once in a while, when life felt extremely hard, we picked them up again.

In a moment of uncertainty, after Mam had said she read something in the leaves, I'd asked Roisin to bring the right man to me. I told her when he was right, I'd know she'd sent him because he would understand my loss, my pain, in some kind of a way. He'd *feel* me.

If Roisin had sent Mr. Kelly to my door, I had no idea why. *Why him?* Why the fuck would she send me a man that made me so uneasy? The more I thought about the way he stoned me with those green eyes, the more I leaned toward hating him for the judgment. I could tell he had something on his mind, and it had to do with me.

Ulterior motives.

Actually, *that* problem was only half of the battle and led me to another. The reason I'd asked Roisin to intervene in the first place was because I was starting to get serious with a man, but my heart was speaking from two sides of its mouth. One voice sounded a lot like my Mam's. The other sounded like mine.

Some days, I felt like I could love him (Mam's voice).

Other days, I wondered where the passion was (my voice).

I couldn't help but wonder whether I was too fucked up beyond repair to actually give love properly and receive it. Was the part of me that died with my sister my ability to love? Or maybe I'd lost my heart, where love was supposed to live.

I loved my parents. I loved my siblings. I loved Mari.

But men? When it came time to switch the light on love, it was always a burnt-out bulb. The men I'd dated always seemed to brighten the room we were in, but not me. Shouldn't I burn for them when they were around?

I couldn't talk to Mari about all of this. Again, she had no clue about Roisin, and she had enough going on in her life. My twisted thoughts on love were the least of her problems. Hell, they should've been the least of mine, but Scott sort of fell into my life, and I'd been keeping him a secret from everyone. My parents didn't know. Neither did my brothers. And again, I decided not to tell Mari.

Things were moving fast with him, though, and I felt utterly lost in a strange place.

If Scott was so right, why did I feel so turned around?

I tried to put the brakes on a bit, slow us down, but when he loved, he seemed to love with all he had. Yeah, *love*. I'd met him in May, it was December, and he had already told me he loved me. He wanted me to meet his family. He wanted to meet mine.

On paper, we worked out. He was older than me, but not too much older. He had a career, and even though it consumed his life, I could respect his drive. He treated me right and respected me. But...I always had a "but" when I thought about all of the things that were right about us.

He's good looking, but...not my usual type.

He has a good job, but...sometimes he's too high on his horse.

He smells good, but...sometimes his cologne gives me a headache.

His touch feels good, but...it never feels like he's truly feeling me. Beyond skin and bone.

I never missed a visit with Roisin in December, on the day she was killed, but it had never felt so important that I go. Maybe it was because I thought Scott was going to propose soon, and I wanted to see if she was going to answer me before he did. She'd been silent all those months since I'd asked.

Apparently, she thought it was wise to send me an Irishman who sent fucking chills up my spine. He showed up and made me feel all weird inside. It was an odd mixture of excitement and fear I'd felt around him—a feeling I'd never forget, but I wasn't sure why.

Maybe Roisin had sent him as an example of who *not* to fall for. It made so much more sense.

I had a hard time imagining my brothers around Scott. Around Kelly? They might tackle him at the door. The phrase "Fighting Irish" had nothing on me and mine. Though, judging by Kelly's size, and something about the set of his face, he wasn't a stranger to a good brawl either.

Why was I still thinking about the bastard anyway? I should've told him to go to hell, but something told me he'd already been there, and he had frequent flyer miles.

A knock came at my bedroom door. Before I could answer, Sierra peeked her head inside. She was my roommate, and even though we were total opposites, our rooming worked. She paid her rent on time. She minded her own business. And, the best part: she was gone eighty percent of the time.

"You have company," she said.

I nodded, taking the picture of Roisin and me at our last birthday party together and slipping it back into the old hatbox I kept it in. Sierra usually didn't ask questions, but who knew when she might start. If I couldn't talk to Mari about Roisin, there was no way I'd talk to Sierra about her.

Just in time, too, because Mari replaced Sierra in the doorway. Like magic, Mari never missed seeing me on the day Roisin was killed. She had no idea, yet she seemed to sense something was off with me on that day, and she made an effort to come and see me.

A huge smile came to my face before I wrapped her in a hug.

"Kee Kee," Mari said, her voice strangled. "I know you missed me, but I can't breathe!"

I stepped back, letting her go, really looking her over. Mari was one of the most beautiful girls I'd ever seen. She had dark hair, hazel eyes, and the prettiest skin. She never got over the kid in our neighborhood making fun of her nose, though. She fixated on the one thing she felt was wrong with her, instead of everything that was right. Which was everything.

But I always judged how she was doing (because she'd never truly tell me) by how skinny she looked. She always looked like she needed to eat for days without a break.

"I haven't seen you," I said, trying to downplay my worry. It was a delicate balance with her. "Where've you been?"

Mari adjusted the old leather backpack she carried everywhere before she tucked a loose strand of hair behind her ear. "Here and there." She grinned.

I narrowed my eyes at her. "What are you up to?"

"Nothing!"

I pointed at her. "Too fast!"

She laughed, and it made me smile. Her life was hard, and with her being so hardheaded about letting people help her, she didn't smile or laugh nearly enough. Her refusal of help actually frustrated me to tears sometimes.

"No." She drew the word out. "Nothing's going on. Your bullshit detector is off. You need to see a handyman about getting that fixed."

"Not likely," I said, making a mental note to get it out of her sooner or later. I was just relieved to see her. Sometimes she'd disappear on me, and when I was close to calling every hospital in New York to find her, she'd pop up. "Where have you been?"

"Slick," she said, adjusting the backpack again, "you just asked me that. But you know I've been doing the same things I usually do. Survive. Work. Survive. Rinse. Repeat."

"Uh huh." I shook my head. "Whatever you're up to, you know eventually you're going to have to come clean."

"Eventually." Her grin was deep. Then she shrugged. "It always seems like I show up on this day, right? It's kind of weird. It's like my internal magnet brings me here. Maybe because Jocelyn and Pops took me in around this time."

"Yeah," I said, turning from her and taking the hatbox from my old vanity. It had been my grandmother's. "Maybe that's it."

"Where are you going?" she said, stepping deeper into the room. "You're all dressed up."

"I took on a shift at a fancy restaurant. I can use the—"

"Extra dollar," Harrison said, coming to stand next to Mari.

I eyed both of them. Harrison could never take his eyes off of Mari. When I first saw Mari, so did he, and sometimes it was a struggle to get him to leave her alone. I'd have to shut the door to my room so he wouldn't bother us when we were younger. He gave her a pathetic nickname, Strings, and treated her like he did me. Like a sister.

Sometimes he was more protective of her than he was of me. It didn't bother me, because we both seemed to have a silent understanding. Mari came to us for a reason after Roisin was killed, even if our Mam didn't see it that way. She hated when Harrison showed Mari attention, even more than she hated when I did.

"You picked Mari up?" I gave Harrison a glower and he gave me a narrow. None of the boys messed with me. I'd beat all of their asses. "Why?"

He shrugged. "I stopped by Home Run to see if Mari needed a ride home, since it's fucking freezing. She told me she was coming here. So was I. Here we are."

"You were coming here, too?"

"Yeah." He gave me a long enough stare to try and communicate silently—*today is hard for me, too.*

I nodded, tucking a wild curl behind my ear.

Mari took a seat on my bed, while Harrison stood in the doorway. They both watched me while I put the hatbox on the top shelf of my closet and then pulled out my nicest coat. It was old, and emerald green, but I'd taken good care of it over the years.

"Mari and I made plans to eat at Mamma's," Harrison said. "We thought you'd come with us, but if you have to work, we'll drop you off."

"Drop me?" I slid the coat over my shoulders. "If you drop me, who's going to—"

"My car broke," my brother said, cutting me off. He glanced at Mari before he met my eyes again.

She must've noticed, because she said that she was going to wait out front for us.

"Just take a seat on the sofa," I told her. "Don't go outside and wait."

She looked like she wanted to argue, but she finally nodded. She was never comfortable around Sierra. The girl was intimidating to some people, but Mari acted exceptionally guarded around her.

"Keely," Harrison said, bringing my attention back to him. "My car broke, and I don't have the fucking funds to fix it. It died in your driveway. I need to borrow your car for a while."

My brother looked so tired. He had graduated law school with honors, but with this market, he couldn't find a job. He was in the same position as me. We were barely making our bills. We weren't as bad as Mari, but we were not far from her, either. The difference between Mari and us, though, was that she was always getting fired.

However, the reason I struggled and refused to go to college was, I had something to accomplish. I'd always dreamed of being on Broadway.

In some odd way, I always thought it was payback from Roisin. I could find a million jobs, but the one I wanted, I could never get. It was the reason I'd held my breath that night. I'd wanted what she had.

"Why didn't you ask Lachlan?" I said.

"He has work."

"Who's going to—"

"I'll pick you up," Harrison said. "What time?"

I threw the keys at him and he caught them with one hand. "Don't worry about picking me up. I'll have a friend from work drop me off at home. You can pick me up tomorrow morning. I took a shift at Home Run."

The real reason he wanted to borrow my car was written all over his face. He wanted to keep his plans with Mari. Any other day, I would've given him shit, but it'd been a long day.

"Keely," he said, grabbing my arm before I walked out of my room. "She comes looking for you on this day every year."

I turned to look at him. "I know," I said. "So let's get going—"

"No. Not Mari. Roisin. I feel her around you. It's...heavy." His eyes searched mine. "She's worried about you. Maybe about all of us. But I have my sights on an opportunity that might pay off, Kee. I'm going to see a man about a job day after tomorrow. He got in touch with me. Said he's been looking for a lawyer with my credentials. It seems promising. Maybe she'll rest in peace once she knows we're all okay."

I couldn't speak, so I nodded, wondering how much peace I was going to find in Scott tonight, when I met him at the restaurant for our date. Since I really didn't have to work.

I BLAMED my entire predicament on my Mam's tea leaf predictions. She'd always claimed to be able to read them, and months ago, when she told me that she'd seen something big in my future, *a huge change*, I thought she meant that I'd be getting a huge part on Broadway.

Broadway didn't come calling, but the guy sitting in front of me did.

I was working at an indoor archery range in Brooklyn when a group of cops came in to take classes. None of them could shoot an arrow worth a shit, and I'd told them so.

One of the most confident ones had spoken up. "If you can do any better, by all means..." He gestured to the target.

"Your name, sharpshooter?" I'd said.

"Scott Stone," he'd said. "Detective Scott Stone."

Scott and I stood about the same height, even though he was wider, and after giving him a narrow-eyed glare as I passed, I shot the hat off his friend's head and nailed it to the board. After Scott had stopped laughing, he told me he owed me a drink. The free drink was a reward for a long week, so I went. Shameful as it was to admit, sometimes I'd go on dates with guys just for the good food and drink, because I couldn't afford it.

I had a decent time with Scott, though. He'd laughed the entire time, and when he had excused himself to use the bathroom, the girl serving drinks told me that he was like one of those cartoon characters who had hearts for eyes when he looked at me.

A month of two after we started seeing each other, my Mam called and told me she saw a heart in her cup. It was meant for me. The big change was going to be love. I'd find it early, just like she did. But there was a catch. It would happen fast. And if I denied it, I'd only be denying myself.

"And one more thing," she'd said before we hung up. "His heart is hidden in his work."

All signs pointed to Scott Stone. His job was his mistress. He'd told me that on the first date.

Oh. So. Fucking. Great.

I had plans. I had things I wanted to accomplish before getting swept off my feet. I wanted to sing on Broadway. Travel the world without worrying about where the funds were going to come from. I wanted to be queen of a country for a day, dammit! Okay, maybe not that, but still, I had plans. And nowhere in my booklet was love first on the itinerary.

Because if I was being brutally honest with myself, I only had two things going for me: the many jobs that seemed to fall into my lap, and the resilient hope that one day I'd sing on stage.

The rest of my life, though? *Shit.*

I barely made rent. I barely had any groceries in the cabinets and in the fridge most of the time. And I had no clue what tomorrow would bring—whether "barely" would turn into "*couldn't make*" and "*nothing in the.*"

Scott was at a different time in his life.

He felt his age. *I found my first gray hair, probably because of the stress of the job.*

He was ready to settle down. *I can see myself getting really serious with you. Having a few kids. Do you think our kids will have red hair like yours?*

He wasn't fond of traveling. *Flying gives me vertigo, and driving for long periods irritates me.*

Whenever we had sex, he always told me what he was going to do before he did it. *I'm going in.*

He didn't like to dance. *Vertigo again. The spinning.*

And he was one of those people who didn't listen to music in the car. *I like to think or talk without noise in the background.*

That was why I preferred to drive my own car. I was one of those people who got lost in the scenery with the radio turned up and the windows down. His lack of listening to music in the car, at one point, had made me think he wasn't a detective at all but maybe a serial killer.

I mean, who doesn't listen to music in the car? Even on low in the background?

But—there it was again—we had fun for the most part. And what if my inability to commit to him would be the biggest mistake of my life? I knew we were inching closer and closer to that point. He wanted to take me to Louisiana with him, where most of his family lived, after the New Year. Then there were the constant hints about my favorite shape—*emerald, round, or oval?*

But... I stopped myself. I needed to stop having so many "but" moments and concentrate on the "what ifs."

What if my forever sat directly in front of me, eating the rest of his steak, and I let him go because he gave me destinations when he touched my body?

I smiled, trying not to laugh at how ridiculous I was being. Maybe letting this play out, without all the thought, would lift some of the burden from my shoulders. Maybe I was holding on too tight because my Mam had put it in my head that it was now or never—no time to decide. Like I didn't have a choice in the matter.

Of course I did. It was my heart. I'd give it or not.

Scott set his fork down, meeting my eyes. "You're terrified, too."

I was about to take a drink. At that, I set it down. "Terrified?"

"Of this." He motioned between us. "But I don't know why they call it falling. Falling makes it sound uncontrolled, an inevitable smash into the ground after you've soared. I've already fallen, and it feels damn good to lose my heart, Kee."

A moment passed between us, a beat, and I smiled. Then he did. Before I knew it, the words tumbled out of my mouth. "I'm ready for this."

That had to be it—the fear. It had stopped me from feeling this—whatever this was between us.

Scott understood. He had just told me he did. Hell, he probably had doubts, too, but fear shouldn't stop what seemed right. Fear shouldn't stop the swapping of hearts. *Give me yours and I'll give you mine.*

But what if this *was* wrong?

Simple.

He'd become a lesson. A steppingstone to something greater. That was the wonderful thing about dating, right? You were free to discover what was right and what was wrong.

Scott had dated more than I had. He was more experienced. So maybe he kept pushing love and marriage because he knew this was right. I wasn't experienced enough to realize it. Time. It would just take time. And maybe the part of me that went fundamentally wrong after my sister died would heal.

I would change.

Be easier to love.

To be around.

I'd be happy with me.

My life would be enough.

A glimpse of Kelly's face shoved itself inside of my mind, but I kicked him back out—he couldn't steal what was no longer available, and that was any more of my thoughts.

Roisin had been wrong, and *that* was *that*.

4

CASH

Compartmentalizing was something I'd always excelled at. It was how I kept the three wars in my head separate. Because no doubt about it, they were separate, although they'd all grown from the same seed.

Even though Scott Stone was on my list, taking back my father's territory was my first priority. The issue with Stone could simmer for a while—it had to—but action was needed to claim what was rightfully mine when my father was killed.

Hell's Kitchen and its streets.

War I went something like this: It was no secret who had killed my father. It was one of the Grady men, who was also working for an Italian family. It wasn't unusual for the Italians and the Irish to work together, so that by itself didn't cause concern. It was the fact that Lee Grady had been trying to get my father to start drug trafficking before his death, but he refused.

He didn't want drugs taking over his streets. He had an old-fashioned way of doing things, and that was mostly keeping his revenue through the docks. My old man knew that drugs only led to other things, and he refused to have any part of it.

So they killed him for it.

This made room for Lee Grady's old man, Cormick, to take my father's spot. He backed Lee's way of thinking, since it was a sure way to make more money, especially since the criminal climate had changed and other lucrative things, like drugs, had already started to take over.

Cormick and Lee had sent one of their men, along with his Italian counterpart, a Scarpone, to kill my father because of his refusal to join the drug game. The setup was made to seem like a meeting, but in actuality, it was going to be a blood bath.

Speaking of which. The Scarpones were one of the most ruthless families in New York, one of the five syndicates, and no one really fucked with them. Arturo Lupo Scarpone, also known as The King of New York, was the head, and he was a dangerous motherfucker. Word on the street was that he had his own son, Vittorio, killed. It was no easy death, either. He had his throat slashed. No one could prove it, nor did they even try, but it didn't take a smart man to figure it out.

Arturo valued power over his son's life, which meant he had zero respect for any life.

Vittorio was considered not only one of New York's most eligible bachelors—he ran in the most powerful social circles— but he was a smart son of a bitch, which was why they some-times called him the Machiavellian Prince of New York. Some say Arturo was threatened by him, by his powerful presence, and that was why he had him killed. There was more to the story, though, and I knew it had to do with orders that were not carried out.

Not long before I left the steel cage, I was made aware of a war on the outside. The Scarpones didn't know who was fucking with them, causing strife between the families. Even the Faustis were involved, and they rarely got involved unless mayhem started brewing on the streets. They stayed out of the way, mostly, but if situations started to stink, they'd step in and right wrongs however they saw fit.

The Faustis were the rulers of the kingdom. When the ruthless did wrong, and no one else could make them pay, it was the Faustis who did. Even the highest have bosses.

Consider the Faustis Kings of the Night. They were the highest animals on the food chain.

But back to the point.

It had only been a couple of months since this tiger's release. I had to bide my time and do most of the work behind the scenes. My father's men had all either sworn alliance to Cormick Grady or moved out of Hell's Kitchen, hoping to honor my old man by doing what he had set out to do.

See to it that everyone in this neighborhood had a better life.

I didn't have my brother to depend on, so I looked to my cousin, Rafferty (Raff) O'Connor, to become my right-hand man. He wasn't my cousin by blood. My old man had married his father's sister, Molly, after we moved to America from Ireland when I was ten.

Raff and I started speaking to some of our old alliances, making friends again, and letting it be known that I was going to take back what had belonged to Ronan "Maraigh" Kelly, and now rightfully belonged to his only heir willing to accept it.

Me.

Things were steadily moving forward until Cormick Grady's car was blown to smithereens. An entire leg was found down the street from his doctor's office. Not even all the king's men could put old Cormick back together again. It wasn't me, though I wished it fucking was. I hadn't gotten that far in war strategy—they knew I was out of the cage, and things were going to get interesting soon enough.

Cormick's son, Lee, assumed it was me. Hell, I'd assume it was me with the way things went down. My father was known for explosives when he wanted to send a message—he taught me well.

Lee was out to get me, especially since I reclaimed *my* streets after Cormick's death. The Scarpones were out for blood, too, since I'd killed one of their men.

More than that, though, what it all boiled down to was money. I was determined to fight the war on drugs. I wanted them off my fucking streets. Businesses would flourish. Children would play without worry. People of this neighborhood would feel safe.

The Gradys were one of the most savage families to ever run Hell's Kitchen. Because of this, men were coming to me in droves, ready to start the work my old man never got to finish.

I had stepped into my father's shoes, the head of a connected Irish family, and no blood had been shed by me. Yet. I could smell it coming, though.

Hell's kitchen was just getting warmed up after being cold for far too fucking long.

———

War II: Scott Stone was never far from my mind.

In general, I never had a real problem with the law. It was one of those things that just worked in life. Without the lawless, there would be no need for the law. Men like me gave them a purpose.

Scott Stone's purpose was to get me.

That was fine, but the problem came when he decided to make his hunt against me personal. The Stones were known for picking a target and keeping at them until they fell, never able to get up again.

At night when Scott went home, badge and gun on his side table, I knew he still thought about me. Just like his uncle in

Louisiana still thought about Luca Fausti, the man who became his worst nightmare.

I never killed one of his, yet my blood stained his soul at night. For what fucking reason? Maybe because his father could never catch mine? Not like he wanted to. Other than that, who fucking knows why one person becomes a personal devil to another?

Yeah, I should've done my research years ago on the Stones, but I never realized what a dick Scott was until he started coming after me not long before my old man was killed right in front of him. He'd caught my scent back then, and it refused to leave his mind.

So it became personal. He didn't want me in a cage for ten years. He wanted me in a cage for the rest of my life.

As for me?

He owed me a heart, a life, and I'd hunt until no one in his life felt safe. I'd steal and steal until the one I knew would cost him the most was mine. And when he saw me with her, that look, the one I saw on his face when my father was killed, would be on mine.

Two imposing wars led me to War III: Keely Shea Ryan.

I had no doubt after seeing her in the cemetery—and several times after, though she didn't see me—that out of all the wars I'd be facing, Keely Ryan would be the bloodiest for me.

Call it a fucking hunch, but she was a strong girl with a sharp tongue, and she didn't seem to know the meaning of the phrase "back down." Even though I was taller than her, and much wider, she still told me she wanted to punch me in the face. If she'd had that bow and arrow of hers? I knew she was capable of bodily harm. She didn't seem to have a filter, nor did she know how to control her temper.

In the months after meeting her at the cemetery, I followed her and Stone, just to make sure that their relationship was moving in the right direction. He was putting the fucking charms on her, and if she wasn't eating them up, I'd allow Stone to call me a bastard for the fun of it. She had convinced herself that she was falling for him. She even agreed to visit his family in Louisiana after the New Year.

She fed her family some bullshit story about going on tour with the archery place where she worked so she wouldn't have to tell them that she was going to meet Stone's family—a collective bunch of cops, except for one cousin who was a firefighter. They called him the oddball of the family. (*Ha ha*—so fucking cliché.)

It was a lover's quarrel after the trip came and went and the fiery Keely didn't ask Stone to meet her family in return. She gave him some bullshit excuse about needing time. His patience was getting thin, and I knew before long, he was going to take matters into his own hands and "accidentally" run into one of her two brothers who lived in New York. The other two lived with her parents in Scotland.

Scott didn't like when he didn't get what he wanted, when he wanted.

We had that in common. Maybe that was why he loathed me. We were too much alike, but on two separate sides of the law. Heroes sometimes walked the line of villain to do what was right, though Stone didn't see it that way.

It was much easier to connect the dots once I hired her brother, Harrison (or as I preferred to call him, Harry Boy), as my personal attorney. He was a smart fella, a good head on his shoulders, but with one major downfall—he had fallen in love with his sister's best friend, a poor girl named Mari. I mean that literally: The girl was dirt poor, and she refused every offer of help Harry Boy offered. He couldn't get his head out of her clouds, so when I started to question him about certain aspects of his life, it was easy to paint a clear picture.

He knew who he was working for, yet he did it anyway, thinking he could convince Mari that he was the man for her. I could've told him he was squandering his time. She looked at him like a brother, but men in the throes of love can't see through the rosy-colored glasses they wear.

It worked out for me, though. All of my chips were falling into place. Every village I'd decided to pillage was mine for the taking. But I was a superstitious son of a bitch, and I believed two things: nothing is ever free, and nothing that looks or feels easy is ever *that* fucking easy.

One of these wars was going to kill me.

If I were to wager, the fatal blow would come from the fiery redhead, the archer. Her arrow coming straight for my heart would be the last thing I saw before hell came to collect me. But before she claimed my heart, I was going to claim hers, if it was the last thing I ever fucking did. And then I was going to smile at Stone as the life drained from my face.

I had no true quarrel with Harry Boy or his sister, but when it came to Keely Ryan's feelings or my own, she'd have to contend with what life was about to hand her.

Me.

Not that it mattered, but I wanted to know what I'd be getting in this one-sided deal, and that was the reason for our meeting at the cemetery. From the moments I spent with her, I was sure of two things: She wouldn't become a blubbering mess, and she wouldn't become so frail that I'd fear breaking her.

Breaking something smaller than me was not in my nature, nor was it my intention. But I knew she was going to be as mad as hell, and there was no doubt I was going to have a vicious fight on my hands.

The thing about hands, though? Just like feet, they can be

tied up, rendered useless. The man about to walk into my office might as well been named "Thread." He called Mari, the girl he was after, Strings, so it was fitting.

Right on time, a knock came at my office door.

"Come in," I said, sitting back in my chair.

No one entered into my personal space unless invited. I had trusted two people in this world completely, my father and my brother. My father was gone, and my brother might as well have been. Therefore, I trusted no one. Which led me to touch the gun I kept close. It was strapped underneath the desk, ready if I needed it.

"Boss," Harry Boy said, entering. "Raff said you wanted to see me."

I looked him over from head to toe before inviting him to sit. The money he was making from working for me was working for him. He'd ditched the flannels and jeans—that attire didn't go over with me, even if my business was unconventional—and had started getting his suits custom-made. I knew a guy who knew a guy. Harry Boy was clean-shaven and smelled of a fine cologne instead of something bought at a drug store. He had respect for the job, for his purpose, which I encouraged in all of my men.

"Sit," I said, motioning to one of two open seats in front of my desk.

He fixed his suit before he took the seat. He looked at me and I looked at him.

"Did you meet with Rocco Fausti?" I said.

"Today. All looks good with your investments."

Rocco Fausti was the son of Luca Fausti, one of the most dangerous men of the Fausti family. Rocco and his brothers were just as dangerous if you crossed them or anyone they considered theirs. However, if you wanted someone to triple your money—or even more—Rocco had a brilliant mind for it.

My father was fond of saying that he could turn a penny into a million dollars.

There was a reason why I sent Harry Boy to the meeting with Rocco. Even though the Fausti family mostly stayed out of business matters that didn't concern them, if wars were erupting between families, or new leaders were trying to make a name, that sort of thing, they kept tabs on the situation.

I was sending Rocco a message: *No need to check on me again. I have things under control. I even have a lawyer who's dealing with my legal shit.*

There were multiple wars going on (or was it just one?), and no one knew who was starting them. All of the five families were blaming each other. At the end of it all? A dead end. So everyone assumed the one they'd originally accused had done the crime against them.

My gut told me that someone was starting shit between them on *purpose*. Whoever did me a "favor" by killing Cormick was going to come looking for payment in the form of a favor sooner or later. And whoever killed Cormick had done it for a simple reason: Favors were highly valued in this life. It was good to keep them close to the vest, ready to pull out when that golden *"get out of jail"* ticket was needed.

Whoever killed Cormick was above average, though. He'd made it look like me. Which also meant that he was starting shit with me, too. A man must kill when he must, and I never took a life that didn't deserve it, but whoever had killed Cormick Grady had set *my* war on *his* terms.

Harry Boy cleared his throat, and I realized I'd been staring at him. I sat forward a little, setting my hands on the desk. "I'm pleased with the job you've been doing."

"I do my best." He smiled.

"That you do." I nodded. "But here's the thing, Harry Boy. My old man always felt the need to meet the families of his workers. I'm keeping that tradition. It makes things more personal. You understand."

"I do." He nodded. "But my family—"

"Your Mam and Da live in Scotland now. Your two brothers are there with them. We'll get to them later." I waved a dismissive hand. "You have a brother here."

"And a sister," he said, nodding before I could even finish.

"And a sister." I grinned. "I'd like you to set up a meeting. We can do dinner."

His eyes narrowed before they lifted. "My brother—"

"He's out of town," I said.

Harry Boy became quiet for a moment, before he nodded. "My sister—" he paused. "She's working at a fair this weekend. You might even enjoy it. It's a medieval Scottish fair being held in upstate New York. Keely—that's my sister—she's savage with a bow and arrow. She's going to demonstrate how shooting an arrow should really look."

"Is she now?" My words rolled out slow. "That's interesting."

Harry Boy brightened. "Yeah, she's...it's hard to explain how accurate she is. She's really good, and she enjoys it, but she's really out to land a part in a Broadway play."

"Grand."

"We could meet at the fair."

I handed him a piece of paper and a pen. "Write down the information. Date and time."

He took the pen and paper, getting to work, jotting down the information I already had.

"It's never too early to meet the family," I said. "It creates a tighter bond. And this business? It's family-oriented."

He looked up at me and smiled, then pushed the paper closer to me. "For sure."

Good boy.

"While I have you." I opened the drawer to my desk, digging

around. When I found what I was looking for, I threw them at Harry Boy.

He caught the keys with one hand.

"Like I said, I appreciate your work ethic. Think of the car as a bonus. It purrs real pretty for its age. '69 Dodge Charger. Completely restored."

He went to hand me back the keys, but I held a hand up. "One thing about me, Harry Boy—once I make a decision, it's done. You hand me back those keys, you insult me. Then we have a problem. You don't want a problem with me, do you?"

"No." He cleared his throat. He held the keys up. "I appreciate it, Boss."

"You earned it. Now get back to work." I dismissed him with a hand. "I'll see you and your sister at the fair."

5

CASH

Raff announced that I had company before I left for the fair.

Rocco Fausti stood from his seat in the waiting room, straightening his expensive suit.

He nodded at me. "Cashel."

No one called me Cashel but my family, since my mother supposedly picked the name, but out of respect for Rocco and his family, I never corrected him.

I held my hand out and we shook. "To what do I owe the pleasure?"

He looked me over from head to toe. "I caught you on your way out."

He could say that. I was dressed in plain clothes, not a suit, and whenever our circle met, we always wore clothes that showed respect to the job, and to us as men. It symbolized that we knew our worth in a world we fought hard to live in.

Instead of addressing my clothes, though, I invited him inside my office. If the Faustis were anything on the outside, it was professional, but whenever one of them was around, I always felt the sensitive spot on my neck—the one that can take even a dangerous animal's life in a second—tingle with warning.

This couldn't be stressed enough:

They. Were. Not. To. Be. Fucked. With.

Period.

Many had tried, and those many were never to be heard from again.

"You first." Rocco motioned toward my office door.

They never walked ahead, always behind. Not because they didn't consider themselves the top of the food chain either. It was because men like them, like me, knew the feeling of that eerie tingle.

He accepted a glass of fine whiskey and then got comfortable in his seat across from me. "Tell me about your graduation."

I grinned at him. "Grand. Just grand. Best education life can afford." I knocked hard on the desk once with a knuckle. "I'm officially a graduate of the school of hard knocks."

He lifted his glass to me and took a sip. After the fine burn of it went down, he set the glass on my desk. "I will not keep you long. You were too polite to tell me you were on your way out, so I will keep this short."

"Don't rush on my account. I have time."

He nodded. "There hasn't been much noise from this end."

"No," I said. "It seemed to fall right back into my palm. However." I lifted a finger and then took a sip from my own glass of whiskey. "I know what's coming."

"A wise man would know his odds before going into battle."

"Ten to one." I grinned.

"Ah," he said, reaching for the glass again. "I'll give you better odds than that. My grandfather and father were fond of your father. If you follow in his footsteps, I can assure you the same fondness will be passed down to you, as well. You will succeed where your father couldn't."

I lifted my glass. "That means a great deal to me."

We clanked glasses and then drained the rest of the liquid.

I set my empty glass down on the desk. "I have every intention of following in my father's footsteps. This area was his heart. His legacy will live on."

"Spoken like a true poet and a good son." Rocco grinned. Then he reached into his pocket and handed me a gold card with black scribble on it.

You owe me.

Mac

The card naturally slid between my pointer and middle finger, and I lifted them up so the card was facing him. I said one word. "Cormick."

He nodded. "It is always wise to have an ally in times of war."

Breaking eye contact, I stared at the card for a moment longer. "One I owe a favor." Then I met his stare again.

He shrugged. "Business is business. We do what we must to close the deal."

"To secure it," I said.

"Neither here nor there. Rest assured. His intentions run parallel with yours, as long as your intentions stay true to course."

It wasn't always what was said in this business that made the difference—it was *how* it was said. The Faustis could be blunt if they wanted to, but the art of subtlety ran through their blood like a unique DNA.

Rocco's words translated: *As long as you don't fuck us over, and whoever this Mac is, he'll play nice with you. We'll play nice with you.*

Mac was offering me an easier way in, which meant that the

Faustis, along with whoever this Mac was, wanted me where I was. But the question still stood: why? I knew better than to ask a dumb question that would go without an answer anyway.

Yeah, kids, there is such a thing as a stupid fucking question.

Rocco slid another card toward me. "You've earned your degree, Kelly. It's been a while since you've seen the city. Dinner is on me."

Macchiavello's. I'd heard it was the new "it" restaurant in town. High-powered business suits and dresses dined there. So did numerous men who had numerous ranks in numerous connected families. Word on the street was that the steak was worth your first-born.

I lifted the card. "I'll try the steak."

"Excellent choice. They also make the best Old Fashioned in the city."

I nodded. "Duly noted." I lifted the card again. "I appreciate this."

Rocco stood, fixing his suit as he did. I stood right after and held my hand out. We shook again, and it was as good as him leaning over the desk and kissing each of my cheeks. Then he gestured toward the door, inviting me to leave my office first.

Once we were outside and he was about to slide into the driver's seat of his $500,000 car, I stopped him.

"Mac," I said. "Any distinguishing marks I should know of?"

Rocco grinned at me, sliding his sunglasses over his eyes. "If I tell you, it will take the fun out if it."

"I'm a boring man," I said. "I'm allergic to fun. It sends me into anaphylactic shock."

He laughed, his teeth bright white, as he got in the car and left.

"CASH," Raff said, looking around. "Where the feck are we? Is this some kind of joke?"

"You know what's a joke?" I slapped him on the back of his head. "Whenever you curse, you suddenly have an Irish accent."

"That's because I *am* Irish!"

"Part-time Irish. The rest of the time you're a New Yorker with a New Yorker's accent."

"It's not my fault my parents immigrated here before I was born. And it's not my fault that the only time my Irish comes out is when I swear."

He looked around again, nodding to a family dressed in old Scottish attire. "Haven't these people got the fucking memo? Medieval is out. Twentieth century is in. We prefer modern-day medicine and boxed mac and cheese. Tell me they have beer. Or do we have to drink *cider*?"

"You drink too fucking much regardless of the name."

He turned around, walking backwards, arms open. "And you accuse me of not being full-time Irish!" He wiggled his eyebrows at two females walking past him. "Tell 'im, ladies. There's nothing wrong with a drink every once in a while. And if it's with a beautiful woman, or two, it's considered socializing, right?"

They smiled at him and he took this as an invitation to wrap an arm around each of their shoulders, kicking his feet together before he walked off with them.

What a fucking winner.

I headed in the direction of the nut roaster. That was where Harry Boy said he'd be waiting for me at the arranged time. Maybe he picked the nut stand because he was busy getting his balls busted by the girl named Mari.

She was working one of the food booths, dressed in vintage clothing of the time, except for the plastic flip flops on her dirtied feet. It was hard to miss her. She reminded me of a young queen in an oil painting—there was something regal about her.

I stopped, stepping to the side of the constantly moving foot traffic.

Fuck. Her face. Either she had face-planted, or someone had used her as a punching bag.

I found Harry Boy eating roasted almonds coated in cinnamon and sugar, watching as Mari served food. I studied his reaction to her for a minute. When she would touch a spot on her face that must've been sore and wince, his jaw would tighten. I wasn't getting involved in his personal affairs, but I was curious as to how he was going to handle this.

However he did would prove to me what kind of man he was. Was he going to kill the bastard who did that to her face? It wasn't hard to tell when a man made that kind of mark on a woman. If it were my woman, I'd kill a fucker for much less than that.

Harry Boy stood up straighter when he noticed me and held out his hand. We shook.

"Nice day to be out," he said.

"Yeah," I said. "The weather is turning warmer."

Even though he looked at me, I could tell he was itching to look at her again. "Your girl," I said. "She have a date with the ground, or someone do that to her?"

"My girl?"

I nodded in her direction. "The one you keep staring at."

"You noticed that?"

"I notice everything."

He nodded, trashing the rest of his nuts. "She's my sister's best friend. Mari Flores. We all grew up together on Staten Island. My sister told me her deadbeat landlord did that to her. He's a fucking prick." Then he really looked at me, at my plain clothes. He'd never seen me out of a suit.

"Harri—" Keely stopped cold when she noticed me standing there.

In less than a second, her eyebrows lifted and then her eyes narrowed. In this light, they were pure blue. Maybe it would've been easier to compare them to the sky or to water, but heaven was all I could think of—a blue only known to heaven. Peaceful. Her fierce red hair made the color seem even brighter.

Keely Shea Ryan was a beautiful woman. Heavenly, in fact. But there was also no doubt that she had a tongue that was made in hell. That temper, too. It matched her hair.

"*You*," she said, and not nicely.

Hell, could I call 'em or what?

"Kee, this is *my* boss," Harrison said, standing taller. He was pissed at how she had spoken to me. He didn't want to lose his job. Or worse.

He knew I was a testy motherfucker, and I didn't put up with much. I might've just gotten out of prison, but I was still known on the streets. It was hard to forget a man called "the marauder": a man who always took what he wanted, damn the consequences.

"Mr. Kelly," Harrison continued, "this is my sister, Keely Ryan."

Keely Ryan looked so fucking ridiculous in her vintage clothes that a smile that I knew pissed her off came to my face. One long curl came loose from the plastic crown adorning her red hair, and she blew it out of her eye with a harsh breath. It didn't budge and she swatted at it.

"We've met," she said, narrowing her eyes even sharper at me.

Her eyes were just as I imagined the gates of heaven would be: narrowed to a slit to men like me.

"Good to know you have a strong memory," I said.

"Oh, it's *excellent*, Mr. Kelly."

"Keely—"

I lifted a hand, stopping Harrison from whatever he was going to say. He was trying to communicate through narrowed eyes that she was being rude to his boss. It was something Killian would've done to me. Manners were never a strong point of mine, though.

"You can call me Cash," I said. "We missed that part at the cemetery."

"You were too busy scaring people, that's why we missed that part."

"I wasn't being quiet. You've seen my feet."

She looked down and then her eyes flew up, catching my grin and scowling at it. A flush crept up her neck and stained her cheeks red.

"They're big and not ashamed of it." I winked. "You were lost in thought. That's why you didn't hear me."

"Cemetery?" Harry Boy said, his eyes moving between the two of us. "You met at the cemetery? When was this, Kee?"

"When I went to visit Roisin on the day she died." She looked at him. "Your *boss* scared the shit out of me."

"I wasn't his boss then," I said. "And our meeting was happenstance."

"Happenstance," she repeated, like she didn't believe me.

Good. She shouldn't. My feelings told me she knew that. Something also told me that she'd thought about me since then. And she hated it. She loathed that I had somehow entered her mind, sifting through her thoughts for the most valuable ones, and marauding things she fought to keep—her time and attention, two of the most valuable things to a person.

I saw the way she was with Stone. Bored. And he had nothing in his eyes but floating fucking hearts when he looked at her. There was something off about the entire situation. Why she was settling for someone who didn't do a thing for her was a mystery. But when she was around him, she played her part well.

She wanted to be an actress on Broadway. She acted every second they were together.

Her...softness when it came to him worked out well for me to a certain degree, though I knew when pressed—and she would be soon—it was only going to make her hard and more determined to see her resolve for Stone through. Like a child.

Too bad I refused to entertain the notion of reverse psychology, or this might be fucking easy.

Harry Boy cleared his throat, and I realized that the archer and me were staring at each other. "Staring" was a stretch on her end. She was aiming arrows at my head through telepathic wavelengths.

"You seem to have a strong dislike of me, Ms. Ryan," I said. "I didn't realize I shook you so hard at the cemetery. Next time I walk through, I'll go through singing a song."

"Oh, cute. An Irishman who can sing!" She made a noise that didn't hide her anger. Her neck was patched with red, and so were her cheeks. "I don't know you enough not to like you, but that never stopped me before. I don't like the smell of bullshit that hovers around you when you come close—"

"Keely," Harry Boy cut her off. But it wasn't harsh. He was more afraid of her than he was of me.

"Don't 'Keely' me," she said. "There's something off about this guy. He's all charming when you invite him into your home, until he comes back later in the night to steal."

"That's why they call me 'the marauder' on the streets. I take whatever I want."

Blunt. There it was. Take it as you fucking please.

Quiet came for a stretch of time after.

Then, all of a sudden, she let out a rush of hot hair, setting her hands on her fine hips. If they were street curves, they'd be labeled deadly. "I don't have time for this!" she hissed. Then she turned toward a man coming toward her with a bow and a quiver full of arrows. The feathers of the fletches were all green

—a real jealous color. The color hovered around her, like it did the arrows.

"Time to start," the man told her.

She settled the quiver on her back and took the bow like it was a toy. She gave me one last scathing look before she turned to go.

I watched her walk away from me, admiring her ass. I had seen it one night while Scott Stone fucked her up against the window in his apartment. The curtains had been pushed to the side, and it was a gorgeous sight, like a full moon on a dark night.

"What do you think you're doing?" She stopped abruptly when I caught up to her a second later.

Scottish drums had started beating in the background, and I knew whatever she was about to do would be good. I wanted to see her in this setting, making those arrows fly with sharp precision.

"Walking."

"Why next to me?"

"Because I can."

She opened her mouth, about to lash out at me. Then she took a deep breath. "This is a huge place," she said. "Plenty of room for you to walk on the *other* side of the field."

"I'd prefer to walk next to you. Seein' as you're packing." I nodded to her gear.

"Why? Lots of people want to kill you?"

"We both know that's true."

She nodded her head, like she could believe that. Then she took a step closer to me. She was tall for a woman, but she still had to look up at me. "Listen. *Cash*. You might've fooled my brother with all your glittery *things*, but you don't fool me. The moment you found me in that cemetery, I knew you were up to no good. I'm not girlie. I don't indulge in fantasies—princes and princesses and all of that fairytale shit. And I don't believe in fucking happenstances. Men like you don't just show up out of the blue. You plan. You scheme. You *maraud*. You met me at the cemetery. Then you hired my brother. And now you're here. Whatever this interest is—" she motioned between us "—stops now."

I refused to hide my grin. She had been thinking about me. No woman comes to all of those conclusions if her mind wasn't on it. Her thoughts were on me. I must've made some impression at the cemetery.

Stone's heart was as good as mine.

I WATCHED HER WALK OFF, knowing I had rattled her some. A woman like her wasn't easily shaken, and later on, it would be both a blessing and a curse.

Later.

Think about the curse later.

Deal with it then.

My eyes followed as she got lost in a crowd surrounding the archery competition. These people were novices, all trying their hands at an ancient sport. I noticed they were all men. The last one had just loosed his arrow, actually hitting the bullseye. When the crowd went up in a cheer, he lifted his bow, cheering with them.

I stood back, crossing my arms, getting comfortable.

"What are we looking at?" Raff said, crunching on nuts.

The noise drove me fucking insane. Hearing people chew grated on me like nails on a chalkboard.

He stopped when he noticed the way I was looking at him. "You have issues, Cash."

"Yeah," I said. "And killing men who chew in my ear is one of 'em."

He went to open his mouth again, but I held a hand up. I narrowed my eyes.

Someone must've given the archer a cape that covered her hair and quiver. She weaved through the masses, making her way to the front of the crowd. She was tall enough to make people move out of her way with ease. A fucking force of a woman. The kind of woman I always said had good bones.

The MC of the archery games had brought the winner up, holding his arm in the air, while the crowd roared with applause. After a second, the MC made a motion for the crowd to settle.

"Scotty Campbell!" He announced. "You have won the grandest of prizes!" His eyes scanned the crowd until he found the archer. The entire crowd seemed to follow his gaze, all heads turning toward her. "Maeve—" Before he could finish her fake name, she threw the cape to the ground, revealing her gear, and started slaying each of the contestants' targets.

She made her way, hitting the bulls-eye where the contestants hadn't, and when she came to Scotty Campbell's prized shot, her eyes narrowed even further as she pulled back the bow. With a collective released breath from the crowd, she let the arrow fly. Upon impact, it penetrated straight through the other wooden arrow, splitting it in half. The Robin Hood shot. Some people called it a once in a lifetime shot.

"Feck me." Raff whistled.

The crowd became silent, not sure where to look the longest, at the shot or at her. She turned toward the MC and Campbell, and without a tremble in her voice, said, "I'm the only one allowed to choose my husband!"

The crowd roared again, and the MC messed Campbell's thinning hair as he cheered along with them.

"That had to hurt his pride," Raff said, one hand clapping against his arm so he wouldn't lose his *fecking* nuts. "She's savage, man. Truly savage. I didn't realize feminists were rife in medieval times."

The archer turned those heavenly eyes on me once again, as narrowed as they ever were, and it wasn't hard to imagine the arrows protecting the gates of heaven piercing straight through my heart, sending my soul to hell. As a prize, she would steal the color of my eyes and use them as feathers on her arrows.

6

KEELY

On the ride home from the fair, I wondered if there was a way to purge my brain. Do one of those detoxes everyone raved about, but instead of doing it for my body, do it for the wellness of my mind.

Because when one infuriating, *probably fucking crazy* Irish *marauder* got into my brain, it was almost impossible to get him out. He kept pillaging around, taking what he wanted—my time and attention.

I refused to give them up.

Yet.

There they went. Straight to him.

Even in that moment, I was still thinking about him and what had happened at the fair. My reaction to him took *me* by surprise. As soon as I laid eyes on him, it felt like my breath had been knocked from my lungs. The man looked fucking amazing in a t-shirt and jeans, as fine as he'd looked in a suit.

For someone who was probably put together in hell, he was heaven to look at.

His eyes were green; his limbal ring thick and black. It made him look wicked. And for the first time, I noticed a tattoo on his neck: a tiger with the same color eyes. The collar of his coat had hidden it when we'd met at the cemetery. It spanned from underneath his ear to the end of his neck, ending right above his collarbone. It looked like it was going to climb out of his skin and devour me.

Heat crept up my neck at the thought of it. *Think about something else. Anything else.*

Happenstance. That was the word he'd used to describe our meeting at the cemetery, and he'd said it with that soft and lyrical Irish lilt.

Happenstance my ass. Even in such a dead place, he was such a life force. His moves were calculated and done with purpose.

Yeah, that wasn't technically thinking about something else, but I couldn't seem to stop.

I'd always go back to our meeting at the cemetery. Something had been nagging me about it, and I couldn't figure out what. Not until it hit me at the fair: this was New York. If you met someone twice, there was probably more to it. Then when *Cash* turned up as my brother's new boss? The one who gave him a fully restored vintage car as a *bonus*? My bullshit meter exploded.

The cemetery. *Bam.*

Harrison's new boss. *Bam.*

Showing up at the fair to "meet" me. *Bam.*

I was waiting for the *BOOM.*

What the fuck did he want with me?

What was even more puzzling—the thought of him made me uneasy *and* excited.

Being close to him? Excited me more than anything. It was also what pissed me off the most. My feelings around him screwed with my mind. There was something about him that immediately made me want to take a step back and then a step forward. Repeat. Repeat. Repeat. I felt like the family in *Beetle-*

juice when they all started dancing because the husband and wife ghosts controlled their functions.

Giving myself some credit, though, I felt like I handled him pretty well at the fair.

On the other hand.

I wished I could extend a fist through time and punch myself for giving him the satisfaction of knowing he had rattled me.

Darlin'. The way he'd said the word, with that sexy voice of his, made me shiver.

I was not an experienced woman when it came to men like him, but I did have a heightened sense when it came to the world in general, and something told me that he was the kind of man who easily read the signs from a woman. And he used them for his nefarious schemes. In his case, he had the perfect weapons: face, voice, body. His fucking *charm* locked it in tight.

Charm—such a pretty word for something that could turn life ugly if used as a weapon. Especially when he used it to get whatever he wanted. And when charm didn't work? There was no doubt he'd get it another way.

I hoped after I showed those men at the fair how good I was at hitting each target set out for me, Cash Kelly would realize that I wasn't to be fucked with. I'd shoot an arrow in his ass so fast that he'd think an invisible foot had kicked him in it.

I grinned to myself, imagining it.

There was one truth that I couldn't ignore, though, no matter how hard I tried. It always led me back to why the bastard excited me. It was nice and simple, clean cut, but with a sharp and dangerous point.

I was attracted to him on a level that felt unholy. Which by itself was okay—attraction was not actually cheating—but it almost felt like I was when I thought about Cash Kelly, even when Scott wasn't around.

Scott—the man who loves you—Stone.

After I met Scott's family in January, he asked me to think about marrying him. I told him I needed time, but he was starting to get impatient. Making a man wait a few months for an answer to such an important question didn't do anything good for his ego, it seemed.

If he was true about his intentions, though, why rush it? It wasn't like he really asked, either. He didn't get down on one knee or give me a ring. He told me to *think* about it.

That was exactly what I'd been avoiding. Thinking about one huge word—yes.

I always found something to redirect my thoughts when they went there. Maybe if he did ask soon, I'd just blurt the first response that came to my mind. I had a teacher once who told me that if I didn't know an answer on a test, I should always go with the one that *felt* right and leave it at that.

"It's probably coming from your gut," she'd said.

It was tiring thinking about the marauder (Kelly) and the detective (Stone) at the same time. I didn't even want to compare them, and for some reason, it felt as if I knew Kelly as much as I did Stone. Maybe even better, which was bullshit, because I'd only met him twice. Still, thinking about them in the same space of time felt like a mind trap.

Enough thinking about men then.

I glanced into the backseat at Mari. She had been quiet, probably dreading the moment we pulled up to my apartment. I knew she had no money. She had told me before we left for the fair that she had been fired. She was kicked out of her apartment and beaten up by the prick Merv, her landlord. Her beautiful face was full of bruises and splits from his fists.

My own fists balled when I thought about him doing that to her over not paying rent.

She and I needed to come up with a plan for her life, and fast. She'd refuse any help outright offered, so I'd have to work around her aversion to accepting kindness without feeling like she had earned it first. I had to think of doing nice things for Mari in terms of a job. She did something for me. I paid her for it. Then she wouldn't consider it accepting something for free.

It was a fucked-up way to live, but she was a kid from the streets. To accept kindness from strangers could get her killed or make her wish that she were dead if she ended up owing the wrong person. So even though I hated that she was that way with my family and me, I never faulted her for it. I understood.

As we pulled up to my apartment, her eyes fell to her old leather bag. I could feel the weight of her situation fall on my back, and I wished there was more I could do. It never felt like enough. It never would. Not until I knew she was taken care of.

"I'm coming in for a sec," Harrison said, shutting the car off. "Give me a minute."

I gave him a narrow look, wondering what he was up to, but I was dying to get comfortable, so I got out. I waited for Mari and we walked together to my apartment. We were both quiet, but I could feel her relief the moment we stepped inside and she realized that my roommate, Sierra, was not home.

My roommate was another kid from the streets, and it was hard to tell who had the hardest life, Mari or Sierra. They both ran a good race for immediate candidates for heaven. As much hell as they went through on earth, I felt they both deserved a direct in. But for all they were the same, they handled their situations differently.

Sierra was not opposed to stepping on anyone to get a hand up. She fraternized with men who could easily put others on an endangered species list. She'd probably cut a starving person for touching her stash of food, even if she had plenty.

Mari was a gentler soul. She kept her head down and worked—when she could keep a job. Mari was terrible with keeping work, even though I'd gotten her plenty of jobs over the years. And even though Mari didn't have a cent to her name, she'd give her last crumbs to a starving pigeon if she felt like she could help it, maybe because not many people tried to help her, and she knew how it felt.

I itched at a raw spot on my side from the dress. The cheap material made me feel like I was wearing one big fucking shirt tag. "I'm going to get out of these clothes," I said, going for my room. "Don't even think about leaving, Mari!" I yelled over my shoulder. I could see her eyeing the door. "We need to work on a plan. We need to get your shit together before you disappear on me. If you do, no fucking joke, I'm going to hunt you down."

Before I made it to the hall, she took a seat on the sofa. It was second-hand and threadbare, but Mari sunk into it like it was made of the finest silk. I sighed, understanding. My feet were on fire from standing on them all day. I ditched the dress —if it wasn't rented, I would've burned the bitch—and put on a comfortable sweater with yoga pants. It took me a few minutes to tame my wild hair into a somewhat respectable ponytail. When I made it back to the hall, I stopped before Harrison and Mari noticed me.

Harrison sat next to Mari on the sofa, talking to her.

My family and I called him "Grumpy Indiana Jones" behind his back. For as far back as I could remember, Harrison was always a man. He was one of those kids that could pull off a suit and tie at two. But around Mari, he never sounded as grumpy as he did with everyone else. So to hear him be nice to her pulled at my heartstrings. She really needed it, but I also knew she hated it, and I didn't need her to find any excuse to run away from me.

"What did you do?" I said, shocking them both. Mari startled like they had been caught doing something wrong. My brother stood, putting some space between them, sticking his hands in his pockets.

"Nothing, Kee," he said. "I gave Mari a gift for her birthday, sort of."

"Her birthday isn't until October," I said, pointing out the obvious. Not for the first time, I wondered how Harrison truly felt about Mari. It seemed to go beyond a brotherly type of relationship for him. He'd never admitted it to me, and I'd decided not to admit my suspicions to her, but sometimes it was hard to see him look at her and not think, *there's more there.*

Harrison shrugged. "I hate being late."

I opened my mouth to respond, but a loud knock came at the door. I looked toward the sound, wondering who'd be coming over so late. Sierra wasn't home, and unless she was, her boyfriends stayed away. Her men went wherever she went.

"Expecting someone?" Harrison asked.

I shook my head. "No, Sierra said she was going to be home late."

"I'll get it," he said.

Mari came to stand beside me while Harrison talked to someone on the other side of the door. A minute later, he came in, followed by two men.

SHIT! The word buzzed to life like a neon warning in the darkness of my mind.

He *wouldn't.*

"Keely," Harrison said. "This is Detective Scott Stone and Detective Paul Marinetti."

Scott stepped up first, offering his hand, playing his part well, but the softness in his eyes was so apparent to me. He let his hand linger a moment too long before the older man offered his. His partner. Scott had mentioned him before. Scott thought that he needed to retire, and he felt Paul was too soft on hard criminals. More specifically, ones affiliated with organized crime.

In general, Scott didn't agree with everyday crimes, but he seemed to have a separate extremely hard spot for anyone associated with organized crime and the like. Scott and his family specifically went after gangsters and the "families" they belonged to with a passion that almost bordered on obsession. It went past the job and became personal.

After meeting his family in Louisiana, I found the reason why: his aunt and unborn cousin were killed by a drunk driver, who also happened to be the son of one of the most notorious Italian crime families in history. The Faustis. They were considered royalty in Italy and beyond, but Scott's family saw them as nothing but low-down murderers who should all be sentenced to life without parole.

"Ms. Ryan," Scott said, a serious look on his face, bringing my focus fully on him. "I regret to have to inform you that your roommate, Sierra Andruzzi, was found dead. We've been trying to get in touch with you, but this is the first time we've been able to."

My legs moved without conscious thought. I didn't realize I'd taken a seat on the sofa until I saw Mari move away from me after she and Harrison had helped me sit. "She..." I shook my head. "She told me she wouldn't be back until later. Her ex-boyfriend. Armino. He was at our door earlier. Mad. She broke up with him. Did he..."

Armino Scarpone was Sierra's latest conquest. He had money. Connections. His family was one of the five, meaning they were connected. He was a good-looking son of a bitch, but I had warned her about him more than once. Something about him rubbed me the wrong way. He didn't seem like the kind of guy who'd take no for an answer.

Sierra had told him no—she'd broken up with him.

He was at our door before Mari and I left for the fair, banging and shouting things at Sierra. She'd told us that he'd get sick of waiting around after a while and leave. Maybe she didn't know him well enough, because he'd been sitting in his expensive car when we left, smoking a cigarette, watching our door.

"From what we've pieced together, Ms. Andruzzi ran to the

store earlier, and that's when she was assaulted and then murdered. It seems like she was headed back here. As of right now, we can't say for sure. That's why we're here. To piece the time together."

"I—" What was I even supposed to say?

"We hate to ask you to do this, Ms. Ryan, but would you mind coming with us to identify the body? We cannot find a next of kin for Ms. Andruzzi."

"No," I said, knowing they wouldn't find anyone to claim her. "She was a foster kid." She'd mentioned once, with a sharp, sarcastic twist of the tongue, that her mom was more concerned with eating pills than with feeding her food.

"My sister is not—"

"No," I said, cutting Harrison off. "I'll do it. It's the least I can do for her. Let me grab my things."

As I stood, Scott handed Harrison his card and told him the address to the place where Sierra was being held was on the back. Harrison told him we'd be there shortly.

Scott gave me a pointed look when he warned us that Armino might be lurking. We were the last people to see him before Sierra was murdered.

Before I went to grab my shoes, my eyes found Mari. She stood in the middle of the room, not sure what to do. She almost looked guilty. I knew it was because she didn't like Sierra, but she felt bad that she had been murdered.

That made the two of us.

Even though their behavior was miles apart, I couldn't separate their situations in my mind. If something ever happened to Mari?—hell no. I refused to even think about it. She was my sister. The only one I had left.

In that moment, she reminded me of a scared butterfly, not sure where to go to find safety. She *had* no place to go.

"Mari?" Harrison said before I could. "Come with us."

I stood next to him, forming a unit.

"No," she said. "I'd rather not."

"You can't disappear," I said, and I made sure that she heard the pleading in it. "I need to know where you are. After what happened to you...and now tonight..." Without warning, I wrapped my arms around her, hugging her tight. It was what I wished I'd done to my sister before she left and I never saw her again.

"Can I stay here?" she asked, her voice breathy. She wanted to step out of my embrace—affection made her uneasy—but she didn't move.

"Sierra's old man." Harrison shook his head. "It might not be—"

"He's not coming back here." Mari took a step back, and I released her. Our relationship was a lot of give and take. "He's probably long gone."

I nodded, eager to agree so she wouldn't leave. "Yeah, he's probably gone. Just make sure to lock the doors."

I tried to keep the fear off my face, to hide the "please don't leave me too" vibe from my body. If pushed too far, Mari would leave, and I'd suffer hell for it. Wondering where she had gone and if someone else had hurt her, maybe even taken her life.

"I will," she said.

"Use the cellphone—" Harrison nodded toward the sofa "—to call me if you need anything. My number's programmed in."

We waited outside of the apartment after we'd walked out of it, listening while Mari locked the door. Then I took a deep breath, not ready to do what had to be done, but determined to claim a girl who never had anyone claim her before.

———

EVEN THOUGH THE girl I looked at was Sierra Andruzzi, my roommate, she looked different to me somehow.

Every person I'd ever seen in death had always looked

peaceful. In death, Sierra looked extremely pissed off. Like she was mad that it took Armino so long to end her life, or that he had actually done it and she wasn't strong enough to fight him off.

Detective Marinetti had told Harrison that her hands were frozen, like claws. Armino had stabbed her to death. Even though Armino was only a suspect, my gut told me he had killed her.

There were times I had worried that one day I'd find Sierra dead, but from something self-inflicted. Though she was hard to rattle, I saw the struggle in her eyes, how tired she was, and she'd sleep for days. Other days, she was so wired that she couldn't sleep. I had tried talking to her about getting help, but she'd always laugh at me and tell me I was the funniest girl in all of New York, and even though she liked me, she'd like me even better if I'd mind my own fucking business.

That was when I knew I could help her, cook her meals when she was too tired to get out of bed, but not directly. After all, Mari was similar. She couldn't accept kindness either.

Mari.

The thought of her made my palms sweaty. She had checked on me, texting with the new phone Harrison had given her as a "birthday" gift. He'd told me on the ride over that she paid him two bucks for the phone. She wouldn't accept it without paying for it. Either way, I was just glad I had a way to keep in touch with her.

Maybe I shouldn't have done it, but after seeing Sierra, I told Mari the conclusion I had come to about Harrison. He was in love with her. I told her not to answer if she didn't want to, but the situation made me uneasy.

I considered Mari my sister. Harrison was my brother.

In his eyes, though, she was a woman. A woman he was in love with. It explained why he was so fucking grumpy all of the time. He must've been harboring his feelings silently since whenever.

That aside, she had texted me that she was going out. She promised me that she'd keep in touch, but it made me worry. What that prick of a landlord had done to her could've easily ended in the same way it had for Sierra.

The entire night felt like a nightmare.

I looked up when the door to the investigation room opened. Scott walked in and sat across from me. He slipped a cup of coffee my way. I took it but couldn't bear the thought of drinking it. I wanted to erase Sierra's face from my mind, but guilt ate me up inside. I was all she had. How could I want to lessen the impact of her death, when I was the only one who seemed to care about her life?

"This isn't your fault," Scott said.

I slid the coffee between my palms. "I know."

"Girl like her." He shrugged. "Bound to happen."

Girl like her. Bound to happen.

Scott's attitude was one of the things I disliked about him the most. It was no secret that he saw things that haunted him. There were times I saw them in his eyes, the ghosts, and I'd know that he was still human because he could be haunted. But there were other times when I wanted to throttle him for being so careless with his words.

It was no secret that Sierra was looking for an easy way out with a rich man. It didn't matter who he was or what he did. She craved security like she craved food after being starved her entire life. Scott, though, acted like she went out every night with a gun in her hand looking for someone to kill or rob. Even though she didn't, he still grouped her in with those who lived by the sword and died by it, too. It pissed me off, as much as organized crime seemed to piss him off.

"Don't give me that look." He sighed. "I didn't say she deserved it. I said it was bound to happen."

"I know what you said."

"And?"

"It sounds callous and cold. She was my friend."

"A friend that was bound to bring you trouble. And she has." He took the coffee from me, taking a sip. "Armino Scarpone is a killer. He knows you and your friend can testify that he made a scene outside of your apartment before you left. Then his ex-girlfriend, because she broke up with him not long before, ends up stabbed to death outside of a store on her way back to your apartment. His family's not fond of leaving witnesses that can testify against them. It's a code. Just like when they kill an entire family because they don't want retribution down the line."

"I'm not worried about Armino. If he comes looking for trouble, he'll find it."

Scott threw back his head and laughed. Then he looked me in the eye. "What are you going to do, Keely? Kill him with your bow and arrow? Shit!" He stood abruptly, the chair almost falling back. "The Scarpones! You're going to stay with me. Do you understand?"

"I'm not leaving Mari—"

"Mari. Mari. Mari. What's with you and Mari? Why do you care about her so much?"

I stood, refusing to allow him to look down at me. "She's my sister!"

"No, she's your friend!"

"And what kind of friend are you? Would you leave a friend who was like a brother to you when he needed you the most?

"We're not talking about me!" he shouted.

"Maybe we should! Maybe we should talk about how big of an *ass* you're being!"

I went to fly past him, but he grabbed me by the arm. I refused to look at him. My heart was in my throat. Tears pushed against my defenses. My neck was on fire, scorching red because of my temper.

"Marry me, Keely Shea Ryan."

From the corner of my eye I could see him digging in his pocket with his free hand. He lifted the ring high enough that I could see it in my peripheral. It was a traditional Irish Claddagh ring. The heart was made from an emerald, and the crown had three diamonds.

Mari was going to tell me it was a bad omen. *Bad things always come in threes, Kee.*

I licked my dry lips. "What?" I whispered, trying to buy time.

"Marry me, Keely. Live with me. I'll keep you safe."

"Is that why you're asking? To keep me safe?"

"No. You know better. I've had this planned for a while. Tonight, after I saw Sierra, it hit me hard. You could've been home at the wrong time. You could've walked with her to the store. I couldn't live with myself knowing that I protect people, strangers, for a living, and I couldn't save the only girl I'll ever love."

"I—"

"Keely—" Harrison opened the door and then stopped, watching us. He had gone out to call our brothers. He kept them informed about everything. Those four were worse than a bunch of gossiping sisters. Harrison's eyes narrowed before he took a step in, looking Scott in the eye. "Get your hands off my sister. Now."

Scott looked between us. "I'm in love with your sister. I just asked her to marry me. We've been seeing each other for months. We're in love."

Harrison stared at Scott with a blank look and then turned his narrowed eyes on me. "Is this true?"

After a minute or two, he took my silence as admission.

"You couldn't tell me?" I could tell my brother was hurt, and even though I hated to see it, he had no room to talk.

And. I. Was. Going. To. Kill. Scott. *Fucking*. Stone.

Who did he think he was? We hadn't discussed this! *This.* Whatever this was between us, and it was moving way too fast. I couldn't stop it.

My Mam. She had predicted this.

And Roisin. I had asked her to send me someone if this wasn't right. And who did she send me?

The wrong man! Who would send a man like him? I knew for certain Roisin would've been the sane one between us. The practical one. Cash Kelly was chaotic. Nothing about him made sense.

Then Mari comes over with her face all busted. No place to live. Nothing in her pockets but old bread. I still had fucking itchy spots from a dress made out of tag material. I figured out that my brother was in love with the girl I considered my sister. He had been keeping the secret close to his *entire* life.

My roommate was brutally murdered.

And now, *this*!

I wished I could store arrows in my eyes for times like these. Even though it wasn't physically possible, I made sure Scott felt them after I turned my glare from him to my brother. "Why couldn't *you* tell me about Mari?"

"What about Mari?" he said, lying through his teeth.

"You're in love with her!"

"Yeah, well, you're in love with Mahoney here!" He nodded toward Scott.

"It's Stone," Scott said.

"Yeah, I got that, bright guy. I was making a *Police Academy* reference. You ever watch a movie?"

"Take me home!" I shouted.

I didn't realize until I got there that Scott had slipped the ring on my finger. I slipped it off as we pulled up to my apartment, not sure why.

7

CASH

Uncertainty and I were old foes. I never enjoyed surprises, or not knowing what the hell to do in all situations. I was a man who always knew which road to take, which man in the room was going to be trouble, which one to kill, what to order, what fork to use at a fancy dinner party.

In a sum, I always had a clear picture of how life was going to play out for me.

Keely Ryan gave me anything but a clear picture. I couldn't decide what I wanted more: for her heart to belong to Scott's fully, or enough to *pretend* that it was.

If she'd given her heart to Stone, then her suffering would undoubtedly be his. Because that was what fools in love did. They suffered for the ones they loved the most.

Once she fell for me, he'd never get over it. Not even in death. Because he was going to love and hate her for falling for a monster.

Either way, though, I knew Keely Ryan was going to try to hand me my ass on a silver platter for fucking with her. She wasn't going to give that heart of hers up without a fight, even if it was only to prove to herself that she didn't have to do anything she didn't want to.

I smiled at the thought of fighting with her, and it felt damn good to smile about something.

A knock came at my office door, and a second later, Raff stuck his head in. "I have a message for you," he said.

We stared at each other for a beat.

"Did you bring the bottle so I can read the fucking thing?" I said after he didn't answer.

"No." He smiled. "It's from Father Flanagan. Message by mouth."

"There's a surprise. I sent you to make an appointment with him."

"Exactly." Raff smiled even wider. "He said to tell you—" he cleared his throat "—'*Appointments are for those who believe God doesn't have His own timin'.*'" His Irish accent was horrible, but I got the point.

I lifted my arm and checked my watch. "He'll see me at 3 then. I have another appointment at 5."

He nodded. "Do you need me at 5?"

I nodded. "Harry Boy and his sister will be joining me in the office. Check them for weapons before bringing them in."

His face scrunched up. "He's been in here more than a dozen times. I've never had to check him before."

"No." I stood, going for my suit jacket. "I don't expect him to have one. The woman? Double check."

"What am I looking for? Specifically."

"If she was able to hide a bow and arrow underneath her clothes, I'd say those. But seeing as she wouldn't get past the front door, check for smaller weapons. Gun. Knife. Poisonous tablets."

"What's this about, Cash?" Raff moved out of my way when I made it to the door leading out to the waiting room.

"I'm going to steal a bride."

His deep laugh echoed around the warehouse. "That's somethin' I guarantee you never stole before!" A second later, after he stopped laughing, he wiped his eyes. "Be serious. Stop fucking with me."

"When do I ever," I said.

"Mr. Cash!" My ancient secretary, Susan, who had also worked for my father, stopped me. "John is here for his appointment."

I looked over at an older man sitting in one of the chairs, waiting. "Mr. Gerald." He stood and I walked over to him, holding out my hand. We shook. "I have to run out, but I've been hearing things. I know why you're here. Don't worry about Martin. We'll get him some help and then see if we can find him some work on the docks. Working for me." His son, Martin, was hooked, and his old man was struggling.

Mr. Gerald nodded. "Your old man would be proud."

I squeezed his shoulder and then told him I'd be in touch with details.

I stepped outside. Raff stopped me as I was setting my Fedora on my head.

"Cash. You're being serious."

"While you're out." I dug in my pocket and handed him a card. "Pick up a ring I ordered at that jeweler. You'll need your ID."

Stone's ring was cliché and not meant for a woman like her. If I was going to do this, I was going to get it right, to show the both of them that I knew her better than he did. Another little nick to his heart.

I was halfway down the street when Raff screamed out my name. I stopped but didn't turn.

"This is not the way it works. You only confess your sins *after* you've committed them—premeditated wrongs are a gray area, Kelly!"

I grinned. "Can't blame a man for trying." Then I figured I'd talk to Father Flanagan about them again when I got there. Gray areas were not my specialty; dark ones were.

"CASHEL FALLON KELLY. To what do I owe the pleasure?" Father Flanagan held his hand up. "Why do I even ask? It's been a while since our last visit. I forgot." He tapped his temple twice. "Follow me."

"It hasn't been that long," I said, following him through the church. It brought back memories of when I was a boy: my father taking us to church to confess our sins. The newsboy hat he made me wear to be respectful. The bitter and potent smell of incense thick in the air. The light coming in through the stained-glass windows, falling on my face. Father Flanagan welcoming me into the room where he'd absolve me of sin. "You came to see me once a week in prison. Four times a month for ten years."

"December," he said.

"That's right. You came five times a month in December."

"A fella should have a friendly face to see around the holidays." He stopped at what I called the "confession booth," but I never called it that in front of Father Flanagan. It was the confessional in front of him. He had old-school ways, like my old man, and he'd take a ruler to my fingers in a heartbeat. "Go ahead."

I entered on my side, and a second later, his voice came through from the other side. "Do you finally have sins that were *already* committed to rid yourself of today, Cashel Kelly?"

"I'm sure I do, Father," I said, attempting to get comfortable. "But the ones I came to talk about today haven't been committed yet."

"Your moral compass still hasn't come in yet." He sighed,

and I imagined him closing his eyes, pinching the bridge of his nose as he did. "What is it that you need my ear on?"

I grinned. Moral compass. Father Flanagan liked to say that I was a late bloomer when it came to getting one of those. I told him to save his hope for someone who could benefit from it. I wasn't born with one, and I doubted this late in life that mine would come through.

"I'm going to steal a heart. Or a bride. Either one works." I'd said a lot of insane things over the years to this man, but this was a first.

He cleared his throat a few seconds later. "Explain in more detail."

I reminded him of years ago. My father. Stone's father. Me. Stone's son. Then I went forward from that point. How it was going to go down.

"The pain ends once the soul does," I explained in a little more depth. "'There are three things that amaze me—no, four things I do not understand: how an eagle glides through the sky, how a snake slithers on a rock, how a ship navigates the ocean, how a man loves a woman.'" I quoted the Bible, because we were taught to know it. That was how my father operated, as a man who feared God but no man on this earth. "I don't understand how a man loves a woman, but I do understand this: when the soul gets attached, it'll hurt until the day it dies when it's separated from the one it loves."

"Are you positive, Cashel Kelly, that Scott Stone's heart is attached to this woman's?"

"Without a doubt," I said. We became quiet for a moment. Something about his voice piqued my interest. I expected him to become serious, to become my moral compass, but out of all my years, I'd never heard a grin in his voice. "You think I'm doing the right thing."

"No," he said, after another long moment. He *was* smiling. I could hear it in his tone. "You are absolutely doing the wrong thing. You're *stealin'* a bride. Stealin', no matter how we turn it, is a sin. You know this, and if you don't, then maybe I should take a deeper look at my life. You and Killian were sent here to test me, of this I am sure. However, there are times in life when we get what we deserve."

"Are you telling me that karma is going to come after me?"

"Somethin' like that."

"That's cryptic."

"Not really." He sighed. "I would have an ear full for ya if ya told me you were plannin' on stealin' money or weapons. But a heart, Cashel? We'll see. We'll just see about that."

"Still cryptic."

He sighed, but this time it was impatient. "Tell me how you plan on stealin' this girl's heart."

"Maybe you don't know much about matters of the heart, when it comes to the opposite sex, but the day I met her, I knew it right away. She was mine. She hated me too much, and that only means one thing. Deep down, she likes me. She's infatuated with me. The bad boy she thinks she can change." I almost laughed at that. A bad boy was someone who did stupid shit. I was a dangerous man who made smart moves.

"Through all my hardness, she wants to find a crack in my bones, so she can go straight through my veins and steal *my* heart. She has no idea, though. I have no heart. And my soul? We both know it's dark enough for light to get lost in. Good souls go on to live another life. But when my soul goes—that's it. One life to live is literal for me."

"What if Stone doesn't truly love her, Cashel?"

"He does."

"You'd bet your life on it."

"The only one I have."

"And you mean to accomplish what by this?"

"I'll steal his heart and his soul will be mine. Everything. I want his everything. I'll have it."

"She's his everything."

"His job is his life. He lives for it. But the fierce archer? She makes him feel the light in the world when he's surrounded by all darkness. Men like me, we touch him and make his life like ours, but in a different way. He fights against it, while we welcome it. And he doesn't want his heart to get tarnished by the darkness. He doesn't want his hope to get stolen by marauders like me.

"He and I both know that I'm the best at what I do. I can go beyond the physical and feel what means the most. He already gave her his heart to keep safe. To keep clean. Even though she has a tongue like a whip, she's good, no matter how much she doesn't want to be. She acts tougher than she is."

"Have you ever loved a woman, Cashel?"

I tried to keep it down, but my laughter still boomed around me. "That's the only thing we have in common, Father. Never. I'm committed to this life. You're committed to yours. Funny enough, neither life leaves enough room for the love of a woman."

He took a deep breath in and then released it slowly. "I've known you since you were a wee babe. As much wrong as you've done, you've never done this particular thing before."

"Like I said, I know *who* and *when. Scott Stone. Now.* He's vulnerable. I know his crack, and I'll slip in like a thief in the night and steal what he stole from me. His entire life."

A noise echoed inside of the booth. It sounded like Father Flanagan had set his hand against the divider. "All you feel is hatred for Scott Stone. All you see is a way in to steal what he claimed as his. But you're forgetting one thing, my son. You're forgetting the innocent woman. What about her?"

"I remember her. Vividly. She's already mine—in hatred and in love. You and I both know how close they are. You're not capable of feeling one without having the ability to feel the other. Indifference is the cold bullet to all feelings. This archer, she hates me now, but her heart is as good as mine. Even if she fights me for it."

"One thing to keep in mind," he said. "A woman's heart was designed with thievery in mind—it was designed so that it couldn't be tampered with. Not even by the best marauder around. You turn the stolen key, or pick the lock, and it might be your heart she claims."

I hadn't come to seek advice. I came to confess. So I sat back, settling in, comfortable with the uncomfortable. "I didn't come here to confess my plans to you, Father. I came here to confess my sins. Or in this case, sin. Through my own hatred, I'm going to use her. Even though it's unfortunate, it's not enough to stop me from doing it."

"It never is," he muttered. "It never was for Maraigh, either. But we'll see what happens this time."

"We shall see," I said. "No one has proved me wrong yet."

That was that.

FATHER FLANAGAN WATCHED as I walked down the street. He'd done it ever since I was a boy. Usually it was Killian and I together, come to say our penance and then off to act like little fools afterward. Father Flanagan used to say that he was surprised we could make it two steps from the church before trouble found us.

Make it a little harder for the devil, will you now, lads. The devil is fond of cheap dates.

Sticking my hand in my pocket, I whistled while I walked down the street, looking forward to my meeting with Harry Boy and family. Family, meaning his sister. I wondered if she was going to finally make good on her threat and punch me in the face, since her bow and arrow wouldn't be allowed in my building. Despite my acceptance of death, I demanded to live long enough to taste the sweetness of revenge on my tongue.

As I passed a warehouse, I noticed two guys standing against it, smoking cigarettes. My eyes didn't linger, but I took notice of them. Halfway down the block, them still trailing me, I stopped in front of another warehouse.

I turned, facing them. "What do you need, fellas?"

"You Cash Kelly?"

Remember—stupid questions. Still, I gave him a brilliant answer for it. "All day."

"Our boss has a message for you."

One of them stepped forward and punched me in the gut. It wasn't hard enough to make me double-up, but the other one decided to land a blow to my nose before I could move. I shook it off, blood splattering in all directions. "You done?" I said.

They both grinned at me.

My fist flew through the air so fast that neither one of them had time to react. I crushed the guy's nose that had broken mine. He cursed, and before he could go for his gun, I pulled mine and shot him point blank in the forehead.

I felt the pressure of a gun behind my head, and the other fella snatched my gun from my hand, taking it. "You're going to die a coward, just like your old man. He was never needed here. Never. He came here from Ireland on a martyr's cause—"

Before he could utter another word, I turned on him and knocked the gun from his hand. It landed on the ground and slid. He was big enough to absorb my punches, but not strong enough to keep up with them. I was quick, and when I hit, I hit hard and in all the right spots. He danced with me while trying to get closer and closer to the gun again. When he went to duck and lunge for it, I grabbed him by the head and stuck my knee in his nose. His eyes rolled and he fell to the ground.

Leaning down, I grabbed him by his hair. "Look at me," I said. "I want you to look at me when I say this."

He blinked at me once, twice, but then closed his eyes. I let his head fall to the ground, before I took a step back, simultaneously looking at him and leaning down to grab my gun.

The fucker was playing possum, because in a second, he had snatched the gun and had it pointed at my head. I kicked his arm a second before the blast shattered it to pieces. The gun went back, but a bullet still whizzed through the air.

This time, I kept my foot on his wrist, picking up the gun again. I was faintly aware that my skull was on fire as I returned the favor. Shot for shot.

He wasn't as lucky as I was. He'd never make another shot again.

I pulled back a bloodstained palm after running it along the side of my head. The bullet must've grazed my skin.

"Jesus, Mary, and Joseph." Father Flanagan stood in front of the mess, making the sign of the cross.

"They weren't as close as two steps." I nodded toward them. "But they found me regardless. Guess they thought I'd be a cheap date." I took my gun from guy two–he'd tucked it into his pants–and then pulled out my phone. "Careful of your robe, Father. You don't want the blood of the wicked to stain your holy clothes.

Then I called Raff and told him to send men to clean up my mess.

8

KEELY

I crossed my arms over my chest, looking out of the window of Harrison's vintage car as he navigated the streets of Hell's Kitchen. "Why? Why did I let you talk me into this? How did I let you do this to me? You know I HATE the man!"

Not even a hundred years would be long enough to not see him, and it had only been a couple of days since the festival.

Harrison gave me the side-eye from underneath his glasses. "You owe me for not telling me about the detective."

"I owe *you* nothing. But maybe I would've told you, if you would've told me about Mari, oh, say, YEARS ago!"

"That's complicated and you know it."

"What's so complicated about it?"

"You would've told her."

"So?"

"Your timing is not mine." He shrugged.

"Fair enough. But still. How did I let you TALK me into this?"

"Hate. Years. Talk. Why did you scream those three words?"

"Stop trying to change the subject!"

"Yeah. Okay. You're doing this for me because we both know who my boss is. And I don't have the option to tell him no."

I studied my brother for a minute.

This guy, the one with the nice car and even nicer clothes, wasn't my brother. My brother was easy-going. He wanted a simple life. A nice house. A decent car. A family. Kids he could teach how to play baseball. *That* was my brother. I'd give him that this car was something he would have bought for himself, but the rest? The fancy lawyer gig? The gangster boss? Wasn't him.

Click. Click. Click. The pieces suddenly made sense.

"You did this for Mari, didn't you?"

He became quiet for a minute before he sighed. "Swear on your Broadway career that you won't tell her."

"Swear." I held up my hand, my fingers splayed.

"I did."

A breath left me that I had no control over. "You need to tell her, Harrison. Tell her how you feel. Life's too short to keep waiting. Fuck timing. We only have this second."

"What about the detective?" He turned the convo on me. "Are you in love with him?"

I'd been avoiding this conversation with him under the pretense that I was still pissed about him not telling me about his feelings for Mari. It was true, but not the real reason I didn't want to talk about it. Like he said, that situation complicated.

"Mam told me that my great love was going to come to me." I shrugged. "Stone came to me."

Even under the sunglasses I could tell his eyes narrowed. "Tea leaves? Are you kidding me, Kee? You're going to let Mam decide your fate with tea leaves?"

"It's complicated, Harrison."

"Mam told me to stay away from Mari because of the tea leaves. She was only going to cause chaos in my life and those around me. Her exact words were, 'a ripple effect from a dark blue stone.' Should I listen to her?"

I whipped my head around. Mam had never told me that, and neither had Harrison. "What did you say?"

He shrugged. "Nothing to her face, but I chose not to listen to her. Not to believe it. I've never felt anything like that around Mari. I've only felt—" He looked over at me and then turned his eyes back to the road.

"Love," I said. "You've only felt love around her."

"Something like that."

I grinned to myself, because my brother was in loooove. Big time. I only hoped Mari felt the same, or would give him a shot. Though, honestly, it would've been a hell of a lot easier if Harrison had fallen for Desiree Gibson. She loved him all throughout high school, and she still asked about him whenever I went to her salon for a trim. Desiree had no ties to our family, and I'd never considered her my sister.

Mari being like a sister complicated things a lot, especially if Mari didn't feel the same about Harrison.

"What's your deal with Cash, anyway?" Harrison pulled the car to the curb, parking right in front of a massive warehouse that looked like it had been redone.

"Deal?"

"Yeah. You've only met him twice, and you've made no secret of your hate for him."

"Those two meetings were enough to last me two lifetimes. And I only have one."

Harrison took off his glasses, set them on the dash, and then gave me the weight of his stare. "I don't buy it."

"I'm not selling anything."

"I don't *buy* that you hate him for no reason. He scared you at the cemetery? So what. It's quiet there until it's not. There's something else going on that you're not telling me. I'm not

Roisin, and I'm not trying to be, but we've always been close, Kee. You're hiding something."

I turned my face toward the window, not wanting him to see my eyes. When I was little and refused to talk, Harrison told me it was okay, that clouds were the words in my mind, and he could make out the shapes in my eyes—because they're blue—and read my thoughts.

It used to make me feel better, like someone out there could understand me without me having to use words, but I didn't want him to see the truth this time. Out of all of my siblings, when Roisin was killed, Harrison stepped up and took me under his wing. I didn't want to lie to him. He didn't deserve it. He didn't tell me about Mari, but when I asked, he gave me the truth.

"Is it Mam?" he said. "Did she say something else? The tea leaves?"

"Do you believe in them?"

He became quiet for a minute. "In a way, yes. We were brought up to. But I also believe that what we believe brings credence to what other people say is meant for us. I refuse to believe what she told me about Mari. And if I refuse to believe, it has no power over me."

"Power over you, huh." I looked at him and then back at the building. A humungous guy, both arms covered in tattoos, even up to his neck, walked into the building like he owned the place. "Cash Kelly. Does he have power over you?"

My brother sighed. "He's my boss."

"Like...you-kiss-his ring kind of boss?"

"He's not Italian."

"The accent sort of cleared that up."

"What do you want from me, Kee? He's my boss. And whether you like it or not, he gave me a good job, moved me out of the nasty fucking apartment I was in, gave me a car, a huge bonus. He gave me a chance at life. I owe him."

"You work for him. He pays you. That's how legit employment works. You owe him nothing if you're doing your job."

"Look," he said, and his tone was sharper. "It is what it is, all right? Cut me some slack. I like working for him."

"I *am* cutting you some slack! That's why I'm HERE! You asked me to do this. I'm doing it. But giving him a second chance is not cutting it for me, *Harry Boy*. What's the deal?"

When Harrison had first asked me to meet with Cash Kelly again, I laughed at him, and then with all seriousness told him not only no, but *hell no*. I didn't even feel bad when my brother started to beg, which he'd never done before. But when he brought up telling my parents about my engagement to Scott, I figured I'd suffer through this ridiculous guise of a meeting and then get on with my life.

And I knew Cash was getting off on this "meeting," knowing I hated him but wanting me here anyway. It almost seemed like he ate it up, like the fires of hell were a delicious meal to the marauder. He probably crapped out firestorms. So I was going to keep my composure around him this time, just to prove a point.

"There you go with the yelling again." Harrison shook his head. "He doesn't say much, but I get the feeling family is really important to him. Raff." He pointed toward the building, where the gigantic guy had been. "That's the guy who just walked in. He's Cash's right-hand man and cousin by marriage. I think Raff is all he has, even though he keeps his distance from him, too. His old man was killed years back on a street not far from here by a rival who wanted to take over, and did. I heard he has a brother, but no one talks about him."

"Did you ask?" I remembered what Cash had told me at the cemetery. He implied that his brother was dead. His twin.

My brother looked at me like my curls had turned into snakes. "You don't ask men like him personal questions."

"Yeah, like why, exactly, am *I* here."

Harrison opened the door and stepped out, then he leaned on it, looking down at me. "I told you. I think he wants to make amends. It seems like he's trying to build something here. Something good for the community. And the families of his employees are important to him. He knows how close we are." Harrison looked at his watch. "Come on. He doesn't like to wait." Then he shut the door.

I sighed, taking a look at the building. Then I opened my door, taking a deep breath. "Yeah," I said to myself, because Harrison was already to the warehouse. "I'm sure Cash Kelly is going to be holding family picnics and singing camp songs with the employee's kids real fucking soon."

As I walked toward the door, I made a promise to myself to keep my mouth shut this time—the longer I was around him, the smarter my mouth became, and he seemed drawn to it, like chaos to peace. And I didn't want to give him another reason to call on me again.

The sooner the marauder was out of my village, *out of my head*, the better off I'd be.

"GET YOUR HANDS OFF OF ME!" I slapped at the big palms patting at my body.

The big guy, Raff, demanded that Harrison and I both be "shook down" before we entered the marauder's layer.

As it stood, I was shocked that the entire place was decorated tastefully, with exposed pipes, tan brick walls, and chrome details, and not done in fire torches, torture chambers, and a bunch of trophy skulls on the wall.

It seemed too upscale for the marauder, but then again, he seemed to be good at putting the charms on people. This all seemed like a trick to put you at ease.

I wasn't buying it.

Even the little old secretary with a potted plant on her desk was hiding something. She reminded me of a wicked creature in a popular book series that I'd both read and watched when they were made into movies: on the outside all sweetness, but on the inside a raging bitch with a vendetta against anything that breathed.

"What's this about, Raff?" Harrison said, giving me a narrow look when I smacked Raff on the head when he touched my leg.

"Cash's orders. He wanted to make sure this one—" he looked me up and down "—didn't bring her bow and arrow in. No weapons on you either."

"I'm sure I could fit an entire bow in my underwear," I muttered. "Genius."

Raff stared at me a second before a huge smile split his face. "I shall call you She-Karma and deliver you to the doorstep of the man demanding your fecking company."

I hadn't heard the Irish lilt until he cursed. What a bunch of winners (my brother excluded) Cash Kelly seemed to surround himself with. I really wasn't sure what his deal was, but I was ready to be in and be done. Especially after Raff started to lead us toward a hallway that seemed to lead to offices, and as we walked, I noticed splatters of blood along the floor.

I elbowed Harrison hard, and when he shot me a look, I nodded toward the stains.

He stared at the blood for a second and then met my eye. He shrugged, but it wasn't lightly. Something about this meeting was bothering him. It was bothering me, too. Why would they have to check me for weapons? My brother, too? From the sounds of it, they had never checked Harrison before. Why start now?

As we passed an office, I knew right away it was my brother's. A framed picture of Mari and me from a year ago was placed on a table behind his desk. Another picture was on his desk, and I had a feeling I knew who stared at him from the other side.

"That's real creepy, Harrison," I said.

"What?" He wasn't paying attention to me. Whatever was going on wasn't the norm. But I couldn't help but give him hell over the picture. He was so straight-laced that I found this side of him almost shocking. He was breaking a rule, but in his own way.

I pointed toward the picture on his desk. "Mari?"

"No. It's of Mam and Da."

"Liar!" I hissed.

"You tell her and I swear—"

"I won't." I nudged him in the side. "I wouldn't do that to you. But I have to say, this side of you is new. I need to dig a little deeper and see what else you're hiding in that shiny office."

His eyes softened but his shoulders stayed tense. They were almost up to his neck. And even though Raff walked ahead of us, I knew he was listening. How could he not?

"Yo, Raff," I said, sidestepping a splatter of red. "You have blood on your shiny, expensive floor."

Harrison turned to look at me and gave me what I called our "mam" face. His lips were pinched and his eyes were narrowed, trying to communicate that I needed to shut up. But my nerves were getting to me. I didn't have a good feeling about all of this, but I didn't know what to do.

I couldn't leave my brother here to deal with these men. Raff was somewhat genial, but he didn't seem like the kind of man you fucked with.

Cash Kelly?

Run and hide seemed like the only appropriate words after he turned off his spinning, hypnotizing, charming green eyes. There was a problem with that plan, though. Running and hiding didn't work on men like him. He'd always hunt for what was his.

"Just another day at work," Raff said, as though blood splatters were no big deal. "Susan—the secretary out front—she'll deal with it."

"Yeah, and turn it into a creature from the faerie forest," I muttered.

"Hey!" Raff stopped suddenly. "You're into Rulers of the Underworld?"

"You know it?"

"Of course!"

"No way!" I said.

"Do faeries love vampires?"

"Everlasting." I pointed at him, repeating what the vampire told his faerie love interest. "I bet you're team vampire!"

"How old are you two?" My brother said, cutting us off. He was on edge, his temper flaring, back to being grumpy Indiana Jones. "Faeries. Vampires. Underworld. Cut it out. I'm in no mood for this."

Raff scrunched his face at Harrison's attitude, making me laugh, but it sounded off. My neck felt hot, but not from anger. It was from something else. On the other side of the door, in an office, sat the man who had wanted to see me.

The idea of him being so close made me anxious.

Part of me wanted to bolt and never look back. The other part wanted to find out why he made me want to run.

The same part of me that commanded my feet to deliver me to him also wanted to see those eyes again. Hear the way the words rolled out of his mouth. Smell him in the air. Take him in my lungs. My hand wanted to brush up against his, just to see what would happen. My heart seemed to melt into my skin when I was around him, like it ached to see how his skin would feel next to mine, whether the weird connection—or was it attraction?—ran deeper than flesh and bone.

The sane part of me warned that he was up to no good, but another part, the rebel in me, wanted to find out more about him. About why I hated him so much when there wasn't a good reason for it, except for the fact that he was able to get underneath my skin and steal all of my thoughts.

He'd been stealing them ever since our meeting at the cemetery, and I knew it wasn't all because of my talk with Roisin and what I'd asked her to do.

That control he seemed to have over me already pissed me off. I wasn't the type of girl to give my heart away so easily. I'd always believed my heart had to be worked for, and then I'd give it away when *I* was ready.

When Cash Kelly looked at me, though, my heart felt like it was already gone.

But it made no sense, because I'd already promised my heart to Scott Stone. I was wearing his ring—that spoke volumes. Even Harrison had looked shocked when he saw it on my finger when he came to pick me up.

"Shit's getting real," he'd said, nodding to my left hand. "I'm going to tell the boys soon. I have to."

The Ryan Boys. My brothers.

I looked at the door, only prepared to deal with one situation at a time.

"You doin' all right?"

I realized Raff was talking to me.

"Why?" I said, my voice thick. "Do I look bad?"

"Nah." He shook his head. "I mean." He squinted his eyes at my neck. "Just flushed."

Yeah, because I heard footsteps on the other side of the door. Heard him clear his throat. Heard the words *come in* in that gorgeous Irish lilt he had. His voice was deep and melodious, and I wondered whether he could sing. Whether his voice had a rasp to it when he did, the kind that gave you goosebumps.

"Cool your blood. You seem stronger than the creature on the other side of this door." Raff laughed and opened it.

"Kee," my brother said, his voice low but urgent.

"I'm okay," I said, though I was lying through my teeth. "Let's just get this over with."

Harrison caught me by the arm two steps in. "This was a bad idea. Let's go."

Too late. The marauder had locked eyes with me, stealing every ounce of my will to move, and before Harrison could turn me, had already ordered Raff to shut the door.

With the *click* of the closing door, I was snared and trapped, a fletching sticking out of a tiger's mouth. Arrows be damned.

———

EVEN AFTER CASH KELLY stood from behind his desk and extended his hand to my brother, it took me a minute to move. After I was able to tear my eyes from his eyes, they went straight to the side of his head, which was stained with blood that had almost turned completely black. Some spots were still ruby with fresh blood. His nose had been broken. It was crusted with blood, too.

"Boss," my brother said. "You want me to get Susan to—"

"Flesh wound." Cash waved him off. "Any blow to the head makes it seem worse than it really is."

Huh. He was an expert in wounds.

He seemed like the kind of man everyone would want to kill. It was clear that if he wanted what you had, it was his. That sort of power came off of him in powerful waves. It smelled like the blood seeping from his head and nose, except it probably came from men who tried to stand in his way.

Maybe even some women. *Their hearts.* He stole their hearts in the metaphorical sense.

In that moment, there was no doubt that I was in big trouble. Cash Kelly was mayhem in a glass bottle, all of the chaos coming from his thoughts aimed straight at me.

What are you up to, Marauder? The tattoo on his neck, the tiger, never seemed more appropriate to describe a man before. No wonder he had it inked over the artery in his neck.

"Ms. Ryan," he said, his voice causing me to shiver a bit. It was low, soft, but with a jagged edge that could slice through most defenses with its sharp intentions. "It's a pleasure to see you again, darlin'."

Good thing my highest defenses were up. He might reduce other women to puddles with his charm, but he'd die holding his breath before I fell at his feet.

"Why am I here?" The words came out blunt, even though my heart was beating too fast and my stomach kept rising only to keep plummeting. My breathing was chaotic, and I hoped he didn't notice how my chest heaved.

"You get shorter and shorter every time I see you." Cash shook his head. Then he nodded toward my brother. I hadn't noticed until then that Harrison hadn't taken a seat. He wasn't getting comfortable, either. "Take a seat, Harry Boy. We have business to discuss."

Cash took a seat on his marauding throne. He probably stole the regal-looking chair from someone more important than him.

"Sit," he told my brother. Harrison stared at him for a moment and then did what he was told. After he did, Cash eyed me expectantly.

"If you expect me to sit, you'll have to answer a question first."

"She always this angry?"

My brother shook his head, but it wasn't to deny Cash's stupid-ass remark. He didn't seem to want to entertain small talk.

"Shorter and shorter, darlin'," Cash said and then sighed.

"Usually after time apart, most people grow, either in height or in maturity. Your maturity always seems to get shrink each time we meet."

"That's because you bring out the worst in me."

"Why is that?"

He settled in his seat, getting comfortable. Like he didn't have fucking care in the world. *La de da. I could be like any other singing Irishman in the world.* Except it would be a grave mistake to believe that about this man.

"Tell me why I'm here so I can go. I have better things to do, and better people to spend my time with. People who don't make me feel like committing murder. Apparently, I'm not the only one who feels that way." I nodded toward his head, which was still bleeding. I also noted that his white dress shirt was stained, too. He was a dangerous animal dressed in an expensive suit.

"You're going to marry me."

Seconds. Minutes. Hours. I had no idea how long I stood there staring at him staring at me.

What.

The.

Fuck.

Did.

He.

Just.

Say?

You're going to marry me.

I wanted to laugh. Laugh and laugh and laugh, like my brother, because he thought this was a joke. I knew better, and so did the muscles around my mouth.

"I'll kill you first."

The tone of my voice made my brother look between Cash and me. Harrison stood abruptly when he realized how serious the demand was.

"Mr. Kelly," my brother said. It was ridiculous to hear him call Cash Mr. Kelly, because they were around the same age, but there was no denying the respect in the tone covering up for the shock. Or was it defiance? "You're joking."

"Not a bit."

It all made sense in that moment. That was why Raff had checked us for weapons. He knew one of us was going to kill him after this. And there was still time. The day was fresh. There was no way in hell I was marrying this marauding animal. This...this...gangster of New York! I was engaged— wasn't I?—to a man of the law!

"You kill me," Cash said easily, "and you doom your brothers. To start. Each attempt on my life will cost you one of theirs."

Harrison came to stand next to me. He put his hand on my shoulder. "Boss. Can we talk about this? Why my sister? She's not—"

I barely heard the words from my brother's mouth as mine opened. I knew Harrison felt like it was his duty to protect me, and I could tell was trying to do that through reasoning, but this was between Cash and me now. "There will be no attempts. Plural. When I aim to shoot, I never miss my mark."

"Don't be so quick to anger, darlin'. Think this through. Be rational."

"I already have. I can't stand to be in the same room as you, much less be your wife." I realized then how deadly my voice had become. Low. Soft. But with enough power to strike him in his heart and make it stop—if he had one.

He leaned forward, steepling his fingers, taking me a bit more seriously now. "Let me be honest. This is not personal. You've found yourself here because you have a heart I want. I'll stop at no cost to have it. Actually. I already consider it mine. You, darlin', are mine. End of story."

"I—" I took a deep breath, releasing it silently, forcing my voice to come out even "—will never marry *you*. And if you even think about hurting my—"

Before the words were fully out, Cash had drawn a gun from underneath his desk, and with a blast that sounded like a bomb going off inside of my heart, shot my brother. He hit the wall and slid down it. I fell to my knees beside him, running my hands along his body.

"Oh my God. Oh my God," I chanted, frantically feeling for my brother's pulse.

"I'm all right, Kee," he said, his voice strained. "My shoulder. He hit my shoulder."

"Then why did you fall?"

Harrison narrowed his eyes at me. "I got hit with a bullet, Kee. Out of nowhere."

I shook my head, applying pressure to his arm. Even though he assured me that it was just his shoulder, he was my big brother, and his wound hurt me as much as it hurt him. I looked up into light eyes that pierced through the darkness that had settled around me.

"Fuck you!" I spat out.

"Later, after I hear your vows." Cash grinned at me.

"Kee." Harrison's voice brought me back to him. "Say no. The boys would want you to do the same. Say no. Run."

"Why?" I said to Cash, feeling the closest thing to weak that I'd ever felt. My brother's blood stained my hands. "Why me?"

"It's not personal," he said causally. "It has nothing to do with you directly. I don't want your body. I'm taking *you*."

"Stealing me," I whispered. "Why?"

"Because I can." There was something in his eyes—knowledge. He knew. He knew that only after meeting twice, not counting this time, he'd gotten underneath my skin.

"No!" Harrison roared, about to get to his feet.

I stuck my finger in Harrison's wound, making him stay put, because the animal had scented blood and he was ready to shed more. Harrison growled again, the pain making all of the color drain from his face, and I looked the marauder in the eyes.

"I'm going to kill you regardless."

"You kill me." Cash shrugged. "My brother will continue to kill your family."

Our eyes held, and something told me he was bluffing, but I couldn't take the chance. He had shot my brother like it was nothing, like it was something he did every day, and maybe he did. I knew he'd kill my brother in front of me, and the more trouble I gave, the further I'd run and hide, the more he'd go on a spree and kill the people I loved the most.

I didn't have much time to figure this out, because I didn't trust him enough *not* to shoot my brother on his other shoulder, waiting for me to agree to whatever he wanted from me. He'd said that I was his already, he'd already decided, but the question kept stabbing me. Why?

Why me?

He didn't want my body. I highly doubted he wanted my love.

What else?

What could he possibly want?

Something about a heart.

My heart?

How can someone steal a heart and not expect to love?

I almost growled in frustration. *Think, Kee. Think!*

I couldn't.

He was staring at me, and fear was the only thing I felt. Not for me, but for my family. My brother kept bleeding.

"Okay," I said, nodding. "I'm yours. Whatever you want."

"Kee," my brother said, and my name on his lips almost made me come apart.

The marauder took a knee next to my brother, patting him on the shoulder. He handed him a glass of whiskey before he set a handkerchief against the wound, over my hand, helping me staunch it. I almost took it away, but I refused. I wasn't going to let him rattle me. Or allow him to see it.

He thought he could steal my heart?

I met his green eyes and grinned. *Game on, you marauding bastard.* There was more than one word for vengeance, and getting even sounded just as sweet.

I WASN'T sure how it happened, but the worst day of my life had also become my best.

After Cash drove my brother to the ER, where we fed them some bullshit lie about a robbery gone wrong, and they took care of him, I received a call about a part on Broadway I'd been after. The name of the show was *The Blood Queen*, and it was based off of a script that felt eerily close to my own life.

That line about art imitating life had never felt so true.

I'd be playing the part of Joan McDougal, a Scottish maiden who refused to marry for the sake of family and obligation. She wanted to marry for love, if she ever married at all. She gave her parents a choice. She'd either marry for love, or she'd bleed her heart dry with an arrow before she settled for anything less. That way, if there was no other way, the man who made her a bride out of obligation would get a raisin instead of a heart.

Was it melodramatic?

Overtly, but my current state of mind was not being rational. I was being forced into marriage by a marauder who couldn't care less about me.

I studied his face as he drove us home from the hospital. This man had a reason for each of his steps, and I knew I was nothing but a conquest that was going to move his journey along in some way. I still couldn't piece it together, though.

I hated to sound like a broken fucking record, but *why me?*

Cash hiring my brother was no accident or coincidence.

The cemetery. Showing up at the fair under the guise that he wanted to meet me.

This plan of his had been in play for a while, based on the timeline, but he had just decided to act on it. What had changed?

Why me?

WHY ME?

As he pulled up to Harrison's car outside of his building, he said he wanted to speak to me alone. Harrison refused to get out of the car at first, but after I told him to go or I'd stick my finger in his wound again, he got out and waited by his car.

Cash sat there a second, gazing out of the windshield. "No one knows about this yet. I'll let you know the time and place, but start packing up your things. Tell friends and family that Harrison fronted you the money for a better apartment. Tell your family about getting the part in the show. We'll have a party at your brother's new place for family and friends. Including the man who gave you that ring."

"That ring?"

He nodded to my left hand.

Scott's ring. I'd totally forgotten about Scott in all of this. The emerald heart was crusted with blood. How was I going to tell him? *Hey, about our relationship? I'm ditching you for a criminal. You know, the guys you usually go after.* Yeah, that wasn't going to go over well. It might even start a war.

"Don't tell him a thing yet." When Cash said "thing," it came out as "ting." "Clear?"

"Whatever you want." I smiled sweetly at him, but bile burned the back of my throat.

He narrowed his eyes at me. "I prefer your lash of a tongue. Sweet doesn't suit you, darlin'."

"Wait," I said, just realizing something. So many things were coming at me at once. "How did you know about my part in the show?" I hadn't even told Harrison. My good fortune and my shitty luck were at war with each other, each trying to vie for the biggest shock of my life.

"These are my streets. I know everythin'," he said. "Just like I know Armino Scarpone won't be bothering you."

"You got me the part! You had a hand in that, didn't you?"

He gave me a side-eyed look. "My wife gets what she wants."

"But I'll NEVER know if I deserved it now! And I'm not your WIFE!"

"Yet. You're not my wife yet," he said. "And you do deserve it. You're good. I watched before I interfered. It was between you and another girl who couldn't act worth a shit, but her uncle's some deep-pocket dick who pulled some strings. I have a deeper pocket, deeper connections, and of course, the bigger dick, so you got the part instead."

"Hold on. Hold on." I pinched the bridge of my nose, trying to stop the raging headache that was about to send *me* to the ER. "My brother's new place?"

"Talk to Harrison." He nodded toward the door. "I'll be in touch."

"Wow!" I said, feigning excitement. "You're such a charmer! Man, what a winner I picked to get married to! Oh wait, I'm being *forced*."

"Keely."

"Yeah?"

"Get out of my fucking car."

"Sure," I said. "But let me tell you one thing before I do. I might be marrying you, but what you're really doing is binding yourself to me. You steal my heart, and yours won't be able to live without mine. It's like a spell. The one who casts it is always connected to the one who's under the spell. Being connected to you in this life—in this way—is enough. I don't need you tagging along with me forever."

I opened the door to his *fucking car* and then slammed it. I marched over to Harrison after, who was leaning against his car, waiting for me. "What's this about a new place?"

"Keely—"

"I just swapped my life for yours, Harrison. The truth."

He wiped a bubble of sweat from his upper lip. I could tell he was in pain, and not just physically. "I bought it for Mari, all right? I fucking bought the house she loves on Staten Island! The one next to our parents' old place. The one she grew up in. The one she still visits when her life gets rough. I want her to feel safe. To...I don't know. Feel loved for once in her life! And I want to give her something without her feeling like she owes me her soul! I want to marry her, Kee."

"All right," I said, my voice lower than I expected it to be. I held my hand out. My brother put his in mine and I smiled. "Give me your keys, lover boy. I'm going to drive you home and take care of you for a while."

He refused to let my hand go. It trembled. "Don't do this, Keely. Run. The boys and I—"

I squeezed his hand, hard. "This is between you and I, Harrison. Your word. If you tell them, or anyone, including Mari, and one of them dies because of me—I couldn't live with that. Roisin—"

"It wasn't your fault."

"Tell that to five-year-old me, okay? Don't meddle in this. I'll get out of it. Sooner or later, I will. He doesn't really want me. This is not about me. I believe him when he says it. So let's figure out his angle. I'll play my part, and once it's done, he'll have no use for me."

"Stone?"

I blew out a warm breath. "This is not about him. He'll have to understand. My family comes first. End of story."

"I did this to you. I'll never be able—"

"Shut up, Grumpy Jones. I've already forgiven you. But only because of one thing."

"Grumpy Jones?"

I waved him off with my free hand. He still hadn't let the other go. "I'm forgiving you because you did this for love. And if anyone deserves love, it's Mari. If she decides she loves you back, you better name a kid after me!"

Harrison grinned. "I'm going to tell her soon, Kee. It's time."

"Agreed," I muttered, pulling my hand from his. I opened my palm and he set the keys into it. Then he walked to the other side and got in.

I'd totally forgotten about the text I'd sent to Mari the same night Sierra was killed, telling her how I thought Harrison was in love with her, until that moment. What worried me, beside my own problems, was the fact that she had said nothing back.

If Harrison was wrong about Mam and her tea leaves? Where did that leave me?

Fucked.

I was truly and utterly fucked.

Harrison didn't believe the truth in them, but I did.

9

KEELY

It had been one hell of a month. We were not even to the end of it yet, and it sort of went something like this: My entire world was turned upside, but at the same time, it was trying to right itself like it never had before.

With Mari's help, I started packing up my ratty old apartment, but Cash didn't tell me where I was going, so that was still a mystery.

In all honesty, I couldn't wait to step out of my old apartment and into something new. Sierra somehow lingered, and I felt like, for once in her life, she was owed the entire space. She came to me in dreams sometimes, and I'd wake up covered in sweat, my heart about to jump out of my chest. But it was only because she seemed to want this place for herself, and everything in it.

I even admitted to Mari that after Sierra had passed, I felt lighter. Like all of the good things waiting not only for me, but for Mari, were going to start happening. It was the shittiest thing I'd ever felt, but there it was.

Those good things I felt were coming? They felt real for the first time in my life. And that was saying something, since I had to marry a marauder in my near future.

There was also something I couldn't ignore, though, that was right for Mari but wrong for Harrison.

The night Sierra had been murdered, when Mari had told me she was going out for a bit, she had met a guy named Mac, who owned one of the most prestigious clubs in the city, and she'd fallen for him. Hard. He asked her to marry him not long after. She said yes. *"You know when you know,"* he'd told her. They were getting married in Italy in the summer.

Sierra had mentioned Mac more than once since she worked at his club. She wanted to marry him. Have his babies. She had said he was the finest man she'd ever seen, and one of New York's most eligible bachelors.

I'd told her I'd have to see this man for myself, and when I tried to search for him on the computer, NOTHING came up. He catered to some of the richest and dirtiest men in the world. By dirty, I meant gangsters. And I couldn't find a fucking picture of him online?

What bothered me the most, though, was knowing that I was going to have to tell my brother soon.

The same day I'd told Mari about my feelings toward Sierra, she told me that she had never felt anything but a sisterly love for Harrison. And after Mari told me she'd like to bring the man she called Capo (everyone else called him Mac) to the party at Harrison's place for my break, I knew he'd lost his chance. I'd never seen Mari so smitten with anything or anyone in her life.

Even though I was happy for her, everything that Harrison had done for her felt like such a waste of his love.

In so many ways Mam was right. Mari's decision to marry Mac was causing a ripple effect. But I couldn't fault Mari for following her heart.

I couldn't fault Harrison for doing what his heart told him

to, either. He had built a life for Mari, hoping once he got his life straight, things would happen naturally. Something told me he was going to come clean at the party, but I was going to have to tell him before then.

The only thing keeping me sane in such a chaotic time was the show, but even then, I found myself not fully into it. I was having trouble focusing, even though I had studied my lines over and over and knew them as well as I knew my name.

Keely Ry—

Keely Kelly.

Keely Kelly.

Keely Kelly.

Yeah, try saying that three times fast.

I groaned and Mari looked at me.

She was hurrying to get ready for the party Harrison was throwing at his place. The one Cash insisted we have. I still hadn't told her about the house on Staten Island, and because she'd just dumped the marriage news on me, I only had a little time to tell Harrison about it. I couldn't let Mari and Mac show up together and my brother be caught off guard.

"Kee?"

"Yeah?"

Mari looked around. "All packed up. Only the things you need have been left out." She waved a hairbrush at me.

I nodded. "I'm glad that it's done. Not that I had much."

Mari studied me for a moment. "What's going on, Kee? Is it the show?"

I took a deep breath and released it. "No. The show is great. It's just so much change at once."

She nodded, but I could tell she didn't buy it.

A knock came at the door and she rushed to answer it.

"Mac," I said when he walked in behind Mari.

Everything Sierra had said about him was true. But. She had downplayed him. He was almost too good looking to be true. Black hair. Tan skin. Ocean-blue eyes that were cold and very intelligent. Model sharp features. Muscles in all of the right places. And if power could create a force field around someone, it had around Mac.

He studied me with what felt like indifference, but at the same time, he seemed to be making sure I was good enough to be around Mari.

Maybe that was why I couldn't hate him.

There was something right about the two of them together. And in all of my years of knowing her, I'd never heard anyone call her by her full name. Mariposa. Because she never allowed them to. She seemed to brighten when he did.

Finally, he nodded at me and stood in the doorway. He wasn't much of a talker.

Mari breezed past. "I'm going to take a quick shower. I won't be long."

I stood, wiping my hands on my jeans, and started toward my bedroom. "I'm going to get there a little early. Help with the setup."

"Wait!" Mari stopped me. "Where do we go? You never said. Is it by your uncl—"

"No." I shook my head, debating on whether to tell her that the party was on Staten Island. Given the fact that I had to deal with my brother first, I decided not to say anything. If she knew what Harrison had done, she might not even go at all. Maybe if Harrison caught Mari off guard, she'd consider his feelings without Mac around. It was a long shot, because I could feel how much Mac and Mari cared for each other, even if their feelings had developed fast, but a shot was a shot. "I'll give Mac the directions. You go jump in the shower so you won't be late."

"I won't be long!" she said again as she moved toward the bathroom.

Mac and I stared at each other for another moment before I

cleared my throat. When I gave him the address, his eyebrows drew down.

"Old man Gianelli's place," he said.

"That's right." I nodded. "You know of it?"

"Yeah," he said, and his voice reflected his eyes. Cold. "Where Mariposa grew up."

"We were next-door neighbors. That's how we became best friends, sisters."

He nodded but said nothing else. Maybe Mari had already told him all of that.

After I collected my purse, I stopped next to him. "Listen. You and I haven't had much time to talk. But I just want to tell you one thing. If you hurt her, I will hurt you. Understand?"

"Your brother is in love with my wife."

He threw me for a second, but I hoped that I played it off well. That force field around him could knock a nun off course. "Fiancé. She hasn't made any promises to you yet."

Right before I opened the door to leave, he cleared his throat. Sometimes his voice sounded jagged. "Have you made any promises to Kelly yet?"

I squeezed the door handle so hard that it bit into my palm. "I know you," I said, my voice quiet. "I know men like you. Sierra and I talked. It doesn't surprise me that you know every-thing. That you control everything. And since you know the intentions of Cash Kelly, then it would be in Mari's best interest not to involve her in my life right now."

Mac's stare felt like ice melting on my back. "Kelly knows better than to come near me or mine. But I have no problem with him, as long as he stays in his lane." He cleared his throat once more. "Mari considers you a good friend. A sister, as you say. That's why I'll leave you and her to it. Your secrets are your own, as long as they don't hurt her."

A shiver tore over me before I shut the door, putting some distance between us. Not even a door felt like enough, though.

These men, the kind I suddenly found myself around, were not ordinary. They were fucking vicious animals in custom-made suits, disguised to look like gentlemen.

I had to get to my brother before he did something that would probably cost him his life. Like tell Mari that he loved her.

I SAT IN MY CAR, staring at my brother's place on Staten Island. He had already started making it his, but I could tell that he was holding out, hoping to get Mari's opinion once he told her how he felt and then asked her to marry him. I knew how my brother's mind worked. Even though he hadn't said as much, he was making plans here—for a wife, for a family, for a future.

A wave of nausea came over me, dreading the talk we were about to have.

My phone rang, and my head popped up from the steering wheel. Scott's name flashed across the screen. We'd been talking lately, but thanks to his schedule and mine, we hadn't seen each other much. The longest we were together was five minutes, and without making a deal of it, I tried to distance myself from him. I wanted to make this as easy as possible, but Cash had told me not to say anything. It was a specific order.

"I'll tell you when the time's right."

Scott had accepted my offer to come to this party. He seemed eager when he realized that my family was going to be there. Mari had mentioned it in front of him. He had to make another trip to my place when her pervert of a landlord had been killed.

Just as I said, "Hey," an expensive car pulled into Harrison's driveway. A second later, Cash Kelly stepped out, wearing a black t-shirt that hugged his muscular frame, dark jeans, and boots. Expensive sunglasses covered his eyes, but his gaze locked onto mine right away and refused to move.

"Kee? You there?"

"Yeah." I cleared my throat. "I'm here."

"Listen." Scott sounded out of breath. "I thought I could make it, but that politician's still missing." He'd told me the day before that he didn't think he'd be able to make it to the party, because all manpower had been brought in, but then told me he thought that maybe he could. That was his life. Making plans to break them for his job.

"Sounds like madness," I said, and the dullness in my voice couldn't be hidden.

Scott was quiet for a moment. "This is my life, Kee. I know it's hard to deal with in the beginning, but here's a deal I'm willing to make: I might not be around all of the time, but when I'm home, I'm yours. I won't even think about a dead body."

"Cute," I said.

Cash leaned against his car, like he didn't have a care in the world. There was that *la de da* attitude. And there I was, my entire world crashing in around me. *Bastard.*

Scott sighed. "I'll make this up to you, I swear. We'll take your mom and dad out to dinner. Maybe it's best if I meet the boys one at a time. They might kick my ass if I just show up." I heard someone call him and then he told me he had to go. "Kee," he stopped me before I hung up. "I'll see if I can make it later. I love you, sweetheart."

Forcing my eyes away from the marauder's, I looked down at my phone, shaking in my hand. My hands had been shaking ever since the day he told me I had to marry him. It caught me off guard because sometimes I didn't even realize they were.

Scott had hung up, but my heart was in my throat.

I should tell him. I should tell him. I should tell him.

One look at Cash Kelly and I knew I couldn't.

He knocked on my window, and I used the hand crank to roll it down. "Can I help you?"

"Who was that?"

"None of your business."

"Nah, that's where you're wrong, darlin'. You are my business now."

"Scott Stone. He can't make it."

His eyes narrowed, and even though his face didn't reflect a particular change, something about him was different, something I could feel rather than see.

"Since you seem a little disappointed that not everyone can make it—" That was when it hit me like a blow to the gut. *Scott.* What did this have to do with him? Did they know each other? Was Scott crooked and had double-crossed Kelly? I didn't want Cash to catch my reaction, though, so I relaxed my features, or tried to.

Cash leaned in a little closer. His cologne smelled like something expensive, but woodsy. If it were anyone else, I would've licked my lips and even rolled my hips if I were on the dance floor. "Cat got your tongue, darlin'?" Then he opened my car door. "This party is not for Scott Stone. It's for you."

"You mean us." I stepped out, and even with wedges on, I had to look up at him. Scott never liked when I wore them because we were the same height. Sometimes I was taller depending on the shoe, and I totally avoided those altogether. There was no way I was going to reach the marauder's height unless I wore platform heels.

I ran a hand down my green silk blouse, ironing out any wrinkles. "Aren't we announcing our engagement tonight?"

"We'll see."

"Always so cryptic."

He followed behind me to the front door, and I could feel his eyes on my ass. I'd felt them the day of the fair, too, and I made sure to swing my hips a bit to give him an eye full.

"What did he do?" I casually threw over my shoulder as I made the steps.

Before I could knock and then let myself in, Cash took me by the arm and swung me around like some dame in an old black and white movie. One of my hands was pressed against his chest to push him away, but I couldn't move. His heart beat steadily under my palm. His entire body was hard and it held me in place.

My eyes were level with his mouth, and I silently sucked in a breath. *Damn me.* He had the perfect shaped lips. I wanted to bite the bottom one hard enough to make him bleed and suck in a breath at the pain.

Scott had soft lips. Not firm at all.

Why am I even comparing? Fuck if I knew.

My eyes made a slow journey to his, and that was when he locked me in again. "You're a little psycho in the bedroom, aren't you, Ms. Ryan?"

"Me? Little?" A boisterous roll of laughter thundered from my mouth.

He made it a point to look down at me, proving his point that I *was* smaller than him. No man had ever made me feel that way before. It wasn't totally physical, either, and that made me uncomfortable. I had finally met my match. If I ever told him to go to hell, he'd probably invite me along, because he'd been there before.

Instead of hell, maybe it was time that I invited him to heaven. I leaned in closer, putting my lips close to his neck, right over his pulse point. I made sure my voice was breathy, so warm air blew over his skin. "Wouldn't you like to know how I am in bed, *Marauder*."

He grinned and then let out a breath of a laugh. I breathed in and then automatically breathed out. I refused to take him inside my lungs. He wasn't my air; he was my suffocation.

"I already know everythin' about you, darlin'. I know how

Scott Stone fucks you up against the wall in the moonlight.
That perfect ass of *mine* sliding up and down the windowpane.
I already know that he tries to claim *mine*, but he doesn't know
how to keep a woman that belongs to a man like me satisfied.
And I already know that *my* eyes, *my* heaven, roll back in your
head, and not from pleasure, but from boredom when he does."

His free hand slipped along my side, and *damn me!*, I shivered at the warmth. It was going to be a fierce game of tug of
war with my heart, but my body had already surrendered to the
enemy's cause. It ached for him to claim me.

"When I fuck you, you're going to go psycho, archer. Your
mind is going to go mad for me. Your skin is going to burn for
me. Those nails are going to claw me until I have stripes. That
mouth is going to bite me until I bleed. You're going to demand
to mark *me*. It'll be *my* heaven to own that entire body of
yours."

"You mean my heart?" I said. "You're going to *try* to steal my
heart to make Scott suffer. *Your* heaven will be *his* hell. What
did he do? I deserve to know that much since I'm nothing but a
pawn in this game of yours."

"He stole from me first, and no one steals from me."

"You're getting even."

"You're the only person he's ever truly loved, apart from his
family."

"He stole your heart," I said.

"I don't have one of those," he said. "All the same, he stole
something vital."

So if Scott hadn't been in love with me, it would've been a
hard pass on Keely Ryan for Cash Kelly. He wouldn't have given
me a second glance, but since Scott was in love with me, truly
in love, I was as good as Kelly's.

Even if this was about revenge, and nothing more, he still
couldn't deny the attraction. His dick was pressing hard into my
belly, and we'd hardly touched.

I couldn't deny the lust, either, and I hated him even more for it. When he looked at me, heat crept up my neck. I'd only ever felt that when I was angry or upset, but never when a man looked at me. And when he touched me? Fire against paper.

There was something between us that felt wild, instinctual, almost...right.

"After you get your revenge?" My voice came out soft. "After you steal his heart, *me*, what then, Marauder? Where does that leave me?"

His eyes were hard on mine. "With me for always. As long as I live, he'll never touch what's mine again. What he's sure is his. Love doesn't just disappear, darlin'. We might move on and breathe, but that love forever marks us. What I'm stealing from him will forever mark him, as what he's done to me scars my lungs. There are days the hurt is so great I can't breathe. There's no return for men like us."

"For men like you," I said.

"There's a thin line between good and evil. Scott Stone walks the line every day, just like I do. We just choose different paths on a regular basis."

"So poetic," I whispered. My eyes were turned up to his, and I wanted to glare at him, but instead I kept blinking, ready to close my eyes, waiting for his lips to meet mine.

Kiss me. Kiss me. Kiss me. Steal that kiss, Marauder. Because I knew once he did, he would realize how strong the pull was between us, and that he wasn't going to get out of this without a few more stripes, or maybe even scars.

He moved us until my back hit the wall of Harrison's house. He stared down at me with eyes that were too beautiful for a soul like his. His entire physical being was too good for what he was, but somehow, it made him more appealing. A man all the girls wanted to tame.

As a woman, I'd turn into his kind of wild before I expected him to change. Because a tiger never changes its stripes.

"You think I don't know what you're up to, archer?" His breath fanned against my lips. "You want me to kiss you, to claim your mouth, so you can mark me, like I've already marked you."

"Hah." The noise was meant to be a bark, but it came out breathy. "You have no idea who you're dealing with. I might want to kiss you, but I'll be damned if I *let* you kiss me. I'm not going to give you what you'll no doubt try to steal anyway. It's called work, Kelly. Learn the meaning."

He moved slow, oh so slow, and went to put his lips to mine but I turned my face. His grin came languorously. "We'll see." He released me, going to stand closer to the door, where Harrison stood, watching us.

How long had he been there? It didn't matter. My entire body was on fire, and I wished I could throw myself into an ocean to put it out. I wasn't sure if that would even work, though.

This fire felt hotter, deeper—somewhere inside of my bones—than anything I'd ever felt before. It was a mixture of lust and rebellion.

Harrison took a step back to let the marauder through his door, but before Kelly stepped in, he stopped. "A secret for your vault. The real difference between Stone and me? I know when you're actin', darlin'. He never did. Remember that." He winked at me and then went inside.

It took me a minute to compose myself, to pay attention to Harrison, who had called my name.

"What are you doing here so early?" my brother asked.

Shaking off my encounter with Kelly, I stood taller and walked toward the porch, looking out at the street. "We need to talk, Harrison."

10

CASH

I t would take time to gain her family's approval. She was the only girl—apart from her sister who had been killed at five—in a family with four boys. So it was their job to give me hell before I earned their sister's heaven. But compared to the animals I ran with, their level of hell served ice water for dessert.

Even though her brothers were a bit cool, most of her family had suspected that she'd been dating someone. Her mother nodded at me in approval, which made the archer scowl. Her father looked me up and down. Quiet for the most part. He would be. He had known my old man, and when his daughter had been killed, he had come to Ronan Kelly for a favor.

We'd get to that later, after I was done dealing with another situation.

Mac "Capo" Macchiavello.

Mari had brought him with her, and upon introductions, Keely had said that Mari was the only one who called him Capo. He was the man Mari was engaged to. Mac was the reason Harry Boy was throwing back more shots of whiskey, eyeing the man with hatred in his eyes. If Harry Boy had any sense at all, though, he'd keep his distance from the man Mari called Capo.

Dangerous animals sense when other dangerous animals are in their territories.

Mac Macchiavello was a hunter, and he was stomping on mine.

Call it a hunch, but I sensed that this Mac was the same Mac that Rocco had mentioned in my office. He was Italian. Part of that world in some way. The tattoo of a wolf on his hand served as a symbol. Or a warning. He was or had been a Scarpone.

It would've been a war right in Harry Boy's backyard if Mac had been anyone else who belonged to that family, but something about him made me curious. Rocco brought me his card for a reason, and if Mac was the one starting the wars between all of the families, and involving me—I'd find out why.

Curiosity sometimes killed the kitty, but not this big fucking cat. I was too smart for a trap.

If this Mac turned out to be as intelligent as I suspected, he knew that and was using it for his own personal gain.

He wasn't just a savage animal. He was a clever savage animal.

His assessing blue eyes were trained on me while a woman at the party held his fiancé's hand up to her nose while she silently judged the ring on her third finger. In the darkness, Mac's eyes almost glowed blue, matching the black wolf's eyes on his hand.

He whispered something in Mari's ear, stood up, and then dumped his empty beer bottle in a trashcan. Grabbing another, he came to stand next to me as though we'd been friends our entire life.

He said nothing.

Nah, he wouldn't. He had come to me.

It was my turn.

I downed a pull of my own beer. "Got your card." Translated: *Message received. I owe you one.*

He nodded, his eyes on Mari, watching everyone who interacted with her. "Harry Boy. He's valuable to you."

My eyes moved between the man standing next to me and the man sitting across the yard from me. Harry Boy watched Mari with an intensity that left no room to question his intentions. He wanted to get her alone.

If all of the pieces fit as I'd put them, Harry Boy had been saving this night to confess his undying love to Mari. And if Mac was bringing the issue to me, Harry Boy had become *my* issue.

I almost shook my head in annoyance, but I didn't. If Rocco cared enough to bring me Mac's card, there was no question of his ranking within the Fausti family. High. My streets took top priority. A war with the Faustis would only lead to certain death.

Still. If something happened to Harry Boy, Macchiavello would mess my shit up. "You can say that."

Mac took a slow pull of his beer. "You gave him a mercy shot. If I aim the gun, it'll be his heart I hit."

Ah. Harry Boy was fucking with Mac's heart. Therefore. Harry Boy's heart would belong to Macchiavello if he kept it up. Threats aside, there was something about Macchiavello that I instantly respected. So I'd squash Harry Boy's schoolboy crush before it ruined my plans. No good would come out of this situation. Because when men like Mac started to catch feelings, it went straight to their heads.

"Noted," I said.

Mac claimed his seat next to Mari again, and my eyes went directly to Harry Boy, who was staring at the girl so hard it was pathetic.

I sighed, shaking my head. Out of all the women in the

world for him to fall in love with, it would have to be one claimed by a fucking savage animal. Her scent was all over Mac —it smelled like the word "mine."

Feeling eyes on me, I turned my eyes a fraction, finding the archer. She was seated in one of the chairs that had been placed around the yard.

Our eyes caught and held.

Not able to hold my stare, she turned her eyes to Harry Boy. She followed his eyes to Mari and Mac and scowled.

Mari looked up when Keely stood abruptly and walked into the house. She whispered something in Mac's ear and then followed Keely. Harry Boy followed in Mari's footsteps. Before he could get to her, or too far inside of the house, I yanked him back by the collar of his shirt.

He went to swing on me but stopped when he realized it was me. He had little to say to me lately.

"You enjoy getting shot, Harry Boy?"

His eyes narrowed. "Can't say that I do."

I took a step closer to him and he held his ground. "Then I suggest you forget about your sister's friend. She's marrying a made man. You know what that is?" He nodded and I went on. "He's more animal than man. You got that? His kind has no idea what the word mercy means. No matter what his name is, all you have to remember is Fausti."

"Your kind."

"You knew what kind of man I was when you started working for me." I lifted my hands. "You wanted fast cash, you got it, and you accepted it, bloodstains and all."

"My family, my sister, was never part of our deal," he said, his voice low and laced with whiskey.

"This is not about your sister. That's a done deal. This is about Mari. Stay the fuck away from her. Her man has the scent of your blood memorized. There's nothing I can do to change the winds, understand?"

A fiery red vision with peaceful blue eyes emerged out of the darkness of the hallway. "I need to talk to you, Kelly," she breathed out. "In private."

My eyes moved between Harry Boy and his sister.

"I'm not going to try to kill you," she said, her voice exasperated. "Not tonight."

I met Harry Boy's eyes again. "Your sister thinks I'm easily fooled. She's trying to give you some time with Macchiavello's girl. You have five minutes to say nothing about love or any of that bullshit to her. Your feelings are no longer relevant where she's concerned. She's off limits. I've been clear enough."

"That's a problem," Keely said, taking the lead after we walked away from Harry Boy. "He's drunk, and whenever Harrison gets drunk, he lets his emotions rule him."

I took her arm and forced her to stop when we made it up a couple of steps. "That wouldn't be good for his health, darlin'."

Her eyes flickered to the kitchen, where Harry Boy had disappeared, and then back to me. "Five minutes," she whispered. "He's earned it."

"He's earned a bullet to his chest?"

"You're going to put one there because of Mari?" Her eyebrow lifted.

"You're far from stupid, woman. You know the man with your friend is not one to be fucked with."

"Like you."

"Like me."

She nodded once, the fear a real thing in her eyes now. She passed me on the step, but before she got too far, I took her arm again, stopping her. "What did you want with me, darlin'? Besides getting me out of your brother's way."

Her jaw tightened when I called her that—darlin'. "To find out when you're going to announce our *engagement*."

"You make it sound like a farce." I grinned.

"It is bullshit."

Before I could respond, her eyes moved away from mine too quickly, and mine followed hers. Macchiavello had come to stand in the doorway of the kitchen. Harry Boy stood in front of him.

"Shit!" Keely flew past me down the stairs. Lachlan, another one of her brothers, had come to stand behind Harry Boy at the same time she'd made it to him. The two of them seemed to defuse the situation before it got out of hand.

Before Keely could make it back outside, Mari stopped her. She whispered something, squeezed her hand, and then turned to leave with Macchiavello. He looked me in the eye on their way out.

Enough said.

The archer watched as they left and then ducked into the kitchen.

She was on a warpath. Opening and closing cabinets, slamming them when she didn't find what she was looking for. She hadn't even bothered to flip the switch back on. The only light came from outside—where bulbs were strung up—through a kitchen window.

"With the amount Harry Boy drank tonight, it's probably all gone," I said, standing with my back against the wall.

This was no beer or wine girl I was dealing with. Keely Ryan had whiskey written all over her.

Her hand paused mid-close on another cabinet and she turned her head a fraction to look at me. "You know *nothing*," she said, almost hissing at me, "about anything. Least of all *me*."

"Ah," I said, standing taller. "I've heard of this game before. It's called Blame Cash. This is where you get to blame me for every problem in the world. I've had much heavier weights placed there, darlin'. A little more won't bother me." I shrugged. "Many have tried before. All have failed. I don't break."

"This *is* your fault! All of it." She slammed the cabinet door and faced me. "Ever since you showed up, so has nothing but trouble!"

I laughed and her neck turned fiery red. "You enjoy feedin' yourself lies, darlin'? Does that make you feel better? Like blaming Macchiavello for all his problems makes Harry Boy feel better. Tell me. Is this a family trait I should be aware of?"

"Are you calling my brother a coward?"

"I'm not calling. I'm telling. He's a coward. No man who has a set of balls sits there for years waiting for the right time to make a woman his. She *is* his. End of story. That car out there." I chucked my head toward the front of the house. "This house." I looked around. "Who gives a fuck? You know your friend better than anyone. Does material shit matter to her?"

Her mouth closed on a snap. She couldn't argue. The red on her neck crept up to her cheeks.

"He was trying to give her a better life! Something you'd know nothing about."

I shrugged.

Her face heated even more. "What's your game, huh?" She took a step closer to me, and I noticed her hands when she did. Trembling. But she flexed her fingers, like she was warming up. Preparing for the attack. "How are you so sure that you're going to be able steal my heart? Last I checked, it was mine to give."

"That's where you're wrong. I'm the marauding fucking tiger." I lifted my shirt, showing her my stripes, scars I'd gotten in battle. "Your heart is as good as mine. You're already falling for me." Letting my shirt drop, I looked down at her silk shirt, the material thin, her nipples pressing against the fabric. "Your body is already down with the memo. It's your head that's tripping you up."

"Bullshit." She tried to snap at me, but her voice came out as a whisper. "All you spew is lies. Lies from that forked devil's tongue."

"It's not that you're fighting this because you don't want it," I said, taking a step toward her. "You're fighting this because you don't want to give in so easily. Pride's a deadly sin, darlin'—beware of that one. Don't deny your pussy to spite your heart."

"You smug son of a bitch!"

In a breath, she was on me, all of her pent-up aggression coming out through her hands. She was trying to beat me with them. I had to stop myself from laughing at her, at how cute she was being. It was a waste to call this warrior woman cute, but she was still a woman, and she couldn't crack my armor.

Subduing her wrists in my hands, I moved her toward the wall, almost slamming her into it.

Her breath came out in pants, and fuck me, I breathed her in. I breathed in the passion she tried to disguise as pure hate. Her heart pounded against my chest, trying to go to war with it. She wanted to claim mine so she could quit the game of tug of war with hers.

She had no idea. I was born without one.

I looked down at her and my grin came slow. Her eyes were narrowed into slits, but I saw the truth she couldn't deny in them. "We'll see how much you hate that forked devil's tongue when it's making you speak in languages you never knew you had."

"Fucking doesn't equal love," she said through clenched teeth. "You might have my body, but the rest—you're going to have to bleed for. Love lives in the heart, Marauder."

"No doubt about it, darlin'," I said. "But I've bled for much less."

"A heart is a bright place. Full of sunshine and rainbows. A real heaven. I can't wait to see you try to steal love out of it." A mocking smile came to her face. It was childish, something I'd never seen on her before. "You speak of pride. Then you should know love doesn't deal with pride. It abolishes it. You, you conceited bastard, will be saying *please* and *thank you* after love gets a hold of you, and there won't be a fucking thing you can do it about."

"Ah, but not all hearts are the same, darlin'. I don't think yours is made of sunshine and rainbows. Princess bullshit, isn't that what you said at the fair? I know yours is the exact opposite. Yours is a fortress. One that needs to be battled for. Bled for. Once inside, it belongs to whoever was *smug* enough to believe he could get past the gates."

I released one of her wrists, my free hand moving a strand of hair from her face. She trembled, and something inside of me echoed the reaction. She closed her eyes, releasing a faint breath. "Then those eyes, those heavenly eyes, belong to *me* alone," I said.

Her eyes flew open, meeting mine, and before I could move, her lips slammed against mine. The heat from her body was like an inferno, and all of my defenses were made of paper buried in snow.

She made wild noises as our tongues warred for more, as her hand searched my body for bare skin to penetrate. When my hand slipped underneath the silk of her shirt, sliding between her tits, a breath hissed out of my mouth that she inhaled.

The same spot that I touched on her, center of her chest, was fucking burning me, like she'd lit it on fire.

She ripped herself away from me in what felt like an explosion to end it all. Not only were her hands trembling, but her entire body. She took slow steps back, keeping her eyes on me the entire time, until she hit a wall. "Where—" She cleared her throat. "What happens next? I mean—my family. This party. Scott."

I took a step closer to her, feeling a bead of sweat roll from my temple to my neck. She tried to take a step back but couldn't. She had already hit the wall. In a move too swift for her to protest, I took her left hand in mine, dug into my pocket, and slipped the ring Raff had picked up on her finger.

"Enough—" I cleared my throat "—said."

"No one is ever going to believe this," she said, not looking at the ring, but at me. "No one. Least of all Scott."

"Kee."

A minute later I turned my eyes to Harry Boy, who stood in the doorway of the kitchen. It took even longer for Keely to look at him.

He looked between us, his eyes narrowed, a frown on his face. "If I wouldn't know any better—" He shook his head, not finishing his thought. "The door. For you."

"Who?" Her voice was low, almost dazed.

"Stone," he said.

I sensed her stomach's reaction. It had taken a deep dive.

"Keep him out front," she said. "I'll meet him in a minute."

Harry Boy nodded and left.

She took a step away from me, fixing her hair, and then she ran a cool hand along her neck, which was on fire. "He's not," she said, the force back in her voice. "He's not going to believe this! What do I say? What do I do? I don't want you to kill my brother if I fuck this up!"

I took her hand, leading her toward the front door. "The truth, you're mine, and not a damn thing else, darlin'. Not a damn thing."

11

KEELY

I didn't get satisfaction out of hurting other people, not like the marauder did, but we were alike in a way that I hated to admit. I did get satisfaction out of getting revenge on people who hurt me or mine.

Did that make me a bad person? I had no idea.

Just like I had no idea how deep this feud between Cash and Scott went. I'd find out after we opened my brother's front door and Scott saw the two of us together. Holding hands. A huge emerald engagement ring on my left-hand ring finger. The one with the vein that ran straight to my heart.

Scott was never going to believe that Kelly and I were together. Not in the real sense. He was never going to believe that I was that kind of woman. The kind to bring two men to my bed at the same time, fooling one of them. He had to believe it, though, or I had no idea what the marauder was going to do.

Cash stopped right before he opened the door, turning to face my brothers, who had all decided to walk behind us.

My brother, Lachlan, cleared his throat. "We'll find out more about the ring on your finger in a minute, but Harrison filled us in on the detective. You were seeing him too, Kee? At the same time as Cash?"

"Yeah," I said, my voice breathy.

Harrison shook his head and leaned against the wall.

"It just happened." For a bunch of men who'd known me my entire life, none of them even blinked at me. At the lie. Usually one of them did if I *was* lying, but it was usually me calling them out on *their* bullshit. Maybe I was becoming a better actress.

"Keely Kelly, Keely Kelly, Keely Kelly," my brother Owen said real fast, but he messed up my soon-to-be name the third time he'd said it. Then he made an *ung* sound when Declan elbowed him in the ribs.

Lachlan shrugged. "It doesn't matter. You have the right to love who you want. But maybe you should've been honest with the detective before he showed up." Lachlan looked Cash in the eye. They stood at the same height. "Is this going to become a problem for my sister? For my brother? Since this is his place?"

I looked up at Cash, who stared back at my brothers like they were, collectively, nothing but easy dinner. He grinned. "No problem at all."

Lachlan nodded. "Let's see what he wants."

Shit! How could I tell them that I'd invited him?

Cash went to open his mouth, but I beat him to it. "No," I said. "I'd rather keep this between Scott and me."

"The three of us," Cash said, and with his accent, "three" came out as "tree." "It's best if the man knows where I stand. And where he stands."

"And where I stand," I said, my voice steadier than my hands and knees.

Harrison stood straighter. "We'll wait right here then." He squeezed Lachlan's shoulder.

I took a settling breath that wasn't settling at all as I opened the door. Scott was looking down at his phone, and I caught how tired he was by the set of his face. When he looked up at me, the look seemed to melt, and a huge smile bloomed on his face.

"Sweetheart," he said. "You're a sight for sore eyes. I hope —" The words died in his throat as the force from behind me slipped a hand around my waist, at the same time moving us out onto the porch, closer to Scott.

Scott. Me. The marauder.

Of course.

In that moment, I was officially the center of this feud between enemies.

"It's so nice of you to join us, detective," Cash said from behind me, his warm breath flowing over my skin, making me tremble. Not from attraction this time, but from the coldness in his tone. "A little late for the party, though."

Scott looked between us, and I couldn't understand the look on his face at all. Not until a second later when he drew his gun and told Cash to either release me, or he was going to take a bullet.

Cash laughed, the sound low, but deep in his throat. "Am I forcin' myself on you, darlin'?"

Harrison. Harrison. Harrison.

I was doing this for my brother! Wasn't I? Even though I hated to hurt Scott, because he'd never done anything to me personally, a part of me—a deep, seedy part of me—actually admired the way Cash was handling this revenge plan. It was clever.

Just like the old saying went, "feed a man and he eats for a day, but teach him how to fish and he eats for a lifetime." Well, Cash's deal seemed to go something like this, "Kill a man and it's over, but wound him in a place that doesn't have the capacity to heal, and he suffers for the rest of his life."

I was the one who ultimately had to do the hurting, though, and it killed me to have to do it. Scott was a decent guy, apart from his attitude toward organized crime individuals.

Cash squeezed my waist a little, and I sucked in a breath before I silently released it. "No," I said, my voice firm. "He's not." I took another deep breath. "I was hoping you would've come earlier. I needed to talk to you about this." I slid my hand over Cash's, and Scott's eyes narrowed. Then he lowered the gun and holstered it. "I'm sorry, Scott. I really am. You'll never know how much. But I can't do this—*us*. I met Cash and— "

I'd been waiting for Scott to interrupt me, to call me out on the bullshit, but he didn't. He believed me. He actually believed me. This *farce,* as Cash had called it. Maybe Cash was right. Scott couldn't tell the difference between the actress and the real me.

"And you fell in love with the bastard!" Scott roared and I flinched a little in Cash's embrace. Scott didn't notice it—his eyes never left Cash's—but it was enough that Cash felt it. He held me a little tighter.

"I—" I was about to say *what?* But then maybe he'd suspect something was up. But how could he not see that I was *acting?* That the only thing I felt for this man holding me was a mixture of disdain and curiosity?

Okay, and lust. I couldn't be blamed, though. The man was frigging good-looking with a healthy dose of virility. I gave myself a pass on the attraction, because my heart worked and the blood in my veins ran hot.

"Fuck, Keely!" Scott shouted, finally looking at me. "Do you have any idea who's touching you right now? Who he is?"

"The marauder."

The air seemed to still, and the only thing that seemed to move was the frantic heaving motion of Scott's chest. "So you know. You know what kind of animal has his hands on you." When Scott looked down at Cash's hand, he noticed mine, the light from the house making the emerald glimmer in the night.

I dug in my back pocket, wanting to get this over with as soon as possible, and pulled out the ring Scott had given me. I stepped out of Cash's hold, then took a step forward, hoping Scott could see the remorse in my eyes. It hurt me to end it this way.

This was only the beginning, though—for the three of us. Cash had sounded the battle cry, and Scott answered it.

"Here." I took his hand and slipped the ring inside, trying to steady my own hand. It trembled. "You deserve to be happy," I whispered. "Another woman, someone different, deserves to wear that ring."

Scott ripped his hand from mine like I was a leper, a disgusted look on his face, before he made a fist with the hand holding the ring. "You fell in love with a savage. A fucking animal that kills for money. You fell in love with my worst enemy. And he played you like the devil plays the weak. I never took you for weak, but I guess I was wrong. About a lot of things."

He looked at Cash. "We're not done, Kelly. You stole my heart—now I'm going to steal your soul—Hell's Kitchen. It never belonged to your father. It'll never belong to you, as long as I'm alive to stop it."

Any reasonable man would've taken one look at Scott's face and cancelled the debt owed, but one look at Cashel Kelly and I knew it would never be enough. He would never be satisfied until Scott Stone cried tears of blood. I knew it was the same for Scott Stone.

It didn't hit me until that moment how insanely dangerous this situation was. Both men's hate and anger were like two open graves. The game was a race to see who was going to fall into one first at the other's hand.

"Kee."

It took a moment for me to realize that Harrison was talking to me. I was out of sorts lately.

Cash turned us around, and my entire family stood facing us.

"You have something to tell your Mam and Da?" My mother glanced down at my hand before she met my eyes and quirked a severe eyebrow up.

"We're getting married," Cash said.

A few seconds later, Scott's door slammed. Tires screeched as he tore away from the curb, leaving behind the scent of burning rubber and smoke.

And that... sealed everything.

12

KEELY

My understudy hated me. All throughout practice she made snide little remarks underneath her breath. *She only got this part because of her boyfriend — or whoever he is to her. She can't even sing. She can't even act.*

Although I knew she was being a bitch because her uncle couldn't secure this role for her, her last comment was the truth. Well, for that particular day.

I couldn't focus enough to get inside of my character's head. My attention was on the marauder.

It had been three days since we kissed in the kitchen. Three days since he gave me the massive engagement ring on my finger. Even though I should've been focusing on Scott, and what I had done to him, all I could think about was my impending wedding and that kiss.

That kiss.

I loathed it.

I loved it.

It chilled me to my bone.

It heated my blood and made my stomach flutter, like my heart was a bird and it had eloped with all common sense, leaving behind loose feathers that swirled every time I thought of him.

That kiss.

I wanted to reject it.

I wanted to keep it for as long as I lived.

Because that kiss? It had blinded me. I'd never kissed a man and had the entire world fade away, and inside of the darkness, it was only him and I. No one else seemed to exist. And no matter what that lying bastard had to say about it or not, he was moved by it, too.

I felt it. How *he* had felt. In that moment, we were connected, and whatever seemed to move through him, moved through me, like a strike of lightning.

What a bunch of bullshit!

He was doing exactly what he set out to do—steal my heart! And I was letting him. *Letting him.* I was probably the easiest heist he'd ever had.

I was the date who didn't make the man work for the kiss, basically.

That wasn't me. At all. I controlled who I gave my heart to. *No* one else, least of all him.

"Damn straight!" I shouted.

The stage grew exceptionally quiet. All eyes were on me.

"I was moved by that last line." I started clapping, and because no one else wanted to seem rude, so did everyone else. My onstage sister had been defending my character, stating that no man would own me—not without shedding blood first.

That impulsive shout went to prove how much strain I was under, though. I was about to snap. I needed to get a grip on my control. I refused to allow Kelly to *have* it all—no fucking way. I was marrying *him*. At his order. The least, the very *least,* he could do was work with me on a few points that meant something to me.

I made mental notes of all the things I wanted to discuss

with him on the way to my dressing room. I was done for the day, anyway. I wasn't doing my character any favors, and shouting out thoughts that refused to quiet wasn't doing my castmates any favors either.

This entire situation was why I'd made a rule for myself years ago. *Never marry someone you instantly fall for.* Those relationships, the chaotic ones, were supposed to burn at a maddening speed, leaving me heart-wrecked but wiser. It was the kind of situation that was supposed to teach me all of the *what-not-to-dos* in love.

Scott Stone was not that kind of man. He was the kind of man you married.

I had surface feelings for him, no doubt about it, but over the years, I would've learned how to love him deeper. He would've learned how to love me. And I would have *given* him my heart. He was my turtle, winning the race of life at a reasonable pace with me. Not a quick-witted and cunning cat that came in, tried to steal my heart, and then set us on a miserable pace until we both burned out. All because of vengeance.

Okay, so maybe I shouldn't have mentally complained about Scott when we were together. I had jinxed myself beyond belief.

I stared down at my messenger bag, stuffing a few things in.

Okay, so maybe Scott wouldn't have been the guy I would've ended up with, but he had potential, didn't he? If not Scott, someone like him.

Stop making excuses, Keely. Listen to your heart.

I refused to. It had betrayed me by already feeling something for the marauder. Especially after that kiss.

"Okay, Kee, we need a plan. Like yesterday. You're not going to get out of this, or get even, if you don't start setting some ground rules now. Even if you do it without him realizing it." My Mam always said the trick with my Da was making him *think* he was the head of the house. "Minds are nothing without thoughts," she'd always say. "I'm the thoughts."

"Thoughts that lead to clever ideas are so important," I said to myself, stuffing some papers in my bag.

"No doubt."

"Ooh!" I twirled around, flinging four or five papers at the man who'd entered my dressing room.

Raff deflected and started laughing. Then he bent over and picked them up, handing them back to me.

"Tell me now if this is a family trait that I should get used to." I stuck the papers inside. "You scare me. Your cousin *constantly* scares me. I mean, you're both big men, why do you both walk like ghosts?"

"I wasn't aware ghosts walked," he said, going to take a seat on the small couch. He grinned at me, resting his foot on his knee.

I waved a hand. "You know what I mean."

"Mean what you say and say what you mean." His grin turned even wider.

"What are you doing here so early?" Cash had appointed Raff my shadow after the party at Harrison's house. But he usually came later to pick me up. I knocked off earlier than usual because of my shitty day.

"Cash sent me to bring you home."

He was keeping tabs on me, but that didn't make a lump form in my throat, blocking airflow to my lungs. It was one word. Home. The marauder's house.

Raff had overseen the move from my old apartment to Kelly's warehouse-turned-palatial-palace in Hell's Kitchen. After Kelly orchestrated that dramatic scene in front of Harrison's house, he told me I had three days to get my shit ready to be moved into his place. He actually used the word "our"—as in, his *and* mine.

If that kiss wasn't enough to knock me on my ass, moving in with him swept the barstool right out from underneath me.

I stared at Raff for second, maybe longer, because he raised his eyebrows at me. I'd been lost in thought.

In the time it took me to walk to my dressing room and pack up some of my stuff, I had come up with plan that might rattle Cash Kelly a little. It was going to take courage to see it through, though. I took a deep breath and said, "Cash's family church, the one he was telling me about?"

Cash said we were going to get married there, since the priest had been a family friend for years—no date had been set, but he'd mentioned it to my Mam and Da after the scene with Scott. My parents were familiar with the church, so my Mam approved. Not that Kelly seemed to care one way or the other, but it was a point for him.

"What about it?" Raff said.

"I'd like to stop there before going home."

Raff nodded. "Yeah, I guess that'd be all right."

I nodded, more for myself, swooping up my bag from the table in front of the mirror. The reflection lit up by megawatt bulbs showed a woman at war with herself, but I'd already made up my mind. "I have one other stop before going to church. It won't take long."

Raff narrowed his eyes at me but came along without protest.

THE SMALL OFFICE inside of the massive church was dim, since the sun was starting to set. Raff had gone to find Father Flanagan and had left me alone with my thoughts and my bags.

At first Raff had directed me to the confessional, but I shook my head and said I needed to speak to the priest somewhere else—a place where we could take my bags and I could keep them close.

Raff seemed to have a clue as to what I was up to, but instead of calling me out, the grin on his face told me he was going to keep my secret. He seemed to like the idea of me one-upping Kelly. Maybe because not many people were able to.

Two chairs were in front of a simple desk in the priest's office. I sat in one, sighing as I did, and then glanced at the bag hanging over the second.

My heart skipped a beat and I took a deep, deep breath to try and regulate it. It was making those feathers flutter again in the pit of my stomach. My fingers drummed against the wood, and my foot had an insane urge to tap.

Five minutes went by, and right before I stood from my seat, too nervous to sit, the door opened, and an older man walked in.

"Father Flanagan?" I said, turning in my seat.

"All day," he said. "Raff said you'd like to have a word with me."

I stood and he stopped cold—his eyes took me in from my head to my hands. I was rubbing my palms against my jeans.

"My name is Keely Ryan," I said, sticking my hand out. "I was told you're a family friend of the Kelly family."

He took my hand, but instead of shaking it, he set his free one on top of mine. "I consider Cashel Fallon and Killian Patrick as close as blood." He paused. "Are you in some kind of trouble, Keely?"

"Trouble." I shook my head. It would do no good to tell this man about the kind of trouble Cash Kelly was, because he probably already knew. "No, that's not the right word for it. But I am glad you consider Cashel Fallon family. Does the branch extend to me? Since he's chosen me for his bride?" I smiled—a cunning smile, as my Mam called it.

Father Flanagan's eyes drifted from mine to the bag

hanging over the chair, and then back to mine again. They were bright blue to go with what was probably once a head full of red hair. "Have a seat." He nodded to the chair I'd been sitting in. "Let's hear your plans."

The grin he gave me matched Raff's, and the smile that came from me this time was true.

———

THE EMERALD SURROUNDED by diamonds on my left finger reacted to the soft lights in the office. Even though it had sat on my finger since Kelly had put it there, I never took the time to admire how beautiful it was.

Maybe because admitting that to myself felt like giving in a bit.

I was having a hard time doing that on principal.

What I was about to do, though? Felt liberating.

An ounce of control made my life feel a little less chaotic, and so I gave myself permission to admire the ring for what it was. Just a ring that looked exceptionally beautiful in this light and on my finger. It was a piece of jewelry that made me feel feminine. I really hated to admit that anything Kelly did had worth, but the ring was stunning and proved that if he had actually picked it out, he had good taste.

"Of course," I whispered to myself. "He chose you, didn't he?"

Then I laughed at myself, because I wasn't his choice at all. Fate. Fate riding on the wings of vengeance had chosen me to be his bride. I should've ended up with a man who was the opposite of Cashel Fallon Kelly. A man who worked hard to earn an honest dime. A man who was predictable and reliable. A man whose touch didn't burn me to my core and put me at ease at the same time. A man who brought me peace, not chaos.

Even the role on Broadway shouldn't have been mine.

Those things—the man who seemed larger than life and the role on stage—should've belonged to my sister. She was destined for big things. Things that Mam had said come with being a star.

So the life I was living? It felt like a big lie.

Before I could get too carried away with the poor-me line of thinking, voices met me from outside of Father Flanagan's office. I didn't bother getting up from my seat this time because I was already standing. I refused to wrinkle anything.

The door opened and Raff walked in first, but he stopped on a dime. Kelly, who had his head turned back toward Father Flanagan, shoved him further into the office, not realizing that I stood there.

Maybe it was the silence from the other two men, but whatever it was, Kelly finally found me in the room.

"We need to talk," I said, not giving him a chance to recover. This was my moment. I'd be damned if he stole that, too.

He said nothing, but his eyes were steady on mine. They were, until light laughter came from Father Flanagan, who was stepping out of the room, Raff following. Kelly narrowed his eyes at me, but a second later, they found the priest and his cousin. His ire was aimed at them, not me.

"Ah, but what a tangled web we weave, Cashel Fallon Kelly," Father Flanagan said before he shut the door behind him and left us alone. Laughter echoed down the hall until it was completely quiet, leaving the two of us to face each other.

When his attention was mine again, his eyes took in the veil on my head and the wedding dress on my body.

I'd gone with Mari to one of her fittings—she was getting married in Italy in June—and while she did whatever she had to do, I had started looking around the shop. Mari was working with a well-known designer, but I decided to scan the shelves. A salesgirl popped up out of nowhere and told me she had the perfect dress for me. It was meant for someone with my stat-uesque build.

Mari came out as the girl argued with me about trying it on. Together they persuaded me to do it. But I only did it because the dress wasn't frilly, and I knew at some point, I was going to have to meet that fate—be it by myself, or with my Mam and aunts.

I'd decided to share the moment with Mari since I hadn't shared with her what was going on. In a secret way, I was able to enjoy the experience with her, even if my circumstances and hers were beyond comparison. Mari was marrying for love. My brother, who happened to be in love with her, had a bullet hovering over his chest if I didn't marry out of revenge.

The dress turned out to be a winner. It was sensual, what the bridal attendant called a sheath, and hugged me in all of the right places. It had a crew neckline, long-sleeves, and the intricate details on the side were made from crepe, lace appliqués, and thread-embroidered tulle with beading. The patterns reminded me of the swirls inside of peacock feathers. The patterns were strictly on the sides, and the back dipped into a V. It didn't have much of a train, but the veil made up for it.

The day after Mari's appointment, I went back and put a deposit down on the dress, veil, and a pair of heels the bridal attendant talked me into. I demanded secrecy from the bubbly girl who had helped me, telling her I was inviting family to a party, but I was going to surprise them with our secret wedding.

If she only knew...

Turned out, it was the partial truth. Instead of inviting family to our secret wedding, I was inviting the groom. He stood across the room from me. Staring. I had no doubt that he would be in a suit—he always wore one when he "worked"—such a gentleman gangster—and he didn't disappoint.

One thing had stayed consistent with Kelly since the first

day we met: He was as handsome as he was ruthless. I knew he'd always be.

Finally, after I realized he wasn't going to respond until I continued, I cleared my throat. "You marry me here and now." I lifted a finger. "I'm saving my parents from this sham of a wedding. I'm their only living daughter, so it's important to me that what they witness is true. I'll tell them that we're so crazy in love I couldn't wait another day." I rolled my eyes. "And Mari. I don't want to tell her yet. I want to keep her out of this, for now."

Kelly said nothing as he stood there, still staring at me. It was making me uncomfortable. I set my cool hand against my neck, to ease some of the burn. A minute or two went by before he moved toward me. I went to take a step back, because he always seemed to cramp my space, but I hit the desk. Even though I demanded this be mine, he was still backing me into a corner.

"You're not saving your parents from anythin', darlin'," he said, his voice cool and confident. "We both know it. And we both know it's not wise to lie in a church." He looked up for a second before his fierce green eyes slammed into mine. "Speaking lies here is the equivalent of lying to yourself. Nothin' but a waste of time."

"I'm not lying," I said through clenched teeth.

"You'd cut off your nose to spite your face." He studied my face for a second before he set a hand on each side of me, leaning in. His head tilted before he moved in even closer, his nose touching my neck before it skimmed up to my ear. His warm breath fanned over my skin, and the smell of his rich, expensive cologne lingered in the air. It smelled so good, I wished it had a flavor so I could taste it. Lick it right off his body.

"You're doing this for control, which is fine by me, darlin'. You're owed that. It'll happen today. Now. You in that dress and me standing here almost tongued-tied because of it. But I won't accept lies. Not here. Not now. So let's be truthful. You don't want to take vows in front of your family and friends because this is no sham to you. You're going to make this as real as I am. Because you're trying to get even with me." He became still, and my skin ached for his lips to close the gap between us and make the connection.

"If I don't take this seriously, you will. To make me suffer. To make me fall for you as hard as you're falling for me. You don't want anyone that knows you to see it—to feel it. The truth you'll give me in front of that altar." He sniffed at my neck. "I can smell the fear on you, archer. Fear that you'll speak those vows with truth and I won't do the same."

Every word was breathed in my ear with that soft lilt of his, and despite all my best efforts, a chill shook my body.

Kelly had shaken the snow globe that was my life, rearranging all of the pieces, and I wasn't sure how they were going to settle around me.

"You're not," I said, closing my eyes. I was a strong woman, and I knew it, but I was also human. And this situation had thrown me inside of a place I'd never been before. Marriage was a serious commitment, one that I'd always expected to honor and respect. "Going to do the same."

"Ah," he breathed out softly. "Now we're getting somewhere."

"This is not real for you. How can it be? This is out of vengeance." I wasn't sure why it was so important for me to find out his feelings on this, but it was.

He might've been using me as a pawn, and I was still determined to give him hell for it, but *I* wouldn't accept lies at the altar. He'd either say his vows with meaning, or...

What could I do?

Nothing.

My palms felt damp all of a sudden, like I was looking down

from a sky-high building on a world full of chaos, about to jump into it. I rubbed my hands against my dress, hoping to find a safety net there.

"This is real for you?" He moved back so that he looked me in the eyes again.

"Yeah," I said. "*You* wanted this. So now it's going to get real. Is that *fine*—" I copied his tone "—with you, Marauder?"

He looked down at me for so long that I wondered if he was ever going to speak. Then he smiled, and I hoped he couldn't hear my knees knocking together. "Grand," he said, his voice a bit raspy. "Just. Grand."

"Wait!" I held out a hand when he went to walk away. "Where are you going?"

"My bride wants to get married." He shrugged, all *la de daaa.* "I'm going to wait at the altar. I'll be there when you're ready."

———

I'D NEVER BE ready for this.

For him.

Ready or not, though, twenty minutes later, I opened the door to the office, taking one last look in the mirror Father Flanagan had brought in for me to use. One last look at the single woman who was leaving this room. Whenever I walked back in, I'd be married to the man known as the marauder.

The thief of hearts.

I took one step out of the door and ran into a solid chest. When I looked up, my mouth fell open. Then it snapped shut. "What are you doing here?" I hiss-whispered at Harrison.

"What am *I* doing here?" He matched my tone. "I should be asking you the same thing! Have you lost your mind? You're choosing to do this, Kee?"

"Wow," I said, drawing the word out. "Kelly has a big mouth."

He shook his head. "We were in the middle of a business meeting when Raff called and told Kelly he had to get here right away. Kelly had me walk with him so we could finish talking. He told me a minute ago to come and check on you. Now I see this. You. Dressed like that. And since we're standing in a church—not hard to figure out."

Oh. I had a big mouth then. I should've felt Harrison out more before I spilled my secret.

I narrowed my eyes at my brother. "You don't get to judge me on this, Harrison! You don't. I'll do whatever I have to do to survive this." I went to walk away, but he grabbed my arm.

"Kee," he said. "I'm not judging you. But listen—just listen! For once!"

I took a deep breath before I turned to face him.

"Whatever you're thinking, forget it," he said. "Whatever you're planning, forget it. It's not going to make a difference. Not with him. It's too late."

"What do you mean?" I said slowly. "Too late?"

"Kee." He shook his head. "The entire family believes you've fallen for Kelly."

"So? Isn't that what they're supposed to believe?"

"We grew up with you, Kee."

"And...?"

"And—how much clearer do you need me to be? You *are* falling for him. That's why you hate him. You know you are, and you don't want to. So you're fighting him because it's the only choice you have. If *I* know it, Kelly knows it."

"What kind of woman does that make me, Harrison?" I whispered, gripping the sides of the dress so tightly that my knuckles strained. "That my heart...it's...not at war with this. It's at war with the *idea* of this. Him bullying me into it."

"Maybe it's just attraction. Just physical. It'll pass. And..." Harrison shook his head, running a hand through his hair, making it stick up. "I don't know, Kee. I have no clue." Then my brother pulled me in, and my head fell against his chest. He kissed me on the forehead. "You don't have to do this. You don't. He got his revenge. It's enough."

"It's not," I whispered. "We both know it."

"I do, but my life is not worth this. You paying for my sins."

I stood, steadying myself. I had my pity party moment. It was time to move forward. "Your life is worth suffering for, Harrison. Because I'm not doing this to pay for your sins. I'm doing this to give value to your love. Mari's truth was a blow, but we both know she's not the type of person to hurt anyone on purpose. So you know what that tells me? Your great love is still out there. You've just been too focused on Mari to see it."

Harrison lifted his hand, fixing my veil. "You're my little sister, and I've never said anything like this to you before. You've always been as rough as one of the boys, if not tougher." He grinned, but it was for memories only. "So maybe this isn't enough, but you're beautiful, Kee. Cash Kelly deserves to have his heart stop when he sees you. He doesn't deserve you."

I smiled. "That's enough, *Harry Boy*." I gave him my arm and he took it. "So you're going to walk me?"

"Right out the door," he said underneath his breath. "Because if Kelly doesn't kill me, Mam will."

"I'll leave you out of it," I said. "Sister's honor."

"Nah," he set his hand over mine. "Let me take this one."

"Honestly? I'd rather marry Kelly a hundred times then have to face Mam once."

"I'm surprised she didn't see this in her tea leaves—the treachery!"

We both grinned—and then our feet stopped. The entire church had been filled with candles, all lit and burning, making the man waiting at the end of the aisle glow. I couldn't tell whether I was in heaven or hell.

"I didn't ask for this," I whispered.

"No, Kelly did," my brother answered.

I nodded. "Let's get this over with."

My brother set his hand over mine as he walked me down the aisle. The green in Kelly's eyes seemed unreal as I moved closer to him, and like the ring on my finger, I wished I could appreciate the color without feeling like I was double-crossing my principals. I wanted to admire his eyes, to get lost in them, to believe that the look he was giving me—all serious and scorching—was true.

I wanted him to want me, and not just out of vengeance.

If that was the case, though, we wouldn't be standing where we were, about to make promises that were built on something brutal and bloodthirsty.

My brother kissed me on the cheek before he handed me over to Kelly. Harrison and Raff were standing as witnesses. I didn't have a bridesmaid, and it didn't really matter. My sister was dead, and my soul sister didn't need to be involved in this. She deserved to believe that all was right in the world and that I wasn't selling out love to save my brother's life.

Kelly's hand was warm on mine as we stood before Father Flanagan and turned toward one another. I repeated the vows I was supposed to, but I couldn't really hear my words, not like I could feel them: heavy, with a lifelong commitment. Once Cash Kelly said his vows to me, that was it. We were both locked in.

Forever was only a few short words from that moment.

"I now pronounce you man and wife," Father Flanagan said, after Kelly had made his promises.

My brother made a low, desperate noise in his throat, but it didn't matter. There was no use in protesting. It was done.

"You may kiss your bride, Cashel Fallon Kelly."

Kelly stared at me a moment before he set my veil aside. I lifted my eyes in challenge, daring him to kiss me again. The look on his face after our kiss in Harrison's kitchen would forever be burned into my memory. He was a pawn to it, to whatever attraction existed between us, just like I was.

As if he could read my thoughts, he grinned at me, and then his hand slid into my hair and he pulled my face closer to his. "That's a real daring face, darlin', and somethin' you should know about me—I never pick truth."

Then he kissed me.

I didn't even realize that someone had busted through the doors of the church. That he was screaming. That I had a trembling hand pressed against my lips. That my heart felt utterly wild, my soul completely lost, my mind locked in battle with the rest of me. Not until Kelly turned away from me, a grin on his face, to face an enraged Scott Stone, who, a second later, had my new husband in handcuffs.

13

KEELY

Cashel Kelly was a fucking masochist if I'd ever met one.

He didn't fight the handcuffs. He didn't even stop smiling as Scott read him his rights. All the while I stood there next to Father Flanagan, while my brother demanded to know the charges against his client, wondering if this was going to be my life.

Reality check. *It is.*

I should've known that our first meeting directed our relationship. How many people meet in a cemetery?

"It's not too late to back out," Father Flanagan said to me, not looking at me but at the scene in front of him. "No papers have been signed."

He had asked me that before, during our meeting, if I wanted an out. He said he'd known Cash his entire life, since he was a wee babe, and how persuasive he could be when he set his mind to something. It seemed Father Flanagan knew more about this situation than he cared to admit. However, there was no out for me.

"No," I said. "Papers weren't signed, but this is a done deal. I made vows I intend to keep. They mean something to me, regardless of the circumstances."

"Ah," Father Flanagan breathed out, and there was something almost funny about the way he had done it.

I turned to look at him and a huge smile lit up his face.

"What?" I said.

"Oh, nothin'," he said, with the same *la de da* attitude Kelly pulled off. "I...I'm delighted! I'd tell you to give him hell, but I'd prefer it if you'd give him a taste of heaven, since..."

I lifted my dress, prepared to ride with Harrison to the police station. "Hell is more his speed."

"Somethin' like that." He put a hand on my shoulder and squeezed. "Go with vigor and grace, my child. You're going to need both."

I met Harrison outside as they put a hand to Cash's head, pushing him into a waiting police car. There were five cars, each one holding two policemen, for one man.

"What are they arresting him for?" I asked my brother.

Harrison shook his head. "Murder."

I turned and really looked at him. He shrugged, like the charge was nothing too exciting.

"Did he do it?" I asked.

"Draw your own conclusions, but they never have enough evidence to convict him."

I let that sink in for a moment. *They never have enough evidence.*

"More than once?"

Harrison sighed. "There were two murders not long ago. They're trying to pin both on him, when the facts show *whoever* killed the two guys—" my brother paused and gave me a "listen beyond my words" look "—did so in self-defense."

"Let's go," I said, moving in the direction of Kelly's building, where I assumed Harrison's car was parked.

Harrison put a hand on my arm to stop me. "We can stop

this, Kee. None of the papers have been signed. You only said your vows."

"What do you suggest?"

"Stone's gunning for him. He's not going to rest. He's not going to stop until Kelly is either locked in a cage for good, or he's six feet under. If I make a mistake—in trial, I mean— maybe I can take care of the first issue and you'll be free."

"What about Kelly's brother?"

"I doubt he'll force you to marry him, too."

"No," I said. *Again.* "Even though no papers have been signed, I'm married to Kelly. It's done."

"You can't move him, Keely Shea! I'm giving you an out, and you're not fucking taking it. He's never been proved wrong. Never. You're not going to change him."

I took a step closer to my brother, hoping my eyes conveyed how serious I was. "You mess up on purpose and he'll know. Do your job, Harrison, and do it right. Get my husband out of jail and out of trouble."

"Your husband." He took a deep breath and then shook his head. "This is not some feral cat you can try to tame. Feeding him is not going to work. Taking him in is not going to work. Neither will compassion. Some men are born more animal than man. Cash Kelly is a wild animal."

I went to walk off when his next words stopped me.

"He's not going to fill the void Roisin left behind, Keely."

I stood motionless for a second, my temper too high to even respond.

"If Mari can't do it—"

I whirled on my brother, my veil catching in the wind, flowing behind me like a flag. It should've been stained red from my anger. "No one will ever replace Roisin in my life. You have no idea what you're fucking talking about."

"Really?" He took a step closer to me and I balled my hands into fists. "What about Broadway, Kee? I know you enjoy it, but do you love it? Or are you just trying to please Mam?"

"What does any of this have to do with Kelly?"

My brother ignored my venomous tone and battled forward. "I don't know." He shrugged. "But somehow I know it's connected. You've never gotten help to deal with the loss. Mam was too blinded by her own grief to reach out for you. All of Roisin's hopes and dreams were put on you, because Mam can't fill the emptiness either."

"None of this is related," I snapped at him. It wasn't, even though I knew his words were the truth. But this had to do with Kelly and the vows I'd just made. There was no way I was letting Stone get even when it was my heart at stake. If anyone was getting even, it'd be me, and I couldn't do that with my wild animal of a husband in a cage. "No matter how you feel about this, it is what it is. Now take me to the police station and do the damn job Kelly pays you for."

I started walking toward the building, and as I did, I heard my brother grumble, "Yeah, Mrs. Keely Kelly, whatever you say, Mrs. Keely Kelly. Serves you right, *Keely Kelly.*"

I shot him the bird.

AFTER A FEW HOURS, they had to let my husband go. Not enough evidence to convict him.

Kelly walked out with a grin on his face, and when he caught the one on mine, his fell and his eyebrow shot up. I wasn't smiling because they had let him go, even though I was getting sick of waiting around in my wedding dress, but because I'd overhead two cops talking about my brother—what a tough-ass lawyer he was.

"What?" I stood, fixing my dress. "Don't trust my smile, Kelly?"

"Not just your smile, darlin'. '*I woke up today to ruin a man's life*' is written all over your face."

I rolled my eyes. "I didn't take you for being dramatic. But here we are." We started to leave together when I stopped. "And I wasn't smiling because they let you go either. Just for the record."

"Noted." He nodded toward the front of the building, ready to walk. A second after we did, he cleared his throat. "You don't care about all of these people?"

"What about them?" I said.

"They're staring at you."

Probably because I was in a wedding dress in a police station, but either way, I shrugged. "They must like what they see, if they keep looking."

Kelly smiled and then laughed.

Like the ring on my left finger, I'd never truly paid attention to it until it seemed to steal my breath. His smile? One front tooth came out slightly more than the other one, and the imperfection made him even sexier. His laugh? It was deep and melodic, like the sound of his voice.

"Good bones," he said, and I had no clue what he was talking about.

"See you next time, Cash," a short policewoman said from her spot at the front desk.

What was it about this guy that made people either love or hate him? There was no in-between. The little woman behind the desk seemed to love him. Her eyes went soft when he walked past her.

"She thinks you're *so* charming," I said. "*La de daaaa!*" I twirled my pointer finger in the air.

"I am," he said.

"Not on your best day. Not to me."

"You have a tongue made from sin, darlin'. If only I was fooled by the lies."

"Are we really going to fight on our wedding day?" I mocked being upset, throwing a hand over my heart.

"Considering I was locked up for part of it?" He shrugged. "I'd say an argument was—"

"Just grand," I said, copying his Irish accent. "Just *grand*."

After a few steps, he said, "No one is indifferent to me."

"No speaking in riddles," I said, demanding to understand this time.

"Love and hate are both driven by feelings. I do something to make another man hate me—" he shrugged "—more than likely, I stood up for my beliefs, challenging his. A beautiful woman falls in love with me—" he grinned "—it means I used my persuasive charms to claim what's mine, even if she had to fall through hate first."

He opened the door to the police station for me and I stepped out first, waiting while he held the door for another woman before meeting me again. We started toward Harrison's car.

"Claim?" I stopped walking. "Or steal?"

He studied me for a minute. "Hearts are stolen every second, every minute, every hour, of every day, darlin'. I doubt anyone would give such a sacred thing over willingly."

"Me," I said. "I was prepared to give it."

"To Stone."

I shrugged. "Whoever."

"Give me the difference between giving and stealing when it comes to a heart."

"Giving means handing over less power. I'm giving it, so some control is still mine. Stealing it—that's consuming. If...*whoever* can steal my heart, *whoever* can steal everything that means something to me. I'm not down with that."

"Ah." The lights from the buildings lit up the mischief in his green eyes. "The safe path. A relationship that's built on something other than animalistic attraction. Or maybe you'd call it passion."

"Sex is sex," I said. "It's good or it's not. Feelings? Those should build over time, because if they run too hot, too fast, they burn everything down around them."

"Sex is sex," he repeated. The look on his face echoed the look he'd given me at church, when I'd dared him with my expression to kiss me. It was a subtle physical change, but it didn't seem to matter. I could feel the changes in him rather than see them.

I shook my head, confused about all of this, and turned to walk away from him. I made it a couple of steps before someone called my name. I sighed, turning around.

Scott stood on the other side of Kelly, like no feud stood between them. Except when you looked at it from my point of view, I was the center. They each stood on a different side of me.

My eyes connected with Scott's before he looked me over from head to toe. I thought I'd see hurt, but I only found disgust. He moved closer after the judgment, stopping when he was next to me. "Marrying him is one thing," he said, his voice a hot whisper. "But coming here to support a murderer? Who. The. Fuck. Are. You?"

I didn't respond, but I refused to move my eyes from his. He stared at me for a minute longer, the disgust even thicker, before he stormed off.

Kelly helped me into the back of Harrison's car, taking care to move my veil from the seat and setting it on the window behind us, and then he slid in next to me.

I looked at my shiny new husband as my brother started the

car, heading toward Hell's Kitchen. "Scott's disgusted with me," I said. "He hates me."

Kelly laughed a little, and Harrison looked at him from his rearview mirror.

"How's this funny, if it's going to ruin your plans?"

"Not funny," he said, shaking his head. "Amusing."

"Amusing. Funny. Same damn thing."

"Harry Boy," Kelly said, hitting my brother's seat, "is it disgust you feel for Mari when you see her with Macchiavello? Or is it pure hate for what you want the most and can't have?"

I met my brother's eyes in the mirror. He said nothing.

"There's your answer," Kelly said, sitting back and relaxing in his seat. "No answer is still an answer. Love does strange things to people, darlin'. It's like a disease—it affects everyone differently."

True, so I didn't argue.

We all became quiet as we drove down the streets of Hell's Kitchen. My new home. The closer we came to Kelly's place, though, the thicker the crowds became. Music thumped from outside. Tables had been set up, lined with food. Clumps of people were talking and laughing. Kids ran around like it was the fourth of July.

The crowd was diverse, made up of many different faces, all coming together to form a party.

My brother, acting like a chauffeur, parked the car in front of Kelly's place of business, and after getting out, opened the passenger side door so he could help me out. Kelly slid out behind me and put a hand to my lower back, urging me forward.

"What's going on?" I said.

"A party." Kelly nodded at a man in passing as we came closer to the thickest part of the crowd.

"Yeah, I can see that. What's it for?"

"Us," he said.

Ooh. On his face, was that...not thankfulness, not humble-
ness, but something close to both of them that wasn't actually
either one of them? Did I dare think something I never
expected? Pride, but not for himself.

"You stare at the devil for long periods of time, darlin', and
it does wicked things to your face," he said.

I laughed a little. "It's not that I'm staring at you because I
like what I see, Marauder. I'm staring at you because I had no
idea this many people *liked* you."

"Like is a strong word. I'd call it respect and then call it a
day."

"Mr. Kelly!" A man who didn't look much younger than
Cash, holding a baby on his hip, came up to us. A woman stood
next to him, holding a little girl by the hand. I assumed she was
his wife and the two kids were theirs.

The man and Kelly shook hands, and then he introduced
me as his wife, full name and all. The man worked for Kelly,
though I wasn't sure in what capacity. He didn't seem like the
marauding type, so maybe he legitimately worked for him.
Harrison had told me that Kelly owned legitimate businesses.

I smiled at the little girl, who was staring up at me. I didn't
give a shit if adults stared at me, but I drew the line at kids.
Most of them were too cute to ignore. "Hi," I said to her.

"Hi," she said, and then she started swinging her mom's
hand back and forth while she sang, "Keely Kelly. Keely Kelly.
Oooh. Keely Kelly."

Her mother told her to hush, but she kept on. Harrison
stood close and started laughing so hard that he had to excuse
himself from the conversation he was in. Raff did the same.

Asses.

After some time had gone by and I'd met too many people
to remember, I decided to grab a drink and take a seat. This was
Kelly's party, everyone wanting a piece of him, so I sat back and
watched it all unfold.

I mean, despite him being a marauding bastard, these people were treating him like fucking Robin Hood. I couldn't claim that he was friendly with them, but there was something about him while he was around them that made me watch him even closer.

Cash Kelly had found a purpose in these people?

Harrison had also warned me about the war going on in Hell's Kitchen—apart from the other one Kelly had started with Scott—because he wanted me to be careful. But here? Among these people? It didn't seem to exist. They were having a grand time. Even the senior men of the group had gotten together and started to sing old Irish tunes for the fun of it.

If I set this scene next to the one Kelly always painted in my head, it made no sense.

Or maybe these people were too afraid of him not *to come and celebrate? He was hell-bent on ruling these streets again, so maybe he did whatever it took to get these people to go to war for him?*

"Sit here, Connolly. Granny'll sit right there."

I was sitting in a beach chair, and I turned to find an older woman taking a seat in the chair closest to mine. A little girl, maybe about seven or eight, sat next to her.

The older lady met my eye. "Congratulations," she said, tipping her head to me. She wasn't your usual "grandma" type. I couldn't find anything sweet about her. She seemed as tough as nails. "I have to say, Mr. Kelly chose a good bride. You look sturdy enough to take on a man like him. I'm not speaking physically, either."

I found no offense to her words. I even wanted to grin, but I held back for the sake of respect. "I hope that's true, Ms...?"

"Maureen will do," she said. She nodded toward the little girl. "This is my granddaughter. Connolly."

Even though her grandmother spoke to her, she looked away, and not at the crowd. She stared at a spot on the building, where no one was standing to block her view.

"What a beautiful name," I said, and I meant it. It fit her. She didn't answer so I tried again after a minute. "Are you having fun?"

Kids her age were everywhere, but she wasn't even bothering to look at them, either.

"Connolly chooses to stay silent," Maureen said.

I looked at Maureen, hoping my face conveyed the question. *Chooses to stay silent?*

Maureen set her hands on the chair and then groaned as she forced herself back up. "Would you mind keeping an eye on her? I'm going to see if she'll eat if I make her a plate."

Not bothering to wait for my answer, Connolly's grandmother headed in the direction of the tables set with food. Maybe it was my imagination, but she seemed almost relieved to have walked off.

I relaxed in my seat, but I was determined to try to talk to her, even if she only listened. The old men were singing a song that put a smile on my face. "I had a sister," I said to her. "My twin. Her name was Roisin. Which is close to Connolly—" she shot me a look "— sort of." I smiled and her eyes narrowed, but I got her to look at me, at least. "She loved this song. She could even dance to it."

After a second, she turned away from me again.

I started to hum along to the song, moving my feet against the cement in a steady rhythm. "Do you know any old Irish songs?"

Nothing. Not a nod. Not a look. Her eyes were glued to dead space.

"Maybe one day, if you'd ever like to learn them, or how to dance to them, I can teach you."

Silence. No movement.

"Yeah, who likes old music anyway?" I said. "You gotta get down with the times, right?"

She sighed, and for a second, I wondered if I was bothering

her. Then I wondered if she just didn't care for casual conversation.

"I understand," I said, my voice low. "After my sister...I didn't want to talk either. It hurt. I didn't know what to say to make it go away." Why was I telling this child this? I had no clue, but the words kept coming.

"Then my brother—" I nodded toward him, even though she couldn't see "—told me that I didn't have to talk. He said he could read the clouds in my eyes. They created all of the words I couldn't say. Maybe one day, if you ever feel like hanging out, I can read the clouds in your eyes on a sunny day, too. Or my brother can. He's the best at it."

It was subtle, and so fucking grown up, but her little shoulders slumped. Like she released a pressure inside of her that had been holding her up. I swallowed down the ball of emotions that were stuck in my throat, because I realized something. Maybe she didn't have clouds in her eyes, but I could understand her silence, no matter what had caused it.

Mam had once told me that money always goes to money, and kindred spirits always find kindred spirits. We were all lost, but other people experiencing the same struggles could find us. Or we could find them.

"Archer," Kelly said, suddenly appearing beside me, holding out his hand. How long had he been standing there? Come to think of it, after Maureen and Connolly had arrived, I stopped watching him and started concentrating on them. His green eyes were unreadable, but he kept looking between the two of us.

I couldn't answer him, so I took his hand and stood.

Maureen came back, setting a plate of cake next to the little girl. She didn't even look at it. With a sigh similar to Connolly's, Maureen took a seat, balancing her plate in her hand.

"Bye, Connolly," I said. "Maybe I'll see you later."

I went to leave, but before I did, a tug on my dress stopped me.

I turned at the same moment Maureen's plate fell out of her hands, and so did a piece of meat out of her mouth. Kelly looked between Connolly and me again, his forehead strained.

Connolly had my dress in her hand. Her eyes were hard on mine, like she wanted me to say something.

"Did I forget something?" I asked.

She nodded.

"Okay." I studied her eyes. "The music we talked about?"

She shook her head. No.

I took a deep breath. "My sister?"

Connolly nodded.

"You want to know more about her?"

"*Was*," she barely got out. Her voice was low and scratchy.

Oh. I'd said "her name was" when I was talking to her about Roisin. Past tense. Connolly had caught it, and she wanted to know what had happened to her, not more about her.

"She..." I hesitated, but I decided to be honest. "She died."

Connolly said nothing, only turned away from me and took her spot, staring at the wall again.

THE PARTY WAS OVER, and my feet were hurting. I slid off my shoes as Kelly opened the door to his massive warehouse, inviting me in. It was spacious and had been redone to look like a home. It was all tan brick and dark brown woods. The floor felt cool against my blistered feet, and my pads relaxed into the sensation as we made our way deeper inside.

"Where are my things?" I asked.

He set his keys on the kitchen counter, and when I turned around, the windows behind him showed nothing beyond but a dark void.

"In your room," he said.

"Is that your room?" We hadn't discussed that part of the deal. Where I'd be sleeping. Or what happened from this point forward.

I wasn't a virgin, so I wasn't nervous about that, but I wanted to know what he expected of me. Was he going to give me a choice or not? The *not* made me anxious. He was game to steal my heart, but what else? Those fucking feathers started to float around in my stomach, making my heart beat faster. It was a strange sensation to crave him sexually while hating him on principal.

I suspected Cash Kelly knew that would be my personal fight long before I did.

"This way," he said, and I turned, finding him standing at the bottom of the metal staircase that twisted and turned as it made its way up.

He'd lost his jacket after the police station, leaving it in Harrison's car, and from the kitchen to the stairs he'd loosened his tie and rolled up his sleeves. He was built like one of those Boston boxers, but with the deep scars of a gangster.

And his cologne, or whatever it was?

The entire warehouse, all however many thousands of square feet, seemed to hold his scent. I took a deep breath in but immediately let it out before I forced my feet to move. As soon as I did, he started up the stairs and I followed. The entire upper level seemed to have more windows than the lower. Actually, except for the brick that separated the rooms, it seemed to be all glass in the back.

He flung a hand in a few directions as we passed— bedroom, bathroom, blah, blah, blah—like he was checking stops off of his list. Then he said something that made me stop.

"Library." He waved a hand at the door.

He kept going, but I stepped inside of the room, wanting to see what kind of library a marauder had. It was fucking fantastic. There were leather sofas placed strategically around the room, all in front of the stretching windowpanes, and the ceiling was made of varying shades of wood. The walls? They were bookshelves.

I ran my hand along one, feeling the spines of so many experiences against my palms.

"That one there," Kelly said from behind me, "you might like."

After removing my hand from the wall, I turned to face him.

He nodded toward an area that had been set up to resemble a coffee shop. It even had a laptop on it.

I moved toward it and picked up the book. Daphne du Maurier.

My father was a quiet man, but there were two things he taught me: how to read and how to shoot a bow and arrow. He'd said both would give me a power that no man could steal.

Reading was something I hadn't done in a while, though, not since I moved out on my own and had responsibilities.

I ran my hand across the cover of the book, knowing Mari would love it here, too. Sometimes when I used to hang out with her in the city, when she was trying to lay low after she left her foster parents' place, we would spend time at the library together.

"Why are you a marauder?" I said, testing him.

Even though I didn't turn my eyes from the book, I could sense his grin. "Why do you shoot arrows?"

Ah, he wasn't just a ruthless gangster with only vengeance on his mind.. He'd read the book.

"Because of the danger, because of the speed, because I might miss," I said, changing the quote up a bit. "I didn't take you for a reader."

"You don't take me for a lot of things. Only one."

"It's hard to know anything else when it's all that surrounds you. Mayhem."

A few minutes passed, and when I looked up, Kelly was beside me, a necklace dangling from his hand. "You say a heart can't be stolen, darlin', but I beg to differ."

I went to take it from him, but he moved it back a bit, grinning. This time when the necklace came forward, I stopped it from swinging back and forth like a pendulum and studied it. The pendant at the end of the gold chain was heart-shaped—a literal heart, veins and arteries included—and it seemed to be a locket. It had a smallish keyhole at the bottom.

"What's inside?" I asked, holding the pendant between my fingers, studying all of the grooves.

He was quiet for so long that I looked up again.

"You'll see when you find your way in," he said. "Just remember. Just because it looks a certain way doesn't mean it is a certain way. There's more than one way inside of a heart."

I took the necklace from him and slipped it over my neck. It sat against my heart, and I wondered if it was going to steal the beats, since its master was a thief.

"If you think things—" I flashed the expensive engagement ring and then the pendant at him "—can buy me, you're wrong, Kelly."

"Rarely," he said, sliding his thumb slowly from my cheek to my neck. "You burn for me when I touch you." He whispered the words, but he'd meant for me to hear.

I hated that he was right. I burned for him beyond relief. His touch had been a caress, barely there, but it had felt like hot wax dripping down my skin. There was no way to hide my attraction to him, not when heat crept up my neck and desire painted me red.

"I am attracted to you." I had to take a deep, deep breath, because my skin was not the only traitor. I knew he could smell the desire on me. His nostrils kept flaring, like he was scenting the air around me, reading signals I hadn't identified yet. "But that means nothing. If you think I'm going to fuck you because you forced me into this, think again. That's *my* decision."

"Let's get a few things straight." For the first time since I'd met him, his features hardened, and I could truly feel the killer in him. He slaughtered the *la de da* attitude to let the animal free of its cage. "You spend time with me while we're both here. You don't." He shrugged. "Your choice. This place is big enough for the both of us. You sleep in my bed. You don't." He shrugged again. "Your choice. I like my space. You fuck me. You don't. That's your choice. That's the one thing I'd never steal."

He took a second, staring me down, before he spoke again. "I don't have a heart, which means no feelings, but I do have a brain. The same one I use to read all of these books. I know the difference between willing or not. 'Not' doesn't get a real man hard, darlin'." He released me from his stare, about to walk out, when he stopped and turned to me. "There is one choice you don't have. You'll eat dinner with me. Every night."

"Eat dinner with you," I repeated. More like blurted out.

"Every night."

"Sometimes rehearsals run late."

"I'll wait."

Then he left me alone in the library with a heart made of metal.

14

KEELY

I t took me a second to realize that I stood in the library alone, one hand clutching the dress, the other squeezing the metal heart.

What the fuck had gotten into him?

Eat dinner with me. Every night.

Of all the things...

Dinner.

It seemed so domesticated. Did he expect me to cook, too? I shook my head, trying to fling some of the chaotic thoughts out. It was a job trying to keep up with him, but one thing I knew for certain.

He claimed he had no heart. No feelings.

I was going to change that.

Not him, but the fact that he thought he was invincible. That he was immune to catching feelings.

He knew my attraction to him was an easy tool to steal my heart. That device worked both ways. His obvious attraction to me was a way for me to get inside of his head, and for once in his life, make him realize that he did have a heart. That he wasn't untouchable.

The block party was proof that he wasn't as heartless as he claimed to be. After spending time with "his" community, I understood why Scott had threatened to destroy his soul. Hell's Kitchen. It was the only thing Kelly claimed as his. Maybe even loved.

Why did it matter so much to him? What made it so special?

Finding my way out of the library and into the bedroom that had all of my things, I slipped out of my wedding dress and decided to take a shower.

My night with Cash Kelly wasn't over yet, though.

After the water ran cold and the usual nightly rituals were done, I slipped on a silk emerald robe and went looking for him. I didn't even bother to knock when I came to his bedroom door.

As expected, the room was huge, but with little furniture or even knickknacks. There was one photograph in an older-looking frame. I assumed the man in the picture was his father. I'd met his widow, Molly, at the block party.

"Empty," I whispered, looking around once more. The biggest thing in Kelly's room was his bed. It looked comfy, and wide enough for two. "Just like the heart he claims not to have."

A distinctive scent lingered in the air, different from his, and I followed it to the glass doors that led out to the fire escape. It was more like a balcony overlooking New York. Kelly sat in a leather lounge chair, his back to me, his feet propped up against the railing. He was blowing smoke rings out of his mouth.

"Isn't that how it starts?" I said, invading his personal space. When I stood next to him, he looked up at me, and I nodded toward the cigar in his hand stuffed with something other than tobacco.

"Are we speaking in rhymes now, darlin'?"

"Addictions," I said. "That's how addictions start."

He looked away from me. "Nothing in this world has power over me. I'm addicted to nothing or no one."

We'll see about that, Kelly. Internally, the villainous bitch inside of me grinned.

Externally, he matched my grin, the villainous bastard inside of him seeming to read my mind.

Fucking perfect. *Listen up, Marauder. I never pick truth, either. And I'm out to prove you wrong, for once in your life.*

He leaned his head back and blew a smoke ring toward the sky. "It's medicinal. It helps me relax." He blew out a wider one. "I get headaches somethin' terrible. It eases those, too."

"Not even twenty-four hours married and you're already needing something to help you relax from a headache. I would've said drinking—" I nodded toward the empty glass on the small table next to him, dregs of whiskey at the bottom "—but I know better. Men like you never drown in the bottle. Gills instead of lungs."

He outright smiled, and something about the imperfection of it made him a hundred times more attractive. It sent my stomach down into my feet and then back up to slam into my heart. I moved past him, deciding not to take the seat next to him, and leaned against the railing, my hands over the side.

After a few minutes, he cleared his throat. "Overcompensation," he said. "It's a real thing."

Every time he said *thing*, it came out as *ting*.

"Are we speaking in riddles now, darlin'?" I copied most of his words and his accent. I grew up in New York, but I also grew up in a house with an Irish father and a Scottish mother.

Even though I couldn't see him, I felt him move forward, and that unique smell became even stronger after I heard the breath leave his mouth. "The loudest voices outside are the ones whispering the lowest behind closed doors. Meaning. Those with something to prove usually have the most to hide."

"Rhymes *and* riddles," I said. "The Irish is strong with this one."

"'Tough. Tough. Tough.' That's what you scream the loudest."

I squeezed the railing, my knuckles straining against skin. "What am I whispering then?"

"You want me, but your pride is standing in the way."

"It's not my pride," I said. "It's my principles." Then I turned to him and unfastened the ties of the robe, letting it fall to the ground. "But since this is my choice, I choose now to say fuck it all. I do want you. I want you to fuck me." Then I gave him *that* look, a look that dared him to take all or nothing.

He stood from the leather lounger, in no hurry. But when he finally made it to me, the tension between his body and mine was as taut as a bow about to release an arrow. His body was close, only a small gap between us, but his heat felt like a raging fire against my skin.

He looked down at me at the same time he took a puff of his cigar. He held the breath in and then slowly leaned down, putting his mouth close to my nose. His breath came out in slow exhales, a little smoke coming out with each release, until he made it to my mouth. I closed my eyes but parted my lips, breathing in, inhaling him like the drug coming from his mouth, until he hit my lungs and rushed into my bloodstream.

I could already feel him inside of me, the high making me feel like I could fly.

Each time he shared his breath and I took his in, the sensation only grew stronger. My limbs weighed nothing, and my head swam in the clouds. I barely felt it when he turned from me, but when he came back with a mouth full of smoke and I sucked in deep, his tongue invaded my mouth. His hands fisted in my hair, rough compared to the slow and delicious rhythm our tongues were moving to.

Remembering that I had hands, I used them to rip his shirt

open. My palms caressed his chest, over his broad shoulders, until I forced the shirt from his muscular arms. My hands were back on him, my nails digging into his skin, ready to draw blood. Though I felt as flighty as a bird, there was this crazy energy running inside of me, waiting for the right time to rule my hands and maul him.

The kiss broke but his mouth didn't stop moving. My chin. My neck. My shoulders. Back and forth. Long, slow, warm kisses. My chest. When his mouth closed over my nipple, I sucked in a breath, my claws sinking into his back, but not enough to draw blood. Just enough to gain some balance. My legs were weak, like they didn't belong to my body, but wrapped around his.

A low noise escaped my mouth, and it didn't sound like me. I'd never made noises during sex. I was too aware of every wrong move by my partner, of all of the problems that existed in my world, of how I'd never be truly satisfied after.

The same noise came again when his mouth moved even lower, his tongue dragging along my stomach, until he was face to face with my hips, his big hands on each side, keeping me in place. His breath was warm as his mouth came even closer. I shivered, the heat of it clashing with the cold that tried to leave my body—not nerves, but anticipation.

As his mouth came between my legs, his tongue tasting me, I let him go and gripped the metal of the fire escape, afraid that I was going to become weightless and lose all balance. A free fall into heaven or hell. My eyes rolled back, and a long, low mewl left my mouth. I was sprawled open against the railing like some sacrificial virgin.

"Fuck. Yeah," I breathed out. I'd never had a man taste me like this. Like he had all of the time in the world, but at the same time, he was too starved to savor.

The orgasm that ripped through me was as brutal as it was beautiful. I screamed out, the noise echoing around us, and for the first time in my life, I wondered if this was how the arrow felt when the bow sets it off. The pleasure overwhelming my body didn't quit even after he did. It fucking lingered, and I wanted another hit. My cheeks felt even hotter, because that had happened way too fast.

He stood and licked his lips before pinning my body against the railing. "Forked tongue, darlin'."

He was right. That forked tongue was made for *sin.*

Before he said another word, I pulled his mouth to mine, like my greed wasn't as sinful as his tongue. He lifted me up like I weighed nothing, setting me on the edge of the railing.

"You," I breathed between kisses that were wilder than some of the sex I'd had before him, "will get life in a cage if you let me fall."

"Ah, my darlin'," he said, his voice slow and low, matching his hooded eyes. *My darling* came out of his mouth as *ma darlin'.* "I'd never let you fall. This arse is too beautiful to bruise."

The world feared this marauder. I didn't have a fucking care in the world when he was this close to me. Maybe it was the stupidest thing I ever did, or the most brilliant, but I believed he wouldn't let me fall. I believed him when he said my arse was too beautiful to bruise.

We were connected in a way that was hard to describe, except for this: what happened to me, happened to him, and vice versa. It was the price we'd both pay for him stealing my heart.

Our mouths paused just long enough for both of us to grin at his comment. Our teeth made contact before his tongue invaded my mouth again and my hands started to work on his pants. Once he was free, he brought me down some, situating me, and then he entered me slowly. His eyes were intense on mine.

The sound that came from his mouth when he was buried

fully inside of me, a deep groan, gave me more pleasure than his dick—and that was plenty enough to keep me satisfied. It fit his build. It fit everything about him. Then he started to move. I closed my eyes, the intensity between us too much to take in.

The more he moved, the more I felt the pressure building and building. I was about to come again. He kept hitting one spot that sent fucking shock waves throughout my body.

Then he hit me so hard that I hissed. It fucking hurt.

He made a similar noise when my nails sunk deep into his flesh. "That's it, my darlin'," he said. "Let go and mark me."

I scratched him from one end to the other, wanting his tongue to go even deeper into my mouth, for him to ram that spot again and hurt me, so the bitter pain would make the pleasure even sweeter. It wasn't a punishment. It was a reward.

"Fuck," he said, lifting me from the railing, carrying me into the bedroom. "You're burnin' for me."

He set me down on the bed, and before he could reach for me, I slammed my mouth against his. Our tongues were at war, like my mind was at battle to keep my heart.

We kissed until I couldn't breathe.

Our bodies were as crazed as our tongues. We rolled around on the bed, his body against mine, mine against his, like we were out to kill each other.

Needing to breathe but also starving to have my mouth on his skin, I placed my lips on his chin, his neck, along his chest, over the muscles in his stomach, using my tongue to make a wet trail down his body. The muscles in his stomach went rigid when I put my mouth around him, tasting nothing but pure male, before I licked my lips and straddled him, taking him inside to the hilt.

I didn't move to a punishing rhythm. I moved slowly, my hair moving against my back like a fan, rolling my hips in sweet, languorous swirls against him. I set my hands against his chest, scratching instead of clawing, using him as a base to lift myself before I lowered myself down again.

As I moved, I dipped my head low, coming down to kiss him. The kiss was as languorous as my movements.

His eyes opened and met mine. Just like that feral green-eyed tiger on his neck, over the pulse point, the wild animal in him seemed to come alive.

With a whoosh of breath, he flipped me over onto my back, and setting my legs on each side of him, slammed into me. His eyes were hard on mine, as hard as he was fucking me. He was wild but in control. Nothing sloppy about him. The relentless pounding kept up, like a savage animal, until he withdrew, and then came back even harder than before.

"Cash!" I screamed. Then my entire body, the fucking traitor, went off like an arrow from my bow. The pressure released me, and I was flying into his territory, about to land. My aim? His heart.

A second later, he came inside of me, a look on his face that I'd never forget. It was the wildest thing I'd ever seen. It was a look a woman could get addicted to.

The only high left in my body was Cash Kelly.

Once I was able to catch my breath, an internal grin lit me up. I'd gotten to him. He had flung me off and fucked me like no man had ever fucked me before because I had. He'd felt something.

I'd felt it, too. A connection that was stronger than just feral attraction between us.

If I was a betting woman, I'd place my money on Kelly being in a bad mood or gone by the time I got up the next day. I hadn't known him long, but what I did know, he wasn't going to like what just happened. Not that I liked the feelings part, either, but I was out to get even, which meant I was willing to make sacrifices for my cause.

He hovered over me, still hard inside of me, and I blinked before my eyes fully opened to meet his.

"You called me Cash," he said, his chest heaving. I didn't think it was from exertion. He'd barely broken a sweat. I was ringing wet.

"Unless you lied," I said, my voice rough, "that's your name."

"Yeah, I suppose it is," he said, but his eyes were narrowed.

He pulled out of me, giving me his hand, helping me up. That daring look had made it back to his eyes, and that animal was still hungry, or out to prove something—that he hadn't felt what he thought he did.

There was no way I was imagining it. It felt too real. It was like getting too close to a raging fire and then ignoring the burns after.

"Where are we going?" I said, hardly able to walk. No man had ever fucked me like that before. *Sleep.* I craved it.

"Shower, darlin'. The night's still young, and so are you."

15

KEELY

I could barely get out of bed the next morning. Cash Kelly had worked my body like no man ever had before. He lingered in the soreness of my muscles and bones. His marks were all over my body, coming up in blue and purple bruises on my skin. In all fairness, I easily bruised, but he was still intense.

He gave me experiences that I would never forget. The son of a bitch was more addicting than what he had smoked last night. There was no doubt—not an ounce of it—that he knew that as well as I did.

After doing the necessary things in the bathroom, I stepped into the deep closet in his bedroom, taking one of his white button-down shirts and slipping it on. It was better than having to search the other room for my things. I was going to move my boxes into Kelly's room on principal.

He wanted me here. He got me. Baggage and all.

Before I found my way downstairs, I stopped and admired the view from the library. The sun was rising, starting to brighten Hell's Kitchen, and the view of New York held me captive to my spot. For the first time in a long time, I took a second to appreciate the start of a new day. It all had to do with my new point of view.

It was different, and in this overcrowded city, something fresh.

The moment the sun fully came up, I moved, looking for Kelly. I found him in the kitchen eating breakfast. He was dressed in a suit, sitting at the table, reading a magazine on the mob. He set it down when he heard me rummaging through the cabinets. I had cereal every morning for breakfast. All the marauder had was oatmeal.

Sighing, feeling like I was five again and forced to eat something that gave me a texture problem, I started looking for items to make oatmeal. If I was going to do it, it was going to be sugary. Bananas. Cinnamon. Walnuts. Brown sugar.

"You don't have any sugar," I said, searching deeper into the pantry. "You're not one of those kinds of people, are you?"

"I don't need it," he said, and I noticed the way his eyes took in his shirt on my body.

I shook my head, deciding that I'd pick up something quick on my way out. I had a fitting for one of my costumes, and then the rest of the day was mine. I'd decided to make myself at home in Kelly's bedroom after, getting cozy.

He stood, fixing his tie, and then grabbed his bowl and cup from the table, bringing them over to the sink. I turned and watched him.

"Work?" I said.

"Every day."

"Must be fun to be you," I said.

"Loads."

Was that an attitude I detected from Cash Kelly? My bet was still strong from the night before—he was either going to be gone or not as *la de da* as usual. Since he stood next to me, his carefree attitude had taken a small hit.

He turned to me but said nothing. He just looked at me. I

wasn't a woman who minded attention, but we stood close, and he eyed me like he had something on his mind.

"What's that look for?" I said, finally breaking the tension.

He looked around. "No mirror in here, darlin.' The only face I see is yours."

"Your thoughts are showing on your face. It matches the hate I feel coming from you."

Without missing a beat, he said, "Maybe I do. Hate you a little."

I grinned, not taking offense. Hate was an emotion, and I considered it a small victory that I'd gotten under his skin some. "It's no fun when someone magically slips over your walls and rages war against your heart, Marauder. Am I right?"

He narrowed his eyes at me in a challenging dare. "I don't have one to war with." He fixed his tie again. "Be ready by five sharp. I'll be by to pick you up." He pulled out his wallet and set a credit card on the counter. "Get something new and expensive."

"Where are we going?"

"Dinner and then a political thing."

"Formal?"

He nodded. Then he stared at me again.

After a few seconds, I said, "Don't you have somewhere to be, Kelly?"

"When I'm ready."

He put a hand on each side of me, one on each side of my waist, his strong arms caging me in against the counter. I lifted one eyebrow, daring him to say or do whatever was on his mind. *Dare for dare.*

After a minute or two, he grinned, and then left without saying another word.

As usual, Kelly sent Raff with me.

We grabbed breakfast down the street from Kelly's place, two bagels and two teas, before we headed back, going for Raff's car. He was going to drive me to the fitting and then to pick out a dress for Kelly's political thing that evening.

"Mrs. Kelly!"

Raff nudged me, and I nudged him back. "Keep your hands to yourself," I said.

He stopped walking and nodded behind him. "Mrs. O'Connell."

"Ms. O'Connell?" I said the name at the same time that I turned. The woman from the block party, Maureen, rushed toward me. Connolly kept step, but barely.

"Yeah," Raff said, narrowing his eyes at them. "She called you twice."

"Mrs. Kelly," she said when she was close enough. "I need to ask a favor of you."

She seemed winded, but I didn't think it was from the walk. I could tell she was a tough old broad, but something about her seemed almost desperate. It was something about the sound of her voice when she'd said my name.

I'll have to get used to people calling me by that name. The name that connects me to him.

Without my response, Maureen barreled right into it. "I need you to keep Connolly for a while. Just until 3 o'clock or so." She took the little girl by the shoulder and urged her closer to me.

Connolly looked up at me and I looked down at her. I smiled but she didn't respond.

"I have a fitting for my job." Not that I minded taking her with us, but she hardly knew me. I didn't want her to feel awkward. "Maybe we can plan a time for—"

Maureen shook her head and pushed Connolly even closer

to me. "Mrs. Kelly," she said, and her eyes were so serious on mine. "I need this from you."

I stared at her for a moment, trying to understand. Nothing became clear to me, though, except for one thing. Maureen was desperate. "Okay." I nodded. "Connolly gets to spend the day with me."

A heavy breath visibly left Maureen's mouth. She touched Connolly on the head and then hustled in the opposite direction.

"Looks like it's the three of us," I said to Connolly. "Do you mind going to work with me for a while?"

We stared at each other, and it seemed like she wanted to say something, but she couldn't bring herself to do it.

I stooped down, trying to get eye level with her. "The clouds are bright today," I said, hoping she remembered our talk from the party. "I know you don't mind coming with me. And after, we'll do a little shopping. A girl has to have a pretty dress. Mr. Kelly's treat." I smiled at her and then stood, offering her my hand. I wasn't sure if she'd take it, but after a few seconds, she put her little hand in mine and my heart filled instantly.

It sunk just as fast when a familiar ringer sounded and my mother's face appeared on the screen of my cellphone.

"Shit," I muttered. Since there was no time like the present, I answered it.

"Keely," she said, like she had to make sure it was me.

"Mam," I said.

She went on about the usual stuff as we all started walking together. After a few minutes, when we'd made it to Raff's car, she made it to the reason she had called.

"The wedding," I repeated after her, knowing it was do or die. "There's no need to plan anything right now, Mam. See. The thing is." Deep breath. "We're married. We got married in a church!" I rushed out, so she wouldn't have a heart attack or combust on the spot. "We couldn't wait. Maybe we can have a reception later. To celebrate."

"You're married," she repeated. She'd heard me, but she wanted me to repeat it again. To torture me.

"I'm married," I said. "The deal is sealed. But we're keeping it a secret right now."

"From Mari?" she said, her voice both suspicious and lethal. Neither one bothered me. It was the guilt trip she was going to take me on that I dreaded.

"Yeah," I said. "Especially from Mari."

I hated how she always brought Mari up first. To make sure Mari didn't know what she did. I didn't want Mari to know, for my own reasons, so it was best if my mam thought she had the upper hand. I'd tell Mari when I was ready.

"My only living daughter. Married without her Mam there to see it." She sniffed, and I resigned myself to the infamous words coming next. The ones that ate at me like acid.

I mouthed the words as she said them: "Roisin wouldn't have done this to me." A second later, she hung up.

I stared at the phone for a second before I stuck it my pocket. A pressure came from my other hand, and I realized that Connolly was watching me, and holding my hand a little tighter.

AFTER MY COSTUME FITTING, I decided on a designer boutique in Manhattan to find a dress for the event. I'd never stepped foot in such an exclusive place, but as soon as I did, one of the salesgirls rushed to help me.

"I have an event tonight," I said to her as she looked me over from head to toe. Maybe trying to guess my size. "Formal. Something in green." Then I gave her my size. I didn't have time to play that game. They either had my size or they didn't.

If they didn't, I'd take my ass to a store that catered to all builds and give them my business.

The salesgirl nodded and said, "I have just the number."

I felt Connolly's eyes on me, and I looked at her and winked. Even though my mam's guilt ate at me, having Connolly around somehow felt like a buffer. I was eager for her to get more comfortable around me. Maybe so she would talk again. She didn't seem as rigid as she had been at the party. She seemed relaxed, though still quiet.

She did roll her eyes at Raff a couple of times, which made me grin. He was a little goofy around her, making kid-appropriate jokes.

Connolly stood with Raff while I tried on the dress. From the moment I slipped it on, I knew it was the one. Emerald, just like I had requested, and sheer, but with a layer of beading. The fit was a size too small, and it had a sexy slit up to my thigh. They say red will knock a man dead, but in this dress, I swore that I'd knock a few beats into that heart Kelly supposedly didn't have.

Connolly's eyes lit up when I walked out and showed it to her, so that was that.

As I browsed the shelves searching for a matching pair of heels, Connolly sat in a chair while Raff stood next to me. His back was to the wall, his arms crossed, his eyes moving with me.

"You're trying to kill my cuz with that dress."

I glanced at him before I picked up a pair of gold heels. "Or steal his heart, at the very least."

He laughed. "Molly and me have a bet going."

"Yeah." I put the heels down. "I hope your bet is on me, or you're on the losing side."

"That's why I bet on you," he said. "You're fucking crazy enough to think you can, so you probably will, Jessica Rabbit."

I quirked my eyebrow up at him.

He waved at my head. "Your hair. It's red."

"Really?" I feigned being shocked. "Someone give me a mirror! When did this happen?"

He laughed and we both turned to look at Connolly, to check on her. Instead of watching us, she was watching as the salesgirls hustled around the shop.

I nodded toward her. "What's the story?"

Raff stared at her a moment before he turned to me. "Her father was killed selling drugs to the wrong people. Her mother died after having her half-brother—who is in the NICU right now. He was born too early and is in withdrawal. Maureen agreed to adopt him so they would always know each other." He chucked his chin toward Connolly. "She's been promised the stars, little Connolly O'Connell, but all she gets is the darkness."

I realized when her eyes met mine that I was staring at her. Tears blurred my world, but I turned without her seeing. I wiped my eyes before they could fall.

"Connolly O'Connell," I repeated.

"Her mom was too high to come up with something different for her first name." He shook his head. "Said it sounded poetic. Like, Connolly, O' my Connell!, after she'd already finalized the papers. Her parents weren't bad people. Just ended up being servants to drugs. That came first."

Her attention to my name—Keely Kelly—made sense. We both shared too many of the same letters in our names.

Not really caring about the heels anymore, I told one of the salesgirls to add a gold pair on to my bill. Then I went and stood in front of Connolly, trying to hide the fact that my heart bled for her.

"Hey," I said. "It's time to blow this fancy joint and get something to eat. Maybe we'll even start with dessert first." I narrowed my eyes some, moving my head from left to right, like I was trying to read something that wasn't clear on her face.

Then I opened my eyes wide and gasped. "Ah! I see you agree! It's so clear in the clouds today!"

She didn't want to smile, but a small grin tugged at her lips.

"Sugar it is!" I held my hand up for a high-five. She placed her hand tentatively against mine and I closed mine over hers, squeezing a bit.

"Lunch it is," a familiar voice said from behind me.

Why did it thrill me so much?

Cash's hand slipped over my shoulder, squeezing a bit. I looked at him, all dressed up in his gentlemen's attire. He reminded me of an old gangster from an earlier time. The man wore the suit, not the other way around.

It wasn't just his clothes, either.

It was the "I don't give a fuck who you are or what you're about" attitude that he carried around like a fine cologne. It lingered in the air around him. Subtle but powerful.

I wondered how many men had moved out of his way because they smelled the carnage on him, and how many women had purposely put themselves in his path because of his hypnotizing charm.

He lifted his hand to the salesgirl. "Box everything up. My man outside will take it home for my wife."

"Right away, Mr. Kelly," the salesgirl said. She was good. She'd already memorized the name on the credit card.

"Don't worry, darlin'," he said, when he caught me watching as the salesgirls looked him over. More than one and more than once. "These eyes belong to you, even though they happen to fit my face."

"Smart," I said, reaching for Connolly's hand. "If you want to keep them there."

I thought I heard Connolly giggle, but I couldn't be sure over the sound of Raff's uncontrollable laughter.

16

KEELY

Kelly left for wherever he was headed after taking us out to lunch. He was quiet during, watching me with Connolly, and I wondered what he was thinking. I couldn't read the thoughts moving behind his eyes.

I didn't have much time to figure it out, though. After we made it back to Kelly's place, I needed to get ready for the event. As I set everything out, I talked to Connolly like she was answering back, hoping that I answered her thoughts. Or got close.

Maureen came to pick her up before I took a shower. The woman looked exhausted, and I understood why. She'd lost her son, the mother of her grandchildren, and now she had two small children to look after. One of the children, an innocent baby, was fighting for his life. When Maureen noticed the look on my face, she nodded, and I nodded back.

No other words were needed. One look sealed our understanding.

Before we'd made it to Kelly's place, we'd stopped and bought Connolly some new clothes and shoes. Hers weren't threadbare, but they weren't the current style either. They'd seen better days. She didn't pick anything out, but I saw her eyeing a few things and just got them.

I told Maureen that I'd bring them out to her car, but she shook her head and said, "Save them for when she comes here. You do plan on spending time with her?" The look she sent me went straight to my bones, because Connolly echoed it.

Maureen was testing me. So was Connolly. Plans in her world were probably constantly broken, like a painful snap of the bone time and time again, until she was paralyzed and couldn't speak from the hurt.

"Whenever she wants." I winked at her. "I'll put CeeCee's new things in her room—she can have it for whenever she comes over." I'd put her things in the room Kelly assigned to me, since I was going to share his space.

"CeeCee?" Connolly's voice was low and scratchy, maybe from not using it often.

"Your initials." I paused. "Well, sort of. If you take the 'O' from Connell." Then I went in a different direction. "Sometimes my best friend calls me Kee Kee. That's sort of like CeeCee, too."

Maureen's face softened for the briefest of seconds before she hardened her features once more. "I don't care what they say about you, Mrs. Kelly. I think you're a fine woman. People hate until they learn to love something new." With that, she grabbed Connolly's hand and pulled her toward the street.

Connolly O'Connell watched me the entire time until she couldn't anymore.

I shut the door, shaking my head. "Say about me?" I said to myself. "What the fuck are they saying about me around here?"

Kelly seemed to be the king of a smallish band of misfits in Hell's Kitchen, in the midst of battle, fighting for a kingdom to reclaim. They all looked at him like he was some kind of anti-hero to admire. And they didn't seem like evil people, which told me that they saw something in him worth the admiration.

Why the harsh judgment for me, though? He did *me* wrong.

Oh well. Fuck it. My happiness didn't depend on other people's opinions.

Unless it's Mam.

I refused to think about the guilt the phone call had caused, so I occupied myself with getting ready.

Kelly's bathroom was spa-worthy, and it was going to be nice to take a hot shower—a long one—before going to a fancy event like this. I used an egg timer in my last apartment's bathroom so I wouldn't freeze my tits off. I had exactly three minutes to wash my hair and body before the water turned ice cold. It was like swimming and then running naked out in a blizzard during New York winters.

At 5 o'clock sharp, I was waiting at the kitchen table, enjoying a glass of fine whiskey, when Kelly walked in. He must've showered and dressed at work. Harrison told me the place had a gym. A workplace perk. Kelly's hard body was a testament to that.

He stopped in his tracks when he noticed me sitting at the table, in the dress, my hair done up, and makeup on my face. He recovered without a hitch, though. Just like I'd done when I noticed him in his suit. It was black and white and made for a gentleman. A gentleman who was anything but behind closed doors.

"You're ready," he said.

"You gave me a time." I shrugged. "Here I am. At that time. Ready." I took a sip of my whiskey and then set it down. "I told you, Kelly. I'm no princess. I'm used to working my ass off for basic necessities, so when I'm told a time, I make it."

He looked down at the table, at the glass of whiskey I'd poured for him. "So you are." He picked up the glass. It stopped when it was close to his mouth. "If I had a heart, it would've stopped at the sight of you in that dress."

I stood to my full height, making sure that the sexy slit was noticed when I made my way closer to him. Maybe some would even call it dangerous. My legs were long, so I worked them to my advantage. When I reached him, my eyes turned up to meet his intense green ones.

A tiger. He had the eyes of a tiger.

"Oh," I breathed out. "I think right about now, you know you have a heart, and it's beating overtime, *darlin'*. I don't need a red dress to bring you to your knees. Nah." I ran my hand along the lapel of his jacket. "The color doesn't matter. It's my confidence that turns you on, Mr. Kelly." I patted the spot where my hand stopped and then went to remove it.

He took my hand and brought it to his mouth, placing a soft kiss on my fingers. I slipped my hand out of his, but I might as well have yanked it back. He noticed how that one act had sent a jolt of electricity straight up my arm. It made my hands tremble for a reason other than anxiety.

He grinned into his glass and downed it like a shot. "There's so much about you that turns me on, my darlin', but nothing makes my cock as hard as the scent on your body. It's a sexual fantasy. It's fucking confidence. It lingers in the room long after you've walked out of it, Mrs. Kelly." He motioned to the front door, for me to go ahead of him.

I stopped when I made it right outside of the kitchen. "You're going to watch me walk out of here, aren't you, Kelly?"

"An arse like that." His eyes moved over me slowly. "It'd be a sin to waste such a blessing."

"Enjoy the view," I said, throwing the words over my shoulder. "And try not to fall in love." I winked at him before I sashayed to the front door.

A ROLLS-ROYCE PHANTOM waited outside for us. A driver in a fine suit, complete with hat, opened the suicide doors just as

Kelly put his hand on my lower back and pushed me forward. My feet had stopped at the sight of it. My ass had never sat on a seat so expensive before.

I ran my hand along the smooth leather. "This is rich," I said.

Kelly took the seat opposite me, fixing his suit, before the driver closed the door and started making his way to the other side of the car. "Rocco Fausti owns a fleet of them. I use them from time to time."

The driver slid in, looking through his mirror at Kelly, and after Kelly gave a nod, the privacy glass rolled up.

We had our own suite in the car. The ceiling looked like it was made of stars. The car moved smoothly, as if we were gliding through the air. A seductive voice came through the speakers a second later, "Billie Holiday, George Gershwin, Ira Gershwin. The Essential George Gershwin." Then she announced, "'The Man I Love.'" A jazzy tune started to play, something that was definitely before our time.

"No champagne?" I asked sarcastically.

Kelly turned to the divider between us and pressed a button. A console came down with two glasses hidden inside. Tucked even deeper was a really expensive-looking bottle of champagne.

"Magic." I smiled a little.

Kelly handed me a glass and then popped the top. He poured me a glass and then took one for himself. We clinked and, without toasting, both took a sip. It slid down my throat like bubbly honey.

"Not magic, darlin'," he said, setting his glass in the holder. "The Faustis. Gold runs through their veins."

"I know." I took another sip. "I know them, I mean."

He nodded. "Macchiavello is connected."

"Their wives have girl nights. Mari invited me." I turned to him a little. "Rumor has it that they're really powerful. Most of them, dangerous men."

Kelly grinned. "Depends on the point of view."

"What's your point of view?"

He sighed, giving me his undivided attention. "We usually stand on the same side, the one with the same view. I have no issue with the Faustis. If I did—" he shrugged "—they'd wipe me clean, but I'd go down fighting."

"Is Hell's Kitchen really that important to you?"

"I'm willing to die for it," he said and turned his face forward.

The things worth a man's soul—faith, rights, a woman's love, that sort of thing—seemed to say a lot about that man. I wasn't sure what that said about Cash Kelly yet. Was he willing to die for the power to rule it? Or for the money? For both? Or for a cause more worthy?

We said no more as the car pulled in front of Macchiavello's. Mari's fiancé owned it, and it was one of the swankiest restaurants in New York. I'd told her that we were going, and she was excited, going on and on about some pasta dish to try. She said after their wedding in Italy, we'd meet up there for lunch.

The driver opened Kelly's door first. Kelly stepped out, fixing his suit and tie, and then made his way to my side. My door opened, and his hand was waiting for mine. I took it, the slit in my dress riding high as I put my heel to the street. A stream of expensive cars waited their turns to pull up in front of the restaurant. People on the sidewalk stopped and pointed at a few of them. Ours included.

The restaurant was as expected. Romantic.

Candlelight made the entire place glow, there were roses on every table, a jazz band played in the bar section, and it smelled beyond amazing.

Kelly handed the man at the door a card, and we were led to a private room. It was so secluded that it seemed like only the two of us existed in the world. The food? Like nothing I'd ever tasted before.

Before I was truly ready, we left for the event. It was being held in a museum, and again, we were lined up with another stream of expensive cars. As we waited our turn, and guests stepped out, I started to recognize faces. Governor. Mayor. Union leaders—one I recognized from our wedding "reception," the head of the longshoremen's union. The kind of people included in little books.

Rocco Fausti and his wife, Rosaria, stepped out next.

Then us.

As soon as we were inside, Kelly started shaking hands and introducing me. The party was a menagerie of high-powered people, but Kelly kept to the local politicians. I knew how charming he could be, and he was using the power on everyone he spoke to. He wasn't ass kissing, though. He was one of those men who oozed appeal without forcing it.

Done with the scene, and not wanting to make an effort to talk to Rosaria, I slipped away from Kelly's conversation and headed toward the bar. I ordered a glass of whiskey neat, and then turned to watch the woman singing by the piano.

A man strode up next to me, ordered his whiskey straight up, and then turned to stand just like I was. "She's good," he said, taking a sip. His eyes were ready to flirt, even if his mouth never said a suggestive word.

"She is." I kept my eyes forward, but I'd already gotten a good look at him. He was probably around Kelly's age, but other than that, there was nothing else to compare. Kelly's scent was all around me, even though he wasn't close to me. It murdered even the thought of another man in my bed. I still hadn't forgotten the ache he left between my legs.

"How did Kelly manage it?" He took a sip from his glass, and the ice danced in amber.

"Excuse me?" I said.

"Kelly." He nodded toward him. "How did he manage to land such a beautiful and willing—I'm guessing—woman?"

I took another sip of my whiskey. "I don't believe we've met," I said, turning to him.

He looked me up and down. "Lee Grady."

"Ke—"

"Keely Kelly," he said. "I've heard the name a time or two."

I nodded. "You're part of the neighborhood gossip mill."

"I hear everything." He grinned.

"You mean you know everything."

"Small distinction." He turned toward the bar, ordering another whiskey for me.

I put my hand over the top, shaking my head. "No more for me."

Lee nodded and then waved the waiter off. Setting his whiskey down, he leaned against the counter. "You're not connected." He turned his eyes to the right, studying me. "It can't be love, because the bastard is incapable. So I'm having a hard time understanding why you'd marry someone like him."

"Someone like him?"

"A marauding bastard who always goes after what doesn't belong to him."

"Maybe he feels like it does."

"Maybe he does," he said, taking another drink. "But feelings and reality are two different things, sweetheart."

"There's nothing sweet about me." I grinned at him. "Don't assume." Downing the rest of my whiskey *without* ice, I went to turn from him, but he caught my arm.

His fingers dug into my skin, and when I went to move, he gripped me even tighter. "I rule Hell's Kitchen," he said, his voice low and venomous. "What comes in and out of it. I'm going to make you a widow soon, Mrs. Kelly. I hope you took out a fat insurance policy on that bastard."

Lee's grip slackened before I heard the tick of a mouth. "You can look, but no one touches my wife but me."

I turned in time to see Kelly take three of Lee's fingers and snap them back. He let out a growl of pain, causing people in the area to turn and look.

Kelly didn't seem to give a shit. He leaned in close to Lee's ear. "We've discussed this plenty of times, Grady. You have to learn what belongs to you and what doesn't. Touching another man's wife is the equivalent of claiming his property. It's disrespectful."

Kelly released Lee's mangled hand, rolled his shoulders, and then offered me his arm. I slipped my hand through, aware that people were watching, whispering, but it was a group of men in the corner that really drew my attention. Hate came off of them in hot waves, and the central fire? Aimed at Kelly.

"Those men," I said, trying not to be obvious about it when I glanced at them. "They're with Grady?"

Kelly lifted my hand and placed a kiss on my fingers, just like he had done before we left, but this time, it was for show. He was staking his claim. "Forget about them, darlin'," he said smoothly. "You'll never see them again."

That was fucking cryptic.

"Are you friends with all of these political people?"

"Half of them had me arrested once or twice." He grinned. "The other half have hired me."

Sighing, I lifted my chin, keeping my eyes forward as we moved through the crowd. People were still staring, but for one main reason.

Cash Kelly had made his comeback.

THE ROOM WAS SO dark that my eyes couldn't penetrate it. I couldn't make out shapes or even see my hand in front of my face. The temperature in the room was a degree above freezing. One thing I'd learned about Kelly right away: he kept his house cold. When I complained, he said, *"The cold helps you breathe and sleep better."* I didn't see how my teeth chattering all night would help me breathe or sleep better—and my blood ran hot.

Maybe he kept his place so cold because if someone were to murder him in his sleep, he'd keep better.

Looking in his direction, I sighed. At least he'd given me all of the covers. I kicked them off and headed to the bathroom. Cold clung to my skin, but so did sweat. My hair was matted to my head, and Kelly's shirt stuck to my body.

I turned the faucet water on cool, and after splashing my face, leaned over the sink, letting the water fall back into the drain.

Maybe I was going to be sick.

I felt movement and then caught it. My heart slammed against my chest, even though I didn't jump. "You're too fucking silent," I said, my jaw clenched.

Kelly leaned against the bathroom door, shirtless with only a pair of grey sweatpants on, watching me. His eyes shimmered from the small, soft light that came on at night anytime you walked into the bathroom. "Had something bad to eat, darlin'?"

"You could say that." I turned off the sink and grabbed a towel to dry my face. After hanging it back up, I went to rush past him, but he caught my arm and I stopped, looking up at him.

"Must've been some real bad food. You're paler than a fucking ghost."

"It didn't go to my stomach," I said. "It went to my head."

His eyes moved, like he was trying to understand my riddle. "Bad dream."

The emotions in the pit of my stomach made it to my throat. I wasn't sure if I could answer. So I nodded.

He used his finger to remove a piece of hair that was stuck

to my face and then, taking my hand, led me back to the bedroom. He didn't stop there, though. He walked through the darkened house, like he could see through it, and then turned the lights on low when we got to the kitchen.

After letting my hand go, he lifted me up by the arms and set me down on the counter. Then he went to the fridge, the light brightening his face and body, and took out a container of soup. He set it down before he went for a pot.

While he stirred the soup, he said, "All of the drink."

"What?"

"My old man used to say that too much drink summoned the devil. You had too much drink tonight."

"I've had more." I shrugged, even though his back was to me. "Your house is new to me. It's always dark and cold, and whenever I'm going through a lot, she comes to me."

I'd never admitted that to anyone, and I wasn't sure why I'd admitted it to him. Maybe because he had a twin and could understand what the distance did to the other's soul.

There was one thing I refused to admit to him, though, and that was how much Lee Grady's words at the event had bothered me. *Make you a widow, Mrs. Kelly.* If anyone was going to kill Cash Kelly, it was going to be me. Not some wannabe punk off the fucking street.

He nodded. "You had a dream of your sister."

"Yeah." I took a minute or two to settle my heart. Whenever I thought about her, my heart hurt. And for whatever reason, when I thought about Kelly being killed because of his dealings, something inside of me twisted. Maybe it was the place where my heart should've been. "She's never young. In the dreams. Not like she was when I saw her the last time. She's always older. Grown up. I can feel her. Actually feel her. Do you have dreams of your brother? I know he's not dead, but any distance is hard."

"No," he said, his voice far-off. "My old man. He keeps me up at night."

I watched him for a minute. He had a beautiful back. When he moved, his muscles rippled. His skin was smooth, except for all of the stripes he'd earned in battle. "Would that have anything to do with your medicinal habit?"

"It has everything to do with it," he said. "It's not a habit, though. It's something I choose to do or not."

"And the headaches, those stem from your old man, too?"

"You remembered."

"I remember everything," I said. "About you. You should always know your enemies better than your friends."

He said nothing while he poured the soup out of the pot and into two bowls. I wasn't sure why I even noticed, but he had given me more.

He set the bowl next to me and then handed me a spoon. He drank his quietly.

We ate in silence, and after we were done, I was warmed and feeling like I could breathe again. I didn't think it was because of the soup either. It was him. My resistance to him, to this, was tiring because of my heart, but my mind kept up the tug of war.

After getting down off the counter, I could feel his eyes on me as I moved toward the stereo system in the front room. I'd noticed all of the old records he had after Maureen had left with Connolly. I'd listened to a few of them while I was getting ready for our night out.

I found one of my Da's favorites and set it to play before I took his bowl and mine to the sink. As I started to wash, I could feel that he was still watching me. His stare hit my back like a rock against glass. I wondered what piece of me he'd steal this time?

My eyes closed as his arms wrapped around me. My head tilted back and I leaned into him, for the first time in a long time giving someone else my burdens to share. Maybe he was stealing those, too, because I felt as light as a feather. Higher than I had been when he was blowing intoxicating smoke in my mouth and I'd breathed him in.

"There's one thing, darlin', that just might have power over me," he whispered, his soft accent lulling me into the safety of his arms even deeper. One arm released me, while the other kept me tight against him, and his free hand ventured against my body. Over my ass, across my hip, around my thigh, and then between my legs.

I sucked in a breath, releasing it in a slow stream, as his breath picked up in my ear. "I never forget. You make me forget. When my cock is buried deep inside of you, I don't know my fucking name, or who I am, or what the world sees when they look at me. I'm just a man inside of a woman, a woman who holds the power to make me forget it all."

"Be careful." My breath was coming out in pants as his fingers worked me higher and higher to the edge of desire. "That's a dangerous direction. It could lead to the loss of a vital organ."

My nails sunk into his arm as the pressure increased, as he started to move faster, as his nose skimmed down my neck, his mouth sucking my skin. "I've already stolen your heart, my darlin'. There's nothing left to lose. All that's left is for you to give in." His words were slow, low, and seductive. "Give in to me, Keely Shea Kelly. You're wasting your time trying to keep what's already mine."

I let out a strangled moan when his arm let me go and his free hand came up, loosening the buttons on his shirt—the one covering my body. He started to tease my nipple. "We both know..." I moaned even louder "...that resisting you is my greatest weakness and my greatest strength."

"You'll be damned if you make it fucking easy on me."

"That's the way of it, yeah. *Ah.*" I sucked in a breath when his teasing became rough.

He grinned against my neck until I moved my ass against him, and he hissed out a breath. I was going to use every bit of weaponry in my arsenal—my eyes, my lips, my legs, my femininity, *my heart*—to get under *his* skin. I was going to make him forget that he didn't have a heart until he remembered that he had one. The situation between us was so ugly that I was starting to find it pretty. Beautiful even.

He stole *my* heart. Now it was set on having *him* and *him* alone.

I started to tremble, giving in, and then I came in an explosion that seemed to echo around the kitchen.

He turned me around to face him, and after staring me in the eye for a moment, he set me back on the counter, situating himself between my legs. I slipped his shirt off my body, throwing it to the side, completely bare to him. I used my feet to shove his sweatpants down, and after he stepped out of them, he entered me in a thrust that rocked my entire world.

He moved in and out, like a thief in the night, finding more and more of me to steal.

Our eyes connected in an intense stare down. My heart was at war with the space where his was supposed to be. It was fighting for this, despite my mind's protests. My heart would pound like a fist until he decided to let me in.

He growled at me. *Fucking growled at me.* Like an animal. A noise came from my throat that was similar to his. My body was going insane, wanting to shatter, ready for stars to shoot behind my eyes, but it was holding on with all that it had, refusing to give in so easily this time.

I was drenched with sweat. He was, too.

I clawed his back, drawing blood, and he pumped into me even harder, but with a control that was perfectly executed each and every time. I squeezed around him, once, twice, and then we both came at the same time. It was loud, and ugly, and had left us both weakened. Fucking him was like going to battle to keep a little of myself in place, before it landed in his hands. He was the kind of man who easily consumed whatever he touched.

We stood that way for a while, him between my legs, me still on the counter, both breathing heavy. When he pulled out, I hopped off the counter, losing my balance. He caught and steadied me. My knees were weak.

I looked up at his face. His pieces fit together perfectly, even if they were put back together a few times, and it was impossible for me not to admire the entire picture for what it was. Art.

"I'm not clear water, darlin'," he said. "Stop trying to see into my soul."

No, and he wasn't rough waters, either. My Da always said that still waters ran deep. A Cash Kelly idiom if there ever was one. It meant that silent people were more dangerous than loud ones. "I wouldn't dare," I said.

There's more than one way into a no trespassing zone, though— and I already found a way into his. Through his skin.

I slid my hand up his arm, nice and slow, and his eyes lowered. "All night," I whispered. "Let's forget all night."

He took my hand and led me back into the bedroom.

I hadn't had a smoke since that night on the fire escape. It was something I did to ease my mind, because if not, I'd fight insomnia. Or raging headaches. I wasn't lying to the archer when I told her that my old man haunted me. It wasn't his ghost, but what he'd left behind. A responsibility to carry on his legacy.

The only opinions I ever honored were my old man's. I respected my brother, but our perspectives had always been aligned differently. He always had the need to ask questions. I went in having trust that our old man would never lead us astray.

He'd fought for and claimed one of the most ruthless areas of New York to run. He'd gained his community's trust and respect, even though he was feared.

Not like Lee Grady and his family, who got into bed with the Scarpones to distribute drugs to his own community. Their drug trade ruined marriages, families, careers. It ruined lives. It took all that my father worked most of his life for, even died to protect, and buried it underneath powder.

My mind refused to accept it. So it kept me up night after

night. Even in prison, because I was a caged animal without an escape.

I thought of Grady nonstop. How he had set my old man up to be slaughtered.

I thought of the Scarpones nonstop. How they had been a part of it for greed.

I thought of Scott Stone nonstop. How he had cuffed my old man and made him an easy target.

Nothing made me stop salivating for the day the streets of Hell's Kitchen would be mine.

Even if the rest of the world was overrun with drugs, my area wouldn't be. We'd celebrate marriage, honor families, and give every man and woman a chance at a career—at a better life.

Stealing a heart out of revenge was at odds with celebrating marriage, but I had every intention of honoring every vow I spoke to Keely Kelly at the altar.

I stopped walking for a minute, thinking about something other than vengeance or chaos in what felt like the first time in my entire life.

No matter how much I fucking despised it, because I knew she'd use it as ammo, the archer put me to sleep like a lullaby. I'd fucked her all night, and then right before the sun came up, fell hard into that space where nothing exists. No noise. No sight. No disruptions.

The archer could've killed me in my sleep and I wouldn't have had a clue.

She was worse than a drug. She was the addiction.

"Power of the pussy," I muttered to myself, opening the door to my office building. "That's all it is, Kelly."

"Mr. Kelly!" Susan, my secretary, popped up from behind her desk. She narrowed her eyes at me after she had really taken me in. "You're late."

"Your watch is fast," I said, checking mine, realizing that I was.

She waved a hand. "Your coffee is in your office. But it's probably cold now." She sat down with a slump and crossed her arms over her chest. It was no secret that she was the head of the club that disliked my wife. Susan and her minions thought my wife was too proud.

I grinned to myself, knowing that the only people I'd ever seen get under the archer's skin was her family, and her friend, Mari. And me.

"Mr. Kelly."

I stopped in the lobby.

Maureen O'Connell stood from her seat. "I don't have an appointment," she said. "But I need to talk to you."

I'd never seen the woman so tired. And she had plenty enough reasons to be. She had worked hard all of her life to make ends meet after her husband died at a young age. When her son got into some trouble and fought addiction, dying from a drug deal gone wrong, and her daughter-in-law from a similar fate, her life got even harder. She was left with two children to raise, and she refused help from most of the women who offered it.

Unfounded rumors and gossip never sat well with Maureen. She had said that the nosy women only wanted inside of her house to know what was going on. "When people know you're down," she'd said. "They'll kick you when no one is looking to keep you there."

Maureen O'Connell reminded me of my wife. She had a backbone and refused to let other people ruffle her easily.

I nodded. "I have time."

Once we were inside of the office, I motioned for her to take a seat. After sitting across from her, we stared at each other until Susan brought in two coffees. Maureen got up and closed the door after.

"Meddling old bitch," Maureen muttered. Then she took her seat again but didn't touch the coffee. I never did either. I had a plant in the corner with a caffeine addiction. "I'm going to get down to the point, Cashel. My grandson is coming home in a day or two. He doesn't have a name."

She called the little boy her grandson, even though he wasn't, not by blood. The little boy was the outcome of his mother paying for drugs with her body. Mad respect for Maureen O'Connell was putting it mildly.

A minute or two passed, and I opened and closed my hands, urging her to continue.

"You'll give him a name. A name to be proud of."

"That's not my place." I'd heard little rumors here and there that Maureen was sick, but I never asked because she talked when she wanted. Maybe whatever she had was affecting her thinking.

She pulled her sweater forward and took out a piece of paper from the pocket. I sat back in my seat, already knowing what it was before she even slid it toward me. My old man would give something similar to a receipt, a piece of paper with his signature, whenever someone had done him a favor. He'd collect them and save them, writing whoever's name down as debt paid, once he was in the good with them.

Maureen's receipt was old and tattered.

"I took him in once and hid him," she said. "Your father. From the police. I didn't want thanks for it, but he insisted."

"Say no more," I said, watching her carefully. "He'll have the O'Connell last name?"

"Unless you can think of a better one?" She lifted a sharp brow at me.

I narrowed my eyes, trying to read her motives, but time ticked. I had a meeting. "Ryan," I said.

"Fine choice." She nodded and then stood. She walked to

the door and then stopped. "Your wife, she's a good woman, Cashel Fallon Kelly. Be sure to treat her right."

The door closed behind her, and after I watched her go, I took the slip and opened it up. My old man's handwriting was scrawled across the threadbare page. It seemed like Maureen had opened and closed it a few times, maybe debating on whether or not to use it when she'd felt she needed it the most.

Opening the drawer to my desk, I took out a pen and wrote *debt paid*, the date, and then added the name Ryan.

AT THE PRECISE time I expected Raff, he knocked on my door and then came in at my word. He took a seat across from me, settling in as usual.

"Their shipments are getting bigger," he said.

I nodded. "Grady wants to be the top distributor, and with the Scarpones backing him, he's getting what he wants."

"There's one problem with the Scarpones," he said. "They're in a feud with the other families right now. Things are tense. Shipments keep getting stolen. Grady is getting wary of them. And they're getting wary of him."

"Yeah," I said, sitting back, putting my hands behind my head, grinning. "He thinks they're lying about the shipments being stolen. That they're holding out on him. Same goes for the Scarpones. They're not sure who to trust, since they can't even trust themselves."

"That's how it seems." Raff paused for a second. "What the fuck is going on with the families? It's mayhem."

"I have an idea," I said.

I thought back to Mari, Keely's friend, and her fiancé, Macchiavello. They were due to marry shortly, and with him in Italy, I wondered if there was going to be a break for the Scarpones and their goods.

Someone had been stealing their shit from right underneath their noses.

I couldn't have done a better job myself. I was able to steal petty shipments lately, but nothing that would really cripple them. If Mac was the person I suspected him to be, he had every right to destroy them. Here was the problem, though—he was a ghost.

Vittorio Scarpone, known back in the day as the Pretty Boy Prince of New York, had been killed. Throat slashed and body dumped in the Hudson for the fish to feast on. The hit ordered by his very own father.

I'd never met Vittorio, only heard stories about how ruthless he was, and when I tried to do some research, it seemed the only thing left of him was speculation. Not even a photograph. I reached out to the older men in the neighborhood who were connected at one time, to get a clear picture of the man, not the ghost.

"Not a man to be fucked with" was the general consensus.

It made sense if he was the one who'd killed Lee Grady's old man, Cormick. Lee would become suspicious of who'd done it. He wouldn't expect the Scarpones at first, but if the shipments kept disappearing, he'd start to wonder why.

His father gone.

His shipments gone.

Who had he been working closely with?

The Scarpones.

If the Scarpones eliminated Lee Grady next, that would give them one hundred percent of the profit, and a shot at claiming Hell's Kitchen as part of their territory.

Relationships were under a massive amount of strain because of the current unrest, which was why Lee Grady got a little testy with my wife at the political event.

I held a finger up to Raff. I got Susan on the line. "My wife," I said to her when she answered. She huffed but connected me.

A few seconds later, the archer picked up. She sounded out of breath.

"Darlin'," I said.

"Hold on." I heard things clanking in the background. "What?"

Raff laughed at her tone. I opened my drawer, stuck my hand in, then a second later, pulled it out, giving him the bird.

"Lunch," I said. "You and me. Sullivan's."

"Can't," she said. "I'm busy. And besides, you just got to *work*. On a Sunday."

"We eat together," I said, reminding her.

"Not every meal. Dinner."

"I changed my mind."

"Too late. Gotta go."

"Keely," I said, catching her a second before she hung up. "What are you doing, darlin'?"

"Wouldn't you love to know." Then she hung up on me.

Raff snorted. "Jessica Rabbit is a fucking spitfire. I like the fox's moxie."

"Jessica Rabbit," I said, looking up at him.

"Your girl. She has red hair and a body that could kill, so..."

The paperweight that used to sit on my old man's desk sat on mine. Too quick for him to dodge, I threw it at Raff's head. His head went back with the impact and it fell to the floor with a clang. It hit him in the spot right above his eyes.

"Next time my wife's body comes to your mind, remember that to fucking knock it out." What the fuck was wrong with this guy? Better yet, what the fuck was wrong with me? I'd just hit my cousin with a metal weight because he'd been thinking about mine.

"You're a fucking asshole, Cash," he said, rubbing the spot. It was already swelling. "Back to business. Our community is growing by the second."

Fucking grand. The hit had knocked some sense into him.

He was back on track. When he said "our community," he
meant the men who'd decided to join us.

"John Gerald's son in?" I said. "Martin?"

"Clean now." Raff nodded. "And working for you."

"Grady's going to start hitting us even harder since we're
growing."

"You're setting off that temper."

"Make sure everyone's on guard."

"You," he said. "Be sure none of that alley shit happens
again. Lee cuts your head off, that's the end for all of us. For
good."

Cormick Grady was known as the Butcher. Lee had that
same gruesome streak, but he saved the massacre for personal
offenses.

"But at least the Scarpones are not getting involved with our
feud," Raff continued. "That saves us some trouble."

"For now," I said. "They're too busy trying to find out who's
fucking with them."

"Works for us." He shrugged.

Silence filled the room, but our thoughts were loud. We
both knew that we needed to make a big move. I was the
marauder, stealing was my specialty, but I had to play this right.
Hitting small shipments wounded and led to bigger wounds
over time. But I wanted to cripple them in one go—and fast.
Grady was tired of working small loads. He was ready to go
bigger, since he'd set this up over the years with the Scarpones.

His first big shipment, his life's work, I'd already claimed as
mine. Unless the ghost, who I sensed was Macchiavello, got to it
first.

A knock came at the door, and Raff and I both turned to
look. Susan came in a second later, holding a plain envelope.

"Urgent," she said, setting it in front of me. "From Mr.
Fausti."

"Ah," I said, opening it, recognizing Rocco's stamp right

away. Inside was a fake bill for his legal services. I knew the difference between the real ones and the ones they used for show. Anyone who worked for them did. It was a way for him to communicate. This bill? I owed payment to Macchiavello. He'd decided to cash in on that debt owed—killing Cormick Grady.

Rocco added a note on his personalized paper: *We need to catch up. I hear Sullivan's has good roast beef. Dinner. Around 7 o'clock.*

He gave me the date, which was around the time of Macchiavello's wedding in Italy. Then he signed off in his regal fucking handwriting.

Rocco Fausti

A slow smile came to my face, and I stared at the paper a few seconds before I met Raff's eager eyes.

"What is it?" His knee bounced up and down.

"Roast beef," I said. I'd give Raff orders to keep his eyes and ears open, but what went on between the Faustis and me stayed between us. No one else knew the details.

Rule number one in this life: never trust anyone one hundred percent.

Back to roast beef.

It wasn't the word that Rocco used, but what he had conveyed through the message. The Italian families, especially the Faustis, were known to speak in code like no one else. Being fluent in their language, I understood right away. Rocco was giving me a time and place for a reason.

This happening during a time when Mac would be getting married was significant. Because it meant he wouldn't be in New York.

My gut told me it had something to do with the big shipment, and if I learned what I needed to know, I had my mark. I knew it was going to happen soon, and Rocco came through just in time.

There was no doubt, though, that Mac was giving me this at

a price. I'd hit the delivery, but he'd get the goods. I wasn't familiar with his business, but this time, I would have to let it go. I could do what I wanted with the small loads, set them on fire like usual, but he had the right to do whatever he wanted with this one.

Then my debt was repaid.

All in all, this was a good deal for the both of us, if it turned out to be the big shipment. No matter what the situation was, though, if Rocco sent word, it had to be something good.

I could taste the roast beef in my mouth now.

Raff went to speak again when a loud bang echoed in my office. Harrison was flying past the windows, his fist landing against another glass as he did. I stood before Raff, wondering why the fuck he was banging on my shit. He'd been a testy motherfucker after his girl decided to marry Macchiavello and after I forced his sister to marry me.

"My sister," he said, after he'd thrown my door open. "She's just been arrested."

I MOVED through the crowd waiting outside of our place as Stone led my wife out of the door, her hands cuffed behind her back.

She wasn't making it easy on him. She was taunting him, telling him that the only way he could control a woman like her was to cuff her. Her neck was on fire with red splotches, along with parts of her jaw. It was also stained with purple paint.

I narrowed my eyes. It was all in her hair, too.

Never did emotions show on my face, but I had to make sure to check myself so Stone couldn't see the fucking fury burning a hole through my chest.

Harry Boy stepped up, demanding to know what the charges were.

"Resisting arrest," Stone said.

"Resisting your pathetic advances," my wife said as Stone walked her past me, a smug smile on his face. He ducked her head before he set her in a cruiser. He shut the door and then smacked the roof twice to signal the patrolman he was good to go. A second later, she was taken away, lights flashing and sirens blaring.

"The royal treatment," I said to him as he stopped in front of me, making sure to keep my voice even. One ounce of emotion and he'd sense it on me—the urge to hurt him physically. No amount of physical pain amounted to the despair I saw in his eyes, though, and that was feeding my need for violence.

"No less for a queen of thieves."

We stared at each other until Raff came to stand next to me, nudging me with his elbow. Stone looked toward the house first, and then I did—police were gathering around, watching us, ready to move if I did.

Harry Boy moved past them, coming to speak directly to Stone. "Where's the warrant, Stone?"

Stone took it out of his pocket and handed it to Harry Boy. His eyes scanned the page, and I didn't miss the name of the judge that had signed off on it. We had a tremulous relationship. He had put me away for ten years.

Finally, Harry Boy looked at Stone. "Drugs. You have reason to believe my client has drugs stashed in his house."

"He does," Stone said.

"Where's the evidence," Harry Boy demanded, getting that lawyer look about him. He was a fucking killer in the courtroom.

Stone nodded to another cop, who came over with a baggie of green, showing it to Harry Boy.

"This?" Harry Boy nodded toward it. "My client has a prescription for it. Written by Tito Sala, M.D."

"We were looking for a bigger shipment of drugs," Stone said, his voice cool. "Those were not found on the premises, but this was. As soon as we get the prescription, Kelly will be in the clear." He shook his head, laughing some. "Tito Sala. Why am I not surprised?"

Tito Sala was the doctor who saw to the Faustis personally. His wife was the sister of one of the most notorious leaders Italy had ever seen—Marzio Fausti, Rocco's grandfather. There was no better doctor than Tito Sala. If he couldn't save you, you were already dead. My old man had been a friend of his, and he'd come to see me every so often when I was locked up. After I got out of prison, he had dinner with me. He wrote the prescription so I could sleep, suggesting that I get my eyes checked soon, due to the headaches.

I hated going to the doctor as much as I hated listening to people chew. Tito Sala forced his expertise on me, usually.

"My sister, you ass," Harry Boy said, losing the professionalism he usually employed, and snagging my attention. I'd been staring at Stone, even though my thoughts had drifted.

"Be careful," Stone said. "I have an extra car ready."

"Take me," Harry Boy said, opening his arms. "I'll tell everyone at the courthouse how she turned you down for Kelly. How you made this personal."

"Better go bail your sister out." Stone grinned and then slapped Harry Boy on the shoulder. Harry Boy's jaw clenched. "I thought she was a woman with a backbone. Turned out she was a chameleon. Her colors change quick, so you better get her before they turn green. Pure evil."

Stone looked me in the eyes and then was caught off guard by a fist.

That was how I ended up having to bail my wife and my lawyer out of jail.

18

KEELY

Being arrested wasn't a shining moment in my life. I was even called a "moll" by the policewoman who stuck me in a cold cell with the hardest seats I'd ever felt in my life.

Moll. She'd meant Mob Moll—a woman who protected a man in the mob.

I wasn't protecting Kelly. I was caught off guard. One minute they were banging on the door, and the next, they were storming through it.

Fucking mayhem ensued.

They were pulling shit out, ignoring me when I kept asking them to explain it again. Drugs, drugs, drugs—that was what they kept saying.

"What about them?" I'd demanded, trying to employ that in-control attitude Kelly always had.

That was when I saw him. Scott. He was watching me, a smug grin on his face. Since it was illegal to put my hands on him, I shot him a look and then went back upstairs. I'd been painting CeeCee's room for her. Purple, because Maureen said that when she colored, she used it the most. I remembered Mari doing the same thing with the color blue and butterflies.

When I reached CeeCee's room, all of the paint had been knocked over onto the floor. They had been digging through the drawers and closet, flinging things around, and some of her new clothes were in it, saturated and ruined.

I'd lost it. Not on the cop doing the searching, but on Stone when he walked into the room and called my name.

It was his fault. He had purposely gotten the warrant issued and took pleasure in being there while it happened. To provoke Kelly, and to hurt me, like I'd hurt him.

Another cop told me to "tone it down" after I started yelling at him. When I didn't, they subdued me, but at that point, my head was void of any reasonable thought. Then they handcuffed me and read me my rights.

Resisting arrest.

The entire neighborhood, including my brother, husband, and Raff, watched as they set me in a car and hauled me away. Paraded me was more like it. They kept the sirens on the entire way.

So, no, my fight wasn't for Kelly. It was for CeeCee, who didn't deserve for her room and clothes to get ruined due to some vengeance triangle that had nothing to do with her.

Okay. Maybe a little for Kelly, because it was a bullshit warrant.

An hour in and the same policewoman came to collect me.

"Kelly," she said. "You've been bailed out."

Harrison stood against the wall, waiting for me, and he looked haggard.

"What?" I looked around. "Kelly didn't even have the decency to bail his wife out?"

"He bailed us *both* out."

I stopped walking, but he tugged on my arm. I only continued because I didn't want to stay at the station.

"What do you mean?" I rubbed my wrists, where the cuffs had chafed some.

"Long story," he said. "I'll tell you later. Right now, we have somewhere to be."

"Somewhere" was the area of the station that belonged to homicide. Harrison led me into a room that had a double window. I could see out, but whoever was in the other room couldn't see me.

Kelly sat at the table on the other side with a cup in front of him. He was alone.

Detective Paul Marinetti stood by the window, watching. He turned when he heard us.

He nodded to my brother. "Ryan." Then he nodded at me. "Mrs. Kelly."

"What's this about?" I looked between my brother and the old detective, suspicious. Did Harrison do something to get Kelly locked up?

"Kee," my brother said, coming to stand beside me. "Detective Marinetti came to me and Kelly with a deal. He'd drop the charges on both of us if Kelly would agree to have a sit-down with Stone."

"Scott wanted this?" The shock was evident in my voice.

"No," Detective Marinetti said. "I did. My partner hasn't been himself lately. He's a good kid, and he's going in a direction I'm trying to change. I don't want him to lose his job. Maybe airing out his grievances will get his mind straight."

"Scott's made this personal," I said.

The detective said nothing, not confirming or denying, but he didn't have to. What Kelly had done, marrying me, had sent Scott into overdrive. I remembered from our time together how obsessed he would get with his organized crime cases. Add that to Kelly being one of his greatest enemies and it added up to something dangerous—between the two of them.

"Seems Stone's been stepping on some powerful toes lately," my brother said. "Not only on Kelly's. The Faustis, too."

I took a step closer to the glass, watching Kelly. He didn't have a nervous bone in his body. That *la de da* attitude was firmly in place.

"What did you do to him, girl?"

It took me a moment to realize Detective Marinetti was talking to me.

"I didn't mean to hurt him," I said. "I had feelings for him, but it just didn't work out."

Detective Marinetti shook his head. "Not Scott. Cash Kelly. He agreed to this right away. In all of my years, I've never seen him roll over for anyone." He paused. "Anyone but you."

I crossed my arms over my chest, feeling a chill all of a sudden. "I'm his wife."

"It shows," Detective Marinetti said. "Still. It's something to see. Like a man walking on the moon."

"He wanted you out," Harrison said, narrowing his eyes at me. "And he didn't want the charges to stick."

I nodded, but my brother kept staring at me. Finally, I mouthed *what?*, and he shook his head and turned to face the window.

A second later, Scott stomped in. He stood across from Kelly, looking down on him.

"Glad you could finally make it," Kelly said, relaxing even further into his seat.

"I'm only doing this for one reason," Scott said, his jaw hard. "My partner."

"Marinetti." Kelly nodded. "There's a man who knows how to do his job and then shut if off at the end of his shift."

"You don't know a thing about his fucking job."

"You're nothing without me," Kelly said, opening and closing his hands around the cup. "I've always known that. You know that. That's why you despise me."

"Nothing without you," Scott spit back at him.

"If I didn't exist." He pointed to his chest. Then he pointed at Scott. "You wouldn't exist."

"You know what wouldn't exist? Your marriage." Scott placed two hands on the table, narrowing his eyes at Kelly. "Mine. You went after what was mine. You manipulated her into marrying you."

Kelly shrugged. "In the beginning, but we both know it's turned into something else."

"What would that be?"

"That's between my wife and me." Kelly's grin came slow. "But you have eyes. You see it. Even feel it."

The entire room seemed to still while Kelly and Stone stared at each other from across the table.

Then Scott leaned in a little closer, a grin to match Kelly's on his face. "You have no idea who Ronan Kelly really was. *Maraigh.*" Scott pronounced the word like MA-RAH. I'd heard some of the men that worked for Kelly call his father the same thing. "You walk this earth like you have a purpose. Like what you do means something. Because it meant something to your old man. Go back home for a while, Kelly, and ask your ma if she has the same hero worship for the man who ruined her life."

I was so stunned by what Scott had said that it took me a minute to look at Harrison, who was staring at me. Cash Kelly's mom was dead. She'd died before he left Ireland with Ronan. Father Flanagan had told me.

Kelly stood to his full height, and even though he hadn't lost his cool, I could tell the tiger on his neck had made it to his eyes.

"Did you ever tell my wife the connection you had to the man who killed her sister?" Kelly paused, and it felt like all oxygen had been sucked from my lungs. "Bert Langster was your father's best friend. He was having marital problems, if I recall, and was chasing after his wife in another car, got reckless in his anger, and killed an innocent child and her grandparents on the way to a Broadway show. Miraculously, the charges were dropped."

"Then, to return a favor he owed, Maraigh had Bert Langster killed."

It wasn't Kelly or Scott who had spoken those words, but my brother. Bert Langster was the man who killed Roisin and our grandparents. A year after they were killed, they found him in his car, dead from carbon monoxide poisoning. He let the car run in his garage for too long. Or that was what I overheard my mam telling one of my aunts.

"What are you talking about?" I barely got out.

"Da," Harrison said. "Ronan Kelly used to buy from his shop in Hell's Kitchen." Then he glanced at Detective Marinetti —he didn't want to say any more.

Our father had opened an imported glass shop when we were little. He only sold things you could find in Ireland and Scotland. He must have gone to Ronan Kelly after my sister was killed, seeking justice through lawless means.

My father.

The man who rarely spoke—we all joked that my mam had stolen all of his words—had gotten another man killed, a man who had walked free of a crime that stole my other half.

I wondered if it was Ronan Kelly or his son, my husband, who had killed Bert Langster.

Like I'd done all those years ago, I must've held my breath for too long, or it was being held in the room with Kelly and Stone, because all of the stars went out and I faded.

19

KEELY

It was hard not to keep hearing Scott's voice echoing inside of my head during quiet moments.

"We didn't have anything to do with him getting set free! Keely, you have to believe me. My father didn't even associate with him after he was arrested!"

Those words seemed trapped in a tunnel, and like the day I'd passed out in that two-way observation-mirror room, the further I got from the memory, the less my hands trembled.

Either way, the man who had killed my sister and grandparents had been a close family friend of the Stone's, and it was something Scott had neglected to tell me. After he found out who I was, it was the first thing he should've admitted to me.

Maybe his family had something to do with the man walking free. Maybe they didn't. But I had deserved to know, especially given the fact that my mother and father would've recognized his name as soon as I'd introduced them.

My mother and father knew exactly who Cash Kelly was when I'd introduced *him*. I should've told her about my wedding, but she definitely should've told me about our history with the Kelly family.

After setting down my lipstick on the bathroom counter, I slipped my feet into a pair of gold heels. Kelly and I had another fancy event to attend, and I chose another green dress to wear. It was my signature color.

The color of his eyes.

Instead of waiting for him at home, though, I decided to meet him at Sullivan's. It wasn't a far walk, and the weather had been nice all day. And I wanted to talk to him in a more private setting. After Scott had insinuated that Kelly's mother was still alive, he had been quiet, and I assumed he was thinking over the possibility.

Why would anyone lie about that, though? His own father? Father Flanagan, too? What did his twin have to say about all of this?

I followed the sound of voices down to the kitchen. Maureen and the kids had been staying with us since the day of the bullshit warrant. She came that night with just two bags between all three of them.

Right before my arrest, I had been outside getting another paint can out of my car when I'd seen her walking. She told me she was going to pick up Ryan, and I suggested that she and the kids come to stay with us for a while, just until Ryan was completely out of the woods.

Maureen seemed like a woman who refused to ask for help, because she was always strong enough to do it on her own, but I worried about how tired she looked. And I loved having the children around. So I was glad when she gave in.

Cash and I were leaving the next day for Mari and Mac's wedding in Italy. I was going to miss the three of them something fierce. Even in such a short time, they filled the house with something that felt warm. When I thought about being separated from them, something in me went cold.

For the first time since I came to live with Kelly, the house was starting to feel like mine, too.

Maureen stood at the stove, stirring something that smelled like cabbage, and when she saw me, she whistled. "Fox!"

"You're Jessica Rabbit in green," Raff said. He sat at the table with CeeCee, coloring.

CeeCee giggled, and the three of us, in our own ways, acknowledged it without trying to shine a huge light on it. It was the same reaction she had when she first saw her room—it didn't take long for the shock to turn into pure happiness. The kind all kids should have.

I went to check on Ryan, who was asleep in the bassinet we kept in the kitchen. I'd taken one look at him when Maureen brought him home and my heart seemed to grow.

All was okay in our home, so I told them I'd see them later and went to leave. Raff stopped me. "Where's Cash?"

"I told him I'd meet him at Sullivan's. Why?"

"I'll walk you," he said. He turned to CeeCee. "Don't color her hair. That's my favorite part!"

She took out a dark purple color and put it between the pages of his book, knowing that he gave the princesses cool hair colors.

We talked books the entire way to the restaurant, and once there, he watched me go inside and then turned back toward our place. I took a seat at the bar and ordered two whiskeys neat.

"Would you like something to eat, Mrs. Kelly?" the old barman asked me.

"No," I said. "Not yet. I'm waiting on Cash. We'll order together."

He nodded and went to check on a guy sitting two seats down from me.

Sullivan's had been in the neighborhood for years and years. It was a place that still held on to its old-world charm. I remembered seeing a picture of my Mam and Da sitting at the bar with a bunch of friends. Mentally, I went through all of the faces, and a few seconds later, it dawned on me—one of them was Ronan Kelly.

The thought of Cash's old man made me look to my left. Molly, Ronan's widow, and Brian Grady, who I'd heard was Lee's uncle, were sitting at a table together. They were a couple, which kind of surprised me, because from what I understood, the feud between the Kellys and the Gradys was the stuff legends are made of.

I was never curious enough about Molly to make an effort to get to know her, but Brian was...different. For instance, he was holding a dart, and instead of throwing it, he was trying to get the sharp part underneath the first layer of skin on his pointer finger. Like the dart was a needle.

He was also missing the middle digit of his right hand.

The bar was noisy enough with chatter and the band playing, so I turned to the guy two seats down. "How long have you lived here?" He was around Kelly's age, if not a little older.

He looked to the right and then at me when he found no one sitting on the other side of him. Or he knew and was just trying to be a smart ass. He pointed at his chest. "You talkin' to me?"

"I'm not talking to myself."

"All my life," he said and turned his face forward again.

I noticed that the barman looked between us before he went back to serving drinks.

"I'm not trying to hit on you," I said. "I have a question."

"He'd rearrange my face, or worse, for much less." He took a gulp of his beer.

"What?" Maybe he was drunk.

"Your husband. There's a reason why men around here keep their distance from you. I was sitting there." He nodded to the seat next to me. "Saw you coming and moved here for the sake of my health."

"Ah," I said. "Because of the tiger that sleeps in my bed."

"He's a tiger and I'm a goat. I can smell him all around you, lady."

I laughed a little and he grinned.

"One question, since you probably know more about the history in this neighborhood than I do." I chucked my chin toward Brian and Molly. "What happened to his bird finger? Seems like an odd digit to lose."

The guy who called himself a goat looked at the barman again. Real subtle, the barman shook his head.

The guy released a heavy breath a minute later. "Ah, what the hell? It's not a secret. The Gradys and Kellys go back years. When Ronan first arrived, he had eyes for Molly. She fell for his Irish lilt and charm. He was older, too, and hell bent on running Hell's Kitchen after he got in good with a previous leader who wanted it back after the Gradys took it from him. Molly decided she wanted Ronan and not Brian, and that was that. But not before Ronan cut off Brian's bird finger after he gave it to Ronan."

"She's sleeping with the enemy."

He took another drink of his beer and sighed. "Molly has a wicked temper. She doesn't forgive, and she doesn't forget. Ronan got her pregnant twice, but there was never a baby. Rumors were that she couldn't have them. Then Ronan brings home his two sons, who were at an age to remember their mother. Molly wasn't her. She hasn't forgiven or forgotten it.

"She would make Ronan prove himself to her by being distant from his sons. If he showed them too much attention, she'd throw a fit and threaten to leave, that sort of thing. Kill made things worse. He couldn't stand her. It wasn't an ideal situation." Then he made a *baaaa* sound and turned around.

I looked back at Molly and Brian, and her eyes narrowed against mine. What kind of woman throws a tantrum over *children* being shown too much attention? A bitch.

A hand slipped around my waist from behind, and I stiffened for a second, before I recognized the touch.

"You're not as jumpy around me, my darlin'," Kelly said, his warm breath in my ear.

"My bones were getting sick of jumping out of my skin whenever you snuck up on me." I grinned. "You're on my radar now."

Though I didn't think I'd ever get used to him. When he appeared, it was like I was stuck in a storm, and during a strike of lightning, the form of a massive cat appeared of out the darkness. His power was the shock of it, time and time again.

"Good bones," he murmured against my overheated flesh, though my arms showed goosebumps. Then he inhaled. "That scent you're wearing lingers. All. Fucking. Day."

Yeah, because it's yours and mine, mixed together.

My heart rose and my stomach dipped at the thought, and the sound of his voice made my eyes lower. I could spend forever listening to it.

The hold on my waist became tighter, constricting, and I had to fight the urge to move out of it. "Another man was breathing in my scent. Making mine laugh. Enjoying my heaven."

He was sending a message— I knew about those, because he usually sent them in the bedroom, when he was fucking me. I should've been afraid, but it turned me on. A fierce ache grew between my legs and a moan was stuck in my throat.

"If it happens again." His voice was ice cold. "He'll be in hell."

The pressure released and I breathed in deep.

The warmth behind my back moved to face me. A gun was tucked behind his suit jacket. "You hungry for something special?" He casually gestured to a menu sitting on the bar, like he hadn't just said those words.

I couldn't answer. I pushed his glass of whiskey toward him, and then grabbed for mine, taking a deep drink. His mouth came against mine a second later, and our tongues twirled, fire between them.

When we parted, he said, "Special reserve of whiskey just for me. The best in the fucking world."

I licked my lips and then motioned to the seat next to mine. "I wanted to talk to you in private."

He looked around and grinned.

I smiled, tucking a wayward curl behind my ear. "Not around everyone in the house."

"That's why we have a private room, darlin'."

"Just sit, Kelly." I nodded toward the seat again. This had to be done out in public, or maybe I wouldn't be able to say all that needed to be said. In our "private" room, it was hard to keep my hands to myself. I wanted to jump his bones as soon as he walked into the house.

He nodded to the guy two seats from me, and after the guy nodded back, he took his beer and claimed a table by one of the windows. Kelly took the seat I'd offered after he did.

We faced each other.

I went to take another drink of my whiskey, but he stopped me with a hand. "Speak what's on your mind."

I nodded. Fixed the damn curl again. "I want to call a truce."

He tilted his head a little. "With who, darlin'?"

It took me a second to cool my temper. Was my fight with him so insignificant that he didn't even notice? "Unlike you, Kelly, I don't have enemies banging on my door every day. A truce between *us*." My hand waved between our bodies, and he caught it, placing a kiss on my ring finger.

"All right." He nodded. "A truce. Between us."

I watched his face for a moment. It showed nothing but a rugged handsomeness that few possessed and could pull off. "You have no idea what I'm talking about." I realized that he never felt resistance from me, because compared to what he was up against on the streets, my temper was insignificant.

"To a degree." He fixed his tie before he looked me in the eye. "I stole your heart without your consent, and you wanted to get even. Now you're seeing this as something that has the potential to be real between us, and you want *us* to give our marriage the respect it demands. The chance it deserves."

For whatever fucking reason, his words stole the breath from my lungs. "Yes," I barely got out. "You have the essence of it."

He tapped the center of his heart with his middle finger once. "No heart." He tapped his temple with the same finger once. "But I'm still aware of every fucking thing, darlin'."

Setting his arms on each side of my chair, he pulled it forward like I weighed nothing and leaned in closer. His mouth was a kiss away, but instead, he ran his nose up my cheek and put his mouth close to my ear after my eyes had closed. "The truth of it is," he breathed out, "some hearts have to be given. Not yours, fierce archer. It *had* to be stolen. Otherwise, you wouldn't have given it willingly. Not to Stone. Not to me. Not to any man. It's a fight to the death to earn your love. You're the most expensive date I've ever had."

"What about yours?" I whispered. "Your heart?"

"What's inside?" He palmed the pendant he'd given me, the chain probably resting between his fingers. I could feel the pull of it as he slowly moved back.

It took me a minute to open my eyes, and when I did, his eyes were burning a dangerous green. I didn't think there was a jealous bone in his body, but the color of his eyes were meant to claim and keep. *His.*

"I haven't found it yet." I entwined my hand with his, the chain coming between our fingers. "The key."

"You haven't looked hard enough." He grinned at me, but it wasn't playful; it was daring. "Prove me wrong."

Oh, I think I already have, Kelly.

Using the chain, he pulled me even closer and set his lips against mine again. When we pulled away, I got the same dizziness that I did when I held my breath. Stars danced behind my eyes, and I grabbed onto the bar to keep myself grounded.

"I'll take care of you, Keely Kelly," he said. "I won't let you fall again. No truce needed."

I tried to pull away, but he wouldn't let me. I had fallen so many times after my sister was killed, from holding my breath, that my Da put a helmet on my head to stop me from damaging my brain. I didn't know how to live without my other half.

Looking at this man who purposely stole my heart, I didn't think I could live without him, either. He had somehow stepped into that empty shadow and filled the void, stealing the guilt and the pain. It didn't hurt as much when he was around.

Meeting his eyes, I nodded once. "I choose to believe you."

He echoed my nod. "*Sos*," he said. "Truce."

The word sounded like "sauce," but he'd said it in that way people do when they're pronouncing a foreign word.

"*Sos*," I repeated, squeezing his hand.

We released the chain from between us, and he stood from his stool, holding out his hand for me. I took it, and he led me to the middle of the restaurant, stopping to pull me close and move me to a slow song that the band in the corner was playing.

"I never got to dance with my bride," he said.

I laughed in his ear as we moved. "That's what happens when you *steal* a bride."

"You get a heart," he said. "So fucking grand."

I laughed even louder as he dipped me.

After our dance, we ate at the bar, and I couldn't remember the last time I'd laughed so much. Kelly had jokes for days, ones I knew Mari would appreciate, and every time he'd smile at me, I found that he no longer had to steal my time and attention. Without ploys and games and barriers—I was giving it.

WE SPENT SO much time at Sullivan's that, by the time we left, it was already dark out and too late to attend the event. Kelly didn't seem to care, and neither did I.

It was a beautiful night to be out, no place to be, and as we walked down the street holding hands, I thought about how nice it was going to be to spend some time with Kelly outside of New York.

He was always preoccupied with his "work." He even worked on Sundays. My schedule was rigorous, and with Maureen and the kids, it seemed like my days were always filled up.

I wasn't sure what it would be like to have more than a couple of hours to spend with each other. It wasn't an extended trip—I had obligations with work. A couple of days, though, with no work distractions, were going to be a change of pace.

I imagined Kelly on a beach in Sicily somewhere, no shirt, and a shot of desire coursed through my veins.

He whistled as he walked, and I smiled to myself, liking the sound of it.

"Can you sing?" I looked at him.

"A little," he said.

"I call bullshit." Then I sucked in a breath and clutched the heart pendant when three men seemed to materialize out of the darkness, no warning.

One stepped directly in front of Kelly, and the other two stood on each side of him. Three guns were pointed at us.

Kelly nodded his head real subtle, behind him, and I caught it. I moved, standing against his back. "Move along, fellas," he said. "Not here. Not now."

"Maraigh might have given passes if the mark was out with family, but you know how we run things, Kelly. And it ain't like your old man. That's why he's dead and you're about to be."

"We'll make this simple, Kelly," another one said. "The drugs. You tell us where they are. We'll let the wife walk."

I looked between Kelly and the three men. This was the first time I'd heard anything about drugs. I knew Kelly was a thief, one of the best, but drugs? Was that what he was stealing and then selling? Maybe the bullshit warrant wasn't bullshit at all.

"Seems Kelly keeps secrets from the missus," Guy Two spoke up, staring at my face, laughing a little. "You didn't know, Red? Your husband steals drugs that don't belong to him and then sells them in the streets for more than we do. He's high class, the marauding tiger." Guy Two hit Center Guy on the shoulder. "Then he lets the children of those parents he sold drugs to live at his place. How's that for repaying a debt? At least his old man was honest about it."

My thoughts went to Ryan, how small he was, how he could potentially be facing life-long consequences for his mother's addiction, and my blood ran cold. I would've taken a step back from Kelly, but the seriousness of the situation kept me in place. These guys were not fucking around.

In my peripheral, I saw someone moving behind the three men. Someone they hadn't noticed. Maureen. She had a bag of trash in one hand and a cigarette in another. She must've stepped out to sneak a smoke under the guise of taking the trash out. Her eyes connected with mine before she tilted her head a bit, maybe realizing what the fuck was going on.

Without trying to be too obvious, I turned my eyes back to the situation, but Guy Two had noticed. His head whipped around but Maureen had already gone.

Maybe she was going to get Raff.

Center Guy was demanding the drugs again. "Where are they?" He had started to sweat. He pointed the gun at Kelly's

218 BELLA DI CORTE

head. "Where the fuck are they, Kelly?" When he didn't get a response, the gun moved and trained on me. "You have two seconds, or you'll be cleaning up your wife's brains from the street you love so much. One."

Kelly made a subtle move, one where either way he was getting the bullet, but on Center Guy's count of two, Maureen swung the garbage bag with all her might, and it connected with his head in a sickening *thunk!* She must've filled it with rocks or something. The crack seemed to echo before all hell broke loose.

Kelly shoved me to the ground. He swept up the gun that Center Guy lost after he went down and shot Guy One point-blank in the head. Guy Two shot Kelly in the shoulder, but a second later, Kelly made two more head shots—one for Guy Two and one for the guy who got whacked by Maureen.

I'd never seen anyone move like that, so quick that it was hard to keep up. *Bang. Bang. Bang.* All three men were laid out on the concrete, blood spreading on the cement.

Kelly stood for a second, his breathing normal, but his eyes were so dangerous that it sent a spike of fear up my chest. It was the kind of look an animal got while hunting. The pulse in his neck was frantic, but it looked like it belonged to the tiger.

I lay on the concrete, my palms and knees burning from the fall. My elbow was bleeding. My ears were ringing. The scent of blood and gunpowder filled the night air.

Kelly seemed to snap out of his thoughts when Maureen picked up the trash bag. He held out his hand. "I'll take it," he said.

She handed it to him without a word. Then she nodded to me. "Come with me, Keely."

Kelly leaned down to help me up, but I slapped at him. "Don't touch me," I hissed.

His eyes narrowed before he looked at Guy Two and then

back at me. The guy who told me the truth about what Kelly's business was all about.

I stood on my own and walked next to Maureen as we made our way back to the house. A few steps away, another gunshot blasted through the air, and I turned, afraid that one of the three guys had gotten up and took his revenge on Kelly. But it was Kelly who held the gun. He had put another bullet hole in Guy Two. Right in his heart.

20

CASH

"Ah," I cleared my throat to speak, but only thoughts came. *It's been however long since my last confession, and after my wife walked out of our place to fly to Italy for her friend's wedding, I'm an animal in a cage who can't stop pacing. This cage feels worse than prison.*

That was not the reason I came to church, but it was the only words that seemed to keep circulating in my head. Instead of trying again, I stepped out of the confessional.

Father Flanagan stepped out a minute later. "What's the trouble?"

"I've come to a point. This." I waved a hand around, the necklace dangling in its grip swinging like a pendulum. "Is pointless. What I'm about to do has been known before I even knew I was going to do it."

"From my understanding, that was never *the* point of you coming here." He pursed his lips at me and then they opened with a pop. "How many times does one man have to repeat himself, Cashel Fallon Kelly? If I've said this once, I've said it a million times. Perhaps our actions are known before, but that doesn't mean they're written in stone. We can change our minds. We can have a change of heart. We all have the right to change our courses while we're here, so we don't have to answer for them after we're gone."

I paced up and down the aisle, my grip on the chain even tighter. I'd given her a metal heart because it was stronger than a real one. A prosthetic replacement for what couldn't be developed in the natural sense.

"My wife left me," I said. She packed up her things and took them to a different room. The next day, after she left for Italy, I found the necklace I'd given her on my pillow.

He was quiet for so long that I stopped moving. We faced each other.

"Ah," he said. "Your discord comes from marital strife."

"There can be no marital strife if only one married person is left."

"Did she leave for good? Or did she leave for her friend's wedding in Italy? Which I believe, if gossip in this community serves me right, you were supposed to attend with her."

"Plans change," I said. "Still doesn't make it right that she believed the words from another man's mouth over my actions."

"Actions," he repeated, like he was thinking over the meaning of the word. "Does she even know why you fight as hard as you do?" He held a hand up. "She knows who you are, *Marauder*, but does she know the plight Ronan Kelly left to you? And why you took it up so fiercely? She sees a community that looks up to Cash Kelly, but no reason behind it. By all means you've done some senseless things in your life, things I'd rather not discuss out in the open. No rhyme *or* reason to them. But the one thing that feels like your salvation, you haven't shared with her."

"There was no rhyme or reason for you to not tell me my mother wasn't dead."

Seconds passed. He opened and closed his mouth. He

shook his head. "She did. In Ireland. What are you talking about?"

"Scott Stone delivered the news."

"He's a liar, and I'll say it right here." He stomped his foot. "Your father told me."

I looked up at him, and something flickered in his eyes that he tried to hide before I caught it. Doubt. Instead of pressing the issue, I let it ride, deciding to believe that he thought my mother was dead, too. He'd never lied to me before.

"Let's get back to the truth," he said, changing the subject. "Something worth our time."

My chest felt winded even though I hadn't taken a step. I stuck the necklace back in my pocket and took out my phone. I found what I wanted and then turned the phone toward him.

He squinted at the screen and then reached for his reading glasses, grumbling. Once they were on his face, he took the phone from me and held it up almost to his nose. "A picture of Mrs. Kelly looking away from the camera."

"Maureen took it of her at the airport and sent it to me." Since my wife was only going to Italy for a couple of days, I sent Maureen and Connolly with her. The baby, Ryan, had round the clock care at Maureen's place from nurses who had cared for him at the hospital and were trusted in our community.

He looked up from the screen. "I'm not following."

I nodded toward it. "That's what Maureen sent, the picture of her looking behind, along with a caption that said, *every five seconds.*"

The light went out on the phone, but his face seemed to brighten. He handed the phone back and then patted me on the shoulder. "The girl was waiting for you to come after her, Kelly."

I turned around to face his retreating back. The smugness rolling off of him was as strong as incense.

"This is a problem," I said. From all of my experience with

women, in the face of Keely Kelly, none of it mattered. I could deal with her games, even her truth, but I had no clue how to deal with her silence, or the reason why she wanted me to come after her if she made it clear she was returning the necklace.

Going after the woman was something a prince would do. My role was the villain in this tale.

"It happens to the best of us!" his voice echoed. "Can't say I didn't warn you, lad!" His robes melted into the darkness of the church, where I usually felt more comfortable, and then he was gone, but his low laughter seemed to linger.

———

As I was walking from the church to Sullivan's, a whistle sounded from behind me. I turned to find Raff running to catch up. I stopped and waited for him.

He dangled a single key in front of my face.

"I'm not in the mood for fucking riddles," I said. "Or rhymes."

"Anybody want a peanut?" he said in an accent I didn't recognize, and then he grinned at me.

I narrowed my eyes at him.

His head came forward a little, naming the movie. When I didn't answer, he sighed. "Your wife loves that one."

Movies. Books. Broadway. My wife seemed to love all of those things.

Movies because her brothers did.

Books because her Da did.

Broadway because her Mam and sister did.

I watched her while she read, while she watched movies, while she performed on stage, and none of those things lit her up like when she was painting the room she had claimed as Connolly's.

After she was arrested, she'd gotten right back to work on it. She even painted a mural on the wall. She'd told me Mari's adoptive mother let Mari pick out anything she wanted to paint on the wall in their house. Mari had picked a butterfly.

Keely painted a pink and purple dragon, with an exaggerated smile and long lashes, because she knew it meant something to Connolly. Maureen had told Keely that Connolly's mother had given her a toy dragon, and the little girl slept with it every night.

Whatever it was between my wife and Connolly was strong. No one was able to bond with the child because she'd been let down by her parents from an early age.

Connolly's parents had been good people—he had a decent job, she was in college, and they had been together since high school. Then he started selling to make some extra money, then he got hooked, and so did she. A little here. A little there. Until he started mooching off of Maureen until she could hardly pay her bills.

My wife, though, she was a fixer. She wanted to fix all things that seemed crooked. Except she was avoiding fixing the one thing she felt she had no control over: the death of her sister.

When she found out about the bastard who had killed her twin and their grandparents, I knew she assumed it was me who had done it.

It was.

She had called a truce at Sullivan's because of it. I'd earned her trust, and even more, had her heart without the tug of war —if I wanted it without the fight. There was more to it for me, though. I still had to bleed to win it, or we would never be square.

Her heart was worth the fight, the bloodshed.

It was worth my blood.

What I had done for her family, killing that bastard, was

payment on a debt my old man owed to hers. This—whatever it was between us—was between us.

One thing still puzzled me, though. She never tried to fix me—the crookedest motherfucker there was. Maybe it was because I didn't give a shit if she loved movies, or books, or Broadway, or even painting. I only cared if she was unhappy. I found myself wanting to kill anything that stood against what was best for her.

"Kelly."

When I blinked, Raff pushed the key closer to my face.

"A key." He smiled. "To one of the trucks that's going to make the load. Vegetables. They're going to hide them underneath a bunch of the earth's best."

Unless Lee Grady had changed the place or time at the last minute, things had happened too soon. Rocco had given me a specific time and place.

"Who?" I said, taking it from him.

"Colin." He searched my face. "He was in Sullivan's. Some of the Grady's have a table. He overheard them talking about a pricey vegetable delivery. Then they handed this kid a key. A few young guys have been going in and out, stopping at the table and leaving with a key. Colin followed him to the shitter and picked it right out of his pocket. Then he tripped him and flung the key to his Granny's apartment next to the kid. Told him his key fell out of his pocket and handed it to him. Doubts the kid even knows the difference."

Colin's granny was my secretary, Susan.

"He got a time and a place?"

"No," he said. "But he thinks he overheard something about a place that distributes vegetables."

"It's happening soon." We stood there, both of us thinking. After a few minutes, I started to move. "See if you hear anything on the street. I'm going to Sullivan's for dinner."

"Watch your back, Kelly," he said.

I lifted a hand, acknowledging the warning.

If I could figure out when this delivery was going to take place, and botch it up, not only would Grady be after me, but the Scarpone family, too. Grady had probably been running his mouth about how it was me stealing from them constantly. It was, but only to a certain degree—I only stole the drugs.

The Scarpones were smart enough to know they had a ghost out for blood. Their shit had started going missing while I was locked up. Grady never connected the dots, which made the Scarpones suspicious of him, but since things were fucking insane on their end with the ghost, it was hard for them to tell who was really doing the damage.

I stopped and turned before I got too far. Raff had his phone out, looking down at the screen. He looked up when I called his name.

"Colin," I said. "Stay clear of him until we talk again."

"Got it, boss." Raff smiled and then winked at me. He started walking in the opposite direction.

Sullivan's was packed with the dinner rush. It made the perfect place for the Grady's to handle their business. It was the perfect place for any of us. Sullivan's was considered neutral territory. We could talk business, even use it as a front from time to time, but not act on violent orders, or be violent, on the premises.

If anyone screwed up, they were never allowed back in again. It was the only rule we all abided by—that, and giving a pass to marked men who were with their women and children.

Grady wouldn't break Sullivan's rule, but he had already broken one that had become my top priority. After how close my wife came to paying for my sins, I gained two more eyes in the back of my head.

She was safe in Italy with Macchiavello and his family, and that was the only thing I truly understood was for the best. Her confusing behavior, though? Still not a fucking clue.

The necklace in my pocket felt like it had a heartbeat. Like she had put a spell on it, making it believe that it could be real.

"Fuck me." I ran a hand over my face, scrubbing a bit. I took out my phone and stared at it for a minute. Then I dialed her number. No answer. I called Maureen, my mole.

"She's staring at the phone." She sighed. "But the poor girl has been having a time of it. I've known a few mothers in my lifetime, but never one who could put the shame and guilt on her child like hers."

"I've never heard you call a girl 'poor,'" I said, not expecting Maureen to sound soft.

"Only another woman can understand the guilt a mother could cause her daughter." She paused. "But I guess sons would know a thing or two about that, as well, when it comes to fathers."

After I hung up, I stared at my phone again, but then I stuck it back in my pocket.

"Kelly, fancy seeing you here," Father Flanagan said, walking up. "Some dinner and a drink, my lad? It might help to ease your sorrows. My treat."

"I'll leave the drinking to you tonight," I said, squeezing his shoulder and then pushing him toward the doors. "Since you're enjoying this so much."

"Life wouldn't be life without a little fun!" He wiggled his eyebrows at me.

Father Flanagan opened the door as a young guy came out. The guy's hand was shoved in his pocket, his eyes averted. He didn't even notice me standing there. I followed behind him, keeping a respectful distance, until we came to Sullivan's delivery entrance. I stood with my back against the wall, watching as the guy hopped inside a truck.

Sal's Fresh Vegetables was scribbled in faded red ink on the side.

The truck came alive with a grumble, shaking some, and

then its lights came on. He put it in gear and took off. When he braked to watch for traffic, I stood behind the truck, memorizing the license plate numbers.

There was no doubt Sal's Fresh Vegetables was a front of some kind, and it was worth looking into. I heard another grumble, and right as I turned to look, a truck came barreling toward me. Its brakes screeched right before they held, and the truck came to a full halt.

Another guy jumped out, leaving the door open. "What the fuck, man?" he yelled. "What do you think you're doing?"

"You hit my leg," I said, tapping at it. "I'm calling the police." I acted like I was going for my phone.

"Hey, man!" He charged toward me, his arms open in a WTF gesture. "You're not going to pin this—"

When he was close enough, I grabbed him by the collar of his t-shirt and pressed my gun to his temple as I shoved him toward the wall of Sullivan's. "You have two breaths to decide if this gig is worth your life. If after two breaths you decide it's not, you have one to tell me where you're supposed to take this truck."

He went to open his mouth.

"One."

I heard the start of another engine, and his eyes flicked to the right for a second before he sucked in a huge gust of air and then told me what the fuck was up. He was given a key ahead of time, and told to come back to the restaurant after normal deliveries for final instructions. Then he spit out the address and time he just received. His code word was "leeks."

"Good boy," I said, patting his head. "Now run along. Not toward the restaurant, but home, wherever the fuck that might be. Because you know the devils in that room, and what they'll do to you—you don't want to know this one."

As soon as he took off, I climbed inside of the truck, right as the other one came from behind. The horn sounded and I put my hand out of the window, signaling for him to give me a second. I made a call to Father Flanagan because I knew the guy was going to rat—better the devil you know than the one you don't. I told the good Father to stop him from getting to Grady's table.

It was against all that he'd vowed to hurt anyone, but he'd lay the guilt on heavy. He'd probably ask him if his soul was in trouble. It was the sort of thing that fucked with your mind even more if it was already in despair. Like a priest showing up to your hospital room right before surgery to read you your last rights—on accident.

If that didn't work, he'd lock him in the closet. Even if the guy knew what was going on with the deliveries, his life would be spared, because I couldn't kill him if Father Flanagan had a hand in his capture. The father and I had made a deal long ago about that.

Setting the truck in gear, I made a call to Raff as I pulled away. "Head to Sullivan's," I said, my entire body jerking from the bumpy ride.

"I'm there now," he said, and I heard the chatter in the background when he opened the door.

"There's a boy you need to save from Father Flanagan's lecture before you take him to a safe house. If he hasn't gotten to him, you get to him without noise. Trucker hat over blonde hair. Plaid jacket. Ripped jeans and boots. Then I want you to call Colin and make sure he's with us for this ride. Tell him we found the place, Sal's, but nothing else."

"*Inconceivable*," he said, quoting that movie again. "You found a way in."

"Vegetables," I said. Then I hung up.

LATER THAT NIGHT, Colin sat in the passenger seat of an expendable car. His leg bounced up and down and he chewed his fingernails. He kept checking the rearview mirror.

"Let's go over this once more," I said. "You know what truck the keys Raff has belongs to, and the drugs are already loaded and waiting at Sal's?"

"I'm guessing about the key," he said, not looking at me while he spoke to me, but at the mirror again. "It has a number on it. And I'm guessing that since the trucks pretending to deliver vegetables to Sullivan's have 'Sal' painted on the side, that's where the drugs are. Or they have something to do with Lee. Worth a look."

I said nothing else the entire ride to Hoboken, and as we pulled in front of the center, I knew I'd been right. Sal's was the real deal. It was a front business for either the Scarpones or Lee Grady. The Scarpones had a few of them, including Dolce, one of the most popular Italian restaurants in the city.

"Where are the other guys?" Colin said, finally turning to look at me when I found a spot to park across the street. Trucks were lined up in the lot down the block from Sal's—ones that were not being used. All identical to the ones that had been "delivering" to Sullivan's. After I had another one of my guys do some digging, he'd found out that Sal's actually delivered to Sullivan's on the regular.

Nothing suspicious about it, until the trucks that came and went that day added up to the magic number seven. Either Sullivan was preparing for a feast made of vegetables, or the truck I stole was going to pick up drugs at the dock after regular delivery hours ended.

Bingo on theory two.

I stepped out of my car, going around to the passenger side, waiting with my back against the hood. A few seconds after I did, I noticed Raff pulling into the parking lot, going to get directions on where to go from there. He was going in place of the guy that was being held at one of the safe houses I had in the city.

Colin stepped out. He looked left and then right. "How are we going to do this alone, Kelly?"

"Trust, Colin McFirth," I said. "Do you trust me?" I looked him straight in the eye. Those were the exact words he had used right after he gave me the story about the key.

A second. Two. Three. He swallowed hard. Nodded. But said nothing.

It took over an hour for the truck Raff was driving to leave. It was one of the last ones. Raff didn't pass in front of us, but after he drove out of the parking lot, he pulled over a few seconds later. I didn't want Colin to see him.

I gave it another two minutes and then hit Colin on the chest. "No more trucks," I said. "We'll check the lot down the street. We can see if the number on the key matches any of them. If it does, we can use it to follow that one." I nodded toward Raff's truck. "We need to hurry, though. If he pulls off, we don't have shit."

"Yeah," Colin said, out of breath. He hadn't taken two steps.

We casually walked down the street, like we were going for a stroll, and then slipped into the parking lot without any trouble. The lot had one small light, and it haloed some, but it wasn't enough to truly see by.

I could see enough, though.

I lifted the key. "Number 22." I pointed to a row across from where we stood. "You check that one. Whistle if you find it."

Each of the trucks had a number painted on the side, toward the bottom, and they seemed to correlate with a number engraved on the key and written on a keychain.

Colin nodded and then hustled across to start looking. I stood with my back against one of the trucks, counting. *One. Two. Three. Four. Five. Six. Seven. Eight. Nine. Ten.*

A low whistle sounded.

Ten fucking seconds to find a truck that was one of many.

"Bingo," he said, when I found him, pointing to the faded 22 on the truck.

My smile came slow. I flung the key at him and he caught it. "You drive."

"Nah," he flung it back, and I caught it with one hand. "I didn't even bring my driver's license. And don't we have to wait for Raff to get in the back? Where is he?" He looked behind me, but didn't find anyone.

The key flew through the air again, this time harder, and it clanked against his silver ring when he caught it. "No time to wait for him," I said, then I took out my gun and pointed it at his head. "Get in the fucking truck and start it. Now."

"Kelly, don't do this."

"Don't do what, Colin? Set you up to get slaughtered? Raff, too?"

At one time, Colin and Raff had been tight. Apparently when loyalties change, so does the value of friendships. Raff had even taken a bullet for him when his girlfriend at the time tried to shoot him in the balls after she found out he'd cheated on her.

He lifted his hands. "I might've gotten the trucks wrong."

Lying to the end.

"It is what it is, Colin. The truck or the gun. You know if it's not mine, it'll be Grady's."

We stared at each other for a second.

"You can think about running," I said, reading the thoughts behind his eyes, "but you won't get far."

"You fucker!"

"Ouch. That hurt my feelings." I laughed, and then I took him by the collar and slammed him up against the truck. "You picked the wrong side."

He spit in my face, and after wiping it on my shoulder, I let go of his shirt, taking the key out of his hand. I opened the door to the truck and motioned for him to get in.

He did, his face determined, even though he was sweating. Then, with a satisfied grin, he started the truck. When it didn't blow, he whooped, shutting the door so fast that it was like he was shutting it on a monster he was able to lock out just in time. He pulled out of the lot, tires screeching, the entire truck tilting as he made the turn onto the street.

Then he hit the brakes to keep the truck from going over. That was when the entire thing went *boom*.

I shook my head, going to the actual truck with 22 painted on the side. I'd put a patch over it so he would assume it was the wrong one. Truck 22 would have blown as soon as it was started if I hadn't taken care of it. The one Colin had started was rigged by me. It didn't go *boom* until he made the turn, because I made it so.

21

KEELY

New York seemed like a battleground when I returned from Italy.

The news was reporting nonstop on the explosion of seven vegetable trucks that were leaving the docks. Masked men had stopped them, made the drivers get out, and then laced the trucks with explosives and blew them up. All of the trucks belonged to a company named Sal's that was located in Hoboken.

Sal himself—who was sweating profusely and constantly wiping his head with a handkerchief while on camera—had no clue why anyone would've wanted to blow up his vegetables. One of his trucks had even been blown up with a driver inside.

The driver of the truck in Hoboken was Colin McFirth, a man known to work for my husband, and he was the grandson of Susan, Kelly's secretary.

The pressure around Kelly's "business" seemed to be closing in because of it. Scott was around more often since the police were involved, and he did nothing but stare at me when we saw each other. And I hated, hated, that he could see something in me that I wanted to hide—the truth. He had been in the right for having the house searched.

I'd even catch Scott at the same grocery or on the same block. That same look he got when he was obsessed with a case was turned on me. He was determined to see a change in me, but he wouldn't.

My time away from Kelly only reinforced one thing. I loved the marauding bastard, though I hated his actions.

How could I justify loving someone who sold the thing that ruined CeeCee and Ryan's lives? I'd truly fallen in love with those children, and as much as I missed Kelly, I had missed Ryan, too. When we returned from Italy, I felt like I was finally home, but then again, it was hard to face my husband, not knowing what the truth was.

He hadn't defended himself or even brought up what had happened after I got home. I went to my room and he went to his, and instead of a hallway separating us, the distance felt further than Italy.

I wasn't budging on this, and neither was he.

The only small thing he did was leave a note on the counter, right by my favorite teacup, that said, *You cannot save people. You can only love them.*

I didn't want to change him, and I didn't want to save him. I actually fell in love with him as is. But I demanded a brighter future for children like CeeCee and Ryan. I never believed that one person could change the world, but one person could make a difference, even a small one.

Our silence stretched on for weeks, and the tension only grew thicker.

Kelly came home with wounds more often, and Harrison was busier than ever. Raff no longer went with me to practice, or wherever I needed to go. Kelly sent Harrison in his place, and if my brother needed to be someplace else, Harrison sent Lachlan.

I'd never met the side of Cash Kelly that was suspicious, but after I returned home from Italy, he appeared like Kelly's missing twin. There were times he ordered Harrison to take Maureen, the kids, and me to his house. Sometimes I would take the kids, and Maureen would go back to her apartment. She said that, in all the years she'd lived in Hell's Kitchen, she had never run from trouble, and she wasn't going to start—she was comfortable in her place. Other times, we'd go to a completely different house in the city.

Winter came, and it was time for my Broadway debut. It was a limited showing, but if things went well, they were thinking of extending dates. The thought didn't thrill me like it should've. After all those years of audition after audition, working hard at odd jobs to keep myself going until I got the part of my dreams...the night fell flat.

I didn't even feel excited. I only wanted it over and done.

My Mam was more excited than I was, and for the first time since I told her about my wedding to Kelly, she looked at me with pride again. It used to thrill me when she looked at me like that, like she didn't blame me for what happened to my sister. But again. It fell flat.

It was a subtle change in me, but one I noticed after spending time with Kelly. He never judged me. He never made me feel like I had to go in one direction or another to get his approval.

Even with Mari. I never showed her who I truly was because I wanted to be the better person for her. A sister she could look up to. The same way I always assumed I'd look up to my sister. Roisin seemed to have this impeccable moral compass, even at a young age. She'd take in wounded birds and they'd trust her right away. I'd throw rocks at car windshields to see how many it would take to make them crack.

Kelly seemed to understand better than most that it was impossible to change someone unless they wanted to change.

He taught me that I didn't need to be fixed, and that it was time for me to stop trying to fix other people.

We had a silent mutual agreement—to accept each other without changing each other—and it was one that I never knew I needed until he came along.

I never knew I needed someone like him until he came along.

His chaos had shaken up my false sense of peace, my life, and made the pieces fall around me differently. The pieces had never landed so perfectly before.

My eyes lifted for a second, catching Kelly through the mirror. After all of my family had gone to find their seats, he stood with his back against the wall, watching me.

"Your hands are shakin', darlin'," he said.

They were, but it wasn't from stage fright. It was from him. My body was highly aware of him at all times. My hands only trembled when he was around. At first, it was from the force, the anxiety, from hate. They trembled from pent-up love now. I hated the thing he did, but I couldn't hate him even if I tried anymore, which frustrated me sometimes.

I gave him a narrowed-eye stare before I turned back to the makeup in front of me, ignoring him like usual.

He spun my seat around, both of his arms locking me in place, and tilted the chair back. My eyes rose to meet his in defiance, even though my heart raced and my stomach plummeted.

"You've lost weight," he said, not looking at my body, but at my eyes.

"You look exhausted," I snapped.

"Someone hasn't been eating dinner."

"Someone hasn't been sleeping."

He searched my eyes before he leaned down to kiss me. I turned my face, giving him my cheek. He growled low in his throat, and it was the first time I'd ever seen him show any outwardly sign of emotion.

Kelly was fucking pissed.

His arms flexed as he held the chair in place. "Do this tonight. Or don't. That little girl will be all too happy to take your place. But from this moment forward, you do whatever the fuck makes your eyes light up. It's time to stop living for a ghost."

He let my chair go and I bounced before I settled. I hopped up from my chair before he left me alone.

"Kelly!" I said.

He stopped, his hand on the door.

"You first."

The arrow hit its mark. His shoulders tensed and his back stiffened. The cords in his neck were coiled tight. He never brought up what Scott had told him that day in the interrogation room, but I'd caught him staring at the picture of his father more than once. I knew he was wondering why the man would lie to him, if it was the truth.

Why hide him from his mother?

If the question lingered for me, it had to be playing nonstop for him. But I wasn't going to allow him to call me out on my shit when he refused to deal with his own. We both had ghosts to expel, and sooner or later, Cash Kelly would have to take a deep breath in and then face his.

22

CASH

She'd called me out on my bullshit.

It was true. I hadn't dealt with my issues. Mainly, did my old man lie to me, and if so, where was the woman I had once called mother?

If. If. If. Fucking *if*. It was triggering my insomnia.

Between my old man coming to me in his old ways and my wife coming to me in new ones, I averaged minutes of sleep every night. If that. It was the strangest thing I'd ever experienced in my life because I couldn't control it. It fucked with me beyond what I felt comfortable admitting to anyone.

I had admitted it to her, though, in my own way. Apart from Tito Sala, I had never told anyone that insomnia crept on me like a silent advisory, night and day. It was the only thing I'd never been able to bend to my will.

Until she came along.

She gave me something no one ever had before: A power that went beyond this world.

Peace.

Then she fucking stole it from me, which was worse than

never knowing what it felt like. Because once I had, it fucked me up worse than the insomnia.

No. It wasn't the insomnia.

It was her.

She was fucking with me in ways I'd never experienced before, and she was clever about it. The smartest adversary I'd ever been up against.

She refused to kiss me.

Refused to kiss me.

Gave me her cheek, like she was offering me her right after I'd assaulted the left side first.

She refused to sleep with me. She refused to fuck me.

If that wasn't cause enough to drive me to the edge, she found a loophole in my one demand: Eat dinner with me.

She didn't eat. Not really.

She'd take a bite or two of her food and then stare at me, arms crossed over her chest, like a spoiled fucking kid. She was losing weight, but it wasn't completely physical.

How did I know that? I couldn't fucking tell you. We were bound together by something I didn't have a word for. It was a feeling. Something that went beyond flesh and bone.

I didn't have bags underneath my eyes, either, and she knew that, too.

We were both at war with one struggle.

Sitting at our table, watching her pick at her food, while everyone—Maureen and the little girl—ate and carried on like nothing was wrong made me want to flip the table over. I'd found peace through chaos before, knew the meaning of it, and I was ready to claim mine again.

I needed fucking sleep like a heart needs an artery.

As if she could hear me, my wife's eyes rose to meet mine. She dropped the vegetable she'd just picked up from her full plate a second later.

The tension in my jaw was tight, sending shocking lines of

heat up to my temples. She wasn't playing games, not on this, and that unsettled me even more. The heart I stole from her was doing a wicked thing to seek its revenge—it had gone on strike and refused to beat. And that beat was what calmed every noise that was causing chaos in the emptiness for me.

I picked up my drink, putting it to my lips, wondering if the glass was going to shatter in my hand. Something soft tapped against my skin before the liquid touched my tongue. I looked down and saw Connolly, who had her hand on mine. She smiled and then inclined her head behind her. I turned to look. Maureen had set out a pie.

"You want dessert?" The sound of my voice echoed inside of the glass. I put the fucking thing down; I hadn't even taken a drink out of it. I glanced at her plate. "You ate all of *your* food." My eyes met my wife's again, but this time she rolled them at me.

Connolly giggled and shook her head, moving her warm hand on my arm and pulling herself up closer to my ear. "Ha-*ppy*," she whispered in a scratchy, low voice.

I narrowed my eyes at her and she narrowed hers back. She was getting plenty of practice in for later—her man wasn't going to know what to do with her someday, either. All female talk was in fucking code.

Instead of waiting for me to understand, she jumped up, going for the pie on the counter. Keely followed her, going to help. It was the only time she smiled, when she was doing something with one of the kids.

Books. Movies. Broadway. Archery. Even painting. Nothing compared to when she looked at those kids.

Connolly's smile was even bigger when she set the plate in front of me and then patted me on the head. Maybe she thought I was a big fucking cat.

"Ha-*ppy*," she repeated, staring at me.

She kept staring at me.

I looked around. Everyone was staring at me. Maureen was trying to hide her grin. Keely was scowling, as if I better do something then and there or she was going to fling the pie in my fucking face. I opened my mouth to speak, but I was met with a mouthful of whipped cream before I could.

I'd never heard a kid laugh so hard. Connolly doubled over, the spoon still in her hand, laughing so loud that the entire table started to do the same.

Except for me.

She'd just spoon-fed me like she tried to do her little brother.

Me.

A grown-ass man.

I tried to ignore it, but my wife's laughter rose above the rest.

A second later, Connolly came back with another spoonful, and this time, when she stuck it in my mouth, I bit down, not letting it go. I growled at her and she growled back. Pie was flying in all different directions, and it was a fucking sugary mess, but the kid was laughing so hard, I worried for her lungs.

In short, though, she was finally enjoying her life. She was comfortable in this house, with us.

I looked up before she came in with another spoonful and met Keely's stare. She was still smiling, but her eyes had changed. They were at war with the rest of her face. She couldn't hide the internal war that raged.

"Okay!" she said when she realized that I'd noticed it. She scooped Ryan up, making him laugh, and stuck him on her hip like he was made to sit there. "Bath time!"

Connolly gave me one more bite and then stuck a finger on each side of my lips, where my mouth dimpled from grinning at her. "Ha-*ppy*," she said again before she ran behind Keely, following her up the steps.

Maureen appeared beside me, going for my empty plate.

"It's not that hard," she said, patting me on the head. Yeah, I was a fucking pet that needed to be domesticated. "If you want to understand our language, you just have to pay attention. Now go get some rest. Because I pay attention, too. It's not only ghosts that walk these halls at night."

I followed the sounds of laughter coming from upstairs. Keely and Connolly were getting Ryan ready for his bath. Keely was helping the little girl hold Ryan.

"That's it, CeeCee," she said, helping her steady him on her hip. "He's heavy, but you can do it, baby girl."

Connolly stuck her hip out, trying to distribute some of his weight, a big smile on her face. While Keely ran his bath water, the entire bathroom smelling flowery, Keely started to sing. Maybe she could hear. Maybe she couldn't. But the little girl hummed along with her.

The change in Connolly was shocking.

Life. She had life in her.

Keely turned around to take Ryan from his sister and caught me standing there. "Need something, Kelly?" Her voice was flat, but she kept kissing his fingers while he tried to stick them in her mouth.

"Nothing but a good night's sleep, darlin'."

"You know which way the bed is," she said, turning around, giving me her back. "And it's not in here."

There was that touch again. I looked down. Connolly looked up. She had set her hand in mine. She pulled me in the direction of the master bedroom and nodded toward the bed. I took a seat, wondering what she was going to do after she left me alone. A minute later, she came back with a couple of books from the library.

"Are you going to read to me, lil' darlin'?" I said.

She shook her head and pointed at her chest.

"I'm going to read to you."

She gave me a sharp nod.

I sighed, staring at her for a minute. Resigned, I took the books from her and nodded to the sitting area in the corner of the room. Keely had set it up with two chairs.

"Pick a seat," I said.

She took the left one, her legs too short to reach the floor. But she settled in, getting comfortable. I read four short books to her ... and then I realized that my eyes had closed, and I had fallen asleep. It was dark outside when I woke up, insomnia hitting me hard in that spot where it usually did. But I had slept, if only for an hour or two.

A blanket covered me that wasn't there before.

THE NEXT DAY, I checked the clock on my dash. Twelve o'clock —lunch—sharp. I was meeting a retired judge who had been friends with my old man.

The valet came out to meet me, and I threw him my keys as I stepped out of my car.

"Mr. Kelly," he said, catching them. "Have a nice lunch, sir."

I nodded to him, walking through the door and breathing in the cool air of the country club. It smelled of old money and whatever was fresh on the menu. Maybe some kind of expensive fish.

I bypassed the people at the front desk. They knew better than to stop me. I had no patience for them, no manners, and I refused to play the power-trip game—they knew I had an appointment, so that was that.

Judge McLean stood as he waved me over to his table. We shook when I was close enough.

"Good to see you," he said, nodding toward the seat across from him. "I ordered you whiskey."

I pushed it toward him after I took a seat. "You enjoy," I said. "I'm driving."

He grinned at me, knowing better. There were only a few places I'd eat or drink from, and his country club wasn't one of them. Too many rats in the kitchen wearing suits and ties that wanted a big cat like me dead.

"I suppose you ate already?"

I nodded. "Big breakfast."

"Ah," he said, sitting back when his plate of fish was delivered. Right on time. They knew when he wanted his food and how it was supposed to be cooked. "Not that marriage has anything to do with breakfast, but I heard you got married. Congratulations." He lifted the whiskey I'd pushed toward him and then drank. "It would've been nice to get an invite to the wedding of the year, though."

Same here, I was going to say, but just nodded and told him I appreciated it.

He wasn't a man to shy away from talking business during lunch, so we went over a couple of things, and then I said something that made him look up from his almost empty plate.

"Adoption?" he repeated.

I nodded, taking the butter knife from the table, standing it up between my fingers. "Tell me about the process."

He wiped his mouth with his napkin and then signaled to the waitress. She came over right away, taking his plate, while another delivered him a slice of cake.

"Depends," he said, after she'd gone. "Through the regular system?" He shrugged. "Could take a while. But if you need this from me—it depends on who's asking." I figured he'd say that. His hands might've been dirty, but he grew up an orphan, and he was a huge advocate for children.

"I'm asking," I said.

His eyes narrowed. "Are you drunk, Kelly?"

I laughed, shaking my head. "No."

"Do you need to be?"

"Not this minute."

He stared at me and I stared at him. He finally sighed and nodded his head. "Tell me about the situation."

We talked for another hour or so about things before I left. The same guy brought me my car, and after I drove off, my front tire started to make noise, so I pulled to the side of the road. The country club was in a private area, separated from the rest of the world by a thick wooded patch, off the beaten path. Not too much traffic coming in or out for me to worry about.

I started rolling up the sleeves to my shirt before I even stepped out, having a clue as to what was wrong.

Yeah, the motherfucker had a flat.

I popped the trunk, going for the jack, tire iron, and spare. My head was lowered while my hands dug around, searching for the end of the cover over the tire so I could pull it up.

I heard footsteps, and before I could turn, something heavy rattled my skull. It wasn't enough to knock me out, but it did shake me some. Hands pushed me from behind, trying to force me into the trunk.

Bracing my knees against the bumper with one palm flat against the inside of the trunk so he couldn't easily shove me inside, I snatched the tire iron. It was a fucking struggle trying to get to my feet. He shoved while I tried to stand. Warm blood ran from the back of my head where he had hit me with a pipe or something equal to it.

The tire iron ended up in my left hand, and swinging blindly over my right shoulder, I cracked him on the forehead with it. He stumbled back a bit, giving me just enough time to turn around and brace myself for his attack.

He came at me again a second later, blood running from the top of his head, down his nose, into his eyes. "You're going to pay for that, motherfucker," he said, swinging a wooden stick in his hand. It whistled as it swung through the air. I dodged it a second before it struck me in the face.

Whoever he was—I had no fucking clue—he wasn't trying to kill me. He wanted to knock me out to get me in the trunk. I acted like I was going to fling the tire iron at his head, to give me time to grab for my gun, but he was too fast. The wooden stick came down with a *whap!* against my arm, sending a shock to my chest when I lifted my arm.

He must've trained using the stick. He swung it like a controlled weapon.

I danced with this guy, getting hit here and there, trying to use the tire iron to deflect his stick. My knuckles were busted from getting in the way too much. On one go, I met his stick in the air, and he pushed against me as I pushed against him. Suddenly, he let go, going back a step or two, and when he came back at me, I kicked him in the kneecap as his stick hit me in the ribs.

I lost my breath, but he lost his balance and fell to the ground. Even with him being down, I couldn't get close to him again. I knew he was going to use that stick to hit at me if I did. It was like a constantly striking snake.

Taking a deep breath, breathing in air and then releasing fire after I did, I took out my gun and pointed it at him. "You have five seconds to tell me who you belong to."

He wasn't with Grady, and he definitely was not a Scarpone. They would've whacked me and then hacked me. Or buried me in the woods to rot.

He lifted his head, laughing a little. "Go to hell," he said, right before he went to reach for something inside of his jacket.

"See you there," I said as I pulled the trigger and hit him in the center of his forehead.

He went completely still after the blast echoed around us and rattled the loose pieces of my skull. Moving his jacket to the side, I found the gun he was going for. He should've just used it from the beginning. Less trouble.

Again, though, he didn't want me dead. Which was fucking

strange. Not wanting to have a debate with myself on the street about it, I took him by a foot and dragged him across the cement, leaving him on the other side of my car. His head left a wet trail of blood.

What was I going to do with this fucking stick wielder?

I looked up as a car was coming from the direction of the country club.

It was an expensive make and model, and judging by the silhouette, a woman. She slowed when she came close, stopping over the main blood puddle. She rolled down the window. She was younger than I expected. "Do you need help?"

"Nah," I said. "Flat tire."

She stared at me for a second before she lowered her designer glasses. "Are you sure?" Her voice went lower, and her eyes were hard on mine, trying to establish the connection.

She could tell I was trouble, and in her plush life, exactly what she was probably looking for. A different kind of dangerous than the one she was probably married to. I was the one her husband called when he wanted someone snuffed out.

"Move along, miss," I said, leaning down to pick up the tire iron. "Your husband is waiting at home for his dinner to be served."

She huffed at me as she pulled off.

I checked my watch. Yeah. It was getting late and I had to get home to my wife. Even if she didn't eat, she still had to sit with me at the table every night while I did.

I touched my head and pulled back fingers stained with fresh blood. Maybe Maureen would be generous enough to stitch me up.

Sighing, I took the fucking stick wielder by the leg, dragging him toward the small patch of woods. More traffic might pass through soon if something was going on at the club. These were high-powered figures who didn't all think so highly of me.

That was the last thing on my mind, though. I kept going

back to why the guy didn't finish me off. He wanted me in that trunk.

It wasn't wise to rule anyone out, so taking that into consideration, it could've been Grady who sent him, or one of his men, or even someone the Scarpones paid. But again, it made no sense. They would've never come in that way, with a fucking whistling stick and only one guy.

It didn't fit.

They would've come in guns blazing—in and out. And not around here. Too many potential witnesses around such a high-profile place. Which backed up my theory about the stick wielder wanting to stick me in the trunk. He wasn't looking to cause a scene, or a mess.

My gut told me it was someone new. Someone unrelated —or not.

It wasn't unusual to be tested and tried. There was always a man, or two, who thought he was more ruthless, more powerful, more cunning than whoever controlled what they wanted. But the timing was too perfect. The man knew exactly where I was going to be at the exact time.

It smelled worse than this dead guy. It smelled like a rat.

I stopped for a second in the middle of the woods, looking around. I'd stick him against a tree and be done with it. I wasn't even going to bother hiding him. Though I'd leave that fucking stick with him. He might need it in hell.

23

KEELY

Nothing was the same.

After the night I caught CeeCee covering Cash with the blanket, I started to hate his actions even more, though on the other side, I loved him even more. Especially when he came home bloody and needing stitches. I wanted to go to him, to take care of him, but the spiteful part of me wanted him to suffer—a physical representation of what he was putting me through emotionally.

Except.

The guilt tore me up inside when I felt that way.

There was no winning with Cash Kelly. I couldn't just pick a side and stick to it. His "business" was a hard no for me. And even though I loved him, it wasn't enough to cover his transgressions.

But what was I supposed to do about it now?

I had accepted him for who he was, without knowing what he did, but whenever I'd look at CeeCee or Ryan, the disappointment would run high. Then I'd remember how he made her laugh when she'd stuffed the pie in his mouth. How he had growled at her and she had growled back. Like a normal kid who had no problems. The world was her friend. A good place to be.

I was in a sticky fucking situation and didn't know how to get out of it, or how to make it better. He still hadn't said a word to me either way. And I refused to bring it up. If he straight-out admitted it to me, I wasn't sure how I was going to cope with living with him—a man who distributed addictions to people who couldn't say no to them, after he acted like his community was worth killing for.

So I kept my distance from him.

Even after *The Blood Queen* had run its course and was coming to a close, our contact was limited. Something was going on that made me anxious.

Cash started acting different. More paranoid. He sent me with Harrison on a regular basis, having me sleep at his place, or at one of the other houses—safe houses—he owned in the city. Maureen would come so I could stay close to the kids. They kept me busy for the most part, which helped, because sometimes I missed him so much I physically ached for him.

And when he didn't show up for dinner some nights?

The grip I had on the television remote bit into my palm. I was watching some fucking sappy romantic movie that I was mad at myself for even putting on. I sighed, resting my head against the sofa, closing my eyes.

Maureen had taken the kids to the zoo. Harrison was at work, but I was going to meet him at home soon. And Raff? I wasn't sure where he was, but I hadn't seen him a lot lately. I assumed it was because his boss was in more trouble than ever and needed four eyes instead of two.

That left...me. And the thought of the marauding bastard.

I took out my cellphone and stared at it. What would I say if I called him? *I hate what you do but I love you more. Which makes me want to hurt you like you're hurting me?*

My phone lit up, interrupting my thoughts, and my heart started to beat faster. Then it calmed some.

"Hey," I said to Mari, resting my head against the sofa again.

"Come over," she said. "I have some cake."

"Cake?"

"The best. You have to try it." She paused. "Thirty minutes?"

"I'll be there."

I had to get out. The silence in the "safe" house was starting to sound like a dripping faucet.

Just from the tone of Mari's voice, I could tell something was going on with her, too. Knowing what I did about her husband and his business, it was no surprise that she was probably dealing with some shit, too.

I chirped the alarm on the car Cash had given me. He told me to consider it a wedding gift. He was sick of seeing my old car collecting rust on the street. It was a beautiful candy-colored green Corvette Stingray. It had tinted windows, and its black rims had matching green strips on the inside.

It was the most beautiful car I'd ever seen, apart from the family-safe car he bought for Maureen and me to use when we were transporting the kids around.

But in that moment, I needed fast. I needed free. Maybe I even needed to feel a little young.

Mari was waiting outside when I pulled up to her place. I shut the car off, but she waved her hands, signaling for me not to get out. She was racing to get in on the other side. Once she was, I took off, faster than she was expecting. Her head hit the seat. At least this time, though, we could take off. With my old car, we could've outrun it on foot.

"Okay." I eyed my rearview mirror, making sure we were not being followed. "Why are we running from your house?"

"I...need a break. I don't feel like being surrounded by men today."

"Ooh. The honeymoon is over. Let the games begin!"

"It's not a game, Keely. It's marriage." She waved a hand. "We just had a fight."

I tried to throw something out there, a random problem, but she wasn't taking the bait. I knew there was more going on than just a regular fight between her and Mac, but I didn't dig. She could sense something going on with me, too, and I wasn't ready to share. So being neutral for each other felt good.

"Answer one question," I said, taking the conversation in a different direction. "Do we hate him or not?"

"Not." She turned to face me. "Who's Cashel Kelly?"

Shit! Just his name made me anxious. I lost the grip I had on the wheel for a second and it swerved. Mari glanced at the mirror, like she thought maybe someone had been following us.

"Cash," I said underneath my breath. "Almost everyone calls him Cash. And Stone told you about him."

"Not exactly. He was fishing for information the night we had dinner."

We had dinner at her husband's restaurant after she got back from Italy. It was a little strained between us, just because of the situation between her and Harrison, but it felt good being together again. Scott had been following me that day, though. He'd watched me walk into the restaurant. So when the waiter told Mari that Scott wanted to see her, I left. She didn't need to be involved in my mess.

I nodded. "What did you tell him?"

"What could I tell him, Kee? I have no idea what's going on!"

"Cash Kelly is Harrison's new boss." Simple. Easy. In a perfect world.

She waited a few minutes. "And...?"

"He's not all he seems to be."

"That seems to be a trend lately. Go on."

I turned to her and narrowed my eyes, but since we were being neutral, I wanted to switch gears again. "Wait. Where are we going?"

She told me about these little figurines she wanted, but she asked if we could just pass by so she could get the name of the shop. I took a detour, heading in the right direction.

"Are you in love with Cash, Kee?"

It was hell when people truly knew you.

But love?

What I felt for Cash Kelly went past love. It was a gray area.

Maybe because my feelings had finally caught up to me, I threw back my head and exploded with laughter. "If New York was a wild cement forest, I'd be the archer and he'd be my target."

"I don't like the picture you painted in my mind. I keep seeing him running away from you, a bullseye on his back."

I grinned and then changed the subject, choosing to harp on the positive for a while. A few minutes later, I found a spot in front of the store. We had some time. I could run in and get them for her. The shop wasn't far from Dolce, one of the most popular restaurants in the area. Maybe we could even have lunch.

Mari shook her head. "I only need the name, Kee! Let's go. We'll go shopping somewhere else."

I studied her face. "Why is your face pale? You have bubble sweat over your lip, and it's colder than a polar bear's oonie outside. Did something happen to you here?"

She bit her lip, fiddling with her purse. "Yeah. I had some bad veal *parmigiana*. Just awful."

My bullshit meter exploded. "Liar." I squeezed her hand but decided we could do lunch another time. "You stay put. Keep the doors locked. I'll just run in and see if they're still there. They obviously mean a lot to you."

I hustled across the street to get to the little shop before she could stop me. She had mentioned that the night she found them, they had been in the window. They were all gone. The shop owner was nice enough, but he said that someone had come in right before me and bought them. He gave me the number to a place in France that might have more. They were antiques.

Bracing myself for the cold, I left the warm shop, walking past a few men coming out of Dolce. I didn't allow my eyes to linger, but I couldn't help but notice the tattoos on all of their hands.

Wolves.

The same tattoo Mari's husband had on his hand. Except Mac's wolf was black with electric-blue eyes.

One of the guys, the one with the hardest eyes, watched me as I walked across the street and got into my car. He stood there, staring, like he owned the entire world.

"Keely." Mari looked even paler. "Get us the fuck out of here!"

"You know them?" I looked in their direction while I started the car.

"Fucking go!" she shouted.

"All right! All right!" I swerved into traffic, barely missing a taxicab. He shot us the bird as he whizzed past. Then he got in front of us and kept tapping on his brakes. "Was that the Scarpones?"

"How do you know that?" She seemed truly scared—the kind of scared she'd avoided while on the street. But something else moved behind her eyes. Hate for them.

"Fucker!" I laid on the horn. The asshole was determined to make me slam into him from the back, or get sick from the constant stop-and-go. This car was smooth and fast, and I whipped around, giving him the bird as I passed him up. Then, because I was on the edge, I did the same thing to him. Cut him off and then tapped on my brakes. "I've heard things. I was curious so I looked them up online. I didn't find anything too juicy, but those tattoos mean something, don't they?"

Again, after I suspected Mac wasn't an average man, I tried to do more research on him. I could never find anything that hinted to anything. Not a fucking clue. Until I asked an old gangster that lived in our neighborhood if he knew what the wolf tattoo meant.

"Yeah," he'd said. "Bad news. Scarpones have them. Which means stay on the opposite side of the world from 'em if you can."

"It doesn't matter." Mari waved off the tattoos, clearly trying to downplay the fact that her husband had one, too. "They kept staring. It scared me."

"It should. They're insane."

"Yeah, I got that."

She had her shit to deal with. So did I. Neither one of us wanted to go there. Maybe later, but the time wasn't right. I knew my husband was in trouble, he was in the middle of a war, and even if her husband was in the same game as mine, it was best to keep our secrets for the time being.

"Bad news." I blew out a breath. "No more figurines."

"What happened to them?"

"Someone wiped them out." I checked my outside mirror and then went a different way. "Maybe you can find another store that has them. They're French, like you thought. Antiques. The seller said they're rare. Expensive. He told me to try a place in Paris. He wrote down the name. I have it in my pocket." I told her to ask her friend Scarlett if she knew of the place. Scarlett was married to Brando Fausti, who was Rocco Fausti's brother. Scarlett had been a ballerina in France at one time.

After a few minutes, Mari looked around. "Where are we going, Kee?"

"Harrison's. I told him I'd swing by later, but then you called. I've been meaning to give him his baseball glove from when he was little. When we moved out of Mam's place, somehow it got mixed with my stuff and I kept telling him I forgot it at home whenever he asked me for it. I took it to Home Run without telling him and had Caspar frame it with his old jersey. I was hoping to surprise him. I never bought him a house-warming gift. And he got a new puppy. I've been dying to see it."

The real reason I wanted to go was because I wanted Mari and Harrison to stop avoiding each other. Even though there was nothing romantic there, they could still be friends. I missed us all being together.

"I don't think that's such a good idea, Kee. I should go home."

"Come on, Mari. You can still be friends with him. We don't have to stay long."

She nodded, but she was quiet on the ride over, checking the mirror every once in a while. I did, too, because for some reason, after we'd pulled off, I got a very bad feeling in that sensitive spot on the back of my neck. Like some wild animal was about to take a bite out of it.

THERE WAS some awkwardness between Harrison and Mari when we first arrived at his house, but I knew after a little time, it would work itself out and things would be fine. We would establish a new normal, and maybe, with more time, Mac could even be welcomed into our group as family.

Harrison had been seeing Mac's cousin, Gigi, ever since Mac and Mari's wedding. Gigi was a big actress in Italy, and even though she made my brother smile more than I'd ever seen him smile—even though he refused to admit it—I didn't like her. She had it in for Mari for some reason, and that didn't sit well with me. It didn't sit well with me that Harrison seemed to be using Gigi to make Mari jealous, either, but that was their problem, and for once, I was keeping my nose out of it.

Though for the sake of the relationship we once had—my brother, Mari, and me—I wanted them to work it out. I missed my brother. I missed my sister. The shit needed to end.

It felt like a good idea after I'd seen them together, but then Mac showed up after Mari excused herself to use the bathroom. It was like he had timed his arrival to the second Mari went into the house.

He strode across Harrison's lawn, a look on his face I'd never forget—a fucking jealous husband out for revenge—and punched Harrison in the face.

My brother saw him coming and rose up to the challenge.

I'd lived with boys my entire life. I let them go at it for a while, because usually, after they punched each other, they were square.

It was a pretty good show, too, since the neighbors decided to bring out chairs and watch them pummel each other like two dogs who'd been released from a cage.

I wondered what Cash would think about it, but then stopped thinking about him when a car made a round or two. Something about it didn't sit right with me.

Again. The tingle.

Maybe I was hanging out with gangsters too much, becoming paranoid, but something told me to keep my eyes open. I couldn't do that with the two animals on the front lawn, rolling around on the grass, starting to draw more blood.

Casually, I took out the hose, set it on the sharpest spray, and then set it on my brother and Mac. It took them a moment to realize that I was blasting them with cold water. Harrison had had the hose on him over the years, but I doubted anyone ever had the balls to pull a hose on Mac.

I'd whip his ass, too, if he had anything to say. I wasn't to be trifled with. I was on edge.

My brother shot up first, his hands in the surrender position. Blood ran from his mouth. Mac stood right after, and I hit him in the chest with the water again, because I could tell the lunacy still ran high in those cold blue eyes.

"That's enough!" I yelled. "The both of you!"

"I—" My brother went to defend his actions, but I hit him with the spray again, cleaning his mouth out.

"Harrison." I kept my voice low. "Knock it off. You know I won't let up until you stop with the excuses. Now get your ass inside before you catch cold!"

"Sissy boy," Mac muttered as Harrison walked off. Harrison shot him the bird.

I hit Mac with the hose again. "You! I'll get you some dry clothes, but only if you shut it!"

He narrowed his eyes at me, and I narrowed back. He wasn't going to intimidate me. If he was going to be a part of this family, he was going to get treated just like everyone else. There would be no tiptoeing around him because he was a badass. He could join the club.

Mac's eyes moved from mine to my brother's porch. Mari had come outside, the dog right behind her.

"What are you doing here, *mio marito*?" she said.

He didn't answer, and I got the feeling he was waiting for me to give them some privacy.

I took the hose and started rolling it up, going to the side of the house. I still heard his answer, though. "I've come to collect my wife. She ran out on me."

Yeah, it was something in the fucking water lately. I would've blamed it on a full moon, but crazy shit seemed to be happening night *and* day.

I rolled the hose up, standing against the house after, my back to it so I could watch the street. A few minutes had passed, and the same car started to creep toward us again. I couldn't see past the windows because they were tinted.

"Have you seen that car before?" I said to them, rounding the house.

Mac and Mari looked in the same direction as I was. He was on his knees in front of her. After he noticed the car, he stood, keeping Mari behind him.

"No," Mari said, moving her head around him to see better. "I haven't."

"I have," I said. "It's passed a few times."

"Down!" Mac roared. His voice was usually jagged, but it came out so clear. He pushed Mari to the ground, but all I could do was watch.

My entire body froze, and I had the weirdest fucking thought when it did. *Cash Kelly.* It wasn't my mind. It was my heart. It cried out for my husband. Maybe because I knew I was about to swallow a few bullets.

Then I was on the ground. Mac's body landed on top of mine as bullets sprayed the house, right where I'd been standing. They sounded like fireworks exploding around me in daytime. Pop. Pop. Pop. Pop. Pop.

I wasn't sure what happened as the sound of gunfire faded. It seemed like everything happened in a blur of time, and I was stuck on the ground, still frozen. But I could hear. I could hear so clearly the words moving around me. They were as loud as the gunfire.

"Call Kelly and fill him in," Mac said. "He needs to know about this. There's no telling who he fucked with and pissed off. This might be retribution in the form of a life he considers important to him."

"How did you know about—"

"Get to work, Harry Boy. It's not safe to chat in the street."

Sirens grew closer.

"Mac?" my brother called. "You saved my sister."

"Make sure you tell Kelly he has a tab."

Hell's Kitchen was officially boiling over, and I'd finally gotten burned.

24

CASH

I ended the call. I stared at the wall in my office for one, two, three seconds. On the fourth, the *boom* exploded inside of my skull and I stood, going for the door. Outside, I unlocked the armored matte black Hellcat that I'd bought from a guy Rocco knew. He actually knew a guy who knew a guy—he was the best in the business, and he only answered to men like Rocco. If he put in the order, you were in.

There was some traffic on the streets, but I made it to my destination without an issue. I parked, turned the car off, and then reached into the console for the knife I had stashed there. Since my suits were custom made, I slipped it inside of the pocket I always had the tailors add inside of the jacket.

I entered the building and went up two flights of stairs. Molly, my old man's widow, answered the door on the second knock.

She said nothing and neither did I for a minute or two.

Molly and I were on all-right terms, but after my old man's death, the thing we had in common ended. I'd see her around sometimes, but that was the extent of it.

My patience was legendary, so with a sigh, she stepped back and opened the door.

Nothing of my old man lingered inside of the apartment. Not even pictures. It didn't take her long to move on. Over the years, I'd hear about the men she'd hook up with, but she had been with the man smoking on what used to be my old man's fire escape the longest. The window was open, and he turned his head, meeting my eye.

"Cash Kelly." Brian Grady took a puff of his cigarette and blew it out in a long stream. "Come to give me an ultimatum?"

Brian Grady was Cormick's younger brother and Lee's uncle. He was a decent fella who didn't meddle in the family business unless they were in a pinch. Lee looked up to him, though, and I knew when he needed an ear, it was Brian who listened to and counseled him.

"You wouldn't!" Big Mouth Molly yelled from behind me.

Killian used to call her that. He never warmed up to her. I kept lukewarm, not caring either way, as I usually did. But the reason she suddenly had such an interest in my coming here was because my old man left eighty percent of the building to me. The other twenty percent was hers.

Since I held the most stock, if I decided to sell, she would either have to buy me out or sell out. She had lived here most of her life, and she was comfortable not having to pay rent, living off of whatever my old man left her, so she didn't want any trouble with me. But her default setting when she was pissed was to yell.

"Move along, Molly," I said, not even turning to look at her. "That temper will get you nowhere with me."

Things became quiet, but I could read her reaction by the look on Brian's face. After a moment, he took another drag off his cigarette and then nodded. I felt the air move when she left. Five seconds later, right on time, the door to her bedroom slammed.

"If I wanted you out of this apartment," I said, "I wouldn't need to own most of the building to do it."

"True," he said, eyeing me. His head was turned toward me, but his body faced straight. "Business then."

"Personal." I reached inside of my jacket, pulling out the knife. "You or me, but either way, you're delivering the message."

He narrowed his eyes at me. "You doin' this for your wife?"

"I'd do much worse for much less done to her."

"I told Lee," he said. "I told him not to fuck with your woman. I advised him not to get involved with the Scarpones either. The boy listens when he hears words. The rest of the time he only hears dollar signs." He shrugged, turning forward, putting out his cigarette on the cast iron ladder.

He took another minute or two, and then he shook his head. "He's going to die regardless," he said. "But I get it. He'll get pissed enough to find you—if the Scarpones don't get to him first." He sighed, stood, stretched his arms over his head, wiggling the nine fingers he had, and then used the window to step into the apartment.

The smell of smoke lingered on his clothes as he rummaged around a kitchen drawer for a minute. He pulled out a knife used for hacking between the bones of an animal about to be put on for dinner. Brian knew his way around a butcher shop, since his brother and grandfather had been butchers.

He lifted the knife up to me. "Mind if I use my own?"

"I'd rather keep mine clean."

"As long as this'll do."

"That or your heart."

"The finger is worth more than a heart. You can get more done with it."

"I have no problem taking your heart, since it's worthless."

He met my eye for a long second before he took a firmer

grip of the knife, proving his words bullshit. He didn't want to die because his nephew was a fucking moron.

He set his hand on the chopping block on the counter. It still had carrot pieces on it. He narrowed his eyes for a second, and then, bringing the knife up, he came down with a hard *thwack!* His middle finger disconnected from his hand as soon as the knife connected with the block. It tilted a little before it righted itself. The nail still had a blood bruise where he must have hit it with a hammer.

He must've done it when he was hanging a picture of him and Molly taken at Sullivan's bar. I'd noticed the hammer and nails on a table right under where the picture was hung when I was making my way through the apartment. It was the same place she had a picture of her and my old man back in the day.

I handed him a dishtowel that was hanging on the oven. He applied pressure for a minute before using it as a tourniquet. He lifted both of his hands, a grin on his face. "At least now they match."

My old man had cut off his other middle finger years ago, when another war had been going on between Cormick and my old man.

"Consider your name Carver Turkey," I said. "One more move against my wife, and I'm going to serve you to your nephew on a fucking platter."

He waved the hand at me, the blood seeping through the dishtowel, like the crazy son of a bitch he was. "Gobble Gobble. I'll be sure to tell him."

Brian was like a father to Lee, and after losing his own, he wasn't going to risk it. Whenever Lee was in trouble, Brian either hid him or got him out of it. This time, though, Brian knew the end game was coming—either from the Scarpones or me. Brian might not convince Lee to give up the entire game, but he would convince him to leave my wife fucking out of it, or he'd be the one paying the price for his nephew's decisions.

As I shut the door to the apartment, I heard Molly yelling from inside. The volume of it rattled inside of my skull until I was about ten minutes away and consumed by my own chaos. The madness went up a notch after I pulled up to Harry Boy's house and found it surrounded by cops.

I nodded to Harry Boy, who was talking to a detective, as I made my way closer to his door. My wife sat on the porch, and when she saw me, she stood. Her face became a mask, but not before I noticed the relief that made it to her eyes before she hardened her resolve.

She could act on a Broadway stage for thousands of people, fooling each and every one, but there was no fucking fooling me. She wanted me here, no matter how much she despised that she did. My theory was further proved right when I took her by the arm, leading her toward the car, and she didn't put up a fight.

After I opened the door for her, she stared at me, like she had something to say. Or maybe she expected me to say something.

Instead, I lifted my hand, and letting my fingers brush across her skin as I did, I tucked a wild curl behind her ear. Her eyes closed and her hand came over my wrist, her grip tight. We stood that way for a minute or two, until she opened her eyes, shook her head, and got inside of the car.

She slammed the door before I could close it.

25

CASH

R occo Fausti came to see me the day after Harry Boy's house was shot up and my wife almost got riddled with bullets.

Which was exactly what should have happened to me if it was Lee Grady or the Scarpones at the country club.

It was hard to pinpoint who ordered the hit, but it didn't really matter in the end. They were in this war together—until they turned on each other. Someone was going to find someone else dead soon. My bets were on Grady floating up first.

The Scarpone family was known to chew off their own legs to save their hearts, and it would take more than Grady to destroy them.

Ah. Lee Grady. This was his big break, and I watched it go *boom* right in front of my eyes. He might not chew off his entire leg to save his heart, but he'd drag the leg, still trying to get a hit in on me before his last breath. Especially since Brian lost a digit.

Either way, between Macchiavello and me, we had almost crippled both operations.

Rocco watched me for a moment, taking a sip of his

whiskey, grinning. "It wasn't the night that I expected, but the end is the end, ah? *Verdura* trucks." He shook his head.

I leaned forward in my seat some, watching his face. "What is Macchiavello going to want for this? That was a lot of money that went up in flames."

It was nearly impossible to break the barrier the Scarpones and Grady had put up at the dock. There were too many men crawling around, looking for any excuse to put a bullet in someone, even when they assumed I was the one who'd been blown up in Hoboken as the deal had gone down.

The Scarpones and Lee Grady had made one massive mistake, though—they assumed.

Instead of guarding the trucks, they put all of their manpower at the dock, not on the trucks leaving with millions of dollars worth of drugs.

Even if they would've had more security on the trucks, I wasn't letting them get past a certain point. So I cut them off and blew them up, but I didn't know what it was going to cost me with Macchiavello.

Rocco took another drink of whiskey and then set it down. He fixed his tie and got more comfortable in his seat. "Nothing. The job is done. However." He took out another card from his pocket and laid it on the table, pushing it closer to me.

Another favor.

I owed him my life for saving my wife, so I picked it up and said, "Consider it done."

He nodded. "You have made your point here. You have done what's needed to be done. Even though Grady is retaliating, he is not as powerful as he used to be. You run Hell's Kitchen now, just as your father did."

He watched me for a minute. "I will be in touch when it is time." He nodded toward the card. "It will be soon. You will need a few of your best men. Men you trust as much as you can. Give very little detail except for this: Their life will be at stake if they do not arrive at the exact time and do exactly what you say. A man's life will depend on the minute—a man I consider blood."

"I'll take care—"

He shook his head. "Take your wife and go somewhere. You run this now." He looked around. "You should be as far as possible from the chaos that will ensue after this. If you prove to the world that you have competent and dangerous men who follow you—" he shrugged "—you will gain respect from my side of the world."

"Stone," I said. "He'll be all over it."

"Everyone who means something will be all over this— there will be a meeting with the families after this is done. Things will change. However, Stone is out of the picture."

I narrowed my eyes. Even though I understood his subtle language, sometimes things got lost in translation.

"He has been suspended from duty." Rocco took another drink and then stood. "No one fucks with my family and gets away with it."

I nodded, standing, and offered him my hand. We shook, and he squeezed my shoulder.

"Tell me about the other threat," he said.

"Same shit, different day." I grinned. It was no surprise that he knew about the country club—whatever that was meant to be. He also knew that before I took care of the problem, I had to make sure my finger was pointed in the right direction.

Rocco seemed to think about it for a minute before he nodded. "*Bene.*" He shook my hand even harder and then went for the door. He stopped before he opened it and said one word. "Dolce."

After he'd gone, I sat back in my seat, staring at the wall.

Dolce.

The restaurant the Scarpones used as a front. It was their personal pride and joy. A place they used for family functions, and on certain Sundays of the month, they got together for family dinners.

The head of the Scarpone family, Arturo, was paranoid about too many people memorizing his routine after a man named Corrado Palermo, one of his closest, had tried to slit his throat. Arturo switched it up every so often to keep enemies guessing. It also made it easier to pinpoint the rat in his family if another attempt was ever made on his life. He kept his circle as close as lifeblood after the first attempt had failed.

I whistled long and slow, then took a deep drink of my whiskey. It went down like honey and caused a nice fire in the pit of my stomach.

Maybe it wasn't the whiskey doing the magic; maybe it was what was about to happen.

Dolce only meant one thing.

Macchiavello was going to end whatever fucking vendetta he had against them, and he was going to use some of my men in the game. After word got around that I was part of it, I'd be considered the real fucking deal to the families, and to my own people, stronger than my old man.

In this life, nothing was ever given. It was fucking hard-earned.

You wanted respect. You had to give up some blood. And I'd donated plenty.

26

CASH

About a month later, I got the call from Rocco. The plan was simple and clean and no problem, but he insisted that I needed to get out of town before the job went down.

I decided to take my wife to Ireland, along with Maureen and the two kids. Keely insisted, since Ryan was old enough to travel.

I hired a private plane, and we took a red-eye out of New York five minutes before my men stormed Dolce with weapons drawn. The instructions were clear—take out these people and these people only. The rest was not my concern.

Rocco phoned me while we were somewhere over the Atlantic to say, "I heard the weather was clear for a good flight." Then he hung up.

That meant whatever debt I owed Macchiavello had been paid in full—we were square.

Before we returned to New York, I was determined to get square with the woman who shot daggers at me as I drove through the streets of Derry in Northern Ireland. I'd made arrangements for Maureen and the kids to spend time with a cousin she had in Dublin. It was a three-hour drive from there, and the ride had mostly been silent.

My wife spent her time taking pictures, only asking me to slow at the Free Derry sign, and then looking it over on her camera after she'd taken a few. Even after we pulled up to the house I spent some years in as a kid, we barely spoke a word to each other.

She stopped in the hallway after I'd placed her bags down. "This place belongs to your family?"

"To me," I said, watching her face. Her neck was tinged red. It seemed like she had a lot to say to me, but she refused. Her temper was creeping up her neck, no place to go, since she refused to say what was really on her mind. "It belonged to my grandparents before."

"Where will I sleep?"

I nodded toward the main bedroom. "With me."

"No," she said, going to pick up her bag, but I put out a hand to stop her. She let it fall with a clang to the floor. "I'm only holding up my end of the deal. I eat dinner with you. That's it, Kelly."

"You don't eat," I said.

"I do."

She looked as scrawny as hell. I looked as tired as the devil himself after he'd tried to convert a hardheaded woman. Our internal wars were finally coming through the physical.

What the fuck were we doing?

What the fuck was *I* doing?

How did I even get here? Caring whether or not this woman ate with me. Caring whether or not this woman fucked me.

I cared because all of a sudden, she felt vital to me. Like a saving grace with heavenly eyes and a wicked tongue that had a dangerous power over me. Her presence softened my guard, like a lullaby, but her backbone, her good bones, made me trust.

I trusted her.

Completely.

Even though she fucking hated the thought of me at present.

I trusted this woman.

What the fuck have I done to myself?

Bad bones, no heart, she still wanted me as is. She hated that she'd accepted me. She hated that she loved me without expectations. She loved me regardless of the things she felt I did wrong.

Her love had her hate pinned down, on its knees, making it scream out in anger before it forgave and then begged for mercy.

She loves me.

I'd stolen her heart, not truly understanding the consequences of actually claiming a heart like hers.

Love was like death in that way. We didn't get to decide.

The realization sent a shock to my chest and jolted me out of my thoughts. I blinked, realizing how hard I'd been staring at her. I had to stop myself from doing it again, from allowing her to completely consume me.

"Kelly," she said, snapping at me. The heat rose from her neck, staining her cheeks. "The look on your face."

"You can't read my face," I said, though I knew she had. How fucking dangerous—not even my old man could read my face. My twin. He was the only one.

She narrowed her eyes, pointing at mine, moving her finger from left to right. "I did. And I don't like what I felt after." Then she shook the digit at me, like I was being a naughty fucker.

"Enlighten the lost."

"You realized something."

"If I did?"

She put a hand to her neck, probably to cool the burn. "I'm mature enough to admit that I know what this means, but I refuse to talk about it. Because this—" she motioned between us "—is what it is. I thought maybe it had a chance to go somewhere, but I was wrong. So fucking wrong."

I pointed behind her, toward the main room. "Your room."

"I'm *not* sleeping with you."

"I'm going to take the other room."

She stood there for a minute, staring at me, waiting, so I took her suitcase and mine, moving past her, leaving hers by the bedroom door.

"Be ready by eight," I said. "Dinner."

"I'm tired," she said.

"I'll wait."

SHE WAS ready by eight sharp.

I doubted she was hungry, only trying to prove me wrong if I'd assumed she'd make me wait until the wee hours of the morning to eat dinner.

She stared at me and I stared at her.

She was wearing all black, and with the color of her hair, she reminded me of a fire in the middle of the night. And those heavenly blue eyes, my heaven, were tinged with red.

"No matter how much you look at me like that, I won't be swayed on this, Kelly." She tucked a strand of hair behind her ear, her wedding ring catching the light for a brief second. She used her pointer finger to wipe at the corner of her eye. Then she looked at me again. "Such a waste."

"Me," I said.

"No." She shook her head. "What's between us—the hope

that it could grow. I accept you. This. For what it is. Because believe it or not, for a time, it felt perfect. How it was supposed to be. Even with the fucked-up circumstances that brought you to me." She touched her neck, over her pulse point. "But when I look at CeeCee and Ryan, in good conscience, I can't accept adding poison to any community. Not like that. Not when it hits so close to home."

Before I could say anything, or she could see the truth on my face again, she moved past me in a whirlwind. Her usual bold scent had changed. It smelled metallic. The scent of her blood. She'd opened a vein right in front of me, not even expecting me to stitch her up, but doing it because she believed in a cause she felt I was fucking with.

I was right behind her as she made her way to the car. I knew it was going to be a quiet trip, and it was. She turned her face away, staring out of the window. We parked, and even as we walked the streets, she kept her distance, keeping herself occupied with the sights around her instead of me.

I directed her to the old pub off of Waterloo, and as I stepped inside, the noise pulsated inside of my head after being surrounded by her silence for so long. I took my wife's coat and set it over my chair at the bar. The black sweater she swore came to her midriff, and her black pants flowed down her long legs. Her hair was a wild storm of red curls, and her blue eyes glowed under the dim lights, making the few freckles over her nose more pronounced.

She was fucking perfect, and it was attracting attention. I stared at one fucking wanker until his eyes moved from my wife to me. He turned away a second later, laughing with his bunch of pussy friends.

My wife flicked me on the hand, and when I looked at her, she had an expectant look on her face. She nodded toward the barmaid. "Bar food good for you, Kelly?"

I nodded, turning to look the barmaid in the eye. "And whiskey. Keep our glasses filled."

The barmaid stood still for a moment, staring at me like she'd seen a ghost. Her hair was black and her eyes were blue, but they didn't hold the same power as my wife's. "Kelly," she repeated.

I grinned at her, and her breathing picked up. "Not the first time you've seen a man who looks like me," I said. "Tell me where he is."

"Who?" she said, lying through her teeth. Her hands shook against the old counter. Her left hand had a gold band on it.

"Killian Kelly," I said, flagging down the man working next to her. "Two glasses. Whiskey." Then I looked back at her. "You can tell me now." I shrugged. "Or I wait."

"Fair warning," my wife muttered, taking her glass from the barman. "He has the patience of a saint."

"You'll be waiting a long fucking time," the barmaid said, suddenly venomous. Her "fucking" sounded like "fecking."

"Doubtful. Once the live music starts."

Her eyes widened. "He doesn't want to see you."

I relaxed, putting an arm behind my wife's seat, taking a drink of my whiskey. A man came from the back room holding a guitar, and the barmaid scrambled to get out from behind the bar, pushing through the crowd.

A man who looked just like me rolled his wheelchair toward the stage, the crowd patting him on the back, letting him through, before he rolled up the incline and took his spot in front of the light.

The barmaid hadn't been quick enough. His entrance had blocked her from reaching him in time. She stood in front of the stage, waving at him, but he only waved back. He started to sing. Instead of watching him, though, my eyes were on my wife. Her eyes were glued to the stage, and when she finally turned to me, she grabbed for her whiskey and downed it in one shot.

"He sings," she said, her breath like straight fire that went to my lungs.

I nodded.

"He can *really* sing," she said. Not, *he's in a wheelchair; he sings.*

"Seems like music is a thing with Irish twins," I said.

"Can you sing?"

"Just because I can doesn't mean I do," I said.

"That's not really an answer."

"If it has stripes and teeth like a tiger—" I shrugged "—it is one, darlin'."

She watched my face, her shock and curiosity waning the longer she did, and then she turned back to the stage. I turned to my food, eating what the barman had brought out. Every once in a while she'd take a bite or two, but she hardly ate anything.

She was still on strike.

Letting my napkin fall to the plate, I sighed, turning toward the stage. He had moved on to the slow, tear-jerking shit. My wife's shoulders seemed slumped. Slowly turning her stool toward me, I found tears slipping down her cheeks. She didn't even bother wiping them.

"This song is for you," she whispered, putting a hand to her throat. She was purposely controlling her breathing, trying not to lose her shit over his shit.

"Nothing is fucking for me," I said, downing another glass of whiskey. "I only exist in songs, in dreams, to him."

The song finished to applause, and after thanking the crowd, he rolled off the stage, meeting the barmaid. She leaned down, and as soon as she did, he grabbed her face and kissed her. When he pulled away, a smile strained the corners of his mouth, and it was always fucking weird to see my face with that kind of freedom on it.

The easy smile melted as soon as her mouth came close to his ear. His eyes narrowed, and he started searching. It didn't take him long to find me.

I lifted my hand and grinned—but it wasn't fucking friendly. I was up against a wall, a version of me that I loved more than myself, and I had to harden my resolve toward the rejection.

The crowd parted for him as he moved toward me faster than he could have if his legs worked. He came to a stop right next to my stool.

"When did this happen?" I said before he could say anything. "Last I checked, in your profession, kissing romantically was forbidden. You did write in your 'Dear Brother' letter that you were moving back to Ireland to become a priest."

"Go," he said, pointing toward the door. His face was flushed from the performance, and sweat coated his skin. It was me after an intense workout to burn off some steam.

"After I get what I want," I said, forcing my voice to relax. His blood ran through mine, and the rejection felt like a vital organ denying its body.

His eyes locked with mine, knowing me as well as I knew him. I wouldn't move until he did. "What do you want?" His voice was low, shredded, full of resentment.

"The truth," I said, standing. I grabbed Keely's jacket, and after she stood, helped her into it. "Tomorrow. Meet me in Gweedore. Bring her with you."

He wasn't staring at me, though. He was staring at my wife.

She eyed him back. Then, without warning, she held her hand out to the woman with black hair and blue eyes, introducing herself. "Keely Kelly," she said, shaking the woman's hand, but giving my brother the side-eye.

"Fuck me," he said, his eyes darting between her and me.

"You got married, Cash. You selfish, selfish bastard." The muscles in his arms strained against the pressure he had on the tires of his wheelchair.

"I doubt you need my name," the woman next to Killian said, rubbing her hand on her jeans, looking at me as she did.

"No, your name doesn't matter," Keely said. "I just wanted you both to know who *I* am." She moved closer to me, no room between her body and mine.

She'd made her choice, no matter who I was, and she was claiming me like I'd claimed her on our wedding night. The scratches, those stripes she'd made on my back, were burning in memory.

I set my hand on my wife's lower back, about to direct her out. "Tomorrow," I said to my brother. "Or we'll be seeing a lot of each other until the truth is mine."

"Still the same marauding bastard," Killian said. "Nothing's changed."

"Not a fucking thing," I said and left.

WE WALKED NEXT to each other in silence, through the music from the pubs spilling out onto the street, until we made it to the Peace Bridge.

I stopped in the middle of it, looking out over the water. It was dark, but the lights from the bridge lit some parts of it. The wind whistled every so often, but other than that, the night was peaceful.

Keely pulled her jacket closer, her hair lifting when a gust passed us like an old ghost. "Maybe he doesn't like surprises." She shrugged.

I leaned against the railing, clasping my hands together, trying to see past the surface of the water. "He doesn't like *me*, darlin'."

"Because of the wheelchair."

"Because of life," I said. "Who we are. We're twins, but we were born to be different."

"He got the man and you got the animal."

"'Some men are born more animal than man. It's just who they are, what's running through their veins,'" I quoted my old man.

We were quiet for a few minutes before she cleared her throat. "Why do you care? The truth, Kelly. Because *I'm* not moving until it's mine."

"The day my old man was killed, my brother took the bullet that saved my life but permanently changed his."

"No. The truth about why you do what you do. Why you fight for a community just to turn around and ruin it. I'm not stupid. I know the game and how it's played. Things that make the most profit are the most powerful, because they bring in the most money. Drugs are high on that list. But you're not trying to run the world, Kelly. You're running one small area of it. A rebel with a cause is stronger than a rebel without one. A rebel with a cause not only has something to kill for, but something to die for."

A thick breath left my mouth, and the fire from the whiskey lingering on my tongue burned the air around me. "I steal them and then destroy them. I lace the trucks with explosives and blow them up. Ruling Hell's Kitchen is not about only ruling it. It's about keeping the bad shit away from the people. Giving them a better way, if possible. It's what my old man did. What he died for."

"What that—"

"Fucking liar said?"

"Yeah," she breathed out. "He wanted—"

"He wanted them back for Grady, but unless he was able to lick them off the ground, he wasn't getting them back."

"That's how you crippled them. Why they want you dead —yesterday."

I tapped my temple. "You're catching on."

She became quiet for a while. "The vegetables. The trucks. Why you didn't come with me to Italy. You—"

"*Boom,*" I said, bringing my hands together in what was meant to be an explosion, but it was quiet. "The biggest load. The most money."

"Your Da," she said and then hesitated.

I turned my head toward her. Her eyes were narrowed in thought.

"Did he teach you how to make those explosives? The ones that blew up the vegetable trucks?"

"Every one of 'em," I said, and then turned back to the water.

"The news..." she started, and then her voice drifted. "You do it because of her. Why?"

Her. The woman I thought was dead. My mother.

"I was told she died of an overdose."

I remembered my father driving her to the hospital, and then I never saw her again. My memories were fucking faulty, though, because I remembered little else about her. And I should've. I was ten. Killian and I lived with our father's parents for a while after we were told we'd never see her again, first in Derry and then in Gweedore, and then our old man brought us to Hell's Kitchen.

Keely said something, but it took me a minute to look at her.

"I was wrong." She hesitated. "And maybe a little scared. No." She shook her head. "Really. I was really scared. Am terrified now."

"Of what, darlin'?"

She took a deep breath, released it, and then took a step, another, until she closed the gap between us. I stood, turning to face her, and her arms came under mine and her head came to my chest.

Three words left her mouth that I'd never heard before.

"Of losing you."

She might as well have said I love you. If she did, I was in so much fucking trouble—because Keely Kelly was the most dangerous job I'd ever done, and her heart was the most valuable thing I'd ever stolen.

27

KEELY

H e'd never looked at me like that.

Not even the first time we'd met, at the cemetery.

Not even when he watched me walk down the aisle.

Not even after he fucked me the first time.

Or the time after.

Or anytime since then.

Not even when he found me in a dress the color of his eyes —a brilliant green—before the first political event.

Not even when I called a truce at Sullivan's.

He looked at me with no pretense, no guise, no holding back. He looked at me with eyes full of truth. It was how he'd looked at me back at the flat in Derry, but he wasn't closing his eyes again.

If Cash Kelly didn't have a heart, like he claimed, he consumed and claimed me with something even greater—his soul.

I never minded the darkness. I'd be his fire until he found his way home. To me.

His hand came underneath my chin, and he lifted it up with

his fingers so that I'd look at him. He whispered something in Gaelic, his voice rough, and then he said clearly, "Keely Kelly, you proved me wrong, my darlin'. So fuckin' wrong. I ripped my heart out at the roots and placed it at your feet long before I even knew I did—a heart that has always known and protected your name."

He leaned down, putting his lips against mine, and our tongues moved in a kiss that intertwined our souls in a way that felt irrevocable. He pulled back first, staring at me, before he took my hand and led me off the Peace Bridge.

WE MADE it back to the flat in Derry in no time, and he instructed me to pack.

"We just got here," I said, but doing it.

"We weren't staying here the entire trip," he said, grabbing for my suitcase after I'd shoved everything inside. I hadn't taken much out, and neither had he, it seemed, since he made it back to the master bedroom in no less than a minute.

He waved a hand toward the kitchen and told me to pack whatever I could from the cabinets. Someone had stocked them before we got here—Kelly said he had someone who took care of the place for him. I found reusable bags and stuffed them with as much nonperishable foods as I could.

Then we left.

He leaned over the seat of the Land Rover, his arm brushing my thigh, and an ache of longing hit me straight between the legs. I had to control the breath that left my mouth in a slow release. He'd worn a flat cap, and his strong bone structure was on perfect display the entire night. I'd refused to touch him then, but my resolve had melted on the bridge, and all that had been caged up had been set free.

When he came back with a map, his hand lingered, and I

knew he was doing it on purpose. I ran my hand up his arm until I found his hand—flesh against flesh—and took the map from him.

"Where are we headed, darlin'?" I whispered.

"To heaven," he said.

"If we can find it, you mean?" My grin came slow.

He looked me in the eye. "Already know the direction, darlin'. You'll just have to direct me on some of the turns."

We sped through Derry, the murals depicting political unrest still standing out even at night, and not for the first time, Ronan Kelly came to mind. I hadn't connected the dots until we were on the bridge.

When I'd gotten back to New York and the news of the vegetable trucks being blown up was scattered on every television and printed in every newspaper, some of the information stated that the explosives used reminded the authorities of a bomb that had been used years ago in political warfare overseas. Authorities overseas still didn't know who'd done it, but they blamed it on radicals.

I got the feeling if Cash's twin showed up with their mother the next day, Ronan Kelly's life, his real one, was going to be front page news, for the first time, to his son.

Derry faded with the night, and Kelly told me to open the map. He pointed out our destination and told me to direct him.

"What is this?" I lifted the map. "And how do I read it?" I was joking, but only a little. If we needed a map, that meant that cellphone service was probably going to be shitty, and that meant only one thing: We were headed into rough terrain.

He grinned. "It's called a map, darlin', and if you don't know how to use one, you best start now. Sink or swim. One wrong turn and there's no tellin' where we'll end up."

I helped him along the way, and in between my directions, we talked. It was the first time I'd ever had him this way, all to myself, for a stretch of time. It mirrored the night we were at

Sullivan's, when I'd offered the truce. I wanted this night to end differently.

As we approached a place called Poisoned Glen, he described it. I couldn't see it in the darkness, so I had to trust that what he told me about the beauty of the place come morning would be true.

He said there was a rumor that instead of the place being called "Heavenly Glen," like intended, something got lost in translation from Irish to English, and it was called "Poisoned Glen" instead.

"The Irish word for heaven is 'neamh,' and the word for poison is 'neimhe,'" he said.

"Heaven and hell," I said. "Separated by two simple vowels."

"It doesn't even take two. One misstep can lead you to one place or the other."

"Give me the story about this place," I said, staring at his face in the darkness.

"There might not be one."

I smiled. "They *always* have one."

His laugh was low. "Balor, the King of Tory, had a gorgeous daughter who he locked up in a tower so no man could see her. Legend has it that she had fiery red hair, blue eyes the color of heaven, five freckles over her nose, and the wickedest tongue in the land."

"Sounds familiar," I said, smiling even wider.

"She was a wild *ting*," he said, emphasizing "thing." "And as wild things go, her beauty couldn't be caged, so news of it spread throughout the land. She was kidnapped—"

I put a hand to my heart, acting a fool. "Stolen? Who would do such a thing?"

"A marauding bastard," he said. "Someone like myself."

"Definitely someone like yourself," I said. "Continue."

He glanced at me. "Yes, *boss*." Then he cleared his throat. "So she was kidnapped and brought to Magheroarty, but her father was on her scent from the start. Balor killed the marauder with a giant stone. One giant stone still stands at the entrance of Poisoned Glen, and it's said that it's the poisonous eye of the King of Tory."

"That's it? The marauder was defeated by a stone?"

"A *giant* stone."

"Where's the action? I mean, where's the story? Did the kidnapper love this woman? How did she feel about all of this? Did she fall for the kidnapper? Did she want to stay with him instead of going with her Da?"

"Not a fairytale type of woman, wasn't that what you said?" He gave me a pointed look.

"What?" I said, narrowing my eyes.

"I'm not the hero," he said. "I'm the villain in this story. Since all of a sudden we're into fairytales."

"Who said I'm attracted to heroes?" I lifted my brow at him. "The villain, I find, is sexy as hell. Apparently."

"You wanted me to come after you," he said. "After you left for Italy."

I twisted my hair up into a messy bun, letting some of my curls fall around my face. "I did. I thought you would—I hoped you would."

"When I didn't?"

"It hurt," I said, being honest. "But I really don't want the fairytale, Kelly."

"Tell me what you want then."

I opened and closed my hands. "I guess what most women desire deep down. To be wanted. To be needed. To be protected."

He didn't say anything, but his eyes turned more serious and he became quiet. The drive stayed that way as we bumped over rough terrain, going through an area so dark that not even shapes were visible to the eye alone. The lights from the car moved up and down, exposing glimpses of an old village, rundown cottages included.

I looked down at the map, and then back at Kelly. "Are we lost?"

His eyes were narrowed on the road and it took him a moment to answer. "You don't get lost in Ireland," he said. "You discover."

"Have we discovered then? Because—"

At the last minute, he took a hard right on a rudimentary lane made of rocks. The Land Rover ate them up, the stones cracking against the teeth of the tires, as we continued along what seemed like a lost road.

It wasn't even on the fucking map.

A jagged electric line forked across the sky before another one shocked it and everything around us. From the momentary brightness of the lightning, I caught a wide glimpse of the land. Water stretched to the horizon on the left. On the right, a great expanse of patchwork land that would probably be shades of unreal green come morning, cottages placed here and there. A few bigger places were set in between. Maybe farmhouses. But all of the houses were acres away from each other. An inlet created from the water sat behind the village, separating it from another stretch of land.

After a minute or so, Kelly turned on to a driveway made from dirt and followed it all the way to the front of a farmhouse.

"Is this where you grew up?" I leaned forward, trying to get a good look at it in the glow of the headlights. It was rundown but in a *this is Ireland's charm* way.

"I was born in Derry," he said. "After my—after she died, we were brought here to live with my old man's parents."

"I thought they owned the house in Derry?"

"True, but this is where they took us."

I didn't say anything, but if I needed a place to hide, or a place to hide *people*, this was prime real estate. I doubted anyone who didn't know about this place would be able to find it. I would've turned back over forty-five minutes ago.

Kelly sat for a minute, staring at the place, his eyes hard.

"Have you been back since you left?" I whispered.

"Once. Right before my old man died."

"Do you feel lost or discovered here?" I felt discovered, completely found, because he sat next to me.

"Lost." He cleared this throat. "I was. So fucking lost. Until I found you." Then his eyes collided with mine.

The breath I'd just taken lodged in my throat. My heart started to beat quicker and my stomach plummeted.

His eyes refused to leave mine as his hand came across and grabbed me by the neck, pulling my face to his. The stream of breath from his mouth caressed my lips, and I breathed in deep, wanting to take him into my lungs.

"I'm in love with you, Cashel Fallon Kelly," I said, my eyes as unwavering as his. "So in love. With you."

The grip he had on my neck became tighter, and I could feel the tremor in his bones. "Say what you mean and mean what you fucking say," he said, his voice hard.

"I'll never take those words back," I said, moving my nose against his, my lips against his skin. "I can't. Those words were inside of my heart when you stole it."

"I'll bleed to set those words in stone," he said, speaking in riddles, right before his lips came over mine in a kiss that stole my breath.

Each of my hands were fisted in his shirt, refusing to let him go, but did when he pulled away to step out of the car. As he did, another strike of lightning lit up the sky. A second later, a droplet of rain hit the windshield, and then another, until I couldn't see the farmhouse from the car.

Kelly tore open my door, rain dripping down from his cap.

He turned me around to face him, his touch rough, the look in his eyes as heated as a flame.

Every breath I took was for him.

Every beat of my heart was his.

Every day of my life. For the rest of my life.

I was *his* and he was *mine*.

My hands were back to his chest, my fists full of his shirt, and I was yanking him to me as he was pulling me out of the car. Our lips met in the rain, the taste of it sweet between our tongues, and I was barely aware that we were moving, until my back slammed against the stone.

His mouth moved lower, to my neck, his kiss warm against my skin, the complete opposite of the storm raging around us. "You've become the most dangerous thing on this earth to me," he whispered in my ear.

His hand slipped underneath my shirt, his fingers trailing a straight line between my breasts, until he stopped over my heart. "It's about to come straight out of your chest," he said. "Right into my hand, my darlin'."

"Easy steal, Marauder," I said, breathless. Rain collected on my lashes and his. His were raven black, making his green eyes seem even greener. They almost glowed in the darkness, high-lighted by the lights from the car. And I demanded to lose myself in the chaos they caused, because he made me feel alive. Perfectly alive in a life that was mine. "Because I let it go—freely now."

"So fucking dangerous," he murmured before he lifted my shirt over my arms, licking the rain from my bare skin. The heat from his body and the cool winds from the storm made a hard shiver pass over me, and my hair stood on end.

Especially after his eyes took in the bodysuit I'd worn under my clothes. It was sheer, with black velvet trimming.

He picked me up, and I wrapped my legs around his waist, kissing him as he carried me to the door. He must've opened it after he'd gotten out of the car, because he turned the handle and walked right in. He set me down on a long wooden table in the kitchen.

He lit a match and a few different sized candles on the counter from it. An old fireplace, dirty from years of use, was in front of the table. He lit that, too.

His clothes dripped water all over the floor, droplets running down his face, and when he came to stand between my legs, one of them landed on my chest, shimmering like a diamond in the glow of the soft flames. My neck burned—my heart on fire—from the desire in my veins.

He ran a finger up my arm, over my shoulder, along my neck, and then down between my breasts, before he circled my nipples, watching the entire time. "You burn for me everywhere I touch you," he whispered.

I reached out for him, lifting the soaked shirt over his arms, over his cap, and then flung it to the floor. He kicked his boots off and unbuttoned his pants. Using my feet, I shoved them down his legs, watching as he stood before me in nothing but the cap.

"Fuck me," I pleaded. "Please."

"First." He reached out and slipped the pants from my legs. His bicep bunched and his back muscles rippled as he turned to throw my pants into the pile with his shirt. "Dinner."

"I'm not fucking hungry," I snapped. Not for food. His shoulders were wide, strong, and I wanted to sink my teeth deep into his skin.

"I'm fucking starving," he said, and with a hand to my chest, pushed me back onto the table.

His fingers trailed up my left leg, and I moved a little for him so he could unfasten the bodysuit. Before he did, he ran his fingers back and forth, back and forth, teasing me. My entire body felt tense, ready to go off, and I almost did when I heard the sound of a snap releasing and felt a breath of fresh air between my legs.

"Soaked," he said, his voice low and rough. His fingers moved, a caressing brush, and then slid between my folds. My breaths came faster, the trembling coming harder. My legs parted even wider as a finger slid inside and his mouth came against me. My back arched off the table, my ass sliding down even further, wanting to be as close to his tongue as possible.

He devoured me like a man who hadn't eaten dinner in a *long* time, and I came like a woman who hadn't felt his touch in forever.

"Cash!" I screamed out, my thighs snapping shut when my orgasm tore through me, even wilder than the storm outside.

Wind howled and rain battered. Every so often the house would be lit with a shock of lightning, and I could see the pure desire in my tiger's eyes. When a roar of thunder would rattle the walls, it seemed to echo the sound of his pounding heart, as if he were on the hunt.

Forget what he looked like. That's what he *felt* like to me—a dangerous animal.

I was still riding the high when he entered me in a thrust so brutal that my eyes sprang open, a hiss escaped my lips, and my claws came out, sinking deep into his back.

"There she is," he said, looking down on me with hooded eyes. "Mark me even deeper."

I tore into his skin as I lifted myself up, meeting him thrust for thrust, the size of him stretching my walls until pleasure clashed with pain. "Oh fuck!" I screamed out. "Oh fuck! Yes!"

I wrapped my arms around his neck, and he lifted me up, our bodies moving together as he carried us toward another room. His back hit a wall first, though, and then he turned us, so that the face of the cold stone touched my skin. The wall was jagged, and as he pumped into me, faster, harder, it left lines of fire down my back.

He was fucking me so hard that my breasts spilled out of the bodysuit from impact and jiggled every time he made the full connection.

Then we were moving again, and after he shoved open a door on the lower floor, he set me down on the bed in the room. He felt around until he hit something solid. I heard a drawer open, a matchstick catch, and then a tiny flame came out of the darkness, lighting up his face. He lit a long taper candle and then blew out the matchstick.

His eyes journeyed over my body as the flame brought me to life. His eyes lowered to almost closed when he found my eyes. He looked higher than he had the night out on the fire escape. "My tigress," he said. "All *mine*." With a growl that seemed to come from the deepest part of his throat, he ripped the bodysuit from my body before he entered me again.

He flipped us over on the bed a second later. My palms were solid against his chest, my hair dripping water down his skin, and I stared into his eyes as I slowly moved up his shaft. I moved even slower when I worked myself back down.

His hands came to my ass, digging into my skin, and then to my hips. I could feel his urge, his desire, like it was my own. He wanted me to tear into him, to ride him hard and fast, to make this about fucking.

Time and place.

I wanted a redo of our wedding night. I demanded to go deeper than skin. I'd coast in his bloodstream, getting him high off my kisses. I'd make his heart thunder in his chest from my touch. I'd make him feel lightning in his balls when he came inside of me.

I'd cause nothing but utter chaos on his body, so he could feel peace down to his soul once I reached it. All of that pent-up *want*—it was going to be released from its cage and set free with mine.

My hands slid up his chest, to his neck, over the tattoo,

where his pulse slammed against my fingers. My tongue slipped up his chin, savoring the taste of salt from his skin, until my mouth met his.

I kissed him slow, my hips moving at the same pace, and a noise I'd never heard before escaped from his lips. It was a deep groan of satisfaction. When I sat up, taking him in even deeper, I couldn't stop the echo of the same noise that left my mouth.

I'd never experienced anything like this before. *Him.* The connection. It was as deep as he was inside of me.

"Ah!" I screamed out when he rocked his hips up so hard that I lost my breath. He flipped me over so fast that I had no chance to stop it. He lifted my leg, positioning himself in a way that I knew he was about to go deeper.

He was going to tear me apart again, fuck me like the animal he felt he was, because he didn't know how to let the man rule this.

A tear slipped down my cheek that I damned to hell. But I let him see. I lifted my chin as it rolled down my cheek until it met the pillow. His chest heaved and his fingers dug into my leg. His muscles strained. His erection was about to tear through his skin.

I closed my eyes when he moved, expecting the brutality of his fucking, but instead of slamming into me, he licked the trail of the tear from my cheek to the corner of my eye. Then he started to move at the same pace I'd set—slow, but with such a contained power that I felt it bone deep.

An animal was always an animal by instinct, but instead of trying to ravage my heart, my will, my stubborn nature, he was accepting me as is, because I was no longer fighting to keep what was his away from him.

We both came in a moment that seemed to rock the house harder than the thunder rattling the panes. My eyes were shut tight, but after a minute, I could feel him watching me. I opened my eyes slowly to meet his, and after studying my face for another minute, he pulled out of me and came to sit beside me on the bed.

The sudden loss of heat, of him, made me shiver, and I curled into myself. He sighed, and the sound of it made me tremble even harder. He moved slowly on the bed, getting a little closer, until finally, he wrapped his arm around me, kissing me behind the ear. Reaching out with his empty hand, he pulled the quilt from the bed over us, and settled in with his head close to mine. We were pressed skin to skin.

"When did it start to storm?" His voice was raw.

I started laughing, real quiet, shaking in his arms.

He grinned against my cheek, his lips lingering where another tear ran from my eye again. He'd broken something in me that no one else ever had before. A tear duct.

"I meant it, my darlin'," he said, "when I said that you were the most dangerous thing to me."

"I know," I barely got out, "that you love me, Cash Kelly. Just as much as I love you."

"Grand," he whispered in my ear. "Just fucking grand."

I intertwined our fingers, holding on tight.

"Keely Kelly," he said.

"Yeah?"

"I need you more than a heart needs blood." He wrapped his hand around my wrist, applying pressure to the pulse there. "The only addiction to ever have power over me. The only soul to ever conquer my chaotic soul with complete peace."

We both stared at the steam on the windows, condensation making strange patterns as it ran down the panes, snippets of the storm coming through the cleared paths. I fell asleep wrapped in his arms without realizing it; the pounding of his heart against my back was a song, soothing the mayhem surrounding us.

28

KEELY

I blinked at the bright light coming in through the windows. The sun had burnt through the night while we slept, and the room had turned stuffy and humid from the storm.

My skin was still against his skin.

His arm was around me, and his nose was close to my ear. He was snoring.

A slow, satisfying grin came to my face at the faint sound of it.

He barely slept, and when he did, it was light. The nights must've caught up to him, like my evenings without dinner had caught up with me. He needed sleep as much as I needed food. My stomach made an obnoxious noise at the thought. But I had other needs that felt more important.

He was hard, and after I pushed my ass into him, he pushed himself inside of me and groaned deep.

"I wasn't hungry for food, Kelly," I said, breathless. "I was starved for *this*." *The connection.*

"When I close my eyes, I dream of this," he said, sinking

into me even deeper. "You fuck up my body and settle my mind."

He worked my body hard—gasping for breath, slick with sweat, his handprints on my skin—before my body submitted to his and his to mine.

Afterward, I felt like I'd taken a free fall from heaven. I sank deeper into the mattress, the pillow, and my eyes closed.

His breath fanned over my ear when he laughed. "No time for sleep, my darlin'."

"There's always time for sleep, my thief of hours," I said. Maybe I dozed off for a second, but when I came to, it was with a jolt. Someone had slammed a fist against the front door, and I heard it open with a creak.

Cash sat up, rubbing his face, and then went to the bedroom door. The golden light coming in through the window lit up his naked body, every spectacular angle of it. He looked around for a second, and after he didn't find what he wanted, he left the room.

"What the fuck, Cashel," I heard the voice say. It belonged to Cash, but it was coming out of another man's mouth. His brother, Killian. "I don't want to see your wanker before I've even had my porridge. Ach."

"Best to knock and wait then," Cash said, his voice low. He must've been picking up his clothes. A minute later, I heard the front door again, and then another minute or two, he came back into our room with our suitcases and all of my clothes from last night. "Get dressed."

I nodded and moved with more energy in my blood. I took a quick shower and dressed in a black maxi dress that came close to sweeping the floor. A row of buttons ran down the front of the dress, which was open from my knees down. I completed the outfit with a tiger-print belt around my waist.

My hair was fluffed up, a wild storm of red, and I didn't even bother trying to tame it, but I did do some light makeup to help my face. Then I stood back, looking myself over. I wasn't sure why, but I wanted to make a good impression on his brother.

I went to touch the necklace, the heart pendant, and as usual, I felt hollow when I found it missing. When I'd taken it off and left it on his pillow, it almost felt like I'd stolen a piece of myself back from him. I hated it as much as if he'd taken a piece of himself from me.

Love should've been spelled I. N. S. A. N. I. T. Y.

I must've been quiet when I entered the kitchen, because his brother didn't hear me. He sat in his wheelchair, at the kitchen door, watching something going on outside. An old song played quietly from a record player in the corner.

When I stood in front of the sink and looked out of the window, my view was the same as Killian's. Cash was unloading the groceries from the car. It didn't seem like Killian wanted him to know, because when Cash started to make his way back to the farmhouse, Killian rolled his wheelchair back, faster than he'd moved the night before.

"Have mercy!" he said when he noticed me. "For a tall girl, you walk with no noise."

"What do you expect me to do?" I lifted a brow at him. "Stomp like a horse in a wooden house?"

He narrowed his eyes at me. "Tell me what you're doing with my brother, woman."

There it was—if the twin thing didn't give it away, the demanding attitude came shining through as family resemblance.

"I'm his wife," I said. "That's what I'm doing."

Cash shoved the door open, setting the bags on the counter. I turned away from his brother, going through them, starting to put the groceries away.

"I'm going to shower." Cash patted me on the hip. Then he looked between his brother and me. "Don't fall in love with him." He nodded toward Killian. "If I steal hearts, he fucking breaks them."

A moment passed and something moved between them—the twin thing—and then Cash shook his head and went to take a shower.

I knew how Cash liked his oatmeal and started to make it. "You like your oatmeal the same way as your brother?" I asked Killian.

"If it's the same way he took it over ten years ago." He shrugged. "The same."

I told him how Cash took it and he nodded. He became quiet after, watching as I worked around the kitchen. The cabinets were empty, but someone had filled the fridge with butter and milk. They looked farm fresh, probably from one of the places around here.

"You're either the most powerful being in the world or the dumbest, woman."

I stopped what I was doing and looked at him. "I have a name. Keely."

"Keely Kelly."

"It's a nice start to a riddle, I think," I said.

"Let's starts the riddle with a question. Most powerful woman in the world or the dumbest?"

"The first," I said, turning to stir the oatmeal.

"You know what he does."

I nodded.

"You know he's more animal than man."

I nodded.

"I'm having a hard time believing the first, then, if you know him."

"I don't see him. I feel him—more than you do." I stopped myself before I wiped my hands on my dress. I looked around the kitchen and found an apron and set it over my clothes. As I made my way back to the stove, I said, "My Mam taught me to stand by my man. Unless he hits me. Then she told me to kill him in his sleep."

It took a second, but a slow smile stretched across Killian's face. It rivaled sunrises in Ireland after dreary days.

"You are crazy, Keely Kelly. Maybe crazy enough to match his level of chaos." He moved his wheelchair closer to me. "There's one thing I can't take away from the marauding bastard. He's got a head harder than stone. Once his mind is set, he'll either seize what he wants or wait until the end of time for it. He'll be faithful to you, if it's you he truly wants. Not even the threat of death will change his mind."

My eyes met his and held. We were trying to read the other's intentions toward the man we both loved. Even though Killian was fighting it, I could tell he loved Cash. Whatever had happened between them, both of them ended up wounded from it in different ways. Some scars come from internal battles, not always physical ones.

Cash cleared his throat, and it took a second, but Killian and I moved in opposite directions. Killian wheeled himself to the table. I started removing bowls and putting oatmeal in them. Then I made us each a mug of tea. When I turned around with two cups in hand, Cash was backing his brother away from the spot at the head of the table, moving him to the right.

Killian held on to the wood for a second before he decided not to fight. "You're lucky I don't have a gun on me," he said, glaring at Cash. "Or I'd shoot you."

"My spot," Cash said, taking the head of the table, tapping the spot where he'd *eaten* me last night.

If I were easily embarrassed, my neck would've turned red, but that only seemed to happen when Cash Kelly looked at me with those fierce green eyes.

After setting down the cups, I made myself a bowl of cereal and set it on the table next to my tea, to the left of Kelly. He'd always move my plate at dinner when I'd try to sit too far from him. So I made things easier on the both of us this time.

We ate in silence for a few until Killian sat his spoon down and cleared his throat. "That's disgusting," he said, nodding toward my bowl and my tea.

"What?" I said, about to take bite. "They're both made with milk."

Cash dropped his napkin, sat back, and gave his brother a pointed look. "You know I'm not much for fucking around." He cleared his throat. "Why are you here so early?"

"About that. Why are you sleeping so late?"

"Answer my fucking question, Kill."

Killian turned and removed a long envelope from the pocket of his wheelchair. He slid it toward Cash. "It's a good thing you're sittin'," he said, "or I'd tell you to take a seat."

BEFORE CASH COULD OPEN the envelope, a knock came at the door. It was much lighter than Killian's. Almost a tap. Loud enough in my ears, though, that it almost rang.

Cash and Killian stared at each other.

"I'll get it," I said, standing.

It was hard to tell if the woman on the opposite side of the door hated to be where she was or couldn't believe that she was standing there. Her black hair streaked with silver was pulled back, emphasizing harsh lines on her face and eyes rimmed red from crying.

"Hello," she said, her voice quiet. "I've come—"

"Come in," Killian said from behind me.

I nodded, opening the door wider. After she entered, I offered her my hand. "Keely," I said.

Her grip was firm. "Keely Kelly," she said. "I'm Saoirse Kelly." Her name came out as *ser-sha*. Her eyes were no longer on me, though. They were feasting on the man sitting at the table, his face turned forward, refusing to give her the power of his eyes.

At her voice, though, I sensed something in Cash. The giant stone he'd told me about the night before? He'd taken a similar one to the gut.

His mother was, in fact, *not* dead as he'd been led to believe.

"Take a seat, Ma," Killian said, nodding to the spot where I'd been sitting.

Saoirse nodded, but she didn't take my seat. She took the one at the other end of the table so Cash was forced to look at her. The same stone seemed to go through him and hit me, directly in the gut, when their eyes met. It was the subtlest fucking thing I'd ever seen, but as they looked at each other for the first time in years, Saoirse's fingers closed over the edge of the table, her knuckles turning white.

"Son," she said, her voice barely a whisper.

He didn't answer her, and the tension in the room grew thick. I cleared my throat and asked her if she would like a cup of tea. She nodded, but she still didn't look away from him. I quickly made her cup, set it down, and then put my hand on Cash's shoulder before I told him I was going for a walk.

"Sit down," he said to me. "Right here." He tapped the spot next to him.

His voice was cold and hard, and even though my first reaction was to resist his tone, I gave in to the plea hidden behind the demand. After I took my seat, I slipped my hand under the table, resting it on his leg.

"Is this where your father hid you both?" Saoirse said, looking around at the house and then at her sons in equal turns. She only got an answer from Killian, though.

"We lived here with Gran and Granda after we were told that you were dead. He took us to New York, after, like I've told you."

"So you have," she said.

The three of us turned to Cash as the envelope crinkled when he opened it, but the sound was like a bomb going off. He pulled out numerous pictures of his father, Ronan Kelly, and numerous newspaper clippings and reports. He spread them out so he could look them over. His eyes scanned the words that described whatever his father had been doing at the time.

Some of the words stood out like deadly debris flying through the air. *Nationalist. Wanted man. Dangerous. On the run. Radical.*

"We were young." Saoirse picked up her tea, slowly putting it to her mouth, because her hands trembled. The porcelain clattered against the saucer when she set it down. "Some say stupid. But we believed in a cause that, at the time, felt worthwhile."

Cash's eyes lifted from the paper he'd been reading to look at her, but they quickly went back to the words in front of him after they did.

"Ronan was an exceptionally smart lad, and when he was passionate about something, he committed himself wholly to the cause. The man who originally brought him in became a hero to him. Patrick was all he could see."

Cash's eyes flew up at the name. They must've crashed into Saoirse's because she closed her eyes, nodded, and one tear fell, then another.

Patrick. Patrick. Patrick...who...?

"Patrick and Ronan were as close as twins. We formed a group, and for a time, the cause seemed worth it. Then I got pregnant. You both came along, and it wasn't as easy as it was before. We would have to run on a moment's notice. Maybe with one babe, it would've been easier, but with two...it became tiring.

"I started not being able to sleep. I was running behind the both of you, and headaches would plague me day and night. I told Ronan that I couldn't keep up, that I couldn't do it any longer. Ireland was doing just fine as it was, but I was on the brink of losing my mind. Our family was in trouble.

"My priorities shifted once you two were born, but Ronan was as focused as ever. Patrick—" she opened and closed her hands around the teacup "—started to see the burden. He fell for you boys and had taken a vow when you were born to watch over you both. He considered you blood, as close as two nephews. He tried talking to Ronan, but there was no changing his direction."

At this, she looked up and met Cash's eyes. "Ronan started to rebel against us because he didn't want to hear the truth. He stopped coming home for long stretches, and then he'd make frequent trips to America. The headaches only grew worse, and after going to the doctor, he found that I have an eye disease. Glaucoma. The only thing that helped ease it was cannabis. Patrick had read something and started bringing it to me. We started to grow closer."

She broke eye contact to look into her tea again, and I couldn't help but wonder what she saw. Maybe she could read them like my mam.

She took a deep breath and then lifted her eyes and her chin. "Patrick and I fell in love. Your father walked in on us one day after we hadn't seen him in a month. I suspected, you know, that he had a mistress in America, but the love between us couldn't be saved at that point. I justified my sins as right because he was committing the same.

"Ronan and Patrick got into an awful fight." She put a hand to her temple and massaged. "I couldn't stop it, and for the sake of you boys, Patrick left. I wasn't sure if I'd ever see him again. But after the fight..." She sighed. "The stress. The headache. I thought I was dying. I swore—I swore then and there, I would never touch another drug again. It had gone further than the cannabis. I had become addicted to other drugs. Harder drugs.

I'm sure you remember me that way." A lone tear fell from her eye then, but she swiped it away before it could run down her cheek.

"Ronan took me to the hospital, accusing me of having an overdose while he drove me. He dropped me off, and that...that was the last time I laid eyes on you, until today." She dug around in the pocket of her cardigan and pulled out a photo. She passed it to Killian, who passed it to Cash, who stared at it.

It was a picture of five people—Ronan, Saoirse, Cash, Killian, and the man by the name of Patrick—sitting at a dinner table. The man. Patrick. Father *Patrick* Flanagan.

"That picture was all that was left when I returned home." Saoirse pulled out a tissue from her pocket and wiped her nose. "My parents died when I was young. I had no siblings. I had no one to help me find you. I tried. I looked every place I could remember. So many places like this one." She looked around, and then her eyes met Cash's. "He left me that picture out of spite." Her tone turned bitter. "His only rule. We always ate dinner as a family, even before you boys came along."

My grip on Cash's leg grew tighter, and the muscle under my hand was taut, so tight that I thought it would pop like a vein in the head.

Tears slipped down her cheeks in a controlled flow. "He left me with that memory because he knew it would hurt me the most. He stopped eating dinner with me *first*." Her hand balled into a fist and she lifted it, like she was going to slam it against the table, but instead it made no noise when it made contact with the wood. "I lost my boys, my husband, and my lover. He never came back for me, either, did Patrick Flann."

"He thought you were dead," Killian said. "Then he was forced into joining the priesthood to atone for his sins. To be able to have the right to see us. Everyone was punished. You. Patrick. Me." Killian stabbed a finger at his chest and then looked at his brother. "Even you."

"But you couldn't remember. You couldn't seem to remember anything that we lost. All you saw was the great Ronan Kelly. You dedicated your life to him, to his cause, without question. You were his perfect specimen—an animal that would attack on command. You're still fighting for a cause you can't win. A cause that he gave you to take on because he knew you'd do it in her honor." He nodded toward Saoirse. "You'd do it because you would remember the worst of her, because all you believed was the best in him.

"He told you she died of an overdose to give you something worthy to fight for while the rest of it was as dirty as sin. He made it okay to kill and steal because he put it in your head that the original cause was honorable. He gave the animal steak to chew on, telling it that it needed to eat, and blood was part of the hunger."

Killian stuck a finger to his chest again. "I remembered, though, Cash. I remembered leaving the hospital, being told that my mother had died of an overdose. That we would be starting a new life soon. I remembered her screaming about a headache, but she was not unresponsive. I remembered the day Patrick Flanagan showed up and stood watch out of guilt.

"I remembered the conversation between them. He wasn't allowed to see us unless he made a promise to never touch another woman again." Killian stopped for a second, trying to catch his breath. "Even though Molly warmed Ronan's bed every night.

"I pieced it together after I lost my legs and you went to jail. I pieced it together because I was fucking allowed to think about it, Cash! You never would. You would never even consider him anything less than a hero! The end always justified the means." He wheeled himself back, showing Cash his legs, legs that would never work again. "What's the cause now, Cashel? What's it worth? The price on these?" He punched his leg.

The door creaked open, and the woman from the pub peeked her head inside a second later. Her eyes narrowed when she noticed how Killian breathed heavily, how his wheelchair was positioned, and the set of Cash's face. It hadn't softened. If anything, it had hardened.

"Should I get the gun?" she said in all seriousness.

"You get a gun," I said, "and we're going to have problems, you and me. I'll put an arrow straight through the wrist holding up the gun and not think twice about it. I'll aim higher if it comes to it."

I narrowed my eyes against hers, and after a second, she stepped inside, taking a seat between Saoirse and Killian.

The room became quiet, no one speaking, no one moving, all eyes on Cash. He hadn't spoken a word the entire time.

Then he cleared his throat. "You sit before me, both of you, and tell me that my mother lives, and my brother knew it, but no one told me until today. Until I came here searching for answers to questions that were given to me by an enemy. You treated me worse than the dead." He tapped the table a couple of times. He stopped. "Consider me dead then. Get out. All of you. Now. Or she will need a gun."

29

CASH

My wife stood out against the ragged Irish coastline, her bow raised, arrow pointed, the wind moving through her hair. The color of it matched the fire left behind from the setting sun.

Her quiver was full of arrows, and a green feather fletch drifted in the wind, landing at my feet. I bent down and picked it up, holding it between my pointer and middle finger.

Seven targets were lined up outside of the farmhouse, and as she moved and released with a quickness that was hard to process, she hit the center seven times in a row. It only took a few seconds for her to reach for the arrow and set up the shot, for the arrow to fly through the air and strike its target, and for her to have already moved on to the next one.

At the rate she loosed arrows, it would only take her a few seconds to clear out a group of full-grown men.

Keely Kelly was not, by any means, to be fucked with.

She'd had an arrow pointed at my chest the first time my eyes met hers, and she claimed a heart I'd had no fucking clue I had.

"Can you shoot?" Her voice carried with the wind.

"A gun." I grinned.

Her grin matched mine. "Don't worry. You have me if there's ever an apocalypse."

"Grand," I said, sticking my hands in my pockets, going to stand closer to her.

She laughed, and a gust of wind swept her hair up. I moved the pieces from her face, tucking them behind her ear. Her eyes closed and she shivered, her shoulders coming up toward her ears. She put her chilled hand over mine, squeezing.

"Stand here," she said, nodding to where she was.

I stood in front of her and she stood close behind me. She handed me the bow and helped me line up the shot, then handed me an arrow.

"Let's see what you can do, *thief* of my heart," she said, her breath warm in my ear. She was watching me over my shoulder.

"How am I supposed to do this with you breathing down my neck?"

"Does this bother you?" Her voice was low, breathy, too fucking seductive.

When she aimed, it didn't even seem like she had to concentrate, or narrow one eye to be able to see better out of the other one. I lined up the shot again, and as I went to release the arrow, she reached around and grabbed my cock, blowing in my ear at the same time.

The shot went wild in a crazed arch and stuck in the ground.

I'd never heard her laugh so hard. I turned around and she pointed at me. "Your face!" She laughed even harder, but she was trying to make the same face I was. Maybe pissed, but it was hard to tell when she couldn't keep a straight face. She was almost wheezing. When she could breathe normally again, she said, "You're not used to being tripped up by a woman, right, Marauder?"

I set my body flush to hers, sliding my hand up her back, feeling the tremble beneath her skin when I touched her. I took another arrow from the quiver. Turning, I set the shot up once more and loosed the arrow. This time it went straight, connecting with the target, but a smidge to the left of her center hit.

"Not bad, my heart," she said from behind me. "Not bad at all. I sense some potential."

She said it casually, like she hadn't called me something other than what she had been calling me—Kelly, marauder, bastard, thief of her time or heart. It felt the same as the first time she'd ever called me Cash.

"What?" She lifted her hair, fixing it so it wouldn't blow in the wind. "I called you *my heart*. Don't make a deal about it. You are my heart, since you stole it."

She turned me toward the target again, setting my body a certain way. With her body guiding mine, we hit each target. The arrows stuck right next to hers, except the last one, when she made the Robin Hood shot. She split her arrow straight through the middle.

"Well done," she said, stepping away from me. "Well done."

I nodded at her and handed her back the bow. She took it from me and rested it against the small building used to house tools and things. I watched her for a minute before I stuck my hands in my pockets and went to walk back to the farmhouse.

"Cashel Kelly," she said.

I stopped.

"Take me for a long walk along the beach." She was next to me before I expected her to be. Her hand slipped into mine, intertwining our fingers.

I sighed and nodded.

We walked the length of the property and crossed the crude road, our boots finding purchase along the rocks that separated land from sea. Water rushed into the cracks every so often, filling the voids, and then rushed back out. She released my hand when I bent down to pick up a rock and throw it.

"Tell me what happened that day," she said. "The day that changed everything."

The day I lost my old man and my brother.

I cleared my throat. "My old man took us to the Bronx Zoo. He'd take us there when he had something important to talk to us about. They had a green-eyed tiger that he called my spirit animal. The keeper used to let us feed him sometime."

I bent down again, looking for another stone to throw. "Our old man told us he had a bad feelin' about something. He had them often. His business was to basically piss everyone else off. Because if you're not pissin' someone off in that world, you're not doing something right. Enemies mean that you've made it. You stand for something that someone else wants." I stood then, four small rocks in my hand. I flung one out and the sea took it.

"He warned us that things were gettin' dicey. That if something happened to him, he wanted us to run things. Take his legacy and make it stronger." I rubbed the stones between my palms and then flung another one, this one going further than the last. "After we left the zoo, we were goin' to eat dinner at my old man's apartment. Molly always cooked a special meal on Sundays, and we were expected to eat with them. A car had pulled across the street before we got inside, and when my old man made eye contact with them, he told us to go inside and wait."

I climbed a mound of rocks, turning to give my wife my hand. She took it and stood beside me, her eyes narrowed against the horizon.

"I didn't. I had a cold feelin' along my neck, like a wild animal was about to sink his teeth into it and cripple me. Because I waited, so did Kill." I flung another rock, this one going wild with a gust of wind. It landed somewhere in the distance with no proof that it did. "My old man was leanin' down, talking to the two men through their rolled down window. They were arguing but keepin' their voices low. It was one of Grady's men and a Scarpone. As they were arguing, a bunch of cops pulled up, tires screeching, sirens blasting. They pulled guns as soon as they jumped out. Stone's old man was screaming at mine to put his hands up.

"My old man did, but he told Stone he had business to finish first. Scott Stone, who was a beat cop at the time, disagreed. Before Stone's father gave him the okay, he cuffed my old man, and as he pulled him back from the car, Scarpone shot him in the chest. Right in his heart. The cops started firing. So did the men in the car. I went to go to my old man, but Kill jumped on me before I could get there. Someone was shooting at me. He took the bullet meant for me."

"And lost his legs," she said, taking the last rock from my hand and throwing it. She put her hand along my side and pulled herself around so she was standing in front of me at the very edge of the rock. "Then you stole my heart out of revenge."

"I spent my entire life, my darlin', waiting to steal the right one."

She blinked up at me, her eyes a true blue. "The right one —the one you found through vengeance."

"If the path to hell can be paved with good intentions—" I shrugged "—maybe the path to heaven can be paved with meant-to-be." I dug in my pocket and pulled out the necklace I'd given her on our wedding night. I dangled it in front of her face, and when she went to take it, I pulled it back. "You take this off, or even try to give it back to me again, you won't be able to sit for two weeks."

She pushed it toward me with a wicked glint in her eye, and when she did, I tightened my hold on it, and she tightened hers. She realized I was being fucking serious.

"I won't," she whispered. "Now give it back to me. It's mine."

I set it over her head, situating it so that the pendant was in the middle of her chest.

She looked down at it, fiddling with it, running her nail through the crevices. "What's inside, Kelly?"

"It's easy enough to find out."

She looked up at me just as I winked.

"Bastard," she mouthed and then grinned. She held the pendant between her fingers, rubbing it.

I tucked my finger underneath her chin. "I wasn't completely honest with you when I said I didn't have a heart. I have many. The men I've killed. I carry them with me. Their sins have become my own."

After a minute or two, she sighed. "Mine? Is it a burden?"

I studied her face, wondering how in the fuck I hadn't realized how beautiful she was until that moment. How her face would be enough if it was the last one I'd ever see. How out of every woman in the entire world, my eyes had decided she was the most beautiful woman I'd ever see.

"No, my darlin'," I said. "When I stole your heart, I found something I'd never felt before. Relief."

Her head came forward, resting against my chest. "You can't truly appreciate peace without chaos." She wrapped her arms around me, turning her head to the side to look out at the water. She pressed even closer to me. "I can hear it, the chaos. It's tearing you apart from the inside. The truth about your Da, the truth he hid from you, is killing something inside of you. Don't let it," she whispered. "My heart is yours now, Cashel Kelly, and if something kills you, it kills me. That's why I called you *my heart*. Because you are, no matter who you are or what you've done. You're mine. End of story."

30

KEELY

W e spent the rest of the month in Ireland, Maureen and the kids joining us after two weeks.

After that, we headed to Scotland, to spend some time with my family. Cash insisted. He said all ghosts had to be put to rest. It wasn't easy breaking the news to my Mam that I wouldn't be going back to Broadway; I would be starting an art class. For whatever reason, she seemed to handle it better when Cash was next to me.

Maybe it wasn't Cash at all. Maybe it was because I'd finally set boundaries on her guilt, and my life was what it was. I couldn't bring my sister back, no matter how many times I held my breath, and it was time for me to live my life. My life. Not hers.

Before we left, my brothers attacked Cash like a bunch of wrestlers during a free-for-all, since Harrison decided to tell them the circumstances of our first wedding in New York. He said he couldn't keep it from them any longer because they'd all decided to work for Cash. He'd funded a pub for them, and he required a certain amount of the proceeds until the loan was paid back. I sensed there was more to it, maybe some criminal dealings, but my brothers were grown men, and I couldn't fix all of their problems, either.

However.

It was decided that my parents would never find out about the circumstances that brought Cash and me together. I had dirt on each of my brothers that I'd sworn never to reveal. Shit was going to get real if they snitched on me first.

As far as I was concerned, I'd found my place in Cash Kelly's life, and I claimed my spot at his table. Our business was our own, and how we got to where we were in our relationship was no one's concern but ours.

After that, Maureen and the kids went home to New York, while we flew to Italy to meet Harrison. He'd been spending time with Gigi, Mac's cousin, and I needed to see Mari. I decided that since I was expelling all of my old ghosts, it was time for me to come clean with her. About everything.

Harrison stood with me and Mari while Cash went out to talk to Mac.

After I spilled my guts, Mari said, "You said you had something to talk to me about. You told me *things*. Plenty of things."

"I guess I did," I said. "I had to. It was time."

She nodded. "I knew about your sister."

I immediately turned to look at Harrison, who held his hands up. "She needed to know."

"When did you tell her?" I asked.

"Years ago."

"You're worse than a gossiping little bitch," I said.

He laughed and so did Mari.

She put her hand over mine, squeezing. "I'm glad you finally told me *things*," she said.

"Yeah," I said, leaning in and kissing her head. "I'm glad you finally told me *things*, too."

"I'll always be your little sister," she said. "But we're all grown-up now. You don't have to protect me anymore, Kee. I'm going to be okay."

"Fucka me," I said, copying her, wiping my eyes. It was something she said that mirrored what her adoptive Sicilian grandfather used to say when bugs would eat the vegetables in his garden. He had an accent, and he would add an "'a" to the end of words sometimes. It must've stuck with her, something to keep him close.

On the plane back to New York, I closed my eyes, my head on Kelly's shoulder while he read a book.

"Tell me one thing, my darlin'," he said, his eyes scanning the page. "Now that you know the reason why I stole your heart. Is it good enough?"

"It all happened the way it was supposed to," I said, leaning in and kissing the tiger on his neck. "You found me through the reason, no matter what it stemmed from." I hesitated. One minute. Two. "I think we should invite Maureen and the kids to come and live with us permanently."

Even though I loved it when it was the two of us, having them around filled something inside of me that I had no idea was missing. When the kids were around, it was like our family was complete. I loved to hear Connolly giggle, even though she still wasn't talking much. I loved to see Ryan smile and experience all of the milestones children achieve as they grow. And even though Maureen could be a grumpy old lady, I liked having her around, too. Her strength was something I admired.

"I don't plan on working as much," Cash said, turning to face me, setting his finger in his book to mark his spot before he closed it.

I adjusted in my seat but still kept my arm locked with his. "Even better."

"It's a little early to start a family," he said.

I turned forward, my head pressed against the seat, shocked at my own words and why I hadn't realized what they meant.

Start a family. Even though it was unconventional, that was exactly what I'd proposed to him. Starting a family—with Connolly, Ryan, Maureen, and the two of us.

I shrugged. "I really like having them around."

"You have a connection with the little girl."

"The little boy, too," I whispered.

"Our place is big enough," he said, opening his book again. "You've already decorated her room."

That was a yes from Cash Kelly, and even though I wanted it, it suddenly scared me. Scared the breath from my lungs and sent my heart into overdrive. It was that feeling of falling in love over and over again, but going deeper every time. I got the same feeling when Cash looked at me, when he touched me, and when I thought about keeping the four of them...Cash, Maureen, Connolly, and Ryan.

Forever.

31

KEELY

I thought returning to New York would haunt me, but having the four of us all together seemed to bring me peace.

We were home.

In the space of time between arriving in Ireland and arriving back in Hell's Kitchen, I had learned that no matter where I went, as long as my family stood beside me, that was the true meaning of home.

I wanted to ask Maureen right away if she and the kids would come and live with us. I didn't want to spend another night worrying about whether she was going to take them to her place for good one day. I enjoyed getting up in the middle of the night, checking on them, making sure they were safe in their beds. It put me at ease.

What was even better was, Cash did, too.

He had taken CeeCee and Ryan to a toy shop down the street so I could talk to Maureen alone.

She was at the stove, cooking up something that smelled good. Though with Maureen, it was hard to tell how it was going to turn out. She found it a personal challenge to use whatever was in the fridge, even if it didn't pair up with whatever dish she decided to cook.

It told me a lot about her, though. She was resourceful when she needed to be. I admired that about her. I'd come to admire a lot of things about Maureen. She was one of the strongest women I'd ever had the honor of getting to know.

I set my chin on her shoulder, looking over at the bubbling —soup?— in the pot.

She smiled. "Don't be one of those hover mothers or whatever they're called. This is going to be ready when it's ready."

I laughed as I took a seat at the kitchen table, though it wasn't as carefree as usual. This—this was a big deal.

Maureen set a beer in front of me before she took a seat. She had one of her own, but she didn't touch it. Neither did I.

"You're a lot like me when I was young," she said. "If I had an itch—" she shrugged "—I scratched it. The world be damned."

I lifted my bottle and we clanked, smiling at each other. "I'll drink to that," I said, taking a long pull.

She didn't. And I wondered—was she sick? I hated to listen to rumors, but it was hard to tell with her. Maureen kept things close to her heart until she was ready to talk. I hoped if she was, she would confide in me. We'd take care of her.

"You've had a lot of practice taking care of other people, Mrs. Kelly," she said, grinning at me. She rarely called me that, but sometimes she did when she got serious. "I've watched. Blood doesn't seem to matter to you, not when it comes to love. Certain women have that way about them, you know. They can love without the bond of blood having to secure anything."

"Cash thinks differently," I said. "He thinks in order for me to truly love him, he has to bleed for me."

"He does," she said, "because he's your man. I'm talking about the love you feel for my grandchildren."

"I do," I said, reaching out for her hand. Like Mari, I knew she wanted to pull out of my embrace, but I wanted her to feel this. "I love them so much, Maureen. Like they're my own."

"Any fool can see that." She squeezed my hand. "And I'm no fool. Never was." She paused. "Well, except for that one time I thought I was in love with Sean McFartin."

I pulled my lips in before I blurted, "Maureen McFartin!"

"Dodged a bullet with that one," she said, laughing with me. "Though I hear he's living the good life. Owns a farm somewhere that's made him plenty."

I couldn't tell if she was joking or not, but our laughter echoed throughout the kitchen. After a minute or so, we both sighed, but not at the same time.

"I told that story to CeeCee," she said, shrugging. "But it didn't get the results I'd hoped for. You. You broke through. We're all meant for someone, you know, and you and that child were meant for each other. I've come to realize that those two children were meant for this family."

"You, too," I said.

Ignoring my last remark, she tapped the table with her pointer finger once. "As unconventional as it is, as unconventional as your husband is, I know there's no place I'd rather my grandchildren be." She stood, going back to the stove, stirring her pot of whatever. "We'll be moved in by next week," she said, her voice soft.

"I didn't even get to ask," I whispered. "I was going to."

"No need," she said. "Your husband already told me so. And when I said I had to think about it..." She paused for a minute or two, and then she lowered her voice, trying to match his, as she said, "I'll wait."

32

KEELY

I suggested that Maureen and the kids move in right away, since CeeCee was so excited about the move, but Maureen claimed she needed a few days to get her things together. I offered to help, but she told me no, she had some personal effects to go through alone.

A couple of days later, that left me with a house full of men. All of my brothers were over, having a poker game in the kitchen with Cash, and since I didn't want to hear it when one of them accused another of cheating, I decided to read for a while in the library.

Cash came in about an hour later and kissed me on the head.

"What's going on?" I said, yawning, looking up at him. Then I inhaled. He smelled like cigar smoke and whiskey.

He showed me his cellphone. "Martin."

Martin was one of the men who "worked" for him.

I nodded but took him by the shirt, keeping him close to me. "I hate to admit this," I said. "But I'm attached to you now."

He grinned, then leaned down and kissed me—he stole my

breath, the marauding bastard. "That's why hearts are a pain in the arse, darlin'. They cause all sorts of trouble when you try to leave them behind."

"Grand," I said. "Just fucking grand."

He laughed, leaving me in the library all alone. A minute passed. Two. Three. On the fourth *tick*, something that felt a lot like fear hit me in the center of my chest. It turned my blood ice cold.

I took the steps two at a time, almost biting it once or twice when I almost lost my footing. Once on the bottom floor, I slid, catching myself right at the entrance of the kitchen. "Where's Cash?" I asked my brothers.

They were huddled around the table, still playing poker.

Harrison pointed behind me. "Just walked out."

I hustled to the door, yanking it open, just before he turned the key in the lock. His eyes flashed up to mine, not expecting it, but then they narrowed.

"You didn't kiss me long enough," I said, stalling, because I had no fucking clue what else to say.

He wrapped his arm around me and pulled me close. He kissed me, but it still didn't feel long enough. My hands were fisted in his shirt, and I wished for claws to sink into his skin so he could never leave me.

He leaned in and kissed me on the forehead, his mouth lingering before he pulled away. Out of all the times he'd kissed me, none of them seemed to mean more than that one. It expressed everything I doubted he'd ever admit to me. How he'd take care of me for as long as he lived. How he loved me, even if he'd never say it.

"Cash Kelly!" I said to his retreating back. It took him a second, but he stopped. "Take care of yourself."

He turned his head a fraction, and I could see the heart-stopping grin from the dim lights on the warehouse. He went to leave again when I called out for him once more.

"I fucking mean it."

He nodded toward me. "I put my heart on a chain for you, darlin'. It's wrapped around your neck. No safer place for it to be."

"That's not good enough." I was surprised that my words came out so strong. A lump had lodged in my throat, a clot coming straight from my gut.

"You love me," he said, like he was having a second revelation of what he'd realized in Ireland.

"From the moment I saw you," I whispered. "I loved you. I love you." He had brought life to me in that cemetery.

"I'm all right then," he said, nodding behind me. "Get inside and lock the door."

He waited until I did, but a minute or two later, I opened it again, looking out. He was gone. He'd melted with the darkness that surrounded him, nothing but his green eyes to bring attention to the force that walked these streets alone.

MY FINGERS WRAPPED around the pendant. Even though he told me I wore his heart around my neck, it felt like he had taken it with him.

"Keely," Lachlan said to me, laying a card face down. "You're going to wear a hole in the floor. Go to sleep."

"Don't tell me what to do," I snapped.

It'd been an hour since Cash left, and even though it was normal for him to be gone for hours at a time, it bothered me for some reason. I kept telling myself it was only because we'd spent so much time together, and my attachment *had* grown strong, too strong for me to feel comfortable when he was gone. I understood then why Harrison used to call Mari "*Strings.*" My heart felt like it had been taken over by hundreds of threads, and every single one was connected to Cash Kelly.

My feet, which seemed to have a direct connection to one of those strings, burned some tension by pacing in front of the kitchen, close to the front door.

"Keely Kelly," Owen said. "You out of beer in this New York mansion?"

"Are you gonna play or complain all night?" Declan said.

I sighed, pinching the bridge of my nose, not sure what else to do. No—I knew. I was about to leave. Surprise Kelly at his office. He'd fuck me on his desk and then carry me home, like some twisted villain in a fairytale written for me by me.

I'd fallen madly, hopelessly, irrevocably in love with that fucking villain in my story.

I swiped my key from the table by the door, my hand on the knob. "I'm going out for a bit," I said.

Harrison stood. "I'll go with you. We need more beer."

"No," I said as I opened the door. "I'll—" My breath left my lungs in relief and my heart lightened.

Cash was coming down the street. His head was down, and one hand was tucked into his pocket. The closer he got to me, though, my eyes narrowed even further. His face. I'd never seen it so hard. His strides were not easy, as usual, but almost brutal. He wasn't stomping, or being loud, but I could almost feel the anger rolling off of him from where I stood.

"I wonder who told him you were in love with Stone and then stole his whiskey?" Harrison said from behind me.

Good, I wasn't the only one who had noticed it.

I didn't want him to think I was a helicopter wife, like those parents at the park who constantly hovered over their children so they wouldn't fall and break something, so I went to close the door. Before I did, though, I noticed another shadow coming up from behind him.

"Is that Susan?" Harrison said.

"Yeah," I said. I had never warmed up to the old bitch. She

was evil wrapped in pink fluff, sort of like ambrosia salad. I'd never met one that I liked. Texture was important to me—even with people.

Cash kept her around because of a debt his old man had owed. She'd needed the job, wanted it even, to keep her busy, and there she was.

Cash had stopped at the same time I'd noticed her shadow creep up. Though the lights were dim, I could see that she was upset. She waved her hands some, and I heard her sniffing. If I really narrowed my eyes, I could see that her eyes were red-rimmed, and the tip of her nose was an even brighter red.

"Like a sadistic Rudolph," Harrison muttered, and I elbowed him. He made a breathless noise before he started laughing—it was quiet, but it was there.

"You better stop that nonsense. Or you might wake up the queen." I rolled my eyes. Mac's cousin, Gigi, was upstairs sleeping. "Come on." I backed up some. "Let's go wait in the—"

Susan called Cash down to her, and as he leaned in closer, she came out with a knife from the pocket of her cardigan and stabbed him in the neck with it.

The roar that echoed in the night was not from Cash, but from me. He stumbled back, and when he did, another shadow grew solid and turned into a man who stabbed him in the back. More shadows started to harden into men, all with glinting knives ready to butcher my husband.

Harrison was already screaming for my brothers to move, but I was already to the closet, pulling out my bow and arrows.

Lachlan held out an arm to stop me before I made it outside. "Kee," he said, his eyes serious. "If Kelly isn't who you—"

"Move your fucking hand or I'll break it," I hissed. I took an arrow, licked it down the center, and loosed the first one before I was out of the door.

It went straight through Susan's neck, blood squirting in all directions, her hand going to grab for it before she fell to her knees. The stunned look on her face was the last thing I saw before I sent another arrow through a man's back. His body arched forward before he fell to the ground. The arrow had gone straight through to his heart.

Cash stumbled, going for something in his pocket, but there were too many of them. It was like they were stabbing at a wild animal, herding him into a corner so they could skin him.

"Not today, motherfuckers, not as long as I'm alive," I said, releasing arrows as fast I could. It took a few minutes for the men still standing to realize where the arrows and bullets— between my brothers and me—were coming from. When they did, they stopped stabbing my husband and came after us.

I didn't even realize that my brothers had guns, and bright sparks along with deafening booms were going off in the night. There were still plenty of them, and I was shooting arrows as fast as I could, all the while making my way toward Cash, who had fallen. He was on the ground, and before anyone else could get to him, I stood in front, my bow raised, an arrow ready, daring another man to come near my husband.

A few tried, but they fell next to the other men who'd come to kill the marauder of Hell's Kitchen.

Something touched my leg and I turned, my bow pointed down, my arrow at the ready.

"You said you'd take my heart with an arrow someday, my darlin'," Cash said. "Do it now." He coughed and blood dripped out of his mouth.

My chest heaved and I couldn't move.

"Kee," Harrison said, touching my arm. "*Keely!*"

All of a sudden, it was like Harrison was screaming inside of my skull and it sent an automatic command to my hands. I dropped the bow and arrow, my knees giving out, right beside my husband on the bloodstained ground. My hands fisted in his torn and soaked shirt, and I set my ear against his heart, listening.

"Look at me," he said, barely able to talk. I sat up some, looking him in the eyes. He lifted his hand, going to touch my face, but stopped. "Too narrow," he breathed out.

Then he shut his eyes and the breath left my lungs on a cry.

33

KEELY

No! *Bullshit!* I sucked up my tears, keeping my husband's shirt locked in my grip. I looked down at him. "No one—*no fucking one*—is allowed to kill you, Cash Kelly, but *me!* Do you hear me?"

I looked up at my brothers, who were all huddled around my husband and me, ready to act if someone else came out of nowhere. "Harrison," I said, "put pressure on his neck. Now!" I looked at Lachlan. "See if any of the other spots are as bad. Hold pressure. You, too, Declan." They all nodded and started to move around me. "Owen."

My brother stood there, staring at Cash. "Owen!" I screamed. He blinked before he looked at me. "Give me your phone!"

"Kee, he's—"

"You don't get to tell me what he is! Give me your phone! Now!" I held out my hand, and he set his phone in my palm. "Keep an eye out," I told him while I dialed the number. Mari picked up on the second ring.

"Kee? What's—"

"Mac," I said, my voice breaking a little at the sound of her voice. "Put him on the phone!"

I heard the phone move and then Mac said, "My wife's friend."

"Your uncle," I said, and another cry left my mouth before I could stop it. I put a hand over my lips to cover it, but all I could smell was blood. I could taste it. "I need him. Here. My husband is dying!"

Mac's uncle was Tito Sala. I'd heard things about him. How he took care of the Fausti family personally. He was a damn good doctor, and if he couldn't save your physical body, no one else could. I'd met him once, seen him around a few times, and even though we didn't speak much, something about him made me think the rumors were true.

"Ten minutes," Mac said. "He'll be there, Keely." Then he hung up.

We all kept pressure on the spots that seemed the worst. They'd cut him up like they were trying to slaughter an animal. Stripes. He was going to have so many stripes after this.

It was the longest ten minutes of my fucking life.

Tito Sala hurried onto the scene, and I finally felt like I could breathe again. He had a woman with him, another doctor—he called her Dr. Carter—and together they started to do what they could on the sidewalk. They murmured back and forth. The main thing that stuck out to me was the word "artery." That evil bitch had almost nicked it. If she had, he would've already been dead.

An ambulance arrived a minute later, the lights going around and around on all of the dead that littered the street. The feathers on my arrows were green, and they looked gruesome in the glow of the red lights.

Harrison put his arm around me as they lifted my husband and set him on the gurney. Dr. Sala and Dr. Carter ran with them, shouting out orders.

I went to run behind them, but Harrison kept me in place. "This is where we need to go." He showed me his phone. Mac had texted him an address. I didn't recognize it.

"What hospital?" My teeth chattered, and suddenly my entire body felt like it'd been hit by the ambulance pulling away from the scene—my heart going with it.

"Kee," Harrison whispered. "They have their own places. Places that are set up with all of the equipment they need. Even the ambulance belongs to them. C'mon. I'll drive you."

We stopped when we noticed two figures coming from across the street. Mac and Rocco. Both men were related to Tito Sala. One by blood and the other by marriage.

Harrison shook Rocco's hand first. Then he hesitated, but after a second, offered his hand to Mac. I wasn't sure what Mac was going to do, since there was some bad blood there, but Mac took it.

Mac looked around. "How many archers are there in New York city?" It sounded like a question, but it was more of an observation. "Ones that can do this much damage?"

All three men looked directly at me as my brothers came to stand next to us.

"We will clean this up," Rocco said, nodding. He touched me on the shoulder. "My uncle will do what he can for your husband. Go now and be with him."

Gigi sat in the front seat next to my brother as we went in search of the address Mac had texted. I'd totally forgotten she'd been there until she touched Harrison on the shoulder, whispering, "My uncle will do what he can for your sister's heart."

For your sister's heart.

I reached for the pendant, clutching it so tightly that the chain around my neck started to dig into my flesh. The lights outside of the car window passed in a blur, illuminating each crevice of the metal heart, stained with my husband's blood.

"If you die on me, you bastard," I whispered. "I'll never forgive you for not showing me what's inside of this heart!"

"It's easy enough to find out," his voice echoed inside of my head, like the sound of waves crashing into the Irish shore.

"Not without you," I whispered back, the panic in me turning into anger. I was so fucking angry at what had happened, at how they were coming at him from all sides, that I wanted to go back and kill them again.

Cash had told me that he carried the hearts of all the men he had killed. Not me. I gave them to the devil as soon as that first blade sliced through his flesh. I had a reason to kill. And it was my right to defend what belonged to me.

Cash Kelly's heart.

My brother looked at me through the rearview mirror, but I didn't want to look back. I didn't want anyone to see that the anger was a shield for a deeper hurt that I knew would never heal unless my husband did.

It only took us a few minutes to get to the "hospital." It looked like an abandoned warehouse from the outside, and when we stepped onto the sidewalk, one of the Faustis let us inside. The place might have looked unused, but it had been recreated into something like an emergency room.

Cash was inside of a room, and it looked chaotic, even with only two doctors and a nurse. Tito Sala made eye contact with me for a brief second before he called out to the nurse to shut the door.

Harrison led me to a chair and made me sit. He tried to hand me a glass of water, but I pushed it away. It was hard to sit and wait and not do something. Every nerve inside of me was wired. Every cell hurt.

An hour went by.

By then, the entire place was filled with people. All of my brothers. Mari. A bunch of the Faustis who told me they knew Cash and respected him. They would light a candle for his soul.

It was an odd thing with the men around me, how they were religious people but killed on the regular.

It was a world that I wasn't used to, but it was mine now. I'd been baptized into the life by the blood of my husband. It was smeared all over my skin.

Mari clasped my hand. "Even though they do what they do, inside—" she touched her heart "—most of them have good, too."

I clasped her hand back, almost losing my shit at the strength in her voice.

An hour and five seconds later, Tito Sala came out of the room. He took a seat next to me, sighing. "Your husband is a lucky man," he said, patting my hand. "The cut on his neck was a close call. A little bit in the wrong direction—" he pinched his fingers close, showing me what a small gap looked like "—he would've died. He is not out of the woods yet, but he will survive this. He has been stitched up and given something for pain. We will let him rest now. He had quite the fight." He adjusted his glasses and looked at me, a kind smile on his face. "You saved him from the worst of it. He told me before what an archer you were, and I have to say, I did not believe it. Until tonight."

Tito stood, but I stopped him before he went back to Cash's "room."

"You know him?" I said. "He talked about me?"

"I knew his father quite well. Father Flanagan, too. We have a beer and lunch from time to time. That's how I ran into Cashel after your marriage." He adjusted his glasses. "I've watched most of these men grow from boys. Father Flanagan takes care of their spiritual needs. I take care of their bodies. And yes, Cashel told me that if he were ever in danger, and you were close, he didn't have to be concerned with his back. I'd say you were protecting his heart, ah?"

"I'd like to see him." I stood. "Now."

Tito nodded. "He is resting, but I am sure he will want to hear your voice."

When I went in, the other doctor and the nurse left me alone with him. It smelled and looked just like a hospital would. Mari told me they had them all over the city, strategically placed, and some were better equipped to handle different levels of emergencies.

Cash was brought to the one that was one level away from an actual hospital, which told me a lot. He'd been just as close to death as the knife was to the artery in his neck.

I took a seat next to his bed, taking his hand, holding it as tight as I could. "You scared the shit out of me tonight, Kelly," I said. "Once you're healed, I'm going to kill you." I sniffed. "What the fuck happened? I knew—" I had to stop myself from going on. I was babbling about trivial shit because I couldn't even find the words to tell him how much I loved him. How all of my worst fears were played out like a nightmare.

As I leaned my head against his, a tear fell from my eye and ran down his face. The tears kept running until I kissed his lips and told him I'd be back in a few minutes. I hated that his blood still coated my hands, my clothes, and I could smell it in the room mixing with the antiseptics. When he opened his eyes, I didn't want him to see it.

I was offered a room in the warehouse to sleep in, and I took advantage of the shower and a clean set of clothes one of my brothers had brought from home.

Sleep was the furthest thing from my mind, though I felt tired to the bone, so I paced the floor, wondering why I couldn't get my heart to settle. Uncle Tito, since he was considered family now and insisted, assured me Cash was going to be okay.

All of our family had left. A few men lingered in a kitchen, eating and talking about trivial shit, in case someone else tried to attack during the night and finish the job.

Someone had tried to finish my husband off.

Was it Grady and his gang? The Scarpones?

I'd heard little things here and there about how Grady was trying to recoup what he lost, but before he did, the Scarpones had had him killed for what happened with the trucks.

Then the Scarpones had been taken out—or that was what had been reported.

So who the fuck wants my husband dead now? Scott Stone? No. He didn't have it in him to kill, unless his life was threatened.

My mind was focused, but my thoughts roamed.

Why did my heart feel so empty? Even though he slept in the next room?

A minute later, reasons came to me.

Three.

Maureen, Connolly, Ryan.

I wanted them close. I knew they were home safe, but with everything that had happened, I didn't want to take any chances. If Cash had enemies, and so did I, there was no telling what they'd do to get revenge. Especially after what I'd done to stop them from killing my husband.

The boys had brought my phone with my clothes, and a set of keys for one of Cash's cars that had been left outside in case I wanted to leave. I wasn't leaving until Cash did, but I wanted to make a call.

"Raff," I said, sitting down on the bed, suddenly feeling so tired.

"Kee? What happened? Where's Cash?"

I shook my head. I couldn't relive it again. Not then. "It's bad, Raff. I can't talk about it right now, but I need you to go get Maureen and the kids. Right now."

"Bring them where? And where the fuck is my cousin? What happened?"

This "hospital" was the equivalent of a safe house, and I was instructed not to give out the address under any circumstances. So I gave Raff the address to one of the houses

Harrison and I had used a while back. I liked it, so I remembered the address.

"That's where you are?" he said.

"No." I shook my head. "But that's where I'll have one of my brothers meet you. He'll stay with Maureen and the kids until things settle down."

I could tell he was angry, breathing heavy, maybe because I was being vague. Then all of a sudden he cursed, but it was panicked.

I jumped to my feet. "What?" My voice echoed his. "*What!*"

"Fuck!" he yelled. "Maureen's building is on fire!"

I FLEW OUT of the warehouse—none of the men in the kitchen paid any attention to me—and found Cash's car on the other side of the building. I wasn't sure what had happened to the man standing guard outside, but I had a feeling he was making his rounds.

It didn't matter. I was going to call Harrison on my way and let him know where I was going. Maybe the boys were still at the house and they could get there quicker than I could.

None of them answered their damn phones. I left a message for Harrison, only giving a rushed version of what Raff had said to me, but by the time I pulled up to Maureen's building, none of them had called me back.

The place was engulfed, but there was no one around.

"Oh, God," I pleaded, almost jumping out of the car before I stopped it. I left it running while I hauled ass for the building.

The heat stopped me in my tracks. I wasn't even that close, and it built a barrier I could feel already singeing my skin. There was no way in. No way out.

"Those babies," I cried out. "My babies!" I hadn't realized until that moment...they had become my children.

My babies.

They made us a family. My blood didn't run through their veins, but every ounce of my love did.

People started to crowd around, their phones out, either recording or calling for help. *Why are they just calling now? Where are the first responders? Where's Raff?* Did he try to go inside and—as the thought came to me, the fire seemed to get angrier, and it sounded like the jaws of hell opening up, swallowing the building. It was starting to collapse.

I fell to my knees, sobbing into my hands, my heart turning to ash in the burning building.

"Kee-*ly*," I heard a strangled voice scream my name. "Kee-*ly* Kell-*y*." It was said in broken up syllables. Then I heard the wail of a baby.

Across the street. In the darkness. Hiding close to a building.

"Kee-*ly*," the strangled noise came again, louder than the baby. It was rough and shredded, but I heard it. "Kee-*ly* Kell-*y*."

I ran across the street, my eyes narrowing against the darkness to try and see better. The fire had the other side of the street lit, but this side was full of darkness and smoke.

I heard coughing, another wail, but it was going up and down in octaves, like someone was trying to shush it.

"Ry-*an*," the shredded voice said. "Ry-*an*, don't cr-*y*."

"Connolly!" I screamed. "Connolly!"

"Kee!"

She was pressed against the building, her eyes wide with fear, but holding onto Ryan with a grip that would've rivaled a grown woman's. She was trying to shake him to keep him from crying.

I fell to my knees in front of them, trying to look over them both. "What happened?" Tears and smoke blurred my vision. "Are you hurt?"

She shook her head. "Gran-*ny*." She sucked in a gust of air and pointed across the street, at the burning building.

It took her a minute, but she told me in broken words that her Granny had talked to a man earlier, Mart-*in*, and then he left. Another knock came at the door, and her Granny told her to take Ryan and go down the chute in their building. It had been used at one time to throw trash down.

I remembered Maureen telling me about it when I was over once. I'd asked her about a picture on her wall, and when she moved it, there was a window-sized square behind it with a handle. Maureen told me that she was afraid Connolly would try to go down it someday, maybe to hide, and it would lead her outside, so she hid it behind the painting.

I needed to call someone—anyone—to come, but I'd forgotten my phone in the car when I'd tried to call Harrison on the way over. I'd load the kids up and get them to safety, and then call Rocco to have the men walk us in. He'd given me his number and told me to call if I had *any* problems. I wasn't taking a chance with these children again. One of the men *would* walk us in.

"Kee," Connolly said, starting to cry harder. She tried to talk to me, but she kept tripping over her words. She was trying to tell me who had knocked on her door after Martin.

"I don't understand, baby," I said, helping her hold on to Ryan, who was still crying some, but she didn't want to give him up. "Who knocked at your door? Who was the other man?"

Her eyes grew wide, and she plastered herself against the building even tighter. Before I could even turn around, she held Ryan with one arm and pointed the other behind me. "Him!"

It took me only a second to turn, to put my body in front of theirs, but before the first blow landed to my skull, I screamed, "*Run!*"

34

CASH

I felt it when her lips kissed mine, felt her tears sliding down my face, but the Doc had me so doped up on meds that I thought I was floating in heaven.

Until I tried to move.

He'd stitched me up like I was made of stuffing and he had to stop all of it from spilling out. Every part of me demanded to move, but I was hardwired with sutures. Never mind the fucking needles in my arms.

Tito Sala was known for making his patients comfortable during, but after, he'd make life hell on earth. Some say he did it so you wouldn't forget. I said he did it because deep down, the old man was playing payback for the many nights he had to put bastards like me back together. A bunch of Humpty Fucking Dumpties.

Two women came into the room. It was dim—someone had turned the lights low—but I could hear the monitors in the background, and their voices.

When the women came closer, I recognized one of them. Clara was a nurse, and her old man had been connected to an Irish family at one time. I'd known her since she was a kid.

The second woman, the doctor, took me a minute longer to place. Alisha Carter. I couldn't remember how she fit, though. Maybe she dated or was married to a Fausti, or someone else connected to the life.

If Dr. Carter was in this room, though, the Faustis trusted her—to whatever degree they could trust.

This was one of their most elaborate setups, as far as emergency rooms went. I'd been in a few of them before. I must've been close to death. If the pain in my neck and shoulder was any indication, the old bitch almost turned me into worm food.

"How close was I this time?" I said, my voice sort of floating.

Clara fiddled with something next to me. "Close enough that Father Flanagan came to check on you." She flicked me on the shoulder. "Your old man would've been pissed that you let it get that close."

"Yeah." I cleared my throat. "The feeling's mutual right now."

"Father Flanagan left, though, so that must mean he feels all's right in your heart." She smiled down at me. "In case you decide to die later."

I didn't have the strength to lift my mouth and grin. Besides, my wife might accuse me of flirting and gouge my eyes out, like she'd threatened to do before. When I said she'd go psycho, sinking her claws in, I didn't only mean in the bedroom. "Where's my wife?" *The woman who'd set my soul at ease.*

"Umm." Clara looked at Dr. Carter. "Have you seen her?"

Dr. Carter shook her head. "Not since she was in here earlier. She went to the private room after, but she said she was coming back."

"How long?" I said.

"Concerned with time, Kelly?" A smug grin came to Clara's face.

"I am, in fact," I said, sitting up some. They didn't even try to stop me. They knew it was useless. My head spun, but I played it off. "Where's my phone?"

"She's in the other room, Kelly," Clara said, about to leave with Dr. Carter. "Not in another country. She'll be in. She's probably tired. She's been upset, worrying about *you*." She slapped my leg, but it was light. "I don't know why any woman would fall in love with any of you. You're all too much trouble."

"Too hard on the heart," Dr. Carter said before they left me alone.

Alone in the silence to think. To remember. My hands curled around the fucking blankets they'd put over me, like some kid who needed to keep warm, and a pulse beat in my ear. If Tito Sala hadn't stitched me up right, I might blow one.

Judging by how stiff I felt, he'd gone a level of tightness too far. Maybe he wanted one to pop so he could do it again—while I was awake, with the biggest needle he had, and without meds. I'd done it before, without meds, but his hand could be as bruising as it was healing when he had a lesson to teach about preserving the temple he considered the human body.

A chirping sounded in the room. At first I thought it came from the monitors, but then I realized it was my phone. They must've cut my clothes off, and my pants were in the corner, the sound coming from my pocket.

"Who the fuck—" Then I realized. It was the ringer Keely had set on my phone.

She said it didn't matter if anyone else had a special one, hers would stand out. She'd picked a picture of an animated green bird, and when my phone would ring, it would appear and this weird birdcall would sound.

It started out as chirping at first, and then it morphed into a voice screaming, "Warning." Squawk. "Your wife is calling. Warning." Squawk. "Your wife is calling."

"Warning," my phone yelled from the corner. "Your wife is calling. Warning."

Why the fuck would my wife be calling if she was in the same building? And why the fuck, if I was awake, or not, would she not be beside me? Even when she hated me, she still refused to budge from her place.

Yanking the wires out of my arms, I moved like a man on a boat during a storm to the corner of the room. Every gash—my side, my back, and wherever else the fuck on my body—caught fire with each step that I took. I'd never been close enough to a raging fire to feel the heat, but my body was lit up in the same way.

Every muscle. Every nerve. Every cell. Burned.

All it took was for the ringing to stop, or maybe the man on the other end heard how hard I was breathing, because as soon as he sensed an opening, *life*, he told me where to meet him.

"Alone, or your wife's dead."

ROCCO'S MEN were not paying attention. They were more concerned with who threatened to come in than who was going out.

Plenty of men had tried to escape from Tito Sala's clutches, though, and those men, they got strapped down to the bed. Then he'd read you the most boring fucking book in the world. The countless men who had been strapped down by his command probably wished they would've just died from the fight instead of having to listen to him drone on and on.

One of the men in the kitchen looked up and nodded at me, but since I swam toward the room where my wife was supposed to be, he probably thought I was looking for her.

Yeah, swam. I felt like I was underwater, but in a hellish version of it. I was sweating while my skin burned to a crisp. I wasn't even sure if I could lift my arm above my head.

I knew my wife wasn't in the room, but these places were

loaded with weapons, and I needed something to bring with me. I was going alone, but I wasn't going empty handed. In the closet I found a leather shoulder holster and put it on. There was only a pair of sweatpants in here, so I was going with no shirt and no shoes.

Every instinct in me told me to fucking run, but my head was at war with my limbs. Whatever Tito had given me was strong, even though pain still existed. Maybe it was wearing off. Which meant I had to get out before he came to give me another dose and found me gone.

I slipped past the men in the kitchen. I knew the man standing guard outside, though, was going to be a problem—a six-foot, four-inch, two hundred and fifty pound, solid-muscle, Sicilian issue. I'd met the guard, Rizzo, who they sometimes called "The Giant" at the door before, and I knew he was from Sicily. The Fausti's reach was long, and they had family in every area imaginable.

"Kelly," he said, squinting at me. He had a red stain on his cheek.

I lifted a gun to his head. "No offense, Rizzo, but I need a set of keys."

"I'll drive you," he said. "Sala gave you—"

I shook my head. "Have to do this alone."

He sighed and pulled out a pair of keys from his pocket. He threw them at me, and I caught them with one hand.

He nodded to an all-black Hummer across the street. "I am going to bust your ass as soon as you heal," he called after me. "I would do it now, but I am too afraid of Sala. You know how he feels about stitches—they are his art."

I pressed the button on the Hummer and it chirped, but right before I climbed inside, I felt someone watching me. I looked over my shoulder but didn't see anyone. I knew, though. That Machiavellian motherfucker. Mac. He was like a ghost, always watching, and when you felt him, that was all it was. A feeling. He was never where you expected him to be.

And if he called Keely "my wife's friend" one more time, I was going to swing on him. It was like no other woman's name was good enough to come from his mouth except for his wife's.

"Keely," I said, as I strained to get inside of the Hummer. It was a road beast, and after I shut the door, I found a clean shirt on the passenger seat and a new pair of shoes on the floor.

I looked around again, but nothing but darkness surrounded me. There was no telling when Mac had arranged this ride and the clothes. Probably as soon as my wife called them for help. Again, he was a smart killer, one of the most dangerous of all. He plotted before he executed.

So how did my wife slip past the men in the house and Rizzo outside?

The stain of red on Rizzo's cheek explained it. He was fucking eating. I could smell the aroma of tomatoes and garlic coming off of him. It was the same dish the guys were eating inside of the house. And if I knew Rocco, and somewhat Mac, they'd just arrived after taking care of the massacre outside of our place in Hell's Kitchen. Keely had slipped out before then. Or they wouldn't have allowed her to leave on her own.

I removed the shoulder holster and slipped the shirt over my head. It rubbed against all of the slices, separate little fires, the material trapping the heat underneath the bandages. It reflected what was going on inside of me. I was a walking fire—about to combust from anger.

The day at the country club, after the attempted hit on my life, I knew.

It was someone who knew me. Someone close. But I'd had to find out how far the operation went before I could take action.

I knew the why, too, but it was hard to concentrate on the reason. Not when my eyelids were heavy and my head kept

going under and coming back up. My skin battled hot and cold
—I was feverish. My teeth clacked.

"Fuck!" I yanked the wheel of the Hummer to the left, clip-
ping a parked car on the right, taking its bumper completely
off.

I shook my head, trying to keep it clear, while I sped
through the streets like a drunk. It wasn't even from the drugs
anymore. The pain was ramping up because the buffers were
wearing off. The motherfuckers must've stabbed me numerous
times, and deep. The one on my neck had the deepest pulse.
And my face. I was starting to feel it again. My nose the most.
One of them must've kicked me when I was down and broke it
—again.

It all came second to the pure determination to get to my
wife, though. The pain reminded me that I had a purpose.

A raindrop hit the windshield. I hoped it would hold off for
a while, but I could smell it in the air. Humidity. Lightning
speared across the sky, followed by thunder.

A few minutes later, the Hummer rolled over the lawn of
the cemetery, coming to a hard stop with my heavy foot. I slid
the shoulder holster back on and bent over to pick up the
shoes. My head drowned before it came up for air and I could
catch my breath. I put the motherfuckers on and almost fell out
of the car getting out.

I was going to have to shoot him before he got to me. I was
in no shape to fight; I could barely stand. He was a strong dude
with quick punches. And I needed to get her out. Once she was,
it was what it was between us.

Keely Kelly had become my life. My entire life. I was
addicted to her peace, to her love, to her. I was in love with the
life inside of the woman. When she restarted my life, she gave
me a first breath again, and I'd give her my last if it meant she
lived.

Following the beams of the Hummer, I made my way

through the cemetery. The gaps between the markers became darker and darker the further in, until the light from a flashlight lit up the area in front of my old man's stone. It wasn't elaborate like some of the ones around.

My old man hadn't wanted that. He'd said that all men ended up in the same place no matter where they'd been or what they'd done in life. A million-dollar casket or a five-hundred-dollar one, it made no difference, because what was inside was still going to perish.

"Ashes to ashes," Raff's voice carried. "Dust to dust... Is that you, Cashel Kelly?"

Yeah, fucking Raff.

Martin had told me that he'd seen Raff give a young guy a key that day at Sullivan's, when Sal's trucks were coming in and out. The guy gave the key to Susan's grandson, Colin McFirth, but Martin didn't think anything of it until Raff told him over beers that some guy had given Colin a key, and the key belonged to the truck that blew up with Colin inside of it. Raff had said the truck was meant for me.

I'd never told Raff what happened between Colin and me. I'd never even told him that I'd rigged the wrong truck and fixed the other one. And I'd only taught one person how to rig anything the way Colin's truck was.

Raff was so caught up in his gloating that he didn't realize he'd busted himself—because he and Colin were in on it. Colin had never sold Raff out. They had been working together against me. My guess was that Colin wanted to kill me off sooner than his partner, but instead, he got the fucked up end of the deal.

It took Martin a minute to piece it together, but when he did, he realized it was Raff behind it all along. Raff had been using me to eliminate all of his potential adversaries, before he eliminated me. It wasn't going to be with explosives, though. Not like he'd taken out his friend. This was personal.

He wanted me to suffer. To beg.

I had the gun trained on him before he twirled out between two stones—one that belonged to my old man, and one that belonged to his—with my wife in his arms. Her head was tilted back, her eyes closed, her hair swaying whenever he moved her. When he turned, like he was taking a last dance with a dead woman, I saw the blood. It ran down her face from her forehead.

Her nose. Her mouth. Her eyes. He'd beaten on the doors to my heaven to get in. Her jeans were soaked, almost black, with blood.

"Keely," her name came from my lips without thought. "My darlin'."

He smiled. "You're losing your edge, Kelly." He nodded toward the hand that'd been holding the gun. It was down, not even trained on him anymore.

I couldn't take a shot, not the way he held her in his arms. It might not even make a difference.

My wife, he'd already... I refused to even think it.

Something inside of me grew weak, but my hand tightened around the gun.

He winced, but then he grinned. "Your wife, Jessica Rabbit, she fought harder than you are right now. We all see who wears the pants in your family." He ticked his mouth. "I shouldn't say family. Maureen. The little girl. The little boy. All dead...and now your wife." He turned a fraction, showing me her face. "I told you to come alone or she'd die. Since I knew you wouldn't..." He shrugged.

I met his eyes as rain started to pour. Lightning forked across the sky, turning it purple for a second before thunder rolled.

"The guns, Kelly." He nodded to the one dangling in my hand. "That's not alone. But I didn't kill her. Not yet. Might want to hurry, though, the bleeding is steady on the outside, but I'm not sure what's happening on the inside." He winked at me. "She can take a hit with a bat, Jessica Rabbit can," he said, mocking my accent.

"What do you want?" I said through clenched teeth.

"You," he said. "On your knees. In front of me. Begging for forgiveness. No gun to your head forcing the words. I want an apology from the soul, since you have no fucking heart."

I threw the gun in my hand to the side of him, and he kicked it so far that I couldn't get to it even if I tried. I did the same with the entire holster. He did the same thing.

Love was the only force that could ever bring me to my knees. My wife had called it the day at her brother's house.

I fell to my knees not in front of him, but in front of my wife. She was all I could see. All I could hear. All I could breathe. I could smell her in the rain, and when he stood over me, holding her, her blood dripped down my face like tears.

"You didn't see this coming, you arrogant bastard of the devil. The marauder of Hell's Kitchen—you don't steal things, you steal hearts. You steal them from men. You steal them from families. Your old man was the devil himself. Everything he touched, he ruined. Like the drugs you fight against." Raff put his gun to my forehead. "Let me tell you a story, a story of how Ronan Kelly ruined a good man's life. My old man owed a debt, and your old man forced him off the street with this band of thugs and brought him to Ginger's."

Ginger's was a bar my old man fronted the money for. He used it sometimes to deal with men who owed money, or worse. It wasn't a neutral place like Sullivan's. If those walls could talk, the FBI would've brought them in for interrogation years ago.

"Over money, Kelly," Raff said, pressing the gun harder against my head. His hand was steady at first, but the more he talked, the more he relived, and it started to shake. "Money. Your old man put a gun to my old man's head, just like this, and forced him to call home. I answered the phone. My old man was crying, begging, and he told me to put my ma on the line."

Raff sniffed. "He owed the great Ronan Kelly a debt, and if we didn't bring enough, we were all dead. Now you're going to beg for something worth more than your life. This woman's life. Your life is not good enough to beg for. Hers? Worth every word from your mouth.

"Kind of like what you did to Scott Stone. You stole her from him knowing he'd never get over her because he lost her to you. The devil's spawn. The thing he spent his entire life fighting against. And his career? His other love? The end of life as he knew it when he lost it. Now you're where many men have been at your word, at your fucking hand, and you're going to lose, Kelly. You're going to lose. Because I've watched. This bitch is worth everything to you. More than your old man's memory. More than your last breath. So what do you have to say?"

I lifted my hands. "Here I am," I said, tasting blood in my mouth. Either hers or mine.

"Here I am." He looked up at the sky and laughed. "Is that all you have to say for your fucking self? Where's the begging? The pleading? The crying?" He turned and slammed my wife's head against my old man's stone at the same time thunder seemed to crack the sky in two, and more rain started to fall. "You'll cry—"

My heart screamed out her name, but a roar left my throat when heat surged up inside of me, and I slammed my body into his. We collided so hard that he dropped my wife, trying to protect his body from mine, and as soon as we went down, we started fighting.

He had me on my back in no time, hitting me in all of the spots he knew were weak, missing one vital spot.

My neck.

I could survive the rest.

But not my neck.

I didn't give a fuck about my life. I had to get my wife help. We were in a cemetery. The land of the dead. She wasn't going to be one of them. If she was, we'd go together. I'd break open the vein in my neck before anyone lowered her in the ground before my eyes.

He kept landing punches on my back, on my sides, and then he hit me right over the spot in my neck. The wind left my lungs in a fucking wheeze, and rain poured into my mouth as I tried to breathe.

Raff rolled off of me, crawling to get to the gun he'd lost when I'd slammed my body into his. He stood no less than a second later, going for Keely again, and with every ounce of air I could steal, I screamed out his name.

"Raff!"

He stopped and turned to me.

"Fuck you," I said. "And fuck your old man. He was a pussy." I whipped out the gun from behind my back, shooting him once in the head and once in his heart.

He fell to the ground as I climbed to my knees and crawled to my wife, who was lifeless on the ground, the rain pouring on her face, trying to wash the blood. It was too much, coming too fast. Using my old man's stone, I propped myself up, pulling her with me, roaring with pain when I did. I set her against my chest, holding her tight against me, not sure what the fuck to do. Besides her face, I wasn't sure what he'd done to her. I wasn't there to protect her. Or those children. Or Maureen.

Our family.

My head swam in and out again, but even in the darkness, all I could see was red.

Blood.

Our blood ran and mixed in the rain.

I turned my head up to the sky and cried out. I cried out so loud that my lungs trembled. "Please," I begged. "Please." Lightning lit up the darkness, showing me her face, and I begged once again in Irish Gaelic. "*Le do thoil!*"

"It's about time you begged for something, you no-good bastard."

Lee Grady. The man who was supposed to be dead. A fucking ghost in a cemetery. He stood over me with a gun in his hand.

I went to move my wife, but he shook his head, pointing the gun at her. "She's going first. After what I just heard, she's worth more than what you stole from me. You'll live long enough, after I finish the job Susan couldn't, to see the life drain from her before it drains from you. Very poetic. Your old man might've even been proud you went out this way."

A whistle sounded. Like a bird. Singing. Or talking to another one. It came and then went when another roll of thunder drowned it out. It came back, closer this time.

I could see Grady in the light of the flashlight Raff left behind, but he couldn't see who else was out there.

Grady aimed his gun toward the left, toward where the noise was coming from, his eyes narrowing. "Who's there?" he shouted.

Nothing but the downpour of rain answered him, and then the whistle, which came and went again. My old man might've had a simple stone, but big statues surrounded him. Whoever it was seemed to be moving between them, letting Grady know he wasn't alone.

Grady pulled the trigger on his gun. A flash of light, and then the blast rang and seemed to echo in the night. He must've hit a stone, because I heard it crack.

"Who's there?" he shouted again, ready to pull the trigger once more. Before he did, though, a man appeared out of the darkness and put one bullet in his head and two in his chest. He lay at my feet, his eyes still open, rain pooling in his unseeing eyes.

When the man showed his face in the light, I cleared my throat. "It wasn't her. I forced her into it. Take her." I tried to lift her, but my arms felt like they were weighed down with lead. "She needs help."

"I know you forced her," Scott Stone said, kneeling to feel the pulse in her neck. "But I also know she's not the kind of woman to be forced into anything. She fell in love with you." He sighed. "Get me my job back and I'll get help. You've said it enough. We can't exist without each other."

"Done," I said, but I wasn't sure if the word actually left my mouth.

"I'm not sure about you, Kelly." He sighed again. "But I need something to live for besides myself."

"The fucking truth," I said, holding on to her tighter. If she didn't survive this, neither would I.

A second later, it seemed, people were running through the rain with lights, coming toward us. Too soon for him to have just called someone.

I heard Scott Stone say something about how he had been following me after I clipped the car. He'd lost me at some point, but then figured out where I'd been going. I heard Mac. I heard Rocco. I heard him say they left the Hummer for me in case I wanted to go after Raff when I was healed. The Hummer had been tracked.

I heard Tito Sala cursing in Italian at all of them.

Pulling my wife even closer to my chest, I said two words that I never remembered coming out of my mouth before. "Thank you." Then I closed my eyes.

35

KEELY

7 MONTHS LATER

The evening sun poured in through the windows of the library, highlighting all of the stories on the many shelves.

I tugged at the pendant around my neck, studying all of the crevices with a narrowed eye. Some were still stained with blood.

His and mine.

Two bodies that shared one heart.

Love is never easy, because true love, the kind I made vows to, meant that the days would be long, the years short, and not all of them good. One thing I knew for certain, though. It would be worth it.

It already was.

No matter how hard our road became, I would always make the choice to walk beside Cash Kelly and our family in love.

It took me time to get to that point. It wasn't easy to heal after what Raff had done to me. He had beaten me senseless. Beat me until I'd passed out from the pain. He had broken bones and torn muscles.

The one he almost killed—my heart—still beat. He left me

bruised and tattered, and he left my husband the same way, but he was still here. And so was I.

Any sacrifice to have him would be worth it.

He was enough for me. And so was our family.

Ryan giggled and ran into the library, my arms open as he crashed into me. My arms were full, and so was my heart, even if I still had no clue what filled the metal one against my chest.

CeeCee ran in right behind Ryan, pretending like she was the dragon on her wall, going to eat him up. Her speech was getting better and better with each day. She picked books from the children's section of the library each night, and it was Cash who read them to her.

"Grand," she would say as he tucked her in. "Just gra-*nd*."

It wasn't easy for her to lose Maureen—it wasn't easy on any of us—but she flourished with us, and I was thankful every day that Maureen had the foresight to see that ahead of time. She'd made the transition easy for CeeCee, and in a lot of ways, she had prepared me for the family we had.

Father Flanagan had told us that Maureen wasn't sick, like everyone assumed, but she wanted to be certain that no matter what, her grandchildren would be loved beyond measure and taken care of.

When I'd told CeeCee to run, she did, straight to find Father Flanagan. He caught her in the street as he was heading to the fire, and she'd told him what had happened.

Even in death, Maureen was directing CeeCee, and I was positive she always would.

Ryan settled into my lap, the sun highlighting his dark hair. CeeCee grabbed a book before she took a seat next to me.

"No one invited me," Cash said, striding into the room. "I'm offended."

My tiger was riddled with stripes, but it only made him more beautiful. I took great pleasure in licking each one every night, tasting the sacrifice he made for these children, for me, on my tongue. Letting it settle in my bloodstream and go straight to my heart. Reminding me of how bittersweet a time it was.

"Grr!" CeeCee growled at him. "You are mad. You will get happ-*y*."

Ryan lifted his arms for Cash to take him. Cash held him close to his chest for a moment, stroking his head, and then sat next to me. We stared at each other for a minute, getting lost in all we had, before we both grinned.

The marauder was still stealing my fucking breath. Maybe because I had nothing else for him *to* steal. He had me, all of me, for the rest of my life.

"Here," CeeCee said, shoving a piece of paper at me. I looked away from Cash to take it. She'd drawn four dragons, all different, but each one represented each one of us.

Under Cash's dragon, the scariest one, the name said Daddy Cash. Under Ryan's was Baby Brother Ryan. Under hers, it said, Big Sister CeeCee. Under mine, it said simply, Mom.

My eyes rose slowly to meet hers.

She shrugged. "We are a famil-*y*. I pick you as my mom. And—" she touched Cash's shoulder "—Daddy Cash."

Cash's face lit up when he smiled. "Has a nice *ring* to it."

I pulled Connolly to my chest, crying into her hair but laughing at the same time. "I pick you as my baby girl," I said, kissing her on the head even harder. "And you as my baby boy!" I tickled Ryan on his belly and his shoulders came up, his nose wrinkling, as he laughed.

"Me," Cash said, pointing to his chest. "Do you pick me?"

"As long as we both shall live," I said, placing my hand against his heart. He set his over mine, pressing it even harder against him. "You bled for this—for me. You conquered my heart. You can write that on your stone."

Ryan tugged on the chain around my neck, gazing at the pendant. His eyes narrowed for a second, before he took his finger and tried to stick it where the little lock would go. His nail came between the crevices that would open the locket to reveal what was inside of the heart.

And it did. It opened.

A simple gold ring fell into my lap, one that was too big for my finger. I held it up, looking through it, letting the sun move through the everlasting circle.

"'You proved me wrong,'" I said, reading the inscription.

"You did, my darlin'." He grinned at me, but there was nothing cocky about it. For the first time, it touched his eyes. "You proved me wrong. You *prove* me wrong. Every day."

"You love me," I breathed out.

"More than life itself." He looked me in the eye and then turned his eyes to Connolly Kelly. "More than life itself." He looked at Ryan Kelly. "More than life itself."

I took his hand and slipped the band on his ring finger. "A leash on a tiger," I said.

"Grand," he said. "Just fu—" CeeCee put her hand over his mouth, and he pretended to bite her. She laughed and moved it. "Just grand. You'll never lead me astray."

We kissed and then started dinner.

EPILOGUE

CASH

Two Years Later

"**G**et the door!"

I grinned at my wife before I went to answer it. Ryan was on her shoulders, hitting at the balloon animal she had around her head, laughing his ass off. Her hair was full of glitter, and she had a tigress painted on her cheek. Connolly ran around with her friends, hyped up on too much sugar.

I had warned my wife about the dangers of sugar and kids mixing, but she ate it with them, so she said there was no excuse not to give it to them. She was of the mind that we should practice what we preach.

The grin was still on my face when I opened the door. It fell when I was faced with three people.

"We were in the neighborhood." Killian shrugged. "Thought we'd stop by for my niece's birthday party." He was wedged between his wife and Saoirse.

"This house is invite-only," I said.

"We have an invite," Kill said, looking behind me.

I turned and found Father Flanagan, but he shook his head. He didn't invite them. I'd told him about the situation with Saoirse after what had happened to my wife and me at the cemetery. He was as shocked as I was that Saoirse was still alive, and that Killian hadn't told him. When I asked him if he was mad or was going to hold a grudge, he told me no.

"Holding a grudge only turns you bitter," he'd said, "because only you can live with you. I'm not the one to judge." He pointed up to the sky. "That's a burden I'm blessed not to have to carry. When I chose to walk in love, I chose the hard road. It's not the path of least resistance, but in the end, it'll be worth it. Because when we go, Cash, we all go alone, and our sins are our own. I'll only be judged for what I've done. 'He did it first' or 'he hurt me first' will not be good enough. Not for—" he nodded up again. "And not for me."

That was that—until this moment. Until his eyes connected with Saoirse's for the first time in years.

Kill cleared his throat. "Father Flanagan didn't invite us."

I looked at my brother, and he nodded behind me. My wife stood there with our children. She smiled and waved at me.

"After I spoke to Kee, and she told me that *someone* refuses to sing for her, I decided that someone—" he pointed to his chest "—has to teach those children how to sing." Kill grinned. "Properly."

"Daddy two," Ryan said, lifting up two fingers, trying to figure out why there was another me on the other side of our door.

"Daddy," Connolly said, coming to take my hand. She had dropped the "Cash" part a week after she decided to give me the name. "Who are they?" Her eyes jumped between Kill and me, focused on the same thing Ryan was—how much we looked alike.

"I'm your uncle," Kill said. He introduced his wife, whose name was Megan. Then Saoirse.

"You can call me Gran," Saoirse said, "if you want."

Connolly smiled. "How about Grandee?"

"I'd love that," Saoirse said, wiping her eyes. "Very much."

Keely slid her hand around my side and Ryan took my other hand. After a tense few minutes, I sighed and moved back some. Keely gave a low whoop and moved aside so the three could enter.

Before they did, I stuck my foot out, stopping Killian from entering. I looked each of them in the eye before I spoke. "For my children," I said, "since you played on their sympathies. But not for me."

Killian met my eye, reminding me of myself when I was determined to get whatever the fuck I wanted. "We'll wait," he said, and then he rolled into our home.

The kids ran after them, excited to get to know new people. We were an unconventional family, but our connection was even stronger than blood. Even Keely's mam gave Saoirse the evil eye when Connolly introduced her as her new Grandee. Those children belonged to all of us.

Keely stared at me for a minute and then wrapped her arms around me, looking up. "Life doesn't always go the way we want, thief of hearts," she said. "But no matter what, good or bad, it goes. It moves forward. Bad times come. They go. Good times come. They go. But forever. That's us. You and me. And them." She nodded behind her at our children laughing in the background.

I searched her eyes, my entrance to heaven, wondering what I'd ever done in my life to deserve her. The truth was, nothing. Not a fucking thing could ever be compared to her. I'd never be worthy of her love. It was mine, though, and I'd never let anyone else get fucking close to it. We couldn't even mess it up, and we'd been chaos and spite in the beginning.

"Good bones," she said. "Remember?" She tapped my temple.

"Forget the bones," I said, giving her a tap on the chest. "Strong heart."

"You should know," she said, taking my hand, leading me back to the party. "You stole enough of them. And I'm not only talking about men in the game. I'm talking about women, too. *Molls*." She rolled her eyes.

"Only one that counts, my darlin'," I said. "Yours."

"Grand," she said, laughing. "Just grand! Now it's time for you to sing for me. *La de daaa*."

"No way in fucking hell," I said.

"Been there, Marauder. Have to do better than that."

I stopped her before she made it to the crowd, turning her toward me. No room between her body and mine. I started slow dancing with her. And then I put my mouth to her ear and started to sing.

"Your voice is like a lullaby," she breathed.

"You sing me one and I'll sing you one," I said, grabbing her ass.

"*Shh* the talking. Sing for me again."

I did.

When the song came to an end, she inhaled and then exhaled. "Sing for me only," she whispered, her eyes closed, tears slipping down her cheeks, "until the day that I die."

"Until the day that *I* die," I said. "You, and only you, my darlin'."

"You bled for this heart, Cash Kelly," she said. "It's yours until the day you die."

"Grand," I said. "Now put the arrow meant for me away for good, archer. Because we're finally even."

AFTERWORD

Do you remember this question: *How do you see me now?*

Villain or hero?

More animal than man?

A modern-day Robin Hood?

Perception.

It causes two people to see the same situation in two different ways, even though they're looking at the same thing.

If you read Scott Stone's story, which he doesn't have, you'd undoubtedly see me differently, but at least in this story, I fucking tell it like it is.

I don't give a fuck what people think of me. Never have. Never will. Those who scream the loudest have the most to hide. Remember that.

Me.

I hide nothing.

I hid nothing.

I am who I am.

Niccolò Machiavelli said, "Men judge generally more by the eye than by the hand, for everyone can see and few can feel.

Everyone sees what you appear to be; few really know what you are."

Even if you see me for something I'm not, my wife never will. She feels me. And if you have one person who feels you, compared to a million who see you—consider yourself one of the lucky ones.

I do, because a woman did something no one else ever could. She proved me wrong. She let me steal her heart.

Yeah. She fucking *let* me.

She made me think I was stealing it without her permission. What Father Flanagan told me about a woman's heart was true. But he forgot to mention one thing—her mind was designed to outsmart any man's.

Remember that. It's coming from one of the smartest men I know—myself.

My wife gave me the key long before I "stole" it. I just didn't realize it until the truth was something I couldn't ignore anymore. When I said some hearts had to be stolen, what I meant was, some hearts had to be worked for.

Before I ever laid eyes on her, she had claimed mine. I was always a cheap date, though, and she knew that just as well as the devil did.

As the old saying goes, *that* is fucking *that*.

ABOUT THE AUTHOR

Bella Di Corte has been writing romance for seven years, even longer if you count the stories in her head that were never written down, but she didn't realize how much she enjoyed writing alphas until recently. Tough guys who walk the line between irredeemable and savable, and the strong women who force them to feel, inspire her to keep putting words to the page.

Apart from writing, Bella loves to spend time with her husband, daughter, and family. She also loves to read, listen to music, cook meals that were passed down to her, and take photographs. She mostly takes pictures of her family (when they let her) and her three dogs.

Bella grew up in New Orleans, a place she considers a creative playground.

ALSO BY BELLA DI CORTE

The Fausti Family:

Man of Honor

Queen of Thorns

Royals of Italy

Kingdom of Corruption

War of Monsters

Gangsters of New York:

Machiavellian, Book 1

Mercenary, Book 3

Coming Soon:

The Fausti Family:

Ruler of Hearts

Law of Conduct

King of Roses

Printed in Great Britain
by Amazon

81567139R00223